PENGUIN BOOKS

Lost and Found

ABOUT THE AUTHOR

Lucy Cavendish has spent most of her life working in journalism. She writes for the *Evening Standard*, the *Sunday Telegraph*, the *Observer* and a variety of glossy magazines. She lives in Oxfordshire with Michael, a graphic artist, and their four children.

This is the second novel in a trilogy, following *Samantha Smythe's Modern Family Journal.*

Lost and Found

LUCY CAVENDISH

PENGUIN BOOKS

PENGUIN BOOKS

Published by the Penguin Group
Penguin Books Ltd, 80 Strand, London WC2R 0RL, England
Penguin Group (USA) Inc., 375 Hudson Street, New York, New York 10014, USA
Penguin Group (Canada), 90 Eglinton Avenue East, Suite 700, Toronto, Ontario, Canada M4P 2Y3
(a division of Pearson Penguin Canada Inc.)
Penguin Ireland, 25 St Stephen's Green, Dublin 2, Ireland
(a division of Penguin Books Ltd)
Penguin Group (Australia), 250 Camberwell Road, Camberwell, Victoria 3124, Australia
(a division of Pearson Australia Group Pty Ltd)
Penguin Books India Pvt Ltd, 11 Community Centre, Panchsheel Park, New Delhi – 110 017, India
Penguin Group (NZ), 67 Apollo Drive, Rosedale, North Shore 0632, New Zealand
(a division of Pearson New Zealand Ltd)
Penguin Books (South Africa) (Pty) Ltd, 24 Sturdee Avenue,
Rosebank, Johannesburg 2196, South Africa

Penguin Books Ltd, Registered Offices: 80 Strand, London WC2R 0RL, England

www.penguin.com

First published 2009
2

Set in 12.5/14.75 pt Monotype Garamond
Typeset by Rowland Phototypesetting Ltd, Bury St Edmunds, Suffolk
Printed in England by Clays Ltd, St Ives plc

ISBN: 978-0-141-03019-7

www.greenpenguin.co.uk

Penguin Books is committed to a sustainable future
for our business, our readers and our planet.
The book in your hands is made from paper
certified by the Forest Stewardship Council.

For Leonard

The first place that I can well remember was a large pleasant meadow with a pond of clear water in it. Some shady trees leaned over it, and rushes and water-lilies grew at the deep end . . . When I was young I lived upon my mother's milk, as I could not eat grass. In the daytime I ran by her side, and at night I lay down close by her. When it was hot, we used to stand by the pond in the shade of the trees, and when it was cold, we had a nice warm shed near the plantation. As soon as I was old enough to eat grass, my mother used to go out to work in the day time, and come back in the evening.

Black Beauty, Anna Sewell

A Stormy Day

For the first time in his life, Edward is wearing clothes on the beach. I am watching him from where I'm perched on a sand dune. I'm trying to pretend I'm not looking at him as I know he will be cross if he thinks I am: now, aged ten, 'or nearly eleven', as he puts it, he has become aware of his body. I see him looking at himself in the bathroom mirror. He has hugely long legs and dangling arms. Sometimes he smells a bit and I have to remind him that he needs to use soap.

'Why?' he'll say truculently.

'Because when you start getting older and you play more sport, you start to sweat and when you sweat you –'

'But you don't need to use soap for sweat,' Edward usually chips in. 'I asked Robert and he told me that if you leave your body alone, it looks after itself.'

'Who told him that?'

'Auntie Julia did.'

'Well, I think she was referring to hair. Some people say that if you leave your hair long enough it'll replenish its own oils and –'

'No, Robert said Auntie Julia told him your whole body can clean itself so I'm not going to use soap.'

'Right,' I'll say firmly. 'If you don't use soap, you won't be able to play on your computer at the weekend.'

He'll glower at me a bit. 'Where is the soap, then?' he'll say accusingly, as if I've hidden it. 'There isn't any!'

'Yes, there is.' I'll point to his younger brother's soap dispenser, a plastic frog that squirts out something that smells of a chemical version of strawberries.

'Not that soap. That's for babies. Where's the sort big boys use?'

Over the past few months we have had many such encounters and now I have had to accept that, on top of hating baths, Edward feels he has to cover himself when I'm around. When he was younger, and I was a single parent, after his father, John the First, had upped and left, he discarded his clothes anywhere and everywhere. On a visit to London Zoo on a hot summer's afternoon it occurred to him, aged three, that he would like to be as free and unfettered as the caged monkeys. 'I wanna be like a monkey, Mama,' he said, as he pulled his T-shirt off over his head. 'Yes, Edward,' I said, 'but you are not a monkey. You are a small boy and small boys keep their clothes on.'

He also had a very exciting time in TGI Friday's, where the loos had some spraying mechanism so he came back soaking wet and utterly naked, having drenched everything else in sight as well, including the loo rolls and the hand towels.

'Sorry,' said Edward, looking very sorrowful. 'I just can't help it.'

So, nudity is not alien to Edward. His brothers, Bennie and baby Jamie, the children I have had with my current husband John the Second, are happy to be naked. I always think of them as cherubs in the sky, looking down on us, tooting their horns, held aloft on golden wings. Maybe that's what babies are, cherubs waiting to come to earth, watching us from above and picking out the mothers and families they like – although God knows why anyone would pick me. When Edward was a tiny baby he cried all the time, especially when I was trying to bath him (see? Thinking about it now, he's never liked having a bath). One day, my mother found me crying with him.

'What on earth's the matter?' she said. 'Why are you both crying?'

'He doesn't like me,' I wailed. 'Everything I do is wrong. I tried to give him a bath and he threw his arms out and looked terrified and –' I wailed some more. 'He *hates* me!'

My mother made me a cup of tea and sat me down, picked up Edward and held him. 'You need to support his head when you bath him,' she said, wedging Edward firmly in the crook of her arm. 'Maybe he doesn't feel properly supported. That's why most babies panic.' She took him to the bath, put him in and swooshed him around. He cooed happily. 'You see?' she said. 'He's a perfectly affable little chap.' Then she looked at me. 'Babies choose their parents, you know, so, believe it or not, Edward chose you. I'd get on with it and stop feeling sorry for yourself.'

Now I know two things. First, Edward isn't really an affable chap. He's amazing and magnificent, and probably the love of my life, but he's not affable. He's odd and scratchy and sensitive. He knows this, too, and I think it bothers him. His brow furrows when children in the playground tell him he's weird, which, according to Edward, they do quite often.

'Am I weird?' he'll ask, and I'll do that thing my mother used to do, which irritated me beyond measure, and reply, 'Well, Edward, it takes all sorts of people to make a world.'

Edward will think about this. Then his face will clear and he'll say, 'Yes, it does, doesn't it, Mummy?'

I also know that Edward and I probably did choose each other. We're two units that have become a whole. I like being with him more, perhaps than I like being with anyone else. Maybe this is why his father left all those years ago.

Today, on the beach, Edward is going to extreme lengths not to be seen. He is wrapping himself in a towel, taking off his T-shirt, clutching the towel round his waist, then trying to wriggle out of his underpants.

'Do you want help, Edward?' I call.

He glowers at me.

'Do you want me to hold the towel?' I say.

'No,' says Edward. He looks around for his swimming trunks. He can't see them. Of course not. I have them – because I have everything. I always have everything. I have packed the boot of the hire car with all the things we might need and among all the things we might need, Edward's swimming trunks are in one of the bags I have brought down to the beach. Now I can see that Edward is a little panicked. He looks confused, then turns to me and it's as if sunlight has shone across his face. He smiles at me as he always used to do.

'Mummy,' he says, 'do you know where my swimming trunks are?'

For a moment I wonder if I should say, 'No. Didn't you pack them?' After all, I spend hours moaning to John that I feel taken for granted, that my children are too dependent on me, why can't they pack their own bags and make their own tea and clean their own teeth? John points out patiently to me that, yes, that's all very well for Edward but what about Bennie, who is four, and Jamie, who is two? Then I wonder why John can't do the packing. Why is it my job? Then again, he did try to help pack for this holiday – he put in raincoats, and some tiny nappies, which Jamie grew out of at least a year ago.

'It's April,' I said to him. 'We're going to Crete, one of the hottest places known to mankind even at this time of year.'

'Great,' said John.

'So why are you packing raincoats?'

'Because it's not the summer holidays, is it? It's Easter and maybe Crete's cold at Easter.' He wandered off, and I had to unpack and start again. I wasn't sure that anything John had put in was suitable for an Easter break.

So, here we are, on the beach. I'm about to delve into one of my bags for Edward's swimming trunks when Jamie tugs at the hem of my dress. I had deposited him next to me on a beach towel and the last time I looked, thirty seconds ago, he was playing happily with his bucket and spade. Now he's trying to climb up my leg and on to my shoulder. He's shrieking and hopping from foot to foot. He has managed to manoeuvre himself off the towel and is now standing on the sand. He hates sand, especially on his feet. I have taken him to endless sandpits and encouraged him to play, but all he does is cry. The first time I took him to one, I rolled up his little baby trousers, took his tiny shoes off and helped him toddle into the sand-play area. He reacted with horror. As soon as his feet hit the sand, he let out a high-pitched squeak, then did a bizarre dance of irate disgust, turned, buried his face in my skirt and tried to climb up me, his podgy little fingers clawing at my clothes. Since then, I've tried everything. I have taken him to play parks and shown him lots of other children having a good time. Last summer, when it was deliciously hot, I found a park with a sandpit and a large paddling pool. Jamie and I watched Bennie take off his clothes and wriggle into the warm sand like a snake. But it made no difference to Jamie. He squealed every time I took him near the sand. In fact, now I think about it, he was no more enthusiastic about the water.

'Oh, Jamie,' I say, 'is it the sand? Is it too hot?'

He looks at me rather sadly.

'Is Jamie ever going to talk?' Edward says, shuffling towards me, his towel round his waist. 'This sand's hot.'

'Of course he is,' I say, picking Jamie up before he starts to cry. 'He's just a baby, Edward. You didn't speak for years. I had to get you speech therapy and – '

'Oh, forget it, Mum,' says Edward. 'Look after Jamie.'

He turns his back on me. In one motion, I deposit Jamie on my hip, his little feet all curled up, and hurl Edward's swimming trunks at him. He puts them on and mooches off towards the sea.

'I love you, Edward,' I say to his back.

'Yeah, right,' he says, not turning.

I sit down and stare at Jamie, whom I have plonked back on my towel. 'Jamie,' I say, 'what is the matter with you?'

He sits wiggling his toes and burbling.

'Jamie!' I say sternly. 'Why don't you like the sand?'

'Dada,' Jamie says, giving me a doleful look.

'No, Jamie,' I say. 'I am not your daddy. I am your mummy.'

He gives me one of his heart-melting smiles, then hauls himself on to my lap and cuddles into me. 'Dada,' he says happily, and pops his thumb into his mouth.

We sit there for a while, him and me. I gaze out at the glistening sea, the sand and the sun, and feel rather elated. I can imagine how I look: long tousled hair pushed back by my sunglasses, tanned arms and face, beautiful blond baby. God, I feel good. This is a wondrous place. Even though it's only April, the sun is warm, the sand is golden, and there's only a handful of people here. I like watching the sea, the gulls and the flocks of other birds that wheel overhead. I have our picnic hidden in the shade of a rock, sandwiches, fruit, a salad, water for the boys and a bottle of white wine for me and John.

We're having a good time here, John and I. So much of our lives is spent passing each other in a chaotic muddle. He goes to work. I look after the children. Sometimes I do some work and he runs around, trying to get the children ready for school or nursery. 'Where are your socks?' he'll ask Bennie.

'My socks?' Bennie will say. 'They're here.' He'll grab a pair of Edward's that I have left out in the hope that

Edward might find them and not put on yesterday's. Then he will run into the garden brandishing them above his head.

'Those are my socks!' Edward will yell, running after him, and Jamie will put his socks into his mouth. Five minutes later, John will come in, wild-eyed, and find me getting ready in the bathroom. 'I can't seem to get the children dressed.' I will go outside and persuade the children to behave.

Then I'll try to find the car keys – usually in the dog-basket – hang out the washing, come back in and find that still none of the children has his socks on and that John is playing a mad game with them, which involves John hiding behind the sofa while the children creep up on him until he roars and chases them back into the garden.

''Bye,' I'll say, heading towards the front door. Everyone will ignore me until, on my way home, I'll get a call from John, who by now is exhausted. 'When on earth are you coming home?' he'll say.

So, our minds are always befuddled, which is why I write everything down. I make endless lists, then insist John makes his own endless lists. Sometimes our lives seem to run on these bits of paper inserted into our diaries. We spend evenings staring at dates and booking in time – for Edward to go on a sailing course, for Bennie to get used to the idea of starting school in September, to persuade Jamie to speak.

'You're spending a couple of weeks at Edward's school in the mornings before the summer holidays,' I tell Bennie.

'Why?' Bennie will say.

'To get used to it. It'll be fun!'

Then John tells Edward he must speak c-l-e-a-r-l-y to Jamie so that he can learn to talk.

'I do speak c-l-e-a-r-l-y,' Edward will say.

Then John and I try to make time for us. Sometimes we go out for dinner. Sometimes we see friends. Often we just like to hang out together. Yet somehow, on this holiday, I feel we have found each other again. I didn't know we had lost touch but here, well, we have been happy. Here we have found what we have always known, what has never really gone away but somehow faded into the background – that we love each other.

Every night we have made a fire on the beach, then told the children stories and watched them as they've drifted off to sleep, happy, tanned and tired. Then we have taken them back to our hotel room, tucked them in and spent time drinking wine, laughing and making love like teenagers, quietly and surreptitiously in the dark.

Even Edward, truculent Edward, is happy. Look! There he is. I can see him lunging into the waves, diving through them, his brown hair flattened on to his head like a seal's. I put my hands over my eyes and squint. I see John and Bennie in the waves near Edward. Is that John and Bennie? Yes, that's John. I can tell by his outline – tall but with that stuck-out middle, like a bear. 'It's my curve of pleasure,' John always says. Sometimes, when I'm feeling particularly witty, I ask him when the baby's due. 'Next spring,' he'll say, laughing, but the buttons are popping off his shirts and his jackets don't do up any more. Ah, and Bennie's with him. Bennie is a mini-John.

He has exactly the same figure, even the same bottom – cute and round but flat at the sides. Bennie has taken off his clothes, as usual. I can see his blond curls now, long and straggly over his shoulders. I can see his rosebud mouth, open, as he screams with delight as John swooshes him in and out of the waves. Look at Bennie! He's almost hysterical, he's laughing so much. And John is throwing him higher and higher – and maybe a little bit too high, I think, and Edward is leaping into and through the waves now alongside John. They are big and rolling and John grabs Bennie and hurls him forwards into them. Hurl. Splash! Crash go the waves as they plummet down and smash on to the beach.

'Oh, Jamie,' I say, as he snuggles further into my arms. 'Don't you want to go into the water? It's so lovely and cold and refreshing.'

He gazes up at me.

'Oh, I love being on holiday,' I say, and kiss him. I kiss his little snubby nose and his face turns towards me and and I kiss his little pinky mouth and –

Suddenly the wind catches a noise and brings it to me across the beach. I strain to hear it. Someone is shouting. Who? Then I see a long-limbed figure running towards me. It's Edward. It is he who is shouting. Oh, God, what's happened? I put Jamie on the sand and leap up. He starts to cry.

Edward is yelling now. '*Muuuuum!*' I can see he's shouting something else too but I can't hear it because the wind snatches it away. He sounds panicked. What is it? Has he stepped on an urchin? No, he's not limping. I hear Jamie crying. I do nothing about it. I can't concentrate on him right now. I know something's happened. I look for John but I can't see him.

'*Muuuuum!*' yells Edward, still struggling up the beach towards me.

I look for John again. I still can't see him. I run to Edward. His face is white. I can hear Jamie crying behind me. I keep going. Where is Bennie? Thank God. There's John. I can see him in the water. His head is swivelling around. He has lost something in the water. Then I look for Bennie again.

Where is Bennie? I can't see him. John is looking this way and that, yet I cannot see Bennie. I start to panic. Suddenly John dives, but he comes up alone and there is still no Bennie. Now I can see only John, silhouetted in the sea against the sun, and Edward thrashing across the sand towards me, now breathless and half crying, half yelling. I can hear Jamie wailing behind me and then, finally, I hear a roar. It is not the sea. It is not a flock of sea birds with their wings beating heavily through the air. It is John. 'Benneeee!' he yells, and the sound of his voice breaking, cracking, is carried across the water to echo all round the perfect inlet of Elafonissi beach.

And that was it. In that moment, before John dived one more time, found Bennie at the bottom of the sea and pulled him up, cold and seemingly lifeless, then dragged him out.

Before the Greek doctor who happened to be on the beach with his family brought him back to life, before I knew whether Bennie was dead or alive, I knew something very important. I knew that it was me and me alone who had this ability to create these children and love them and keep them. It seemed to be the only thing that made any sense. Bennie was mine and only I could take the decision to lose him. No one else had the right to take my child away from me. And in the moment it took that doctor to force air into Bennie's body, with the breath that wrenched him back to life, I knew something else. I wanted another baby. And that knowledge made me put my hand fleetingly on my belly. Once Bennie was breathing regularly, I let myself smile a secret smile.

A Fair Start

It is seven fifteen in the morning, two months after our holiday, and I am lying in bed. Normally I would be excited about this. Normally I would be doing a little horizontal jig. I would be thinking, Here I am *in bed* and everyone else is downstairs. Then I would experience a small, secret swell of excitement, starting in my belly and moving to my brain as I realized I didn't have to deal with what was going on downstairs. For what is going on downstairs at this time in the morning is chaos.

Edward is usually watching television. He will have been downstairs goggling at it, from the relative warmth and safety of the Chair, since about five thirty. He likes to watch television from the Chair because it is the only comfortable thing to sit on in the house. Everything else has been ruined. The sofa in the sitting room, which was once plump and glorious, is now put-upon. Its fine deep blue lustre has become matt. Its cushions are bedraggled, its covers torn. The carpet is covered with dog and cat hair and, probably, fleas. When our neighbours moved out rather suddenly – she had told him she didn't want kids although a nanosecond later she was pregnant by someone else – we filched five cans of home de-flea spray from their skip. I felt almost uncomfortable rifling through what was left of a life together. There was an entire sofa, a bit worn in places, but we would've grabbed it if it hadn't been an especially rainy spring, which meant it was sodden and too heavy to lift.

I'm thinking about this as my head sinks back into the pillows. How marvellous and unexpected to see the clock's hands tick round and know that your husband, your beautiful loving husband, is downstairs making breakfast and you can stay in bed and doze. Doze! What an attractive, heady sensation dozing is. So here I am, happy, sleepy, on the verge of – *Bringggg!*

The alarm goes off. Oh, God. I'd almost forgotten that I have to take my temperature every day and note it in a little book with *How To Get A Girl* on the front. Two months ago, when we came back from holiday, I went on to the Internet and found a company called Choose Your Baby!

I told the doctor who saved Bennie that I had decided to have another child. We were standing on the beach. The doctor was dripping. He had run into the surf to help John as he brought the limp Bennie back to land. He had forced his mouth on to Bennie's and given him the kiss of life, and once Bennie was breathing, he had rocked back, stunned. Edward was crouched over his brother, holding him and whispering, 'I love you, Bennie,' into his ear. I was standing, Jamie on my hip, jabbering thanks like a madwoman. John was staring out to sea.

'I'm going to have another child,' I said to the doctor, in a rush. 'I'd like to name it after you or your wife to honour you for saving my son.' I grabbed the doctor's hand as I told him this. I wonder now if he was embarrassed. What do you say to someone who has just saved your child's life, who has telephoned his hospital for a fully-equipped ambulance? Do you say, 'Oh, thanks'? I couldn't think of anything else to say so I cried and promised him the only thing I could think of: a child bearing his name.

'My name is Stavros,' he told me. 'My wife is Maria.'

'Wonderful names,' I said. 'Beautiful.' I told him we'd send them a photograph every year of Bennie so they could see how he had grown, and how grateful I was because he would not have grown without Stavros. I told him we would write to him, that we'd never forget him, but then the ambulance arrived and we had to leave him and Maria and wave goodbye to them as we drove off.

I held little Bennie's hand for what seemed like hours on that journey. He just stared into space. The blankness of his gaze made me cry. I had no idea what he was thinking. I'd thought we'd lost him for ever, and wept for his life, the shock he had been through, and tried to imagine what it must have been like for him, abandoned to the power of the sea. The enormity of his terror made me shiver.

But Edward seemed unaware of this. He talked to Bennie all the way to the hospital. He told him tales of Jack and his beanstalk and Slinky Malinki the cat, and I had to bite my tongue to stop myself telling him to shut up.

John drove behind in the hire car with Jamie, and sometimes I would peer out of the back window and see him with his shirt open, bare chest exposed, eyes dark and hollow. For a minute, I was so angry I wanted to hit him. But by the time we got to the hospital I had tired of that emotion, of everything, really, and it was only as Bennie was rushed off to A and E that I realized Edward was still in his swimming trunks. He left small trails of sand like Hansel's breadcrumbs on the floor behind him as he followed us. Maybe he thought we'd never find our way out again.

But we did find our way out and, as we left and as Bennie's head sank on to my shoulder, I pushed John away when he held out his arms for his son. I whispered, 'I love you,' into Bennie's ear and he murmured back, 'I – I – love you too, Mama.'

What It Is to Be Loved by a Child

Every child's first love is for their mother. Goodness, how children love their mothers! It is overwhelming and all-powerful. The thought of your mother abandoning you, of taking away her love, is so dreadful, so terrifying that the child who fears this will cling to its mother as if possessed by demons.

One of my first memories of my mother is of her lying on my bed reading Black Beauty *to me and my sister Julia. I loved those evenings, the three of us curled up quiet against the wintry night. My mother would come in with two cups of cocoa, set them down, then lie between us, holding the book so we could see the etchings in it. She'd won it in 1939, as a prize at primary school, and her name was written in it in brown ink. I loved that book. It smelled fusty when she opened it.*

Some nights, my mother wouldn't read. She'd tell us she was going out and we'd stand, dejected, watching her get ready for a party with my father. She would be in her bathroom and we would peer at her through the crack in the door. My father would be downstairs, ironing his dress shirt. My mother wouldn't iron. She'd say, 'I was born to do many things. Ironing isn't one of them.' We would hear her singing in the bathroom. We would go to the door. She would turn and smile. She'd beckon us in and we'd perch on the side of the bath as she 'put her face on'. We would watch her rub rouge into her cheeks, paint kohl on her eyelids, then make her lips into a pout and smear on bright-red lipstick.

She'd go to her bedroom and leaf through her wardrobe, humming and hawing, looking for the right dress.

That wardrobe seemed cavernous. Julia and I could fit into it together. We'd rummage around and then we'd sit down, squashing my mother's leather shoes, with their high heels, her dancing shoes covered with navy satin, tuck our legs under us and wait for someone to find us. Sometimes it would take ages. I'd hear her calling for us: 'Samantha! Julia! Where are you?' But we'd sit there quietly, breathing in the mothball scent, mixed with material.

We loved my mother. We wanted to be near her. I remember this when I see my children's need for me in their eyes. I see their delight as they rip off their pyjamas and get into the bath with me, even when there is no space beneath the bubbles. Even when I want to yell, 'Get out!', I cannot bring myself to disappoint them. They love to feel my skin on theirs, to sidle up to me, soapy and warm, and snuggle their heads on to my chest as I pour warm water over them, soap them and gently wash their hair. Then I wrap them in towels and cuddle them on my bed. For it is my love that they need. And I am convinced that it was my love that saved Bennie.

So, John and I went home with our family. We sat in silence on the aeroplane, but when I looked at John, I thought he was going to cry so I held his hand and he squeezed mine. I told him it wasn't his fault, that it could have happened to anybody, but he wouldn't meet my eyes. We both knew how close we had come. It was a warning, maybe.

And now, some few months later, with Bennie spending a few mornings at school before he starts full time in September, we seem to have got back to normal. John is working and I, well, I haven't dismissed the idea of having another child. This is what families are about, isn't it? They chop and change, expand and contract, only this family stopped the contracting part when we went from three – John the First, myself and Edward – to two. Now we just keep getting bigger and bigger. But we can encompass all. With every growing child, so my capacity to love them grows. I just find more love somehow.

'Look,' I said to John one day. 'I've found this website that says it can get us a girl.'

We were having another diary discussion in which he was telling me what he was up to – 'Being successful!' I said, as he explained he had a new project on – and I was trying to explain the logic of having another child in, ooh, let's say nine months' time.

'Mmm,' said John, who was also trying to fix a door handle. He used to be hopeless with practical stuff – strange for a set designer, I always thought, but he maintains he's a creative type who designs things that other people make – but now he's quite good.

'There are all these testimonials from people saying how ecstatic they are that they had a baby of their choice.'

'Great!' said John, hammering away.

'We can buy a girl kit,' I said.

'God, it's like a supermarket,' he said. 'You don't believe this, do you? You *can't* believe that this company, which is going to charge you two hundred dollars, can give you the baby you want?'

'Why not? It says you can have your money back if you get the wrong sex.'

'Oh, yippee.'

'Seriously, John, I've been researching it. It's all about when you ovulate and stuff. Female sperms swim slower than male ones. If I find out when I ovulate we can have a girl.'

'How?' he said suspiciously.

'It says on the website that we have to have sex constantly until two days before I ovulate, then stop.'

'How long for?'

'For ever.'

'Forget it!'

'But we do have to have sex every day, maybe twice, for five days.'

'Buy it!'

'John,' I said, 'I have the feeling you're not taking this seriously.'

He put down the screwdriver with which he was about to attack the door, came over to me and put his arms round me. 'I am taking it seriously,' he said gently, 'but I'm not sure we should have another child.'

'Why not?'

'Well, I just think we should concentrate on the three we have.'

'I do nothing but concentrate on them. Ever since we

got back from holiday I've concentrated on them so much I think I'm going to burst.'

'And you're tired,' said John. 'Wouldn't a baby make things worse?'

'Maybe it would reinvigorate me.'

'What on earth makes you think that?'

'It's not just any baby I want, John. I want a girl.'

John looked away, but when he turned back, I could see he was worried.

'I know, and I do understand, but what if we don't get a girl? How would you feel if we had another boy?'

'Fine,' I said brightly.

'Really?'

'Absolutely,' I said. 'Anyway, we're not going to have a boy because I'm going to get a girl Choose Your Baby kit and then I'll be like those grinning parents on the website. I can say, 'Thank you, CYB, for giving me the baby girl we always wanted. How can I thank you? Here she is and her name's Angel.'

'Angel?' John groaned.

'OK, what about Clemency?'

'Yuk.'

'Marlene?'

'God, no.'

'Beauty, from *Black Beauty*?'

'She's not a horse. How about Claire?'

'*Claire?*' I said. 'I get one shot at naming a girl and you want to call her Claire!'

'What's wrong with Claire?'

'Everything. I want a romantic name like Maria or Tallulah or Sheba . . . Actually, we have to call her

Maria after Stavros's wife – remember? We promised him.'

'Well, I didn't.'

'How about Elizabeth?'

'All those names are dreadful,' said John, 'and, anyway, aren't you being a bit previous? You haven't even bought the kit yet.'

It arrived four days later. I sat and read the *How To Get A Girl* booklet from cover to cover and felt terribly excited. The kit contained a thermometer, charts and ovulation sticks that you used as a test five days a month, and some funny little pills called nutriceuticals, which you took every day to make your womb more receptive to girls. I wanted to be pregnant again. A brood-mare, that's what I am.

So, every day I have to take my temperature, and when the thermometer bleeps, it means it's read it. I mark it down on the chart, take my nutriceutical pill and work out whether or not I need to use my ovulation monitor. The monitor is everything. It tells me when to use my test sticks (it shows a little picture of a stick on the tiny screen). I must use my monitor when my temperature does a sudden leap upwards because that means I'm ovulating. If the monitor shows a picture of a test stick, I have to wee on one and slot it into the monitor, then wait to see if a green or red light comes on. A green light means John and I must have sex immediately for that is when we can get a girl: 'You must have sex as soon as you see the green light come on,' the booklet says. 'This is your chance to Get A Girl so it is important you act immediately.'

Apparently we are to have sex only in the missionary position. The man should ejaculate more than once – lucky him! – but the woman must not orgasm or go to the loo for at least an hour. If you fail to have sex on the green-light day, or you fail to get pregnant despite having had sex, you can buy more monthly *How To Get A Girl* kits for another two hundred dollars a pop.

The booklet listed all the things I should eat to get a girl – fish (not tuna), lean meat, wholewheat pasta, dairy products, fresh vegetables, unsalted nuts and peanut butter – and all the things I shouldn't: red meat, processed cheese, sausages, ham, burgers, soy sauce, frozen dinners, pickles and sardines. I told John it sounded very complicated. He grimaced.

Edward came in while I was studying the booklet. 'What's that?' he said, looking at everything I'd laid on the table in front of me.

'It's my *How To Get A Girl* kit,' I said.

'Are you pregnant again?' he said, excited.

'Not yet, but we're going to try.'

'Can I call her Sparkle?'

'Yes,' I said.

'What – Sparkle Smelly-bum Smythe?' Edward was giggling now.

'No.'

'Oh,' he said, deflated. Then he thought for a bit.

'Oh, God,' he said. 'That means you and Daddy are going to have to have sex, doesn't it?'

'Yep. No other way, I'm afraid.'

'That's disgusting.'

'No, it isn't, Edward,' I said. I had rehearsed this one

in my head. 'It's an act that's jolly good fun between two adults who love each other.'

'Should I have sex with Stanley? I love Stanley, you know, we're very interactive* together.' (* Note from Edward: 'My mum has put lots of stars in this book because she says I get my words muddled up. She has written about it right at the very end. You go past the bit that says The End and there it all is.')

'Ah, yes, I know you love Stanley but you're not adults so you can't. However, if you get to be over eighteen and you and Stanley feel you still love each other then –'

Wendy, our new au pair, appeared. 'Then you're a pair of raving poofters!' she said, in her broad Australian accent.

Edward was giggling again.

'Come on, Edward,' she said. 'Your bros are all ready for tea.'

'What is it?' said Edward.

'Kangaroo bollocks and raw prawns Aussie-style!'

Edward was giggling uncontrollably now. 'I love kangaroo bollocks,' he spluttered.

On her way out, as she blocked the light from the doorway, Wendy said, 'Ah'm having a night in, me, some tinnies and the footie. Join me, eh, and we'll make a party of it! 'Sall right with you, yeah?' And then she walked out.

The Hunt

I'm not sure if I was right to let Wendy into our lives. I'd always thought I could cope without childcare but, one day, I realized I couldn't. 'I need help,' I said to John, and those words felt like an admission of failure.

'Do you?' said John.

'Yes,' I said. 'I'm desperate. I'm stuck in the middle of nowhere with three children and a vague job and I want more help.'

'Mm,' said John. We had a discussion – interrupted constantly by the children, who were bickering over a toy fire engine – about whether or not we could cope with someone living in.

'We'd have to get them a car,' said John. 'We'd have to buy their food, give them a television in their room and hear about their emotional problems.'

'I could share my car,' I said, 'young girls don't eat much, and au pairs never talk to men about their problems. It's always the mother they go to.'

'Do you want that?'

'No,' I said. 'Not really.'

But when we got back from holiday, it started up again.

'I'm dying,' I groaned to John one night, as I peered out at him from under a huge pile of washing at ten o'clock.

'No, you're not,' he said. 'You're just overworked and stressed out.'

'I need someone to help me,' I said.

'I can help you,' he said. 'We don't need anyone else.'

'We do. You can't help me because you're always working and, anyway, I wasn't put on this planet to spend my life shopping and ironing and sorting out children's clothes and doing the school run. I've thought about it, John, I really have, and I need someone to be here every day.'

'Why?'

'Why? Because I'm tired and I've turned into a domestic drudge and we never go out because we can't find a babysitter and I'm the only one who ever remembers things and juggles things and I'm tired of it all.'

'I remember things.'

'But not in the same way. I mean, what day does Edward have his swimming lessons?'

John stopped and thought a bit. 'Hmm,' he said. 'Thursdays.'

'No. It's every other Tuesday.'

'Oh.'

'What time does Bennie come home from school?'

'Oh, that's easy. Three forty-five with Edward.'

'No, midday while he's acclimatizing this summer term and full time in September.'

'Oh,' said John, a bit upset. He prides himself on being a good father – and so he should: he's a very good father. He took Edward on from the age of just four and morphed so quickly into being Dad that most people assume he's Edward's father, even though he isn't. 'Are you cross with me?' he asked. 'Am I a crap and useless dad?'

'No, darling. You're a truly wonderful dad, but you're busy so the boring minutiae of the children's day is not embedded in your brain as it is in mine.'

'Well, what do you feel you need?'

'Another me, really.'

'Well, I can't be another you,' he said, 'so I suppose you're right. We need some help.'

We discussed it for ages. John said he was coming round to the idea of a live-in au pair. We spent the night drawing up a list of what we wanted. I wanted someone kind, reliable, efficient, self-motivated, optimistic, artistic, sporty, a good cook, good fun, a driver, non-smoking, wonderful with children, easy to get on with and over twenty-five. John wanted someone under twenty-five and pretty. That was all. Young. Pretty.

'For God's sake,' I said, 'is that all that matters to you? What about our children? What about their needs?'

'OK,' said John, 'I also put on the other side of the page – see? I've written PTO at the bottom of the page – good at cleaning.'

'Good at cleaning?' I said. 'Is that it?'

'Yup,' said John.

I was about to explode when I caught his eye. He was grinning. Then he caught me round the middle and bundled me down on to the sofa. 'Get your clothes off,' he said, trying to undo my belt.

'Oh, no, kind sir,' I said, in a fake Spanish accent. 'Meeses Smythe will not be pleased with me.'

'Mr Smythe is very pleased with you.'

'Oh, no, kind sir. Not unless Meester Smythe has protection.'

'Your accent's putting me off,' said John.

'Oh, sorry,' I said. 'Anyway, you seriously need protection because, according to my *How To Get A Girl* kit, now is the wrong time to have unprotected sex.'

'That bloody kit,' said John. 'It's ruining our lives!'

He went and got the telephone directory.

'What are you doing?'

'Looking up au pair agencies.'

'But, Meester Smythe, me thought you wanna hanky-panky?'

John came back and kissed me, then said he thought we ought to start ringing agencies in the morning but, right now, we should plan where the girl could sleep, and off he went, talking about how maybe Edward should move upstairs to the front room so that the au pair could have his room, which had a lock . . . I wasn't really listening. He had turned me away. John, my John, who had always wanted me, always desired me, had never let me down, had turned away from me. Why now?

'John,' I said.

'Mm?' He was drawing plans of who should sleep where.

'Don't you want me any more?'

'Of course I want you.'

'But why did you stop kissing me back then?'

'Did I?'

'Yes.'

'It was that silly accent. It put me off.'

'I'd stopped doing the silly accent.'

'Oh.'

'John, are you sure you want another baby?'

'Yes.' But he didn't look me in the eye.

'Do you think it will change things?'

'Babies always change things, don't they? I don't think women are the same after they've had children, are they?'

The next morning I called the agencies and told them what I wanted. A live-in? Yes. Own bedroom? Yes. Own car? Yes. Own bathroom? No, shared. In a city? No, a village. Near a town? Yes. Babysitting required? Yes. Yes. Yes. Yes. The fifth agency I called was run by a lady called Anne who lives near by.

'I need an au pair desperately,' I said, cutting to the chase.

'Luckily for you, I've got just the right girl sitting in front of me now,' said Anne. 'Would you like to talk to her? Her name's Wendy. She's Australian and she came over to work for a family but they can't have her because the gentleman' – here, she hushed her voice right down – 'has *lost his job*. Wendy has no employer, no job and nowhere to live.'

'Right,' I said. 'Has she any experience with children?'

'I've got her CV right here. Let me see. She used to be a nursery nurse in Adelaide, has three younger brothers and a younger sister.'

'Crikey!' I said. 'That's a big family.'

'She has good written references – I'll follow them up, of course. Do you want to speak to her?'

Yes, I did want to speak to Wendy. I can't remember what I said. I can't even remember what Wendy said. I just remember thinking that she could be the answer to my problems.

'She sounds great,' I said to Anne, when she came back on the telephone.

'Great!' said Anne. 'I'll chase up the references and you talk to your husband. If you're both in agreement, she can start tomorrow.'

'So fast!' I said.

'That's good, isn't it?' said Anne. 'Strike while the iron's hot. It's fate!'

Before she rang off I told her I needed to ask her one more thing. 'How old is she?'

'Twenty-three, I think.'

'And is she . . . is she . . . Oh dear, this is going to sound dreadful.'

'I know what you want to ask, Mrs Smythe. All women want to know. And you needn't worry. Do you understand?'

'Yes,' I said. Good. Not pretty. I breathed a sigh of relief.

Wendy showed up the next day, tall, blonde, tanned and huge, with massive feet encased in what looked like flip-flops made from tyres.

'Oh, my God, she's on loan from the Wallabies,' said John, as Wendy came up the drive.

'Don't be horrible,' I said. 'It's probably puppy fat.'

'At twenty-three?' He snorted.

Wendy took one look at me, dropped her rucksack on the ground, strode the last few yards, took me in her arms and gave me a bear-hug. 'We're gonna be great mates,' she said. 'Y'know, you can be like me mam. Me mam's me best mate. Me dad ran off with another woman when I was ten. Me mam told me he was as lazy as a koala. I love me mam and you're like me mam because you saved me! I had nowhere to go and you rang when I was in that posh lady's office and now I've got a home and I couldn't be more . . . Thanks, Mrs S. That's what I've decided to call yer, kinda matey but respectful. What d'ya think?'

Just as I was about to tell her that Samantha was fine by me, the children ran out to meet her.

'Oh, look at these beaut nippers!' she yelled. She ran to the children, scooped up Jamie and Bennie, somehow ruffling Edward's hair at the same time. 'I come from a country where crocodiles bite yer toes off!' she roared, pretending to nip Jamie's toes with her fingers. He squealed in delight.

'Do you have kangaroos in your country?' said Edward.

'Yeah,' said Wendy. 'I got a kangaroo bag for one of you!'

'Wh-wh-where?' said Bennie, having wriggled out of her arms. 'Look at me! I'm a kangaroo!'

'They don't jump like that, Bennie,' said Edward.

'Y-yes, they do,' said Bennie, his mouth forming a crumpled O.

'No, they don't. They don't really hop. They bound, don't they – What's your name again?' he said to Wendy.

'Wendy,' she said.

'I'm no good at names,' Edward told her. 'I don't even know what my mum's name is.'

'It's Samantha!' said Bennie, leaping up and down in a most kangaroo-like fashion.

'I was only joking,' said Edward, witheringly, to him.

'The roo bag's in me rucksack,' said Wendy. 'And I've

got a mock-croc tail for someone else and some bonza sweets I brought all the way from Oz and –'

'Are they all in your ruck-whatever-you-call-it?' said Edward, eyeing Wendy's rucksack.

'Yeah,' said Wendy.

'G-get them out! Get them out!' said Bennie.

'I'll show you to your room, Wendy,' I said.

'No, I'll show her,' said Edward, roughly pushing me out of the way.

'Edward!' I said.

'Don't shove your mam,' said Wendy, grinning. 'Now, where were we, Edward? Your mam's told me a lot about you, y'know.'

'Did she tell you I liked sharks?' said Edward.

'Yeah, she told me you think sharks are bonza!'

'Yes, I do think they're whatever that word is you said I think they are. I think they're great! I know everything about them. I . . .'

And off they went to the house, with Edward chatting on about Hammerheads and Oceanic White Tips and Great Whites and I could hear Wendy saying, 'I saw a Great White off the coast of Queensland once,' and Edward saying, 'Nooo, tell me about it,' and Wendy saying, 'It swum up to me and I inflated myself as big as I could get and I yelled, "Yullaboobahooba," at it and I waved me arms around and I punched it on the nose and it swam away!'

'Punched it on the nose?' Edward said thoughtfully. 'Yes, that was the right thing to do, er . . .'

'Wendy,' supplied Wendy helpfully.

'Yeah, that was the right thing to do, Wendy, because

sharks hate being punched on the nose. It probably tried to eat you because it thought you were a sea lion.'

'Right,' said Wendy.

'God,' said John, as we followed them into the house. 'You've hired the female equivalent of Crocodile Dundee.'

But everything about Wendy, in terms of the children, turned out to be almost miraculous. She seemed to have an innate understanding of Bennie's newly acquired stutter.

'It started after he had an accident, did it, Mrs S?' she said, before I'd even had a chance to tell her that Bennie had spoken the Queen's English before he'd nearly drowned.

'Yes,' I said.

'My little brother, can't remember which one, stood on a scorpion once and it bit him so hard he didn't speak for a whole day, which is saying something in my house, Mrs S.'

'Yes,' I said. 'But Bennie does speak. He just –'

'Can't spit his words out, yeah? Same thing, Mrs S.'

Jamie seemed to adore her. She carried him around everywhere on her hip, as if he were a bushbaby, and even Edward, who had complained bitterly about having to leave his beautiful, relatively remote bedroom, was proud of his sacrifice.

'Your new room's fab!' Wendy told him on the first night, and then, within a week, she'd got him some glow-in-the-dark stars and a mobile consisting of all the planets in the solar system. His room was transformed. She put butterflies all over hers. 'We get big 'uns in Oz,' she told the children. Then she bought more glow-in-the-dark stars and an aquarium for Bennie and Jamie.

'Maybe that's a mistake,' I said nervously, when she arrived back from the pet shop laden with it, four goldfish and two beautiful black shubunkins. 'Nah,' she said. 'It's good for nippers to have a pet. My brother had a piranha once and he took care of it really well. It became quite matey.'

She turned to Bennie. 'What do we do with the fish?'

'Be – be careful with them,' said Bennie, solemnly.

'Yeah, little mate, and what do we feed them?'

'F-fish food.'

'Do we feed them a lot or a tiny bit?'

'Tiny bit.'

'See?' said Wendy, galumphing up the stairs. 'It'll be fine.'

And, for a while, it was, until one afternoon while Wendy was out with Bennie and I was at home with Jamie, the cat got upstairs. We found him with a fishy tail sticking out of his mouth.

'Ooh,' said Jamie.

'Honey!' I shouted at the cat.

Bennie was inconsolable. Then, a week later when Bennie and Wendy were out, I found Jamie in his and Bennie's bedroom with two wet hands and a fishy tail sticking out of his mouth. 'Jamie!' I said. He had grabbed a shubunkin. I tried to resuscitate it but it floated upside-down.

When Wendy came home I took her to one side. 'Jamie tried to eat a shubunkin,' I told her.

'Right, he's copying the cat, yeah?'

'Obviously. But I've put it back in the tank and it's dead.'

'How d'ya know it's dead?'

'It's upside-down.'

'Sometimes shubunkins like swimming on their backs. My sister had a fish like that once and he flipped over and never came up the right way.'

'Well, maybe that was because the friendly piranha had taken a nip out of it.'

'Nah. That fish was alive. It outlived the piranha.'

'Well, this one is dead and I don't know how to tell Bennie.'

'No worries. I'll tell him for ya.'

Wendy went into the kitchen where the children were having tea. 'Hey, Bennie,' said Wendy, 'your little bro ate one of your fish.'

'A-ate my fish?'

'Yeah, one of those cute little black ones.'

'J-Jamie ate it?' said Bennie again, his eyes wide in amazement.

'Yeah, poor fish, eh?'

'P-poor fish,' said Bennie, and that was that.

A Friend in Need

This morning I try to lie very still in my bed. It is not easy as the children usually come in and bounce on me. Wendy is supposed to help me get them up but of late she hasn't bothered. This has made me rather annoyed with her. I keep telling John it's her job to get up, but he just shrugs and goes back to sleep. Sometimes he says, 'Well, why don't you do something about it?' which is what my best friend Adele says when I moan about Wendy.

'Well, what do you want her to do?' Adele will say a bit tartly, as I go on about how Wendy used to be brilliant but has ceased to be so.

'I want her to get up in the morning and help,' I say.

'Well, make a list of her jobs. She'll be clear about what you want and you'll be clear about whether or not she's prepared to do what you want.'

'But I told her when she started that she had to get up and help get the kids ready in the morning.'

'Did you?' Adele says. 'Did you make a list?'

'Not exactly.' I know the type of list Adele means. She loves lists even more than I do. She makes lists of everything. She once made me a list of all the things I had to do with Beady. On it she wrote, 'Feed Her, Walk Her, Wash Her Coat'. John and I giggled over it for ages because we thought Adele must think we're morons.

'You need a list that you pin on the board so everyone's clear about what their responsibilities are. Are you capable of doing that, Samantha?' Adele said the other day, when I called up for another Wendy-moan.

'Yes. Why wouldn't I be?'

'Because you're one of those hopeless middle-class liberals who wants to avoid conflict. Your problem is that you want everyone to like you.'

'What's wrong with that?'

'It doesn't work with staff. They try to become your friend and stop working effectively. You have to be straight-talking with Wendy. You have to tell her to bloody well get up in the morning or she can move out. Get it?'

I told Adele I did but somehow, all these weeks later, I have still failed to talk to Wendy about her morning non-appearance. Whenever I think the appropriate moment has arrived something else happens: a child needs food/water/their knee bandaged, the telephone rings, someone drops by for a coffee . . .

Anyway, this morning I'm not budging from my bed. I've made it clear to John that if we're to get a girl, I can't do anything when I wake up.

'Oh, God,' said John, when I dug him in the ribs about an hour ago. 'Why do I have to get up? I mean, I love the children and I'm dying to see them but –'

I poked him in the ribs again. 'My *How To Get A Girl* kit told me that, in order to get an accurate reading of my temperature, I can't do anything before the thermometer bleeps.'

'Nothing?'

'Absolutely nothing,' I said. 'The book's very clear about that. I mustn't move a muscle.'

John groaned a bit, but, as I rummaged around for my thermometer, he got up, put on his robe, found the thermometer, gave me a kiss and disappeared downstairs.

I stuck the thermometer into my mouth, and now I'm lying here, letting my head sink back and – *Bringgg.* What's that? *Bringggg!* The telephone. *Bringggg!* I'm not answering, I've got a thermometer in my mouth. If I move a muscle or open my mouth all will be lost. *Bringggg!* Click. Someone downstairs has answered it. Mmm, I shall sink back into my pillows and –

'Mu-um!' It's Edward. I shall ignore him. I know Edward. He'll just shout and shout and never bother to come up the stairs to find me. If I lie here and do nothing, he'll go away.

'Mu-um!'

I reach for my earplugs. I love them. They're called Ear Fit, spongy and yellow. I bought them originally to block out John's snoring but then they proved handy in making Jamie's crying seem distant so now he sleeps well and does a good line in babbling when he wakes up rather than out-and-out yelling.

'Mu-um!'

Why is Edward still calling? I can hear him coming up the stairs. I dive under the duvet. I have a thermometer in my mouth. Why doesn't John take the call? Why is someone calling me so goddamned early? I hear the door open.

'Mum,' says Edward, ignoring the fact that I'm hiding

under my duvet. 'There's a telephone call for you. I've been shouting for *ages*. Why didn't you answer?'

'Urgh,' I say, trying not to dislodge the thermometer.

'But, Mum, it's Adele. She says she has to speak to you.'

I crawl out from under the duvet and reach for the phone.

'Adele,' I say. 'Are you OK? What's the matter?'

'I'm fine, painting my toenails.'

'It's just gone seven in the morning. Isn't it a bit early to be doing that?'

'Only time, when you're busy for the rest of the day. What are you doing? Has Wendy got up?'

'Erm, yes,' I lie. 'I was sort of sleeping.'

'How restful! Are you trying to boost your *chi*?'

Adele always says things like this. For an organized person, she's rather New Agey. She spends half her life getting her *chakras* read and taking her daughter, Nancy, to the kinesiologist to see what foods she's allergic to (everything, apparently). She's very intense about such things and has absolutely no time for anyone who disagrees with her. 'Why haven't you taken Edward to see the kinesiologist?' she'll say, as she watches Edward career round the garden with his mouth open as if he is catching flies.

'Why? What's wrong with him?'

'He's hyperactive.' Then she'll announce that he's probably allergic to wheat and dairy products.

When Adele isn't preparing wheat-free food for Nancy, she's having non-invasive facelifts, spray tans, and balancing her amino acids, which apparently affect her moods.

Yet she's very devil-may-care, is Adele. She drives at breakneck speed, her blonde hair flowing out behind her, talking on her mobile, drinking coffee and steering with her knees.

Edward is fascinated by her.

This morning, Adele tells me she has to meet me at the school gates.

'Why?' I say, a bit crossly as I'd had no intention of going anywhere. 'John was going to drop the boys off on his way to London.'

'Samantha, listen to me. You must get out of bed, have a bath, do your hair, put on some makeup and wear a skirt.'

'I don't have makeup or a skirt and, anyway, why must I?'

'Oh, God,' she says, rather tetchily, 'don't you read the local paper?'

'No,' I say.

'So you don't know, then?'

'No.'

'Gary White's just moved into the area. He's bought that big house down the road from you. The Dower House, isn't it?'

'He's bought it?'

'Yes – for millions! I can't believe you didn't read about it.'

'But who is Gary White?'

'*Who's Gary White?* Are you mad? He's that Cockney footballer who's always in magazines.'

'I don't watch football. I don't read magazines.'

'Surely you know who he is. He's retired now but he

used to play for some London club. He was really very famous and he's very, very good-looking. His wife left him for his accountant. It was all over the papers a few months ago. You must have read about it.'

'No, Adele,' I say. 'I didn't read about it and I have no idea what it's got to do with me.'

'I've told you. He's just moved to the Dower House *in your village* and he has a seven-year-old daughter, called Rowan, and she's starting at our school, and guess what?'

'What?'

'She's in Nancy's class!'

'Lucky old Nancy.'

'That means she's at Edward's school, too, dimbo.'

'And?'

'Oh, Samantha!' Adele sounds frustrated now. 'He's gorgeous. He drives a red Ferrari. All the mothers are so excited.'

'Why?'

'Because he's a celebrity! It's the only chance any of us has ever had to get near to one.'

'He's a *footballer*,' I say. 'In fact, he's a former footballer.'

'God, Samantha,' says Adele, laughing now, 'you can be such a snob sometimes. Come on! He's single and sexy and worth a look. It's called fun, you know.'

'It's only just past seven,' I remind her.

'It's Gary White! He's super-famous. Come on, nothing exciting ever happens round here. The least you could do is meet me at the gates and have a little look at him. You won't believe what you see. I promise you.'

*

I decide that Adele is mad and that there's no way I'm going to drive the children to school. Then John appears from making his usual morning mess in the bathroom – shaving foam spread everywhere, sometimes on the ceiling, hairs in the bath, stubble in the sink, grooming products scattered over the dresser – and says he has to leave *right now*. Apparently his co-worker Charlotte, or 'Charlie' as he calls her, needs him. They're working on a set design for an open-air play-cum-circus-cum-aerial-spectacular being put on in a specially made circus tent and Charlie has just text-messaged him to say that the revolving system he was using to create something involving flying unicorns has broken down.

'I've got to go!' he yells, as I look at the text. '*Cum now. St br dwn. C x*'

'How on earth do you know what that means?' I call. He is noisily flossing his teeth.

'What what means?' he says, from the bathroom.

'That message.'

'It's obvious.'

'Not to me.'

'It means, come now, set broken down.' He reappears and gives me a funny look. 'Don't you understand text messaging?'

'You know perfectly well I don't. I don't even know how to do it.'

John knows this is true. I have spent hours jabbing at my phone with disastrous results.

'Everyone does it now,' he said, grabbing his car keys and his bag. 'It's so cheap.'

'But I don't,' I say.

'That's because you're a Luddite, as everyone knows.'

It's true that, in the past, I've told everyone I know that I can't text-message but they still insist on sending me them. My sister Julia has perfected some kind of teenage jargon that only Edward can understand. When I asked her why she kept sending me messages in gobbledegook, she said, 'I've got teenage children! That's how they communicate. It's terribly handy, you see, because they've pared down the English language. For example, if you've said you'll meet someone for a drink, but then you don't want to, you just text them you're busy like this.' She typed 'bsy 2mr'. 'See?' I told her I didn't. I told her I had no idea what 'bsy 2mr' meant either.

By then Edward had appeared through the door and was moaning about why he couldn't have a mobile phone or a PlayStation or a game cube and I replied, as I always do, that I didn't want him to turn into a moron. My sister said that in her studies, and in the studies of childcare guru and American academic Dr Zachary Hofman Junior, with whose work she seems to have become obsessed as part of the PhD she's doing on children's cognitive behaviour, playing games for an hour a day is constructive to the male brain.

'See?' said Edward accusingly. 'Did you hear what Auntie Julia said? It's *good* for me to play computer games. I bet Robert plays them and he's super-intelligent.'

'Well, I bet Stanley isn't allowed to,' I said.

'No,' said Edward, morosely. 'He's not allowed to play anything.'

Now John is abandoning us and I'm not happy. 'Couldn't you just wait twenty more minutes and take the boys to school?' I ask, as he bends to kiss Jamie goodbye. 'It means so much to them.'

'Samantha,' says John, smiling, 'I have to go. We're doing the first performance in less than a week. If it's a success we could go up to Edinburgh. Apparently we can erect a big top in Princes Street Gardens and stay there for the whole of August while the Festival's on. This is the most ambitious project I've ever done so I really need it to work. My reputation depends on it as well as my salary. Do you understand?'

'Yes,' I say, feeling a bit silly.

'It can earn me serious money. And we need it, don't we?'

I nod.

'So Wendy can do the school run, can't she? Actually, where is Wendy?'

'In bed,' says Edward. 'I went up to see her and she told me to tell you she's got a hangover. She said, "I've got a bloody hangover," and I said to her, "You're staying in bed a bit early,* aren't you?"'

'Great,' I say. 'I didn't think she was getting up.'

'She's only young,' says John, as he walks out. 'We'll talk about it later.'

Ten seconds later he's back.

'I didn't kiss you goodbye,' he says. He bends down and gives me a long, tender kiss. 'I do love you,' he says, 'and I'm sorry about all this work, really I am, but this could be the big-time for me. I've worked so hard and –'

'Don't worry about it,' I say, smiling. 'I love you too.' I kiss him back.

So, I get up and get breakfast – eggs for everyone

except Edward who hates eggs so he has an alien bagel* instead. I drag on my jeans and a T-shirt, find Edward's schoolbag under the cat, pack his lunch. As I pass the mirror in the hall I catch sight of myself. I look wan and harassed, laden with schoolbags and a lunchbox. I stop for a minute, put the bags down and stare at myself. My skin is dry. I have wrinkles. My boobs are huge and they sag. My tummy rolls over the top of my jeans. I pull the skin on my face towards my cheekbones. Hmm. Better. I look five years younger. Adele gave me a pamphlet about having a natural facelift. 'You owe it to yourself and your husband,' she said. Maybe I should find that leaflet.

'Muuum!' yells Edward, breaking into my reverie. 'WE HAVE TO GO NOW!'

I look at the clock. We're five minutes late. I grab Jamie. 'Noo dada,' he says.

'No, I'm Mummy,' I say.

I frogmarch Bennie, who is hiding behind the dog, out of the house.

'B-B-Beady is hurt,' says Bennie, protestingly.

'No, she's not,' I say.

'Sh-she is,' says Bennie. 'Sh-she whispered in my ear that her paw hurts and that she wants me to stay and look after her.'

'Well, I'm here, Bennie. I'll look after her until you get home from school.'

'I–I don't like school.'

'I know, Bennie, but it's so nearly the end of term. You've got a long summer holiday ahead of you. Come on, now.'

We go outside. Edward is already in the car. I shove Jamie into his seat, then buckle Bennie in.

'Ow!' he says. 'You hurt my hand.'

'Sorry,' I say, reversing rapidly out of the drive.

Beep! A car tears past us on the road.

'Mum!' says Edward. 'Do you want to kill us all?'

'K-kill us all?' echoes Bennie, nervously.

'I'm not killing anyone,' I say, and we set off up the hill to school.

'I love this hill,' says Edward, munching the remains of his bagel, which he has spirited into the car.

I remember how we came down the hill the first time into this beautiful English village we now call home. Often, on the hill, I've stopped the car and told Edward how, one day when I'm dead and gone, he'll come back to this place. 'I wonder what you'll think then?' I always say to him.

'I'll think of you, Mummy,' he says.

'What words would you use to describe this beautiful hill on this magical morning?' I ask Edward now.

Edward smiles. This is a game we often play. It started when he was five years old and had just begun school. I was called in by his teacher, who told me she felt he needed help with his language skills. I went to see Mrs Desmond, whom John insisted on calling Norma Desmond, as she was rather melodramatic about everything.

'Edward is a lovely boy,' she said, clasping my hands and looking at me earnestly. 'He really is the most lovely and charming boy, but he has a few problems.'

'Yes,' I said. 'I know. He's always had problems. He

used to bite terribly when he was little and I was always concerned it was because his father and I separated and –'

'No, no, you misunderstand me,' she said. 'He's a little . . . How should I put it? A little *behind* the other children.'

'Right,' I said, feeling as if I was the worst mother in the world.

'I am not trying to say that he is *backward* or that there's anything wrong with him . . .'

'No?' I said miserably.

'Not at all, just that he may need extra help.'

She went on to describe the form it would take. 'I thought he'd enjoy being taught by Pip,' she said.

'Who's Pip?' I said.

'A puppet,' she said. 'He can be very useful in accessing children's intrinsic problems, the ones that are holding them back, the ones that make a bright boy such as Edward not trust his true potential, the ones who are damaged or unhappy.'

'Damaged or unhappy?' I said, feeling as if I was about to cry. 'You think Edward is damaged or unhappy?'

'Oh, no, not *Edward.* Others. Some children are obviously very unhappy. You can see it. Why, in Edward's class, I can think of at least three children who are underperforming and there seems to be no reason why. They're just switched off.'

'Why?' I was fascinated now and rather relieved. It wasn't just Edward who was backward, it was other people's children too!

Then Norma Desmond leant forward and whispered, rather dramatically, 'I think they're being pushed too hard too young by over-competitive parents. Sometimes they're doing so many out-of-school activities that they're exhausted and their brains are fried. Sometimes they're wrapped up in cotton wool and even by the age of five they don't dare to speak their minds. But Edward isn't like that, not at all. He just needs his brain synapses sparked up and he'll be fine.'

To help Edward 'catch up', as his teacher put it, I made up a game. If we liked something, we thought of as many words as we could to describe it. So, if we went on an aeroplane, Edward would say, 'Big, huge, loud, noisy, smelly, dirty,' and so on. We did this until, after Pip the Puppet and his girlfriend Pippa had taught him for a year, he was up to scratch. Norma Desmond was delighted when I told her about our wordplay.

'You've worked so hard with Edward, Mrs Smythe,' she said. 'You're an inspiration!' It made me feel really rather proud.

'This hill's steep,' says Edward today, 'almost vertiginously so.'

'Ooh, that's a good one!'

'I think the sunlight's dappling through the verdant undergrowth,' he continues, 'and that the Tarmac's sweating in its repose.'

'Hmm, I don't think Tarmac can be in repose.'

'Yes, it can. I think the leaves are unfurling in a supine fashion.'

'Edward! You're being ridiculous now. Leaves cannot be supine. Lions are supine when they lie in trees.'

'Lions don't lie in trees. Leopards do.'

'OK, leopards, then.'

Edward carries on: 'It's a sweltering day and, later on,

we should all be allowed to consume a sumptuous ice cream.'

'Edward . . .' I say, but on he goes as we slowly drive up the hill.

Cockneys

By the time we get to school, the gates are shut. A few mothers I don't know are chatting as they wander back to their cars. I look for Adele, or anyone I might know, but I can't see any familiar faces. I decide that, unless she's later than I am – unthinkable in Adele Land – she's done what she usually does, which is to go off with a select handful of others for coffee in the local Starbucks.

'Is Nancy ever late?' I ask Edward.

'I don't know,' he says. 'She's not in my class. Ask Bennie. He might know.'

But when I turn to Bennie, he's asleep.

'Bennie,' I say, 'time to wake up.'

'Ooh,' says Jamie, waving his legs in an upward trajectory so that his feet came up to his nose. How do toddlers do that? They're made of some kind of stretchy material that has no solid mass. They can put their toes in their mouths and squat on their haunches without thinking about it. They can fall out of low windows and bounce back up. They are truly amazing little people.

'Come on, Mum,' says Edward. 'We're late. I need you to get me buzzed in.'

'Can't you go by yourself?' I say.

'You know the rules. You have to report to the office if you're late.'

'Can't you just sneak in and no one will notice?'

'No, it's not allowed.'

'Who says so?'

'The school rules.'

'Well, sod the rules. I'm only suggesting today that you go in quietly so that I have time to wake Bennie up. Then you won't be late.'

'But I *am* late. The gates are shut, in case you hadn't noticed.'

'Of course I'd noticed. I just thought that – Oh, forget it. You'll have to wait for Bennie. I'll have to wake him.'

'But, Mum! That'll take ages. Bennie hates being woken up. He'll scream and you'll have to comfort him and then he'll scream more and you'll get cross and it'll be first break by the time I get through the door.'

I sigh. He's right. 'Well, I'll carry Bennie and you'll have to carry Jamie because I can't leave him on his own in the car.'

'Mum,' says Edward, 'Jamie's two. He's not a baby. In case you hadn't noticed, he can walk.'

I get Jamie out of his car seat and tell him to hold Edward's hand. 'Wait here, Edward. Don't cross the road without me.'

I reach into the back to extricate Bennie. As I take off his seatbelt, he stirs. 'Wh-where are we?' he says.

'At school,' I say.

'S-school!' wails Bennie, tears welling in his eyes. 'I hate school. I don't want to go to school. I want to go home. I want to –'

Suddenly I hear a growling noise behind me. It's getting louder and louder. Something's coming up the hill, very fast. Blam! I hear a squeal of brakes. Oh, my God, where's Jamie?

I wheel round to look for him and Edward but smash my head against the car's door frame. 'Ow!'

'Sorry,' yells a male voice.

For a second, I can't focus, my eyes hazy from the bash on my head. 'Sorry what?' I say. 'Sorry who? Where's Jamie?'

'Who is he?' says the voice. 'Is he the little boy about to cross the road?'

Then I hear Edward say, 'Cool motor.'

'Edward,' I say, my eyesight now returning to normal. 'Are you all right? Is Jamie?'

'Yeah, Mum,' he says. 'We're fine. That's a cool car.'

'What's a cool car?'

Then I see, in front of me, on the road, a red Ferrari, with a man and a child inside it. I look down. Jamie is holding Edward's hand.

'Why did you slam your brakes on?' I say, suddenly angry, to the man, whose window is open. Jesus! I'd thought Jamie was in the road and that the man in this stupid car had nearly hit him. 'Were my sons in the road?'

'No,' says the man.

'So why did you slam on your brakes and give me the fright of my life?'

'I couldn't see them. I thought I might hit them.'

'Oh, you thought you *might* hit them. Why *might* you hit them? Is it because you were going too fast up the road? You shouldn't speed here. There's a school.'

'I know that,' says the man. 'I'm late delivering my daughter, Rowan.'

Rowan? I squint at him. I see a tanned face and lots of

brown hair. He has a Cockney accent and a red Ferrari. This must be the famous Gary White.

'Is that a Ferrari?' Edward asks him.

'Yeah,' says the-man-I-now-think-is-Gary-White casually. 'It's a 550 Maranello coupé Rosso Corsa with cream.'

'I thought so,' said Edward.

I stand there, gaping.

'Do you like cars?'

'Love them,' says Edward.

'Edward!' I say. 'I've never heard you talk about cars.'

'You don't know everything about me, Mum. Me and Stanley talk about cars all the time. We used to talk about aeroplanes but now it's cars.'

'I'll take you for a ride in it, if you like,' says the man-I-now-think-is-Gary-White.

'Yeah,' says Edward.

'No!' I say. 'It's time you were in school. I thought you were in a bad mood because you were late, and now you're attempting to go off in a Ferrari with a stranger.'

Edward glowers at me.

'Oh, I seem to have caused a problem,' says the man, and drives off, laughing.

The Ferrari shoots a hundred yards up the road, rather noisily, then shudders abruptly to a halt.

'Cool,' says Edward.

'Stop saying "cool"!'

'It has automatic parking,' says Edward. 'This I've got to see.'

'No,' I say. 'You're late enough already.'

Then Bennie emerges.

'I-is that a cool car, Mummy?' he asks.

'No.'

Of course, now I cannot avoid the man-I-now-think-is-Gary-White. I get the children through the gates – with great difficulty in Bennie's case, as he clings to my legs, whimpers and twists so much that I end up saying, as quietly as I can, 'If you go into school without a fuss, Bennie, I'll let you go and play in the man's cool car one day.'

'I–I can go and play in that man's cool car?' says Bennie, perking up.

'Yes,' I say. 'He said we could one day and so, if you walk through the gates with Edward and into the office, you can maybe do it very soon.'

'I–I can do it very soon?' says Bennie.

'But you said I couldn't!' says Edward, picking up on the conversation. 'You said I couldn't go in his car. Why is Bennie allowed in his car and not me?' He looks aggrieved.

'I didn't say you couldn't go in his car, Edward. I merely said you couldn't go right now.'

'I–I want to go for a ride in his car now,' says Bennie, getting louder. 'I'm only going to school if I can have a ride in his car.'

'Bennie,' I say, 'be quiet. Get into school and I'll ask him.'

I can see the-man-I-now-think-is-Gary-White approaching me rapidly across the grassy common. 'Quick! In you go!' I say to Edward and Bennie, and, magically, they run through the gates.

''Bye,' I say, waving and blowing them each a kiss.

'Bye, Mummy,' says Bennie, blowing one back.

Edward says and does nothing.

I turn to gather up Jamie, who is picking daisies with his toes, and find myself staring at the-man-I-now-think-is-Gary-White. He is virtually behind me. Tall, dark, slim, longish tousled hair. Wide mouth. Light linen suit. Loafers. No socks. Hmm. Attractive, if you like that kind of thing.

He looks at me rather cockily. 'How do I get these gates to open?' he asks. 'Do you say "Open, Sesame!"' He waves his hands at them like a magician. His daughter, small and blonde, giggles.

'You buzz the office,' I say. 'You're late, you see.'

'So are you,' he says. He goes to buzz the office. His mobile phone rings. As he answers it – 'Can't talk now, . . . Yes, well I'm . . . Yes, I will try . . . Look, I'm dropping Rowan off at school. I'll call you back' – I take my chance. I pick up Jamie and walk quickly to the car.

But as I'm putting him into his car seat, I hear the-man-I-now-think-is-Gary-White behind me.

'Look,' he says, as I fumble around, trying to find Jamie's straps, 'I'm Gary – Gary White.'

'I thought you were,' I say, finally fishing them out from under Jamie's capacious bottom.

'Oh. Right. How did you know?' asks Gary White.

'You've bought the Dower House.'

'Oh. Right. It's beautiful.' Then he says, 'But how did you know it was me?'

'The Ferrari. It's a dead giveaway.'

'You knew I had one?'

'Everybody does.'

Gary White gives me a smile, then walks back to his

car, but just as he gets there, he obviously thinks of something else. He turns and walks back to me. I'm just about to get in and drive off but he holds my door so I can't close it. 'I wanted to ask you something,' he says. 'I'm new to the area and I don't know anyone. In fact, my mother's just rung and she told me I ought to make some friends.'

'Make some friends?'

'Yes – you know, meet people, ask them round and all that. I want my daughter to feel at home here. She's got lots of cool stuff. I bought her a pony so she could get out and about but she's allergic to horses so if any of your lot like riding . . . and she's got lots of toys that kids like and a trampoline in the garden and one of those motorized tractors and a swing and a slide. They're all new because we've just moved in and . . . my mother thinks if I meet people with kids Rowan won't be lonely.'

'You've bought your daughter a trampoline and now your mother wants other children to come and play on it?'

'Yes. Well, I do too. I was living in London but now . . . it's a long story.'

'I know.'

'How?' he says. 'You seem to know everything about me.'

'It's a small village,' I say. 'We all know everything about everybody.'

'I don't know anything about you,' he says.

'That's because I'm unimportant but you . . . you're a famous footballer so . . .'

Gary White stares at me. 'I'm a famous *former* footballer,' he says. Then he leans towards me. His face passes within half an inch of mine as he peers into the back of my car at Jamie. But, for the briefest moment, I can smell the sweat on his skin, see the pores on his face, the dark stubble where he must usually shave but not today.

'Cute kid.' He withdraws his head.

'Dada,' Jamie says to him.

Gary White laughs. 'I've only got girls,' he says. 'I don't see my eldest. She's with my first wife and this one –'

'Rowan.'

'I only get her occasionally so all her stuff's unused, really. She lives with my second wife most of the time. I'm hoping my future ex-wife will stay around here. That's why I've brought Rowan to check out the school. My mother thought it was a good idea. She thinks that if Rowan likes it round here and makes some friends it'll help her get used to the idea of living in the countryside and maybe my ex would consider buying her own place in the area. I don't think she wants to, really, but . . .' He pauses. 'Hey, what's your name?'

'Samantha – Samantha Smythe, mother of three.'

'OK, Samantha Smythe, mother of three, maybe we could get together with the kids. You should call me. I meant what I said. Bring those boys over to look at the car. I've got quite a few cars, you know, and Rowan's not very interested but boys like them, don't they?'

He fishes out a card. There is his telephone number at the bottom. He walks off, and the next thing I know, he's roaring past me in that infernal car, waving. I find my mobile telephone, which Edward has been playing with, trying to take photographs of the trees. 'Jst mt G wh. Wnkr', I text to John.

I drive home with Jamie, feeling as if I've achieved something for once. But later, as I catch sight of myself in the mirror, tatty and grubby, with a few grey hairs, I wonder what Adele will think when I tell her I've met Gary White when I was wearing jeans, a T-shirt and no makeup. I can imagine her now at the school gates all pristine and beautiful: 'Oh, look, here's Gary White in his red Ferrari! Oh, I want to meet him so much. Do you think he's noticed me? Do you think he might stop and talk to me? After all, his daughter's in Nancy's class.' Then Gary White will drive past her, notice me, stop and wink. 'How's it going, Samantha?' he'll say, and every woman at the school gates will look at me and talk about me. The thought of it makes me giggle.

What Women Talk About at the School Gates

I'm fascinated by the mothers at the school gates. Ever since Norma Desmond told me that some of the children in Edward's class had problems, I've searched every day for these supposedly middle-class, miserable children. Who are they? Which ones have pushy parents obsessed with making them over-achieve? Is it overweight Jane? Her mother, Gail, is as slim as her daughter is large, with the figure of a whippet, constantly dressed in sweat gear as if she's always about to go jogging as soon as she's pushed her daughter through the gates. Gail is renowned for her athletic prowess, always off to the gym, on a run, for a ten-kilometre walk or 'training for a half marathon'. I want to ask her why. I cannot imagine why anyone would want to run anywhere.

Or is it naughty, badly-behaved Josh? He has always been in the same class as Edward, and in the first term he was a sweet boy, but then he changed and became tricky. Edward would come home and tell me how Josh had picked on him. 'He bites and scratches and he tells all the other boys that they shouldn't be friends with me and I don't know why,' Edward would say, close to tears. Liza, Josh's mother, always turns up at the school gates in high heels and makeup, then roars off to make loads of money as an investment banker. She has perfect hair, perfect makeup and designer suits.

Maybe the over-competitive parent is Belinda, but I doubt it. She seems rather warm and friendly with her twin daughters, Saskia and Summer, and her son Jeremy – also in Edward's year – who is the star of the school. He's perfect – maybe too perfect. He's always the lead in the school play and the narrator in assembly. He's in the football and cricket teams and . . . Edward gazes at Jeremy as if he's from a totally different, more exotic country. But maybe Jeremy's pushed too hard . . .

Maybe it's Nicki, with Gus and Jemima. She seems a perfect mother – blonde, casually dressed, slim, attractive without being stunning, unthreatening in every way with her pristine children and very clean SUV. But maybe, under the poise, makeup and blow-dried, hair-sprayed hair, under the cashmere and linen and the expensive gold watch I see twinkling from under the cuff of her laundered shirt, she's an over-competitive harridan. Hard to imagine, though, as I've never thought she was like that. She once admitted to me that she thought she should write a book about diets as she had tried every single one, '. . . and I'm still fat,' she said, which was completely untrue as she's very slim.

But I've tried to embrace this new set of school-gate mothers and, in doing so, I've listened carefully to what they talk about. It's their children: how they're doing at school, what clubs they go to after school, how wonderful it is that they've got into the football or cricket team, or are taking the lead in the school play, what school their children might go to next, how they will or won't be able to afford the fees, and the future of boarding-school. Liza is determined for Josh to go away to school because then, she says, she will be able to concentrate on her work, and Belinda claims to be just as determined that Jeremy will not go to boarding-school because she wants the family to stay together. Nicki has put Gus down for Eton, which Adele tells me is 'an absolute farce': Gus is not the brightest spark in the world, 'like his mother,' says Adele, and it turns out that when Nicki was looking round Eton with her computer-programming husband Colin, they bumped into Belinda who was there with her husband Sandy, a graphic artist with his own company. 'Belinda can't afford Eton!' Adele said to me. 'She must be hoping Jeremy gets a scholarship.' I have, so far, kept out of the school conversation.

The school-gate mothers also talk about their weight, what they eat or do not eat, what diet they're on and how dreadful or successful their husbands are. Nicki keeps telling everyone she doesn't eat wheat, sugar, fruit, dairy products or red meat. Adele always tells me that Nicki looks amazing: 'Her skin's fantastic and she's so slim! What's that diet called she's on because it's really working?' I tell Adele it's called the eat-nothing diet and, anyway, it turns out that Nicki's skin is so good because she has a 'little bit of Botox'. Gail spotted her in the local beauty salon being syringed and told everyone. I thought it sounded ghastly, having snake venom pumped into your face, but Adele was so impressed she booked in for a session the following week. When she came out she couldn't smile or frown and looked like a Stepford Wife, which she seemed bizarrely pleased about. Liza swears by the non-surgical facelift – apparently you get attached to a machine that sends a small electrical current up your facial nerves and tightens them. 'They use it on stroke patients,' she said. Belinda swears by clever makeup and Adele, well, she'll try anything. 'Why not?' she says to me on a daily basis as I slap nothing more than some moisturizer circa ten years ago on my face. 'Has that lasted you a decade?' Adele will say, wrinkling her nose.

But, goodness, these mothers know how to disguise their obsessions. Nicki told me once that she couldn't eat anything much but nuts because the doctor told her a strict diet would help her feel less tired. And Gail claims she doesn't eat wheat or lactose because her nutritionist told her she was allergic to them and that they would therefore bung up her insides. 'I can't run properly with a heavy feeling in my stomach,' she says endlessly and Adele doesn't eat because she wants to stay skinny. They talk about all this when, having dropped their children at school, they go to Starbucks for coffee. There, they sit down with their skinny lattes and the real gossip begins. They talk about who fancies whom and who is having an affair with whom. Adele tells me about this and I pretend not to be interested.

'Caroline Parkinson is having an affair with Mr Durham, the gym teacher,' she'll say one afternoon when we're picking the children up.

'No, she isn't,' I'll say. 'They're both married.'

'So what? That doesn't stop anybody.'

'You're immoral,' I'll tell Adele and then I'll point out that she has no evidence for any of this.

'Gail was out running and she saw them canoodling in the bus shelter.'

'That's a bit public, isn't it?'

'Best place if it's raining and, anyway, no one who's anyone takes the bus, these days. It's full of old people because the rest of us drive.'

I'll say I don't want to talk about this any more.

'You love it!' Adele will say. 'You're only taking a moral stance because you don't get asked to go to Starbucks after the school drop-off!'

This is true. I once told John about it. 'It rankles,' I said. 'Why don't I get invited?'

'You don't get invited to Starbucks,' he said, 'because it's a coffee shop, not a private members' bar. Anyone can go there.'

I told him he was missing the point. 'Of course anyone can go there!' I said. 'But it's not de rigueur *to go after the morning drop-off unless you're part of the in-crowd and I'm not.'*

I see them all – Nicki, Gail, Belinda and sometimes Liza – setting off, with a secret nod and a wave. At nine a.m. they meet to drink latte and if any other mother goes in without having been given that nod and that wave, her reception is frosty. I know this because Adele, who is a fully signed-up member of the club, told me so.

'Caroline Parkinson came to Starbucks this morning!' she said once, with thinly disguised horror. 'No one was expecting her and it was very embarrassing.'

'But why shouldn't she go to Starbucks?' I asked, a touch defiantly.

'She sat down with us,' said Adele, shuddering. 'It was awful. No one knew what to say. She even ate an almond and sultana Danish.'

Apparently no one has spoken to Caroline Parkinson since.

So I'm very aware that you have to be invited to join the post-drop-off Starbucks club and one morning I was. I was at the school gates in jeans and a jumper when Adele swooped up in her Range Rover.

'I'm off to Starbucks,' she said airily. 'Hey, why don't you come?

We could all watch you eat one of those yoghurts with berries on top.'

'What's wrong with that?' I asked.

'Full-fat milk, sugar and fructose,' said Adele, driving off and motioning for me to follow.

So I went.

Every head turned as I walked in.

'Hi,' said Gail, giving me a possibly fake smile. 'How nice to see you here.'

'Adele invited me,' I said. Gail softened.

Adele went to get the coffee. 'What do you want?' she called to me.

'Black,' I said.

'Don't you drink milk?' said Nicki.

'Never have,' I say. 'I hate it.'

'Oh, I thought you might be dairy-intolerant,' said Nicki, hopefully. 'I don't drink milk because I counted up that if you have five cups of tea a day with full-fat milk you consume an extra three hundred calories.'

'It's not the calories,' I said. 'I just don't like the taste.'

We sat in silence until Liza said, 'How's Edward?'

'Fine,' I said enthusiastically, hoping to break the ice.

'And his little brothers?'

'Fine,' I said. 'Really good. Great. Lovely.'

'You've got three, haven't you?' said Belinda, sympathetically.

'Yes, like you,' I said.

'Edward must come over one day and play with Josh,' said Liza.

'Oh, I'm sure he'd love to,' I said.

'My au pair Basia sorts out Josh's play dates. I'll get her to ring you and put something in the diary.'

'Great,' I said.

'Do you have help?' asked Belinda. 'I'm pregnant with my fourth, and I'm wondering if I should look for someone.'

'You're pregnant?' I asked. She didn't look it. 'I couldn't have told.'

'It's early days,' she said, blushing. 'I'm only about four months. Anyway, look at my belly!' She stretched her Lycra wraparound top taut over her belly.

'Oh yes,' I said. 'You do have a little bump.'

'Poor you,' said Adele, appearing with the coffee. 'Imagine having four children!'

'But I want four!' said Belinda, laughing. 'Honestly, Adele . . .'

'I have ten people working for me in my office and it's worse than having children!' said Liza.

'But you've only got one child!' said Belinda.

'Thank God for that,' said Liza. 'My husband would like more but, honestly, I have to sort out everyone's problems at work and my under-manager doesn't like his under-manager and my secretary's boyfriend's just dumped her and she spends the whole time in tears and –'

'That must be hard,' said Gail. 'It must be like running a marathon. Now that's really tough.'

'Not as tough as setting up your own business, like I am,' said Belinda.

'You're not, are you?' said Liza. 'Why are you setting up a business when you're pregnant? Isn't that a mad time to do it?'

'Not really,' said Belinda. 'That's why I was wondering if I should get some help. Now we're having a fourth I thought I'd better try to bring some money in and, anyway, it's not full time. I'm doing this franchise. Lots of mothers do it. It's called Colour Me Wonderful and it involves having these women-only parties

where I work out everyone's colour chart and do their makeup and suggest outfits, that type of thing. I can manage the parties around the baby.'

'Give us an example, then,' said Adele. 'I'd like to be coloured wonderfully.'

'I've only just started,' said Belinda, 'but I'd say you were summer because you're blonde with green eyes.'

'Oh, it's seasonal, is it?' said Adele.

'Basically,' said Belinda. 'Now, you would wear pastels, pale blues, pinks, yellows and –'

'Yuk, I hate pastels,' said Adele.

'Samantha is dark,' continued Belinda, 'so she'd wear purples and russets.'

'I've never worn purple or russet in my life,' I said.

'No,' said Liza, looking at me critically. 'I can see that.'

'You must have a party and try it out on us,' said Adele.

'Oh, I will,' said Belinda. 'I think I'm getting the hang of it and I thought I'd ask you all soon.'

'Can I come?' I said suddenly.

'Of course,' said Belinda, smiling.

And that was that.

My Breaking In

When I get home, I find Wendy yawning, sleepy, frying eggs and bacon in the kitchen. 'Howya doin', little one?' she says to Jamie. 'Howya doin', Mrs S?' she says to me.

'Wendy,' I say sternly, 'why didn't you get up this morning? Are you ill?'

'Ah'm hung over,' she says. 'I went for a walk down by the river with me mates last night and we drunk too many of those bottles that have vodka in them and someone fell in and –'

'What mates?'

'Oh, some people Ah've met,' she says rather vaguely. Then she comes over and ruffles Jamie's hair. 'You comin' out with me, cutie? Ah'm gonna make something yummy for you to eat – maybe even chicken nuggets!'

Those words make my insides groan. What is it about Wendy that makes her eat so much? I spend my life worrying that she suffers from body dysmorphic disorder and when she looks in the mirror she sees a slim, svelte version of herself.

About a month ago when John was in London, working, and I was at home watching television with Wendy, she was sprawled like a stranded heifer on the sofa and I was curled up on the Chair. The children were in bed. Wendy was munching her way through a packet of nachos with a sour-cream dip. She dipped a nacho and put it into her mouth, then again. It was as regular as a metronome. Dip, put in mouth. Dip, put in mouth. How can anyone eat so much? I thought, watching her work her way methodically through the packet. Then I listed in my head all the things Wendy liked to eat. First, chicken nuggets. She was always appearing with bags of them, greasy and deep-fried, from some local fast food outlet. Then came battered cod, chips, chicken Kiev, pizza, baked beans, burgers, more chips, Spam fritters, corned-beef sandwiches, Vegemite and 'Oz choc'.

She was always going on about 'Oz choc', as in 'Have you tasted the chocolate in this country?'

Me: 'Yes.'

Her: 'It's daggy.'

Me: 'Oh. Right.'

Her: 'Y'know. It's not the same as the choc in Oz.'

Me: 'Well, maybe it's the chocolate in Australia that's "daggy". Maybe if I went to Australia and tasted your chocolate, I'd say, "Yuk, this tastes disgusting."'

Her: 'Nah, Mrs S. It's not Oz choc that smells of vom.'

Then she spent about an hour telling me about the sweets she liked and how her mum used to give her money for sweetie cigarettes and sherbet fountains, and how she'd sit in the backyard and eat them. 'I used to eat sweets all day on a Sunday,' she said. 'I don't think I ate anything else.'

I was taken aback. I almost felt sorry for her. Nothing but sweets? I told Edward about Wendy and sweets, but he said, 'Lucky old her.' A diet of nothing but sweets would, in the end, be disgusting, I told him. 'Imagine how sick you'd get of the taste!' I said to him. 'Imagine if you spent a whole day eating nothing but sweets!'

'You'd vom,' said Edward.

'Edward!' I said. 'Where did you get that word from?'

'Guess,' he said.

I thought about Wendy and food for a while and then it came to me. 'She doesn't like food to look like food!' I said to Edward.

'What?' he said.

'Well, she takes a lovely piece of fresh chicken and instead of grilling it with lemon and salt and pepper, she puts breadcrumbs all over it and fries it.'

'So?'

'And she takes a lovely piece of cod I've just bought from the fishmonger, batters and fries it. She could bake it in foil with some herbs, but no. She *disguises* it.'

'I'm not sure what you're saying, Mum,' said Edward, puzzled.

'What did she do with those bananas last week?' I said triumphantly.

'She cooked them with cream and that horrible sweet milk, then called it an offi pie.'

'*Banoffi pie!*' I screamed. 'Yes! She used an entire packet of digestive biscuits, three tins of condensed milk and a huge pot of cream and made that pie.'

'It was disgusting,' said Edward.

'It was inedible!' I said. 'That pie was so huge it was frightening. I could barely open the fridge!'

Then Edward said, 'I think she did something bad to the cherries, didn't she?'

'Oh, yes,' I said, remembering. 'She overcooked them

in Yorkshire pudding batter. Then she took beautiful fillet steak, cut it up and boiled it for two hours to make stew. She put cheese sauce all over the broccoli. I repeat, she cannot eat food that looks like food. She has to turn everything fresh and lovely into something that resembles frozen muck.'

'Oh dear,' said Edward, reaching for an apple. 'I think I'll eat this, then.'

'Well, be quick,' I said, 'or she'll have cut it up and fried it before you've opened your mouth.'

On this particular day, I'd already seen her polish off a huge cheese and ham toastie with chips. She'd offered me one. 'D'ya wanna toastie?' she'd said. 'I've got a joke about that, y'know. This rabbit goes into a bar and asks for a cheese toastie and then he eats it all up and tells the barman it's yum. The next day he goes back into the bar and asks for a ham toastie, and the barman gives it to him and he eats it up and says it's yum. The next day the rabbit goes back into the bar and asks for a ham and cheese toastie and he eats it all up and drops down dead. Do you know what he died of?' she asked.

'Er, no,' I said.

'Mixing-yer-toasties! Geddit?' Then she fell about laughing. But there we were, with me conspicuously eating a salad. I had wanted some grilled organic chicken with it but evidently Wendy had snaffled that.

'Wendy,' I said, having decided to ask her about the chicken, 'you know you're very welcome here . . .'

'Yeah,' she said, eyes glued to the television, hand going to the nachos. Dip, put in mouth.

'And you know you can eat and drink whatever you like.'

'Oh, cheers for the offer, Mrs S,' she said, 'but I got a tinnie right here.' She motioned towards a can of beer at her feet.

'I was just wondering if you'd eaten the chicken that was in the fridge because –'

'Yeah, I fried it and had it in a tortilla with some sour cream and avocado for me afternoon snack.'

'Afternoon snack?'

'Yeah, I get hungry looking after the little critters. You don't mind, do ya, Mrs S? Me mam always told me I should just help myself to whatever was in the fridge to keep me strength up.'

'Oh, right. Well, you look quite strong to me.'

'Is there a problem?' said Wendy, still eating nachos. Dip, put in mouth.

'No, it's just that I thought you were going to do the children some chicken wraps with salad for tea and I was saving a piece for my dinner and –'

'Yeah, but they hate chicken wraps. Edward told me you made them eat them because they were good for them but they told me they'd rather have burgers and chips so that's what I gave them.'

'But we don't have burgers or chips in the house.'

'Yeah, I thought that was weird. I looked for them everywhere and I couldn't find any. Maybe you forgot to put them on yer shopping list, Mrs S.'

'So, how did they get burgers and chips?'

'I took them to that burger place near High Wycombe.'

'You took them to Flames? But they've never been there in their lives.'

'Why not? It's dirt cheap and the food's yum!'

'Yes, but, Wendy, there's a reason why it's dirt cheap. Everyone I know who's had a burger from Flames felt ill afterwards. The burgers are made of wood shavings.'

'Well, I had a superFlame burger and it was very tasty.'

'You had one?'

'Yeah, for me dinner! Anyway, you owe me for it but I won't charge you for mine.'

'Well, that's very generous of you, Wendy, but I'd rather you didn't take the children there again. I really feel –'

'Yeah, Edward said you'd say that. All right. No more Flames.'

'Thank you, Wendy,' I said.

She looked at my wilting salad. 'Aw,' she said. 'I'm sorry I took yer chicken. Now you've gotta eat those horrible green things. Me mam told me never to eat a vegetable unless it came out of a tin.'

'Why?'

'I dunno. I miss me mam.'

While Wendy is bathing and getting dressed, which usually takes her hours, I decide to do some word cards with Jamie. I've been worrying about him. The other day I read a book that the health visitor gave me. She came over to do Jamie's two-year check. I was just telling her how sweet Jamie was when she told me she needed to watch him *quietly* so I shut up. She spent an age staring at Jamie.

'Does he speak?' she asked eventually.

'Of course,' I said, then sat Jamie down and said, 'Now, Jamie, say "sorry".'

'Ga!' said Jamie, waving his hands in the air.

'Say "Mummy",' I said.

'Ga, ga, ga!' said Jamie.

'That means yes,' said Edward, helpfully.

'Interesting,' said the health visitor.

'Say "Eddie",' I told Jamie.

'Bye-bye,' said Jamie, waving to the health visitor.

'But the lady's not going anywhere, Jamie,' I said.

'Bye-bye!' said Jamie again.

'Say supercalifragilisticexpialidocious!' said Edward, dancing from foot to foot.

'Edward,' I said. 'You're not helping.'

'Sorry,' said Edward.

That was when the health visitor found me this book about childhood milestones and the one for two-year-olds went like this: should be able to pile bricks on top of each other; should be able to form two- or three-word sentences; should have at least fifty clear words in vocabulary. *Fifty clear words!* God, Jamie has about three! She gave me a pack of word cards to practise with him. 'You should do a few with him every day,' she said. 'I shall come back in six months, and if he hasn't improved, I'll have to get him looked at by a speech therapist.' That panicked me so now I'm constantly waving the bloody things at him.

'Say "sleepy",' I demand every night, as he's about to go to bed. 'Say "Night-night, Mama."'

'Bye-bye,' he says.

John thinks I should stop worrying. 'There's nothing wrong with him,' he says. 'He's happy.'

But Jamie won't be happy when, like Bennie, he starts school and *no one understands a word he's saying*!

John just laughs. 'Everyone understands Bennie,' he says, 'and he stutters.'

'Yes, but at least Bennie *speaks*, always has spoken and hasn't always stuttered. Jamie just points at things and says, "Da!" or "Bye-bye," and we jump to attention.'

'Well, he's a clever boy, then, isn't he?' said John.

This morning I do his word cards for what seems hours. It involves me sitting in front of him and holding up one card at a time. They have pictures and words and are specifically designed for two-year-olds.

'What's this?' I say, starting with a picture of a dog. I hold up the card and point at Beady.

'Woof-woof,' says Jamie, excitedly.

'Yes, Jamie,' I say. 'Dogs go woof-woof, but what are they called?'

'Woof-woofs.'

'No, dogs. See this one? It's a bath.'

'Buddle bath.'

'No, not bubble bath, just bath.'

'Buddle bath.'

'And this is a cat.'

'Miaow.'

'Yes, miaow like Honey cat.'

''Oney cat.'

'Yes, Jamie! Honey cat.' For a moment, I think we're getting somewhere. 'Jamie,' I say. 'Can you understand what I'm saying?'

Jamie cocks his head to one side.

'Can you understand me?'

'Course he can't, Mrs S!' says Wendy, who has appeared behind me. 'Me mam said I didn't speak until I was four and it's done me no harm, has it, eh?' She scoops Jamie into her arms, chucks him under the chin and marches out of the door. The last thing I hear her say to Jamie is, 'Silly Mummy, worrying about you so when you're such a beaut nipper.'

I now have a rare moment of peace and quiet. For a minute I think I might call Adele and tell her about Gary White. But what would I say? I have no idea. I ought to tell Dougie, my best friend, about him because Dougie's a mad football fan. After his wife Maxine went off with a young plumber and moved out of the area, he was very depressed for a while. To cheer him up we used to have a Friday-night ritual: we went to the pub – the Flying Pig – and had dinner together, and I remember that he would bang on and on about the Premiership and who should manage whom and I tolerated it because I knew how miserable he was. Anyway, it was our time together and John never seemed to mind and I really looked forward to it until, one day, a for-sale sign went up at the Flying Pig and that was that.

I'm not sure if its demise signalled the end for Dougie and me. He'd liked spending his Friday nights with me, having a general rant about his life. 'She left me for a pixie!' he'd say, once he'd downed a bottle of wine. I liked listening to him: I felt sorry for him, and when I've been down, it's always been Dougie who's cheered me up. I met him after my first marriage broke up and there has always been something good about him. He lived in my village, before he moved to London. He can be utterly useless but, then, he's been unhappy for years. Now . . . now maybe he's better. He doesn't have much work for a solicitor, and no one knows how he survives, but he seems to get by. He still sees me often but erratically because, for the last couple of years, he's been having a fling with my sister. Anyway, that's what my sister calls it when I ask if she and Dougie are serious.

'We're having a fling,' she says. 'That's all.' But I wonder if he takes it more seriously than that. My sister was married for ages but her husband went off with an angel therapist leaving her alone to bring up six kids – most of whom are now teenagers and leaving home. About a nanosecond later she was seeing Dougie. Maybe Dougie's an interim relationship, the man she needs to put her back together. Dougie's very good at stuff like that. He can't manage to pay his bills on time but he can make a woman feel good about herself.

I think about all of this as I stare out of the window. I love staring out of the window. I used to do it endlessly when I was a child. I spent days and days just looking at the sky, the flowers waving in the breeze, my father trying to play cricket with my mother and sister – 'Doesn't anyone understand what LBW actually means?' he'd say – the birds swooping into our orchard to eat the fruit. Then I'd watch the horses that lived opposite the house and imagined myself grazing with them . . .

I spent much of my childhood pretending to gallop across those fields, to jump over gates and to eat soft, succulent grass. At weekends, my mother would watch as I put up jumps in the orchard and cantered around, giving a non-stop commentary as I jumped my clear rounds. I remember Naomi, my friend who lived down the road, was there with me. She and I would spend all day outside, neighing and tossing our hair as if we both had a mane. It's a warm and happy memory. Oh, I was so free! In fact, thinking about it now, Naomi and I used to play *Black Beauty* together. It felt very important.

The Significance of Black Beauty *in Our Lives*

I cannot disassociate my childhood from memories of Black Beauty. *I read it over and over again until I was in my teens. Even now, in times of trouble, I turn to it. Sometimes I think about this. Why do I love* Black Beauty *so? Do I go back to it because I crave to relive my childhood? Possibly. Maybe it's more to do with the fact that, for many years, I felt I was the embodiment of that horse. I would stamp my feet (my hoofs) if I felt something wasn't going my way, flare my nostrils and neigh. It drove Julia mad.*

'You're not a horse!' she'd say, and I'd shake my mane and stamp my feet again.

Fortunately, Naomi was as mad on Black Beauty *as I was. She was an only child and, for a large part of our childhood, we were inseparable. It was partly because we were the same age and lived so close to each other, but mainly because we both loved playing at being horses. We would lie in the tall grass of the orchard at the end of our road and read passages from* Black Beauty *to each other, then re-enact scenes. At first we were tentative. We would pretend to be human characters: Naomi was Lady Anne (frail, beautiful, kind, good horsewoman, who rode side-saddle), I was Blantyre (dashing, fair, good horseman, rode out a lot with Lady Anne), but then we morphed into the horses. Although Naomi was small, dark and much more beautiful than I was, she was always Ginger and I was Beauty. This didn't bother me – after all, who wouldn't want to be Beauty? – until I wondered, years later, why Naomi had wanted to be Ginger. She could have been Merrylegs, the pretty pony who ends up with the vicar. She could have been Captain, the proud old warhorse, survivor of the Crimea, who preaches the creed of pacifism and who my mother said was 'a Quaker'.*

'What's a Quaker?' I'd ask.

'Someone who believes in a simple life and not doing ill to anyone,' she'd say, and then she'd tell me there was a Quaker meeting house nearby and we'd go sometimes and look at it. To me, it was like a simple barn on stilts and I imagined all the Quakers in there dressed like the man with the round face and the funny hat who was on the front of the packet of Quaker Oats I had for breakfast on Wednesday mornings, but my mum told me Quakers did not look like that any more.

'They look like you and me,' she'd say. 'In fact, there aren't many left now probably.' Then she would go on to tell me how Black Beauty *wasn't just about the welfare of animals but about society. 'The author, Anna Sewell, wrote it to address other social issues, as well as to promote the humane treatment of animals,' she'd say. 'You see, there was a lot of social deprivation at that time. Women were wives, mothers and ladies of the manor then, not role models for the young women of today – but, still, it's interesting to see the progress we've made over the years, isn't it?'*

I would nod because she'd have her Very Important Voice on, which meant I had to listen to her and try very hard to understand.

Then she'd tell me about Reuben Smith, who injures Black Beauty and drives himself into poverty with his alcoholism. 'Think about Mr So-and-so down the road,' she'd say. 'He drinks two bottles of wine a night and more in the morning and he's just lost his job. Think how his poor wife feels!'

I tried to imagine. 'She must feel dreadful,' I said.

'Exactly!' said my mother.

From then on, when I was reading the book, I tried to imagine everyone as its characters. Mr Grace, the nice man who delivered the coal and logs and worked seven days a week, became Jeremiah Barker, the kindly cab driver who owns Beauty for three years. His son Graham, a capable boy who helped with the load, was Harry Barker. Naomi's father, Gordon, was Squire Gordon, a kind but relatively distant man, by dint of his name, which meant that Naomi's mother, Eileen, had to be the sickly Lady Gordon, even though she'd never been ill in her life. My dog became Merrylegs and Naomi's, Spotty, was Captain. Julia, my sister, unfortunately had to be Beauty's brother Rob Roy, who dies at the beginning of the book when he falls chasing a hare with the hunt, but I let Julia come back in as Dolly Barker, a little girl who is also kind to Beauty.

And Naomi, of course, was tragic, put-upon Ginger, the horse who has a horrible start to her life, maltreated and abused until she kicks and bites She has brief respite when she meets Beauty but by the end of the book she has died, beaten, confused and disillusioned, at the hands of her horrible master. Ginger's final scene, as we children imagined her death, was something Naomi and I would enact over and over again. Naomi would say her lines to Beauty from the middle of the book because, although these were not the final words Ginger spoke, Naomi was particularly keen on them: 'And so here we are – ruined in the prime of our youth and strength – you by a drunkard and I by a fool. It is very hard.' Then we would both sigh and hang our heads and think about how Reuben Smith had ruined me by galloping me over stones in a drunken state and how young Lord George had galloped and hunted and raced Ginger until she was worthless, and we would almost wail in sorrow for ourselves. Then Naomi/Ginger would decide to die and she'd lie on the ground on her side, her limbs splayed out every which way, and make a piteous moaning noise and I would whinny and whicker and nose around her, breathing warm breath on her, trying to persuade her to get up, but Naomi would sigh, then suddenly sink down and die in a silent, heart-breaking fashion.

We played this game over and over again and, every time we did, it made me cry. I would go back to my house in a terrible state and say to my mother, 'I couldn't save Ginger,' and she would roll her eyes and say, 'If this game makes you and Naomi so unhappy, why do you play it?' I tried to explain to her that I really felt I was Beauty and it was my responsibility to look after the broken Ginger. 'Don't you understand?' I'd say to my mother. 'It's my job to look after Ginger!'

'Yes, but you're always going to fail,' my mother would say, 'because Ginger dies in the book, and as long as you and Naomi won't stray from the story she'll have to keep dying.'

Once, as Naomi and I were cantering around in the field across the road, then grazing happily in the lush grass by the stream, I suggested to her that maybe we change the ending for Ginger. 'Naomi,' I said, 'why does Ginger always have to die?'

Naomi looked at me with her big brown eyes. 'Because she is mistreated by her master,' she said sadly. 'Because no one, apart from Beauty, really cares about her from beginning to end.'

'That's in the book,' I said, 'but maybe sometimes we could

change the ending and Ginger could live happily ever after with Beauty. That would be fun, wouldn't it?'

'Not really,' said Naomi, 'because that isn't what happens.'

'Yes, but it could happen, couldn't it? I mean, Beauty loves Ginger so much and is so hurt that Ginger dies that I was wondering if we could change it. That's all. Beauty and Ginger could escape and go and live in a field somewhere together.'

'No,' said Naomi. 'It couldn't happen. Ginger dies and that's it.'

I thought it could happen, though. Ginger could live, and sometimes when Naomi lay dying and I was pawing around her and wanting to cry, I'd imagine that Ginger wasn't dead and that I hadn't failed her and that, in fact, Beauty and Ginger were going on to have a fantastic life together, and then I didn't feel so bad. I told my mother I'd decided that she was right and that life, after all, was rather like Black Beauty.

'It's about bringing up foals and why some people are nice to horses and some people aren't, isn't it?' I said to her.

'Yes, it is about that. It's about human kindness and how we should look after each other but, in the end, it's only a book, Samantha. I didn't mean you to read too much into it.'

But sometimes, even now, as a grown woman, those words come back into my head: 'And so here we are – ruined in the prime of our youth and strength – you by a drunkard and I by a fool. It is very hard.' They seem as valid now as they did then.

I close my eyes to enjoy the peace and quiet – and the telephone rings. Damn. It's always ringing at the wrong time. I pick it up.

'Samantha!' says a male voice. 'How are you?'

'Dougie,' I say. 'That's weird. I was just about to call you.'

'Why?' says Dougie, in his cheery voice. 'What's the matter?'

I love Dougie when he says things like that. He always listens to me and always has. 'I'm upset,' I say. 'I've been thinking about the plot of *Black Beauty*, the bit where Ginger realizes she's doomed. She tells Beauty they've been ruined by a drunk and a fool and –'

'Nope, I'm not following you,' he says. 'What are you talking about?'

'I used to read *Black Beauty* with my mum and she told me that the book is an allegory for our lives.'

'So which one am I?'

'Sorry?'

'The drunk or the fool?'

I giggle. 'Both,' I say. 'Or maybe you're one of the servants who look after the horses. They're all nice but simple.'

'Charming,' he says. 'Anyway, I haven't rung to discuss some childhood book with you. I've called to say I might drive down and see you tomorrow.'

'OK, but it's the last day of term,' I say. 'Edward and Bennie are only at school half a day and Stanley's coming to play.'

'Great,' says Dougie.

'And I thought we could pack a picnic and go down to the river for a walk and a swim after school.'

'That sounds perfect,' he says. 'I shall pack my picnic kit.'

I'm just about to ask what his picnic kit is, when I

remember how appropriate it is that he has called. 'Actually, talking of the end of school, I was just about to ring you. Guess who I saw today?'

'I don't know. Erm, Edward's head teacher who told you he was the quirkiest, most talented boy she'd ever met?'

'No. Gary White!'

'Gary White?'

'He's that former footballer.'

'I know who he is, Samantha,' says Dougie, suddenly sounding terribly overexcited. 'Gary White? I can't believe it! My God, I used to worship him.'

'Yes, I thought you might have done,' I say, cheered by his enthusiasm. 'Well, he's just moved in down the road and his daughter's started at Edward's school. He drives a red Ferrari.'

'But why has his daughter just started if term's about to end?'

'I guess he wants her to see it for a couple of days before she begins properly in September. His mother suggested it, apparently.'

'Mm. What's he like?'

'I don't know, really. He drives too fast.'

'Do you think I could meet him?' he says. 'He really is a hero of mine.'

'Oh, I don't know. I only bumped into him at the school gates.'

'Yes, but maybe he's lonely and doesn't know anyone. We could take him a cup of sugar for his tea.'

'A cup of sugar?'

'Isn't that what neighbourly people do?'

'But you're not his neighbour.'

'You are!' he says triumphantly. 'And I used to be. Oh, please, Samantha. I only want his autograph. It's not too much to ask, is it? I mean, if Black Beauty had moved into the area, I'd have taken him a carrot.'

'Black Beauty's fictitious, and I told the children I'd take them for a picnic,' I say.

'Yes,' he says excitedly, 'but wouldn't they rather see a Ferrari?'

'No,' I say. 'And, anyway, why on earth would we just appear on his doorstep?'

'You could bake him a cake.'

'But I can't bake, Dougie.'

'We'll buy one and take it out of its packaging, pretend you've baked it.'

'Don't be ridiculous!' I say. 'Gary White is probably a very private person who has moved out of London to be left alone, not have mad fans turning up on his doorstep bearing fake cakes.'

'Oh, Samantha, you've lost your sense of fun!' he says. 'Gary White used to be a famous footballer! All famous people like being recognized. It's like oxygen to them. He's probably dying to meet some fans and he'd no doubt love it if I came round and asked him about his matches. I remember one against West Ham where he did this amazing header and – I think I've still got my ticket somewhere! He could sign it, couldn't he? It'd be worth a fortune and –'

'Look,' I say, 'we can talk about it tomorrow when you come down but I'm tending towards the picnic and swim. OK?'

'Oh, all right,' says Dougie, and rings off.

A minute later he calls back. 'Look, if you say we can go round I promise I'll read *Black Beauty*.'

'Dougie . . .' I say, and he puts down the phone for the second time.

My Early Home

John comes home late that evening. Wendy's out again. I asked her where she was going but she just smiled. After she'd left, I thought I might get some work done but now I feel pleasantly dozy. I often feel dozy. I spend half the afternoon and all weekend yawning and counting the hours until the children go to bed.

I remember what it was to be tired from working hard. Before I had Edward, I used to travel all over the place, asking specialists if red wine could ward off cancer or what really were the life-prolonging properties of broccoli. Then I started my celebrity-fridges job, which has been fun but, recently, I've wondered why I'm doing it.

I told John about my concerns when we came back from holiday. We were lying in the garden in a hammock that he and Edward had nailed to a tree.

'I bought this hammock in Crete,' John said, as we swung back and forth in it lazily. It was early evening and turning chilly after a warm spring day. The children were inside squabbling over the Chair and who was watching what on television, and we were snuggled up, jumper-to-jumper, our bare feet touching, still warm from the patio stones.

'I don't remember you buying it,' I said. 'When did you do that?'

'When we were in Chania, that day we went to the market. The man with the beautiful honeyed apricots sold it to me.'

I screwed up my face. 'Oh, yes,' I said. 'God, they were lovely. Bennie ate about ten and said he felt sick. You had to rub his tummy. Do you remember?' I turned to him and he nodded. Then we were both silent, remembering what had happened the following day. I was just about to mention it but stopped myself. Later, I asked myself why I didn't ask him how he was feeling. I knew how I felt. But I didn't know where the conversation would lead and, somehow, it seemed to be the last thing either of us wanted to talk about. Instead I said, 'I don't want to keep doing my job.'

'Why not?' said John, astounded. 'You've been doing it for so long. I thought you liked it.'

'Well, I don't. I have no idea why I still do it, and I was thinking that maybe if I stopped doing it and stayed at home full time, Bennie would be happier.'

'But, Samantha, you get paid well. It's not a hard job, is it? And why do you think Bennie's unhappy?'

'He's been odd since the holiday. He hates school, he's not sleeping well and he stutters.'

'I know that, but I'm sure the stutter will go.'

'And he's very clingy.'

'He's at that age,' John said carefully. 'He's just started school. I don't think it's that unusual, is it? When I first met you, Edward was stuck to you like a limpet and Bennie's not much older than Edward was then.'

'Yes, but I worried about Edward then and I'm worrying about Bennie now. I feel I should be here for him. I feel it's my job as his mother to do that. I feel he needs me at the moment.'

John looked at me quizzically. 'What's all this about?'

'I don't want to do my job,' I said. 'I want to be here with the children. It's coming up for their summer holidays and I want to make sure they have really good ones so that when the new term starts Bennie feels more confident and happy about school.'

'And you think staying at home is the answer?'

'Yes. I can always try to find another job in September.'

'OK. Well, let's see. Maybe the magazine will compromise. Why don't you ask if you can take a sabbatical? Maybe you could do something else for them.'

'Like what?'

'Oh, I don't know. An overview of all the fridges you have met or something.'

I laughed, but that night, as I was leafing through a coffee-table book on people's loos, I suddenly wondered if he was right. If you can sell a book on loos, why not one about fridges?

I called the editor the next day and told her my idea. 'I want to take a sabbatical over the summer and pull together the words and pictures for a coffee-table book called *Our Fridges, Our Selves*.'

'*Our Fridges, Our Selves*, eh?' she said, musing.

'Yes,' I said emphatically. 'These celeb coffee-table books are very in now, and I'm sure it would sell like hot cakes.'

The editor said she'd call me back, and the next day she rang to say that, yes, she thought it was a good idea. Apparently she had a friend in publishing who was already interested. 'You get it together over the summer,' she said. 'Only the good fridges, mind.'

When John came home, I was ecstatic. 'I'm going to spend the summer at home writing a book called *Our Fridges, Our Selves*!'

'What?' said John.

'They bought the sabbatical idea. I'm going to do a round-up of all the fridges I've looked at – Booker Prize winners, glamour models, reality-TV-show contestants.'

'Well done you,' said John, giving me a hug.

'But it was your idea,' I said. 'You're really very clever.'

'Great. Then might I suggest you do *All The Fridges I Have Never Seen* as a follow-up?'

'Ha, ha,' I said.

But this book is not getting done. Every time I sit down to do it, the telephone rings, one of the children wakes up, or I read and reply to emails, which takes an age, or I try to buy the children pyjamas on-line. In fact, even now as I sit down to write about some rock star's fridge that had nothing in it but beer, I see the little email sign flashing at me.

There are two new ones: one from my sister saying she has something momentous to tell me and can I ring her, and one from Naomi. I feel a pang when I look at it. How weird! First Dougie rings when I'm about to ring him and now, on the day I'm thinking about *Black Beauty*, there's an email from Ginger/Naomi. Gosh, Naomi and I used to be so close. She meant everything to me. I almost had a crush on her. For years I saw her every day. We used to hang out at her house because although I lived in quite a large family home with an acre of garden and a vegetable patch, she lived with her Irish mother Eileen and American father Gordon in a bungalow.

I loved that house, and that everyone knew what everyone else was doing. In my house you could go all day without bumping into anyone. My father was at work and my mother was busy in the garden, planting out seedlings, and my sister was always squirrelled away reading a book. You couldn't help but bump into someone in Naomi's house. Her mother was often in the kitchen, making stews, cookies and cakes, and her father was always banging around fixing things or creating new things in the garage. He made Naomi a doll's house and a Wendy house, and he converted the corner of the small garage into a summerhouse for us. When she wasn't being Ginger, Naomi used to pretend to be Mother. Her father had put a rusty old stove in there with some plastic pots and pans, and Naomi would pretend to make tea for me when I came home from work because I was the man of the house. I used to speak in a gruff voice that frightened their old cat, who used to sleep on the stove. 'Hello, my darling,' I'd say, as I came through the door. Naomi would have on one of her mother's lacy pinnies and I'd borrow her dad's trilby. Quite often I'd ask if we could change roles, but Naomi would never agree. 'You're taller than me,' she'd say, 'and husbands are always taller than their wives.'

One day Gordon made us a camp in the old orchard at the end of the road. He found some railway sleepers and tarpaulin and constructed a rather special upstairs-downstairs den for us. The camp leant partially against a tall apple tree, which he had used to make the upstairs. Naomi and I would climb up the tree – her father had hewn some footholds in the trunk – to our bedroom. Once we were reading *Black Beauty* up there and crying at the Ginger bit and Naomi wailed, 'Imagine if we were separated from each other. Imagine if something happened to one of us and we never saw each other again!' Then she thought a bit and said, 'Why don't we carve our names in the tree? I saw these girls do it in a story I read. Then we'd never forget each other.' I thought that was a good idea so we got down from the tree, went back to her house and found one of her father's penknives.

'Should we carve our own names or "Ginger" and "Beauty"?' I asked Naomi.

'Well, I suppose we're more like Ginger and Beauty to each other, aren't we?'

So we carved those names into the bark, then etched a misshapen heart round them and felt as if nothing could ever part us.

It was not to be, though. Maybe on the very afternoon of the pledge Naomi guessed at something I didn't. Maybe that was why she had chosen to be Ginger for all those years. I think even then she knew more than I did about the tragedy in people's lives. My own tragedy, my marriage break-up, was years ahead of me. Neither, at that time, did I understand that families are mutable things. Some people leave, others stay behind. Maybe Naomi could understand, in some vague way, how defenceless, loving creatures who are not given a warm stable and a kind word when they're young are scarred for the rest of their lives. She'd say to me, often, 'It's OK for Beauty because his first master protected and cared for him while Ginger had a master who beat her and didn't care about her.'

I didn't think about it then but now I wonder if she was making a reference to our families. My parents were kind and loving. They were good masters. Her parents argued a lot. It was impossible not to notice. We'd hear them in the evenings when I was having a sleepover. I never heard my parents argue but you could hear Naomi's clearly. Her mother would go on and on about how disappointed she was with her life and how sick she was of doing nothing but cooking, and Naomi's poor, sweet father would apologize in this small sad voice.

'You've let me down, Gordon!' she'd yell at him.

'I'm so sorry, Eileen,' he'd reply.

One night, when I was there and Naomi's parents were rowing again, Naomi said to me, 'Squire Gordon and his wife don't shout at each other in *Black Beauty*, do they?'

'No,' I said, because I was pretty sure that they didn't. 'Squire Gordon and his wife leave Birtwick Park never to come back, though, and all the horses are sold.'

'Why do they leave?' whispered Naomi.

'Because she's sick,' I said.

'Hmm,' said Naomi.

I found Naomi's mother confusing. I was very fond of her father, who seemed approachable, but her mother was an unknown quantity. She seemed unlike a mother. Despite all that baking, she could be fierce and terrifying. It was impossible to judge her mood. One morning I would appear at their door and knock, hoping that Naomi would answer, but it would snap open to reveal Eileen Cooper glowering at me. 'Naomi has to go to church right now,' she'd say, or 'Naomi has been naughty so she's not coming out to play,' or 'Naomi has to tidy her room this morning,' or any number of other things, including, quite regularly, 'Naomi cannot come out to play as she has to wash her hair.' She'd say it with such venom that she'd make me feel as if it was my fault that Naomi's room was messy or that her hair was dirty. Other times she'd smile and let me in, make me cocoa, give me a biscuit and tell me how happy she was that Naomi and I were friends. It was disconcerting, and although I knew she wasn't very happy because if she and Naomi's father were happy they wouldn't argue like they did. I never understood why Naomi's father seemed to love her so much.

I concluded that it was possibly because Naomi's mum was so beautiful. Her skin was like Naomi's, the shade of alabaster, and she had green eyes and long black hair.

I now know she was a control freak or had emotional difficulties. I'm not sure which, but she could be pretty nasty to me and Naomi. She kept crisps and sweets in the pantry which she would dole out to Naomi and me as a reward when we were good. She made it very clear, time and time again, that this was the only time Naomi and I were allowed them. 'This pantry is my pantry,' she'd say. 'I give sweets but I can also take them away. If I ever find you have stolen anything from here, woe betide you.' She said it so often that Naomi and I were under no illusion what would happen if we were ever tempted. 'I'll lock you in the coal hole,' she said. But tempted we were, and one day Naomi's mother left the pantry door open – did she do it deliberately? The sweets and crisps were winking and waving at us and there were so many that, as one, Naomi and I thought maybe her mother wouldn't notice if we just crept in and . . . I took a packet of Monster Munch and Naomi had a Turkish Delight, wrapped up in shiny pink paper. We buried the wrappers in the garden and thought we'd got away with, it but later that afternoon Naomi's mum came into the garage where we were playing mummies and daddies and she shouted at me, white with fury, then marched me home, tugging me along by my ear, which really hurt. She told my mum I was 'a thieving tinker'.

After she'd gone my mother hugged me for ages and said it wasn't me that was the tinker, but I didn't know what she was getting at. After that I kept out of Naomi's mother's way.

It never occurred to me that things were hard for Naomi. I knew her mother *had* locked her in the coal hole after we'd stolen the sweets but Naomi said it was only for half an hour so I didn't think much of it. After all, Naomi said she'd pretended to be Ginger when she'd got locked in the coal hole and that, when she thought about it, getting locked up was a very Gingerish thing to happen. But after another stint in the coal hole for swearing, she burst into tears, as we sat in the low branches of the apple tree in her garden, and told me her father didn't have a job. That was why he managed to spend most of his time making things for us. By then he'd added a beautiful wooden sledge to our toy collection, a go-kart, a mini-wheelbarrow and a stall for us to be Black Beauty and Ginger in on the other side of the garage. Naomi and I purloined a bit of hay from the horses that lived opposite and put it there so it felt like a real stable. He also came home with Spotty – we used to make him sit on the back of the cart as we wheeled it along the road.

One day, as we were pushing Spotty up the drive, we saw Naomi's dad talking to my mother, and the next thing I knew he was doing a bit of gardening work for us. I remember hearing my mother discuss it with my father after dinner one night. 'He needs the work,' my mother was saying. My father had asked why we were paying him to do the garden when we already had a gardener and my mother was a pretty dab hand too. He nodded sympathetically and I never heard them talk of it again.

I think my mother must have felt sorry for Naomi because I remember Naomi coming to stay at our house a few times and my mother looking at her sadly as Naomi cantered round the orchard and then, of an evening, would come in and pick her way through her salad. One memorable Friday night, my mother had even splashed out and put sweetcorn on top, which irritated me as I hated tinned sweetcorn on salad. In fact, I still do. I fail to see why it counts as salad, but there was no telling my mother that. She had her set menu and, for all the years I was a child, it never deviated.

This is how my mother's menu went:

Monday
Breakfast: boiled egg (runny, yuk!) and toast
Dinner: Alphabetti spaghetti

Tuesday
Breakfast: fish fingers (yum!)
Dinner: spaghetti casserole, which involved my mother tipping a tin of spaghetti hoops into an ovenproof dish, chopping onions and bacon into it, then putting it into the oven. She left it for half an hour until it was cooked and bubbling.

Wednesday
Breakfast: Quaker Oats (yum!)
Dinner: rice, boiled mince and peas

Thursday
Breakfast: poached eggs (underdone, yuk!)
Dinner: baked potatoes with cheese and bacon on top

Friday
Breakfast: toast (neither yum nor yuk)
Dinner: salad, followed by a slice of Mr Kipling's walnut cake but only if you'd eaten up *all* your salad.

That particular Friday, I remember my mother offering Naomi some cake and I had to bite back words because I could see that Naomi had certainly not finished her salad. It was inconceivable to me to forgo the cake. Nothing would have stopped me and so, that night with Naomi, I had bravely eaten the sweetcorn and the beetroot and the limp leaves and every little bit, and then I looked over and found, to my horror, that Naomi had barely touched her food.

'You have to eat your food,' I hissed at her, 'or you won't get cake!'

Naomi just looked at me with her big sad eyes and I decided she didn't really care whether she got cake or not. But when my mother came back from the larder with the cake, she cleared up our plates without looking at them. Why wasn't she looking at them? Could she not see that Naomi hadn't finished her salad? Apparently not, for she still gave both of us a slice. I glowered about it all night.

One day, when I was about thirteen, I went over to see Naomi and she was crying. All her mother's things had gone. By then we were far too grown-up to play Ginger and Black Beauty and instead spent our time reading teen magazines and worrying about our hair and whether or not any boys fancied us. The stall in the garage had been empty for a while. Naomi told me her mother had run off with a man from a nearby village and they'd gone to Ireland.

About two months later I was invited to go with Naomi to see her. I don't know why Naomi's mother asked me to come along. Maybe she thought Naomi would be bored without a friend. We were excited to go but when we got there we realized that things weren't working out. The man for whom Naomi's mother had left her husband – Fergus, handsome, in a threatening way – used to go out drinking at all times of the day. I remember him leering at me and Naomi when he was drunk and every night Naomi and I would creep out of their tiny house to the caravan in the back garden where we were sleeping and lock the door. Neither of us said anything. Fergus's obvious ill-intent remained like a secret but I had a secret that was worse. Sometimes, in a horrible but fascinating way, I sort of enjoyed the attention we were getting from Fergus. It was the first time I had experienced it, the power, the pleasure, a woman can get out of being attractive to a man. It was sort of heady, in a really awful way. I would watch Fergus watching me. He would stare out of the upstairs cottage window in the morning, his gaze lingering on the window of the caravan near where I slept. I would stretch out my long tanned legs and feel him looking at me. Then I'd swing my legs over in an arch and place my feet on the floor and stand up. I would be wearing my short nightdress, with my bottom just hidden, and I would imagine Fergus mentally lifting up that nightdress to gaze at my body. I found it strangely exciting, but when he came back to his house, drunken and stinking, shouting at Naomi's mother, I'd shrink away, for then it was real and frightening, far removed from my teenage fantasy. One night we found Eileen hammering on the door of the caravan and crying. 'Help me, Naomi,' she said. I retreated to my bunk but I heard them talking. I'll never forget Naomi begging her mother to tell her why she had left her father. 'You can't help who you fall in love with,' was what her mother said and then I heard them both crying.

After we came home, Naomi moved away with her father. She told me he had a job in the States. She was very sad when she told me, so we climbed the tree of our camp one last time – we hadn't been up there for years! – and traced our names, now just visible under the lichen that covered the tree trunk. 'Are we still Ginger and Beauty?' Naomi asked me sadly, and I nodded and told her that somewhere, deep in my heart, we always would be. 'I will always try to save you,' I said to her. 'I will always protect you and look after you.' We vowed to keep in touch and, for many years, we did. Naomi would write – she would sign herself as Ginger, a joke, I thought – and I would write back as Black Beauty, but our lives were changing and soon I had forgotten to put BB at the end of my letters.

I went off to university, grew up a bit and met boys! men! Gradually my letters to Naomi got less and less frequent. Naomi, though, kept going, despite my crushing silence. It wasn't that I didn't enjoy getting her letters but I could never seem to write back.

Her letters were full of her life in America and how much she loved it there. She wrote that she'd done well in her exams and that she was going to college in San Diego. Then she wrote that she'd met a great guy and that they'd moved to Los Angeles because he was a film producer and she was in film PR and . . . my life seemed so tame in comparison. I remember sending her a picture of Edward when he was a baby and she sent me a picture of her daughter, born the same year as Edward and . . . What was her daughter's name?

Naomi rang once and we had a stilted conversation because I suppose we felt like strangers to each other. That's certainly how I felt. I didn't even tell her what had happened between John the First and me. How do you catch up on twenty-plus years of life gone by? She seemed so contented at a time when I was anything but. Then I gave her my email address and she started emailing and, when I had time, I replied.

But seeing her email in my inbox now makes me feel

guilty. I resolve to stop being so useless. She was my Ginger all those years ago. She'd got locked in a coal hole because of me – well, partially. If she can continue to make an effort to stay in touch, then so should I. I vowed I would never let her down and I must honour that vow, so open her email. In it she says she's coming to the UK with her daughter, Alexa, who everyone calls Lexie, to look at schools.

I want Lexie to have a good education so Lexie's father and I are thinking of sending her to boarding-school in the UK. It's something we want to do and Lexie is very excited. I have a demanding job in film PR for a top Hollywood studio so I can see her when I'm over doing business. Her father also has a very demanding job so can't come with me this summer. There are a few schools around where you live that interest us both so I shall be over in July. I'd love Lexie to go to school near you because then I can visit you, too. Also, Lexie is very important to us. She's our only child so I've told her that maybe you could keep an eye on her if anything goes wrong. I'd feel so much happier if someone I know was on hand. I hope you don't mind. Anyway, it would be great to meet up even though we haven't seen each other for a long time. Are you around? Gxx

'Am I around?' I type back, suddenly realizing I'd love to see Naomi. We could catch up on the past and on Gordon, Eileen and Fergus. I wonder what happened to them. This is my chance to find out, to make up for my lack of communication. I am already beginning to plan the things we can do together: take the children to the river to swim, go to Starbucks for a gossip and a coffee – as it's nearly the summer holidays I don't suppose I have to get an approved pass from the school-gate mothers. Maybe we could go and find that tree. That would be weird, wouldn't it? To look at the names we carved as adolescents all those years ago? 'I wouldn't miss seeing you for the world!' I type back to Naomi. 'Where are you staying when you're over here? You must stay with us if you're in the area. I have a son the same age as Lexie, I think, and it's the summer holidays and we have lots of fun things planned and can't wait to meet you and her so call me asap. Sx.' I retype the last bit. 'Call me asap,' I write, 'love BB.'

Just as I hit send, the telephone rings.

'John?' says a breathless female voice.

'No, Samantha,' I say. God, do I sound like a man?

'Oh. Right. I need to speak to John.'

'He's not here.'

'Oh, no.' She sounds pretty desperate. 'When will he be back?' she says.

'I don't know. I haven't spoken to him.'

'Oh, no. I have to get hold of him.'

'Have you tried his mobile?'

'It's off.'

'Well, I'll get him to call you when he comes in. Who should I say it is?'

'Charlie. I work with him. I'm on set now, the runners won't work and we're opening in two days' time and –'

'I'll get him to ring you,' I say, and hang up.

Half an hour later, John walks in. He looks tired and dishevelled. 'Samantha, my love,' he says, coming over and kissing me.

'John, I –'

'Kiss me again, Samantha,' he says, running his hands through my hair. 'I'm so tired and fed up and the train was delayed and I haven't seen you or the kids all day and – please kiss me and get me a glass of wine, my darling wife.'

So I kiss him for a long time and feel his shoulders relax. Then, as I'm getting him a glass of wine, I tell him about Charlie.

'Oh, God,' he says crossly, taking a slug of red wine. 'I've just got in.'

'She said it was important – something to do with the runners.'

'Those blasted runners,' he says. 'I'm sorry, I'm going to have to call her. Do you mind?'

'Not at all,' I say.

I go back to my work but I can't concentrate so I wander into the study.

John has his head in his hands, the telephone receiver cupped under his chin. 'All right,' he's saying. 'I'll come back as early as I can. Thanks for holding the fort, Charlie. See you tomorrow. 'Bye for now.'

'Oh, John,' I say to him, laying my hands on his shoulders. They feel very tense again so I start to massage them.

'I'm sorry,' he says. 'I'm going to have to leave early again tomorrow. This blasted set, it keeps going wrong and I can't seem to fix it properly. If it wasn't for Charlie, who seems to be working all the hours God gave her . . . Can we go to bed?'

'What about dinner?'

'You're dinner.'

Later, in bed, as we lie entwined, John asks about my day. 'What's going on in your life, my love?' he says. 'I seem to be away so much and . . . I miss you and the kids. I want to know everything about them.'

So, I tell him about how Wendy didn't wake up and I took the kids who, by the way, were fine, to school and how we'd met this man Gary White who'd nearly run us over and –

'Oh, you sent me a text message?' he says. 'Something indecipherable. What did it say?'

'Oh, that Gary White's a wanker or something.'

'Poor man,' says John, kissing me sleepily, then yawning. 'Who is he?'

'A former footballer, and his wife has just run off with his accountant.'

'Oh, even more poor man. What makes him a wanker?'

'He has this horrible red car that looks like an ashtray on wheels and drives too fast. He nearly ran over Jamie and then, when I complained to him, he had the audacity to ask the children over to see the car!'

'Mmmm,' says John.

'Oh, and it turns out that Dougie's Gary White's biggest fan and he's coming down tomorrow and wants me to buy a cake and pretend I've baked it so we can go round and get an autograph . . . And – are you awake?'

'Mmmm.' He rolls over and starts to grunt.

John is a past master of grunting. His primary, and most important, grunts are used when he can't be bothered to wake up at night and see to some fretful child. They go something like this.

Me: 'Darling, the baby's crying.'

Him: 'Grunt, grunt.'

Me: 'Maybe he's teething. Do you think he's teething?'

Him: 'Grunt, grunt.'

Me: 'Oh, John, listen, now the baby's screaming. Oh, he's in pain. Aren't you going to get up and see if he's OK?'

John will give a protracted grunt that sounds as if he is trying to say something like, 'Well, why don't you bloody well get up and check him if you think he's in pain?'

But he doesn't actually say this, in the same way that I don't reply, 'Because I had to go through hell to give birth to our healthy boys and then I had to breastfeed them and sacrifice my breasts to a life of droopiness, and now I will never be able to laugh or sneeze again without vaguely wetting myself and every week I think I should really go to the gym to get any semblance of a figure back, which is boring and I would hate it, so, please, John, could you open your eyes and get your lazy, unaffected, unstretchmarked, untouched-by-childbirth body up those stairs and see to your youngest child?' No, I don't say that for, by the time I'd said it, John would be fast asleep again.

He has other grunts. He has the I-want-to-have-sex grunts, which usually happen late at night when I'm too tired to think, let alone be gentle and loving or, God forbid, passionate. Then there are the grunts he makes when he's about to go to sleep, and the grunts when he's come back drunk from the pub and is trying to talk to me but making no sense.

Tonight it's his I've-just-had-sex-and-am-pretty-happy-but-very-tired grunts.

I lie and listen to him. I hadn't realized how much I've missed this easy intimacy. He's been working so hard and I've been so involved with the children and . . .

I hear the patter of feet. John's grunts change. He's heard it too.

'Bennie!' I say, as Bennie's blond head appears round the door.

'M-M-Mummy, there are monsters in my room,' says Bennie, climbing into bed with me.

'There are no monsters, Bennie,' I say. 'None at all.'

'Th-th-there are. They're waving at me.'

John grunts a bit more.

'Monsters don't wave,' I say.

'Wh-wh-why not?'

'They just don't do that sort of thing, really.'

'Wh-what do they do?'

'I think sometimes they may growl.'

'G-g-growl?'

'Yes, like this,' I say, opening my mouth wide. 'Grrrrr!'

'Samantha!' says John, suddenly, sitting up. 'I thought we weren't supposed to be encouraging Bennie to get into our bed.'

'We're not,' I say. 'I just wanted to reassure him that there cannot be waving monsters in his room because monsters don't wave.'

'Th-they say, "Grrrrr," Daddy,' says Bennie.

John groans. 'Why can't we get this child out of our bed?' he says, getting out of bed himself.

'Where are you going?'

'Bennie's room,' he says. 'I'm tired. I need to sleep.'

Why We Can't Get Bennie Out of our Bed

We have had so many conversations about getting Bennie out of our bed that I have now come to one awful and stunning conclusion. We're just useless tired people who have no determination. We talk about getting Bennie out of our bed and do nothing about it.

I pointed this out to John the other day as we were having yet another such conversation.

'We'll have to persuade him not to come in,' said John.

'I know that,' I said, 'but how? We talk about this all the time yet, at the end of the day, we're both too exhausted to do anything about it.'

John agreed that maybe we should wait until his play was on, the problems had been ironed out and he didn't have to work so hard. 'I don't think I can cope with sorting him out now,' he said. 'I need all the sleep I can get.' He said he didn't mind sleeping apart from me temporarily, as long as we all got a good night.

But now John is virtually inhabiting his son's room. This must be the umpteenth night in a row he has ended up sleeping there. It started when we got back from Crete. Bennie crept in then and I didn't have the heart to take him back. Then he started the trial mornings at school and it got worse. He cried on the first morning and hasn't stopped. I keep telling him it should be an exciting time of his life, but Bennie stands at the school gates and howls.

'Come on, Bennie,' says Edward, on the days he's feeling help-

ful. 'I'll look after you. It'll be all right.' But it hasn't been so far.

I've tried everything. I've even tried something Julia, who has a degree in childcare studies, calls 'positive reinforcement'. 'Bennie needs to associate school with good things,' she said. 'It's often the case with Oedipal children, like Bennie, that they can't bear to leave the mother they adore. Subconsciously, they think their father, whom they hate and want to kill, will move into their territory and take their mother away. To protect themselves, and their special relationship with their mother, they refuse to do the thing that threatens them.'

'What are you talking about?' I said. 'Bennie isn't Oedipal. I haven't noticed him trying to kill his father. It's almost the other way round. Anyway, no young children ever want to go to school. Edward was just as bad, if not worse.'

'Exactly!' said Julia, triumphantly. 'I remember asking him what his interests were and he thought for ages, then said, "My mum." Oedipal or what?' I told her I felt this was slightly more explicable. 'I was on my own with him!' I said. But Julia ignored me and went on to tell me I must bear in mind that our family had been through a traumatic experience.

'I know that,' I said. 'It's why I'm taking a sabbatical from work and writing a pointless book about celebrity fridges. I've done it to be here for Bennie.'

'Ah, yes,' said Julia, 'but I'm not talking about Bennie. I'm referring to John. He's been through a traumatic experience. It must be very difficult for him to know it was his fault that Bennie nearly drowned.'

'It wasn't his fault,' I said.

'No, of course it wasn't,' she said, 'but he may think it was and, underneath, maybe you do too. Maybe that's why you're having

problems getting Bennie to sleep apart from you. Subconsciously you may both be willing him to come into your bed to give you a good enough reason not to talk about what happened or discuss the state of your marriage.'

'You're going mad!' I said. 'Nothing's wrong with our marriage. Everything's fine. The problem's with Bennie.'

'Just think about it,' she said. 'In most marriages, the busy wife and mother often puts the husband last on her list. It's something they need to look out for so I'd do something about it – and quick. If you talk openly to John, I bet Bennie will leave your bed.'

But, of course, I do *know how to get Bennie out of our bed because the health visitor – back again to watch Jamie – gave me a book about it. It says I should march Bennie up the stairs, say goodnight to him and leave. Then, when poor Bennie slips under our covers, I should take him by the hand and lead him firmly back to his own bed while saying this and this only, 'Bedtime, Bennie.' Then I should turn round, and walk purposefully away. If Bennie gets out of bed, I should do all this again. I must not look him in the eyes. I must not smile, play or laugh. I must not let him drink water, eat an apple or do anything but get back into his bed. 'There must be no deviation,' said the book.*

'No deviation,' I said to it in return.

I tried it one night. In came sleepy Bennie and as he slipped between the sheets, I found his trusting little hand and propelled him back to his room. 'Wh-what you do, Mummy?' he said, opening his eyes, round like saucers.

'Bedtime, Bennie!' I said firmly.

'Wh-why you not sleep with me?' His face crumpled.

'You must stay in your own bed,' I said, a bit more softly. I lifted him in and went away.

A minute later he reappeared, looking very tired. 'I wanna sleep with you,' he said. 'I wanna do a wee-wee. I'm very thirsty. I wanna have water.'

I hardened my heart, took him back, said my piece and went away.

Fifteen minutes later, I was still plonking Bennie back into bed and he was still reappearing like a particularly stubborn ghost hell-bent on vaporizing into our bedroom. Back I'd take him. Back he'd come. Eventually, on the tenth time of putting him back to bed, he made so much noise that Edward appeared.

'Jesus Christ, Edward!' I said. 'What are you doing? You should be asleep.'

'How am I supposed to sleep with all this racket going on?' he said, hotly.

'Go back to bed,' I said. 'You've got school tomorrow.'

'Sch-sch-school tomorrow?' said Bennie, trembling.

'How many times have you put Bennie back to bed?' said Edward.

'Ten.'

'Oh, that's not bad. Stanley told me the other day that he was terrible at sleeping and that one night his mum had to put him back to bed two hundred and forty-eight times before he stayed.'

'Don't be ridiculous!'

'It's true. He told me she's in the Guinness Book of Records.*'*

'Under what, Edward? Surely there's no category called "Woman Who Put Son Back To Bed The Most Times In One Night"?'

'It's true. Stanley told me.'

I put Bennie back into bed again as Edward went to his room. 'Bedtime, Bennie,' I said desperately.

I went back into my bedroom and curled up in bed. Soon I heard the telltale sound of feet coming towards me.

'Bennie!' I said.

'Number eleven!' sang Edward.

A Job-Horse and his Driver

It is seven thirty a.m. and I'm lying in bed with the thermometer stuck in my mouth. I'm beginning to dislike the thermometer. It beeps when it's ready to divulge my temperature, but today it has got a bit erratic. Fifteen minutes ago, when I first attempted to take my temperature, it beeped after about five seconds and told me my temperature was 22 degrees C, which, essentially, means I'm about to die or am already dead. I shook it harshly. 'Don't be ridiculous,' I said. 'I have to be thirty-six degrees or above to be alive!' Three minutes ago, having somehow pressed the beeping button on the thermometer so many times it's now, unhelpfully, going to tell me my temperature in Fahrenheit rather than Celsius, I put it back into my mouth. So far, it hasn't beeped. I want to go to the loo but I'm not allowed to move.

The telephone rings. I glower at it, but as my thermometer is still not beeping, I give up and take it out of my mouth.

It's my sister. 'Oh, hello, good morning and all that kind of stuff,' she says.

'I'm in a hurry, Julia,' I say. 'I've got to get the kids off to school.'

'Oh. Right,' she says. 'Well, I've just called to say that I'm moving to Los Angeles.'

'What?' I say, momentarily stunned. 'How can you be moving to Los Angeles?'

'To further my career,' she says. 'I want to do some research for my PhD at the university. I have a bursary and it's a great opportunity, so I've said yes.'

'What about the kids?' I say, still in shock.

'Robert's in the sixth form. The older two girls have pretty much left home as they are at university and the others will live with their father. His job is taking him to Scotland. The children have to have time with him. Why not now?'

'But he left you. I thought you hated him.'

'Now, Samantha,' she says, 'how can I hate him? He's the father of my children. I couldn't do the job I do and not let the children see him. It would be hypocritical. And, anyway, I've got all these childcare specialists to meet and it's very exciting. The kids can come and stay in the holidays.'

'But when are you leaving?'

'Erm, tonight.'

'*Tonight!* How can you be leaving tonight? You've only just told me you're going. How can I say goodbye to you?'

'On the telephone.'

God, Julia sounds so calm, it's infuriating. 'But . . . when will I see you? And what about Dougie?'

Suddenly Julia snaps, 'I'm not responsible for everyone else's well-being, OK? I need a break, Samantha. Be happy for me, please.'

I tell her I am but –

'Oh, Samantha, really,' she says. 'Don't you get it? I need a future. I need some me-time. Everybody does.'

'I hardly get any,' I say.

'That's because you're not resolving your issues. Few men will move out of their bedroom to make way for a four-year-old and not demand their oats somewhere. Think about that!' she says, and rings off.

John comes into the bedroom and tells me he has to go back to London.

'The runners for the set . . .' he says, kissing the top of my head.

'I know.'

'I love you,' he says, kissing me again. 'How's the getting of the girl going?' he asks, from the door.

'I'm trying to check my temperature now,' I say.

'Do you think we've got one yet?'

'No, the light hasn't been green so far.'

'Oh. And where's our grown-up girl?'

'I'm sorry?'

'Wendy. She's not downstairs with the kids.'

'Oh, she was out again . . .'

'What's going on with her?' he says, coming back into the room to get his shoes. 'Do you want me to have a chat with her?'

'No,' I say.

'Look, Samantha,' he says, 'I know you. You don't want to upset her because you never want to upset anyone. It's one of your most endearing qualities but, really, you're going to have to get over it. You put yourself out for everyone, but Wendy's paid to be here, to do a job, so just tell her to get on with it.'

'I can't,' I say miserably. 'It's not in my makeup. I'm hopeless at things like that.'

'Well, change your makeup,' says John. 'We got Wendy to help and now you're doing the school run all by yourself.'

'I know,' I say.

'OK, well, can you get them to school this morning?'

I think for a bit. 'Yes, of course I can. It's the last day of school. Even Bennie will be happy – and you're right. I'll talk to Wendy, I promise.'

It turns out that Bennie *is* happy. He and Edward sing the whole way up the hill.

'She'll be coming round the mountain when she comes!' sings Edward, slightly out of tune. 'She'll be coming round the mountain, coming round the mountain, coming round the mountain when she comes.'

Bennie joins in. 'With an ai ai ippi ippi ai. With an ai ai ippi ippi ai. With an ai ai ippi, ai ai ippi, ai ai ippi ippi ai.'

'What's the next verse?' asks Edward.

'She'll be wearing pink pyjamas when she comes,' I sing. 'She'll be wearing pink pyjamas when she comes . . .'

Edward and Bennie giggle and then we all sing, 'She'll be wearing pink pyjamas, wearing pink pyjamas, wearing pink pyjamas when she comes . . .'

I can see in my rear-view mirror that Jamie is clapping.

'Look at Jamie!' says Edward. 'That baby may not speak much but he's certainly got rhythm!'

We're all so busy clapping with Jamie and yelling 'ai ai

ippi ippi ai' that I fail to notice a car right behind me. I only see the red Ferrari with its top down when it cuts violently in front of me. I slam on the brakes. Jamie catapults forward but is, thankfully, yanked back by the belt of his car seat, as is Bennie. Edward flings an arm out and cushions himself on the dashboard.

'Bloody Gary White!' I say, as I hit the horn. *BEEEEP!*

The Ferrari pulls over and I move up alongside. Edward winds down his window.

'What the bloody hell are you doing?' I yell across him at a sheepish-looking Gary White.

'Sorry,' he says. 'I thought I was late and –'

'I don't care!' I say. 'What *is* the matter with you? My children could have gone through the windscreen!'

'I didn't realize I –'

'You cut me up on a hill, on a bend. Do you have some desire to kill yourself or kill me or –'

'Would your eldest son like to come in my car to school now?' he says.

'No!' I say, as Edward says, 'Yes!'

'The school's only there,' says Gary White, pointing round the next bend.

'Yes, I know,' I say sarcastically. 'I do live here.'

'I promise I won't kill him.' Gary White is smiling now.

'Oh, get stuffed,' I say. As I pull away, I mouth, 'Idiot,' at him.

'Mu-um,' says Edward, pulling a petulant face. 'I'm never going to go in that car, am I?'

'No,' I say. I think I'm going to cry, I'm so cross. 'Listen, Edward,' I bite at him, 'money doesn't mean anything. Gary White is a careless, cruel man, who doesn't think about anything but his bloody car. He isn't even talented! All he can do is kick a bloody ball so, no, you'll never be able to go in his car. Just stop talking about it.'

Edward bites his bottom lip and turns to stare out of the window.

As we pull up to park near the school, I can see Belinda getting out of her people-carrier. When she sees me she waves. I wind down my window. 'Belinda,' I say, 'you look amazing.' She smiles at me. Goodness, she's wearing makeup and she's got that bloom all pregnant women have in the early months. Her skin is plump and fresh, her eyes are twinkling and she has on a dark purple jersey wrap-around maternity dress that shows off her neat bump and her shapely tanned legs. 'You're wearing makeup,' I say.

'It's part of my new job. I've come as autumn.'

'I'm sorry?' I say.

'I'm wearing dark autumnal colours because that's what my personal Colour Me Wonderful makeup chart said suits me.'

'Well, it looks very good.'

Then I turn to the other mothers parked near her and find that they look pretty good too. Nicki – 'It's Nicki with an I not a Y' – is wearing a white blouse, a lightweight baby pink cashmere jumper, deep blue pristine jeans and high boots. She has her blonde hair tied back in a ribbon, as does her daughter Jemima, who is getting out of Nicki's recently cleaned sparkling silver Volvo SUV. Behind Jemima, I can see Gus's shiny shoes emerging, then his head, with his hair brushed and wetted down. Do Nicki's children always look so smart? Why don't mine? I turn to Bennie, who has his hands down the back of his school trousers.

'What are you doing, Bennie?' I hiss, as Nicki turns to me.

'M-my bum hurts,' he says, 'so I'm trying to stick my finger up it to itch it.'

'Well, don't!' I say.

'No, don't,' says Edward, 'or else it will smell.'

'W-will it?' says Bennie, fascinated.

'Like your bottom,' says Edward.

'M-my bottom?' says Bennie.

'Of course it will!' I say. 'Now, get your hands out of your trousers. Anyone would think you had worms.'

'Can you get worms in your bum?' asks Edward. 'Really, can you? I never knew that. I can't wait to tell Stanley.'

'Edward,' I say, a bit desperately, 'please don't start telling people your family has worms. I don't think even I could cope with that.'

Gail is coming up the road, clad in a skintight pair of black Lycra leggings and a bright pink cut-away-at-the-sides sports top. The outfit leaves nothing to the imagination and, as she passes, everyone stares. She power-walks up the hill to the school. A hot and bedraggled Jane is trying to keep up with her but trailing. Gail stops when she gets to Nicki and gives her a beaming smile.

'Breathless?' says Nicki, looking very cool.

'Not at all,' says Gail. 'You know I like to keep fit.'

'I was talking to Jane,' says Nicki, who has noticed that Gail's daughter is now gasping.

'Oh,' says Gail, and hands her daughter the water-bottle

on a special holder round her waist. 'Have some of this, darling. It's a glucose drink and it'll make you feel better.'

'Don't you have a personal trainer?' says Nicki. 'For all those marathons? Don't you have Adam?'

Gail looks momentarily confused. She takes a glug of water from another chrome bottle attached to the belt round her middle. 'I don't think I know who Adam is,' she says.

'Yes, you do!' says Nicki. 'He's that trainer Liza works out with. You know, black, good-looking, fit.'

Then Gail spots me in the car and waves. Jane tries to wave too but she's still breathing hard and holding her sides with one hand. Just as they are about to come over to me, just as I have my bottom out of the car door and I'm fiddling with Jamie's straps, I hear the familiar purr of the Ferrari. God! I'd almost forgotten about Gary White. I'd assumed he was already here and parked. After all, he was only just behind me. Where has he been? The thought suddenly occurs to me that he's been waiting to make an entrance. Surely not. What kind of self-obsessed idiot would . . .

The Ferrari is inching its way down the hill. I keep expecting it to pull in for Rowan to get out, but it passes every available parking space. It's moving my way. I get out and perch Jamie on the roof of my car. Edward is now on the grass verge, watching the Ferrari with Bennie standing behind him.

'I love that car,' Edward says, as if in a trance.

But I'm not watching the car. I'm watching the mothers. They have lined the road as if they're watching a parade. Nicki reaches up, tugs at her ponytail and lets her hair loose. She shakes it out and it falls to her shoulders. She pulls her two children in front of her. Gail must have dabbed her face with powder for now there is no hint of shine and, unlike Nicki, she has pushed Jane virtually behind her. Belinda is further up the road, smoothing her dress over her bump and applying lip-gloss in the car mirror. Everyone has stopped what they were doing. I catch sight of Adele. She has just parked, a bit further down the hill. She leaps out of her car. She's wearing a simple white dress, teamed with some flat, Grecian-style gold sandals and snaky gold bangles winding up her arms. She's so tall, slim and lightly tanned that, to me, she's like a goddess.

'Why has Adele come to school dressed as a gladiator?' asks Edward.

Adele comes towards me at speed, with Nancy trotting in front of her. 'Is that him, do you think?' she says, pointing at the road.

I stare at her face. She has what I call her 'nude' makeup on. Her eyelids are glistening. Her lips are glinting. Her nails are painted the palest pink. Even her hair seems to glow. 'You look so glossy,' I say admiringly. 'Have you come as summer?'

'What are you talking about?' she says.

'Belinda's wearing autumn colours and I thought you might be summer because you look so, so . . .'

'And what have you come as?' she says.

I'm suddenly aware – too aware – of my dirty jeans and milk-splattered T-shirt. 'Oh, I'm a fashion disaster,' I say. 'It's called the hands-on-mum look.'

But Adele isn't listening. Her eyes are fixed on the

approaching Ferrari. It's just passing Gail and Nicki who both, for some reason, start waving and giggling.

'Is that *him* in that car?' says Adele again.

'Yes,' I say. 'It's him. Why on earth are Gail and Nicki waving? He's not royalty.'

Adele gives me a look. 'But how do you know it's Gary White?' she says, making a *moue* and turning to face the Ferrari.

I'm just about to explain to her that not only did I meet Gary White yesterday but that today he'd almost caused me to swerve off the road and give my children excruciating whiplash, when I see Edward waving excitedly.

'Edward!' I say, but it's no use. The menacing Ferrari comes to a halt beside Adele and me.

'Oh, my God!' says Adele, as if she's about to faint. Out of the corner of my eye I see Gail and Nicki coming towards us.

Gary White is sitting in his car, sunglasses on, shirt slightly open to reveal a hairy chest. 'I'm at the school gates again,' he's saying into his mobile as he winds down Rowan's window. 'I really can't talk now. Can I . . . Yes, she was fine yesterday . . . Yes, I have met someone. In fact, she's standing right next to the car now and I want to ask her something . . .' Gary waves at me. I ignore him. 'Yes, she has children of her own . . . No, Mum, not *now*!' He puts down his phone and leans over to open the door for Rowan to get out. As he does so, he looks Adele up and down.

'Hi,' she says, blushing.

Gary White winks at her, then turns his gaze on me.

'Samantha,' he says, pushing his sunglasses to the top of his head.

I'm about to say something – I don't know what – when I feel a little pair of feet kicking me in the back. I spin round to find that Jamie is about to slide off the roof. I grab his legs and hoick him on to my hip. He nestles his head into my shoulder and I kiss his hair.

'Samantha?' says Gary White again, a bit more persistently.

'*Samantha?*' says Adele, shocked.

'What?' I say to her.

'I'm sorry about earlier,' says Gary to me, ignoring Nicki and Gail, who are now positioned just behind me on the grass verge.

'Oh, that's OK,' I say, trying not to look at him. Instead I watch Adele's face as she looks from Gary to me, then back again.

'I mean, I'm sorry if I hurt you,' says Gary.

'You didn't!' I say, and glance at my watch. 'Oh, goodness. Is that the time?'

'Can I make it up to you?' says Gary, bobbing his head to get into my vision. 'Should I buy you dinner or something?'

'No!' I say, as Gary's mobile rings again.

'*What?*' shouts Gary, into his phone, as I bend down to put Jamie on the ground. Gary tucks the telephone between shoulder and chin, then leans out and grabs my hand.

'Get off!' I say, trying to pull away as he motions desperately for me to wait.

Just then the car behind him sounds its horn. I snatch my hand back.

'Ring me,' he says to me. 'You've got my number. No, not you,' he says into the phone. 'I know you've got my number. You're my mother! No, I was just telling Samantha . . . The lady with the children! I was just telling her . . .' The car behind him beeps again. He rolls his eyes at me and drives off.

I wait for Adele to say something but she's still in shock. I grab Bennie and tell Edward to take him, Rowan and Nancy to the school gates.

'Do you know you have worms that live up your bum?' says Edward to Rowan, as I push them towards the road.

'Edward! You're nearly late,' I say, as I see who is in the car behind Gary. It's Liza. She swoops to park in front of me and Adele, then brakes suddenly as she sees the children step out to cross. She mouths, 'Sorry,' at me, then jumps out of her car, swiftly followed by Josh.

'Good God,' I say, as Liza, clad in nothing more than a microscopic miniskirt and a tie-dye cheesecloth top that just about covers her breasts but leaves her midriff bare and taut for everyone to see, comes to the verge to speak to us all. She's clacking along in a pair of high wooden mules.

'Hi,' she says, smiling.

'Hi,' says Adele, clocking what Liza is wearing and finally coming back to her senses.

'Who was in the Ferrari? Was it Gary White?'

I nod.

'Damn,' says Liza, pursing ruby-red lips. 'I really wanted to see him.'

'Well, I'm sure he would've noticed you,' says Adele. 'You are, after all, dressed for the occasion.'

Liza frowns. 'But I always wear this type of thing when I'm not working.' Then she notices Gail and Nicki, who are standing just behind us. 'Gail! Nicki!' she says, and bends forward to air-kiss them. 'Did you two meet the new celebrity within our midst?'

They shake their heads.

'Not really,' says Nicki. 'He was talking to Samantha. But we did see him and he's really good-looking and Adele says he's single.'

'He was talking to Samantha?' says Liza, astounded. She hasn't missed my dirty jeans and grubby T-shirt. 'Really? Was he?'

'Oh, yes,' says Adele, a bit sarcastically, I think.

'What was he saying, Samantha?'

Just as I'm about to tell Liza that he was saying nothing much, really, Adele says, 'He was asking her for dinner.'

'Asking her for dinner?' say Nicki and Gail in unison.

'For dinner? Really?' says Liza.

'No,' I say, as Adele says, 'Yes.'

'Is he good-looking, Samantha?' Liza asks.

I'm about to reply when Belinda walks up with Summer and Saskia, clasping a hand each. 'Who-was-talking-to-Gary-White-I-bet-he-stopped-to-speak-to-you-Adele?' she says, all in one breath.

'Actually, it was Samantha he was talking to,' says Adele.

'He asked her for dinner,' says Gail.

'Did he?' says Belinda, now also in shock.

'Yes,' says Adele, raising an eyebrow.

'He didn't, really,' I say. 'And he did talk to Adele.'

'No, he didn't,' says Adele. 'He just winked at me.'

'Are you going to go, Samantha?' Gail asks. 'You *have* to go. He's the only celebrity for miles! I mean, most women would climb a mountain to get to him.'

'Yes, are you going for dinner?' says Belinda, a bit more seriously.

'Of course not!' I say. 'Look, I don't think you understand what's gone on.'

'Well, what *has* gone on?' asks Adele, raising her eyebrows again.

'It's not like that. It's just that I was late getting to school yesterday and he was late and . . .'

Liza's mobile phone rings. 'Hi,' she says, answering it. 'Oh, hi . . . Yes, oh dear . . . Yes, I'm on my way now . . . Yes, right now . . . Yes, I'm coming now this instant.' When she rings off I notice she's blushing. 'Adam, my personal trainer,' she says. 'I have to go. In all the excitement of Samantha's dinner date with the former footballer I'd forgotten he's at my house waiting for me to do a workout.'

She air-kisses everyone goodbye. When she gets to me she shakes her head. 'You're a dark horse, Samantha. The wonderful Gary White fancies you. Who'd have thought it?'

She gets into her car, pulls out in front of a van and drives off.

'I have to go, too,' says Belinda, still staring at me as if she can't believe her eyes. 'I've got to get the twins sorted out – but, Samantha, you'll let us know what's going on, won't you?'

'Nothing's going on,' I say.

Then Gail notices that Josh is still waiting at the school gates. 'Oh, no,' she says. 'Liza's forgotten to say goodbye to Josh again.'

We look at him. He seems sad and also angry, kicking stones venomously. They are rebounding off the school fence with some force.

'I'll take him in,' she says. 'Are you coming, Nicki?'

'Yes,' says Nicki, eyeing Josh sympathetically. 'I'll ask him if he wants to play with Gus this afternoon. That'll give Liza more time with Adam.'

As they walk off I turn to Adele. 'What's all that about?' I ask. 'Why did Liza forget to say goodbye to Josh? Why would she need more time with Adam? How long do her sessions last?'

Adele raises her eyebrows.

'Oh, for God's sake, stop raising your eyebrows, would you, and talk to me?'

'Talk to you?' she says. 'Why should I talk to you?'

'Well, why wouldn't you?' I say, now rather confused. 'You're my friend. We always talk to each other. We share things, don't we?'

'Oh,' she says, 'like what's going on between you and Gary White? You've certainly shared that with me, haven't you, Samantha?'

'You're being ridiculous,' I say, somewhat crossly. 'For a start, nothing's "going on" between me and Gary White. I find it a bit upsetting that you and the others assume that, even if something was "going on", he must be mad to choose me.'

'He would be! God, that man could have the pick of

any of us and he's chosen you. Wonders will never cease. What's it about you, Samantha? Is it your *essence de* stale milk or your bare-faced appeal? Just watch yourself. You'll be the talk of the town now, you know.'

Ginger

By the time I get home – having been to the greengrocer for my second fruit-and-vegetables shop in a week and stopped off at the pharmacy to get Jamie his pull-up nappies that everyone forgot to buy yesterday – it is almost eleven o'clock. Wendy is up and wandering round the house in a rather sophisticated bright blue silk kimono. 'Hi, Mrs S,' she says, yawning. 'How was school?'

'Good,' I say brightly. 'How was your lie-in?'

Wendy giggles. 'Oh, it was great, *Mum*,' she says. 'Ah'm calling you Mum because you sound just like mine and Ah'm missing her, Mrs S – I mean, Mum – really I am. She was always waking me up to go to school and all I wanted to do was sleep.'

'Yes,' I say. 'It's a bit tricky when you've an education to get, isn't it?'

Wendy doesn't catch the sarcasm. 'Yeah, it's a drag.'

I'm about to explain that it's her job to get up in the morning and help with the children when I notice that instead of her usual breakfast of three muffins, a crumpet and a bagel smothered with cream cheese, she's helping herself to my muesli. I'm so surprised that thoughts of giving her a talking-to go right out of my head. 'You're having muesli for breakfast,' I say. 'What's going on?'

'Ah'm having a change,' Wendy says nonchalantly. 'I've

seen you eat it so I thought I'd try it. It looks like those daggy things that hang off a rabbit's bum but I thought it might taste all right.' She pours on some semi-skimmed milk and takes a mouthful, then chews ruminatively, like a cow.

'Well? Do you like it?' I ask her.

I think she says something like 'disgusting', but it's hard to tell as her mouth is still full. Then I think about the semi-skimmed milk. We never have anything but full-fat. 'Where did you get that milk?' I ask. She points to her purse.

'Yeah, I bought it by meself,' she says, swallowing hard. 'Blimey! I'm not surprised rabbit food's good for you. It takes half an hour to eat one mouthful!' Then she says she's going upstairs to get dressed and that she and Jamie might go to the park for the morning. 'It's a beautiful day, isn't it?' she says. 'Ah said Ah'd meet me mates there, then you and your friend can have a nice chitter-chatter in peace, eh?'

'What friend?' I ask.

'I dunno,' she said. 'Some woman called up and said you'd asked her to come round and she's coming . . .' Wendy looks at the clock '. . . about now, really.'

'But who is it?' I ask again. 'I haven't asked anyone round – '

'You're losing your mind, Mrs S,' says Wendy. 'I think me mum had so many nippers she lost hers in the end. Do you know what she did before I came here? She got some paint and a roller and told me she was going to take in a lodger! In my room! As if! I said to her, "Mum, Ah'm only gonna be gone for a couple of years and when I get back I want me room to be the same as it always was," and she said she needed the rent money so I said –'

Just then Beady starts to bark.

'Oh, that'll be your mate, eh?' says Wendy, and wanders upstairs, followed by Jamie.

There's no mistaking who is standing on my doorstep. When I see her, I catch my breath. I peep out of the sitting-room window, beneath the linen curtains, and there she is, still petite, still dark, and looking like a grown-up version of my childhood friend, Naomi.

'Naomi!' I shout, as I run to the door. I open it. She is smiling at me. Same smile, same pale skin, same curly dark hair. 'Oh, Naomi!' I say.

'Samantha!'

For a split second I'm not sure what to do but Naomi hugs me and kisses my cheek. 'Oh, Samantha!' she says again, sounding rather emotional. 'It's been so long since I saw you and . . .' She pulls away and I notice her eyes are glistening. I find this rather touching. It makes me feel close to tears too.

'Do you need a handkerchief?' I say, taking her hand.

'No, I – I'm just so pleased to see you.' She hugs me again.

Her hair smells of grass. Delicious. I push her away and hold her at arms' length. 'You look amazing!' I say. 'You've barely changed.' She's wearing a pink polka-dot tea-dress cut quite low to reveal a mere hint of white broderie-anglaise bra and a pair of simple white ballet pumps. Her waist is as tiny as it was when she was a girl. Her skin is clear with barely a wrinkle. 'God, have you found the secret to eternal youth?' I ask her. 'And why do you smell so good?'

Naomi throws her head back and laughs. 'It's an American perfume called Green Grass, and as for looking so young – well, you're too kind! You always were. Oh, Samantha, I've thought about you so much and here you are, looking exactly the same yourself and . . . Gosh, I feel so emotional seeing you! I can't believe it.'

'But, Naomi, I'm twice the size.'

'No! You're exactly the same. Look, you even have your hair in a ponytail. You wore your hair like that when you were a girl.'

'Oh, God,' I say, laughing. 'I can't bear it that I haven't changed.' Then I realize we're still standing on the doorstep. 'Oh, come in!' I say. 'Have you just arrived from the States? I only got your email last night. You must be exhausted and jet-lagged and –'

'Don't be silly,' she says, laughing. 'I've been here for a week. At least, I think I have. My life's been so topsy-turvy.'

'But where have you been staying?' I ask, as we go into the kitchen. 'Are you going to be around long because if you are why don't you stay here? I'm sure we can find you some space and we have so much to catch up on.'

'What a lovely kitchen,' says Naomi. 'And what a big house! I thought you wrote that you lived in a cottage.'

'It's a large cottage,' I say. 'There are five of us living here, six if you count Wendy, the au pair.'

Half an hour later we're in the sitting room, drinking coffee, eating biscuits and talking madly. Naomi has her legs tucked under her bottom as she nibbles a custard cream and lets out peals of laughter as we try to remember everything that happened to us as children.

'Do you remember we used to pretend to be horses?' asks Naomi.

'Yes,' I say. 'I was just thinking about that before I got your email. You signed yourself Ginger.'

'Did I?' says Naomi, pleased. 'Oh, I didn't mean to. I must have had my mind on other things.'

'But it was lovely,' I say. 'It brought it all back to me.'

'You mean how we used to build jumps and do all that commentary – you know, "Here comes Ginger now, over the second, and moving on to the third"?'

'Exactly that! And how you spent all your time dying.'

Naomi laughs. 'Oh dear, was I a bit melodramatic?'

'Just a bit.'

'Yes, but you were always such a good friend, my Beauty.'

'Yes, I was, wasn't I? Do you remember how I kept trying to save you but you absolutely refused to be rescued?'

'Oh, yes, I did, didn't I? I must have been a terrible attention-seeker.'

'No, you weren't,' I say. 'I just think that, somehow, you identified with that character.'

'I also remember carving our names into that tree.'

'I was thinking about that after I got your email,' I say. 'We really identified with those horses.'

'And do you remember when I climbed up the tree to the second floor and did a wee on your head?'

'Oh, my God! I'd totally forgotten but I do now! You

were disgusting! I had to pretend to my mother that I'd got rained on and it was a gloriously hot summer's day. She was very suspicious.'

'She was always suspicious of me,' says Naomi, suddenly looking a bit more serious.

'She wasn't. She liked you. She let you eat a slice of cake when you hadn't finished your salad. No one else in the history of our household got to do that.'

'Oh, God, that salad! It was horrible.'

'Disgusting,' I agree.

'I never felt comfortable in your house. I never felt your mother liked me.'

'Why not?' I say, rather surprised. 'As far as I can remember, you always liked coming over to mine, didn't you? I thought you did.'

'But we spent more time at my house, didn't we?'

'I suppose we did. But I thought that was because your dad made us such fantastic things and your house was much cosier than mine.'

'There was something a bit cold about your house.'

'My mother refused to heat it. I only had a bath once a week, remember?'

'No. It was more than that. Honestly, your mother didn't like me. I've been thinking about it over the years and I reckon she looked down on me.'

'She's not like that.'

'I think she thought I led you astray, that I wasn't the right friend for you, that I was an attention-seeker.'

'She didn't.'

'She hated me being Ginger. I remember her watching me once out of her bedroom window as I was dying and you were trying to lift me up and she looked really cross.'

'She never said anything to me about it.'

By now our cups are empty so I tell Naomi I'll go and make some more coffee and she asks if she can look round the house while the kettle's boiling. I stand in the kitchen and stare out of the window. I feel a bit disturbed. Why was my mother so cross about us playing in the garage? It's certainly true that she was but I can't remember why. Was she threatened in some way by my relationship with Naomi? But why would she have been? We were just children. It's true that I can remember her being horrified when I told her Naomi got shut in the coal hole. She'd say, 'That's a dreadful thing to do to a child,' and then, when she saw Naomi again, she'd hug her and find more bits of cake for her to eat. All I can remember about my mother being cross was that she was concerned about the garage being so run down. I'm sure that was it. She didn't want us playing there in case a beam came down and hit us on the head. She said, 'It's a dangerous place and you're not to play there.' I'm sure that is how it was.

When Naomi reappears, I tell her that I am sure my mother was cross only because the garage was structurally unsafe.

'No,' says Naomi determinedly. 'It wasn't that. She resented how close we were.'

'But she liked me having you as a friend.'

'That's not how I remember it,' says Naomi and then, somewhat petulantly, 'Why don't you ring and ask her if you don't believe me?'

I tell Naomi I'm not saying I don't believe her and, anyway, my mother's away. 'She's gone a bit mad on cruises,' I add apologetically.

'Well, that's nice for her, isn't it?' says Naomi, slightly bitterly. Her tone surprises me. It occurs to me that she might not be very happy – but isn't she married to a film producer? Isn't she in film PR? Her life hasn't turned out like Ginger's.

I'm just about to tell her that she's doing well for herself when Wendy appears with Jamie on her hip. He almost lives there.

'Hiya,' Wendy says to Naomi.

'Oh, hi,' says Naomi, standing up. 'Are you Wendy?'

'Yeah, Ah'm Wendy and this little tyke's Jamie.'

'Oh, Jamie!' says Naomi, reaching out to him. 'Aren't you a beautiful boy?'

He hides his head in Wendy's bosom.

'Don't worry about him,' I say. 'He's very shy.'

'Is he your youngest?' asks Naomi, brightly. 'I remember you wrote to say you had three. Where are the other two?'

I tell Naomi all about my boys and then we sit down again and she asks about John, and seems so fascinated to hear about everything I forget the momentary hint of tension between us. She seems to hang on my every word. She says things like, 'You've done so well for yourself, Samantha!' and 'Goodness, your husband sounds amazing!' until, fifteen minutes later, Wendy wanders in again to say goodbye.

'Ah'm off to the park to give Jamie a swing and then Ah'll go and get the others from school. OK, Mrs S?'

I ask if she's remembered it's a half-day and that Stanley's coming home with us because we're going on a picnic.

'Oh, yeah?' says Wendy. 'Right, well, me and Jamie will go and pick up some yummy stuff, then.'

I tell Wendy I've made a list on the board and she goes off to copy it down on a piece of paper she's found scrunched up in her pocket.

'Salad?' she yells, from the kitchen. 'Tomatoes? Cucumber? Oh, Jeez, Mrs S. You know I hate that blaady stuff!'

I tell Wendy to take some money from my purse and buy herself something she likes. 'She'll come back with sausage rolls and pork pies,' I say to Naomi.

She giggles. 'I thought you hated salad too,' she says.

'Only my mother's,' I reply.

We hear the back door close, then Wendy's footsteps on the gravel as she goes round the front of the house to the road.

I'm just about to ask Naomi her plans when Beady barks and there's a knock on the front door.

I open it to find Wendy there, with Jamie still on her hip. 'Is there a problem?' I ask.

'There's a girl in that car opposite,' Wendy says, pointing towards a silver hatchback, 'and she wants to know if it's OK for her to come in to see her mam.'

'I'm sorry?' I say. 'What girl? Who's her mother?'

'She says her name's Lexie and that your mate's her mum.'

Suddenly Naomi appears at the door. 'Lexie?' she says to Wendy. 'Does Lexie want to come in?'

'Lexie?' I say, confused.

'She's my daughter,' says Naomi.

'But why's she in the car?' I ask.

'Oh, she's a bookworm,' says Naomi. 'She insisted on staying there to read, and she can be very determined when she wants to be, but I'll get her now and bring her in. She's so looking forward to meeting you.'

'I wouldn't leave a dog in the car for that long,' says Wendy, as Naomi crosses the road to her car. 'Anyway, see you later!'

I watch Naomi as she comes back from the car. She has her arm round a girl who looks Edward's age and is almost identical to Naomi. She has black hair, pale skin and is very slim, maybe too slim. Her shoulders are hunched. I can't see her face as Naomi's is bent towards it.

They get to the doorstep. 'This is my daughter, Lexie,' says Naomi, smiling and pushing Lexie in front of her.

Lexie doesn't smile.

'Hi, Lexie,' I say. 'I'm Samantha. Are you all right? You must've been in the car for an hour or more and it's so hot. Do you need a drink or something to eat?'

'Some water would be nice,' says Lexie, quietly.

'Your mother says you were reading your book.'

'Yes,' says Lexie.

'You must have read it to the end!' says Naomi. 'And that's why you've been in there so long, isn't it? And on such a hot day, Lexie . . .' Then she turns to me. 'Honestly, Samantha, what must you think of me? I told Lexie she should just read one chapter, but you know what girls are like – although, Lexie dear,' Naomi turns back to her daughter, 'you could have come and knocked on the door. You're not a little girl any more.'

'I didn't know I was supposed to knock,' says Lexie, 'and I was perfectly happy with my book.'

'What are you reading?' I ask, as I stand back to let Naomi and her daughter into the house.

'*Black Beauty*,' she says.

'*Black Beauty*!' I say. 'You're joking. Your mother and I were just talking about that. It used to be one of our favourites.'

'Did it?' says Lexie, looking at me with shining eyes. 'I've just got to the bit where Ginger dies.'

'Oh, no,' I say.

'Yes, it's awful, isn't it?' Lexie looks very sad now.

'I always cry when I read it,' I say.

'I try not to,' says Lexie.

'Oh dear,' says Naomi, who has been into the kitchen and reappeared with a glass of water for Lexie. 'Why are you trying not to cry?'

'Because Ginger's dying,' says Lexie.

'Oh, poor you,' says Naomi. 'That's a dreadful bit, isn't it? It's not the end of the book, though. I don't know if I've ever told you, but Samantha and I were obsessed with *Black Beauty*.'

'Were you?' says Lexie.

'Oh, absolutely,' says Naomi. 'Weren't we, Samantha?'

I nod. 'Actually, Lexie, your mother was Ginger and I was Black Beauty.'

'Why weren't you Beauty, Mum?' asks Lexie.

'I don't know,' says Naomi, smoothly. 'I think it's because Samantha was more suited to being Beauty.'

'I'd want to be Beauty,' says Lexie.

'Naomi, you liked being Ginger, didn't you?' I ask.

'But Ginger dies,' says Lexie.

'Do your children like *Black Beauty*?' Naomi asks, changing the subject.

'No,' I say. 'They're all boys and I don't think it's a boys' book. Edward, my eldest, doesn't even like reading much.'

'Oh, if I had a child, I'd read *Black Beauty* to them every day,' says Lexie enthusiastically. 'Wouldn't you?'

I laugh.

'Would you like a girl?' says Lexie.

'Oh, yes, Lexie,' I say. 'I'd love one.'

All the Reasons Why I Want a Girl

I don't want a girl just so I can read Black Beauty *to her,* Jill Has Two Ponies *and all these other horsy books I loved so much as a child. I also want one because I know girls are different and, to me, they seem different in a good way. I once went on holiday with my sister and her six children – she has five girls and one boy. The girls spent their days drawing pictures, painting each other's nails, reading and playing mummies and daddies. It was so peaceful that, as I lay in my sun-lounger 'babysitting', I nodded off and got roundly scolded for failing in my duty.*

Robert always refused to join in these games. Instead he careered around with Edward, even though he's seven years older. At ten, playing trains with a three-year-old was preferable to being with girls. All I wanted to do on that holiday – other than sleep – was play with my sister's girls. I wanted to plait their hair and dress them up in pretty clothes. I wandered around shops with them and bought them flouncy dresses and ballet cardigans. There's nothing nice for boys, just tracksuit bottoms, horrible nylon hooded tops and T-shirts. I could have dressed girls in pretty rosebud-print smocks and brushed their hair a hundred strokes every day like princesses in fairy stories, I could have made them a Wendy house and we could have got out their miniature china tea set because you can buy girls pretty things: they don't throw them against walls to see if they'll smash, as boys do. Then we could have read books such as Ballet Shoes, Anne of Green Gables and, of course, Black Beauty. Later, we could've baked cakes and made necklaces and bracelets, and when they were older still, we could have gone shopping together, swapped clothes and talked about men. As mother-of-the-bride, I could have fussed around, finding a beautiful dress and hat, then cried copious tears, and when they had their babies, I could have been prime grandmother, rather than the interfering mother-in-law whom my son's wife hates. None of this will happen if I don't have a girl.

When I told my mother I wanted a girl, she said, 'I had you and your sister and you were both a nightmare. I always wanted boys.'

'Why?' I asked her, a bit shocked.

Because they play like puppies and they're more fun.'

I told her I didn't think my boys played like puppies, more like small-but-just-as-aggressive gladiators.

'They're supposed to be like that,' she said. 'They have to be boys, you know. You should encourage aggression and competition. Stop being so pathetic.'

I rang up my sister and asked her what she thought about the boy-versus-girl issue. Julia said, 'I don't think it's to do with boys versus girls.' Then she told me that, as part of her thesis, she was *covering the issue of gender and childhood problems. 'I've been reading some research papers by Zachary Hofman Junior. He's a specialist in this area and he says people always like to stereotype the sexes. He believes that boys are generally told to be brave and tough. If they fall over and hurt themselves, they're told off if they cry. They're encouraged to take responsibility, to protect the family, to be a man, especially if they're the oldest child. They're praised for being good at sport, fast and physically strong. Girls are praised for being pretty. A lot of attention is focused on how they look, how clever they are. They're asked to help more in the home, and with younger siblings, in a more maternal role than is necessarily appropriate for their age. They're encouraged to enhance their femininity.'*

'Oh,' I said. 'But what's this doctor's conclusion?'

'That we should try not to stereotype the sexes. We should praise boys for being pretty . . .'

I snorted.

'. . . and girls for physical achievements.'

I said that although I could understand what Julia was saying, I remembered spending my own childhood – when I wasn't being a horse – climbing trees, scrumping apples, pouring petrol from the lawn mower on the gardener's head hoping he'd set himself alight when he lit one of his cigarettes and putting on the clothes in Naomi's dressing-up box.

'Hmm,' said Julia. 'That's true. I also remember that you and Naomi threw our mother's jade figurines out of her bedroom window to see if they bounced.'

'They didn't, did they?'

'No. And you melted her welly boots when you were seeing what sort of things went up in flames and what didn't when you put them in front of the fire. And you and Naomi picked all the vegetables from the vegetable patch and sold them round the neighbourhood.'

'I remember that!'

'Ah, yes, but you're not very girly,' said Julia. 'Maybe that's why you have boys. That's what Mum thinks.'

'What?'

'She thinks you're so masculine that you'll never give birth to a girl.'

'In what way am I more masculine than you? You've got five girls!'

'Well,' Julia thinks for a bit, 'you don't like doing girly things.'

'Like what?'

'You hate art and craft. You never wear makeup. You never wear anything other than jeans. You were very naughty.'

'I wasn't!'

'You were. You were as naughty as a boy. I rest my case, I suppose. It's not a boy-versus-girl thing. It's a character thing. You just have to accept it.'

But I can't because I envy Julia her girls. I can see how close they are, and I can see how closed Edward is becoming, and one day a wife will come along and nick him. Then someone will nick Bennie, and then Jamie, and then I'll be all alone with John, and the thought scares me.

I'm about to tell Naomi and Lexie my plans to get a girl when Naomi spies the clock on the sitting-room wall and gasps. 'Oh, God, I've got to go!' she says.

'Where?'

'I've got an appointment and I'm late already!'

'I'm sure they won't mind,' I say. 'It's to see a school, isn't it?'

'What? Oh, yes, a school,' says Naomi. 'It's with the headmaster and he's a very busy man.'

'Which school is it?'

'I can't remember,' says Naomi, frantically. 'All I know is that it's half an hour away and I've got –' she looks at the clock again '– only twenty minutes to get there.'

'Oh dear,' I say, 'and we've got so much more to talk about.' I turn to Lexie. 'Sorry not to spend more time with you,' I say. 'I was really enjoying meeting someone who likes *Black Beauty* as much as your mother and I do.'

'So was I,' says Lexie, fervently.

'Then why don't you stay for the afternoon?' I find myself saying. 'Why doesn't she?' I say to Naomi. 'It's such a hot day and we could go swimming in the river and . . . it's just an idea.'

'Yes!' says Naomi, in a rush. 'Yes, yes, Lexie. Why don't you stay with Samantha?'

'Oh, but doesn't Lexie need to see the school?' I say to Naomi, suddenly remembering that she should.

'Oh, not really,' says Naomi. 'She's seen so many and it's very boring for her, really. It would be much more fun for her to stay here with you, wouldn't it, Lexie?'

Lexie looks at her doubtfully.

'Oh, yes, it would,' says Naomi. 'Samantha's got a child the same age as you . . .'

'A boy,' says Lexie.

'Well, there's nothing wrong with boys! And they're going for a picnic – aren't you, Samantha?'

'Yes,' I say, 'to the river, and boys can be quite nice sometimes.'

'You love rivers, Lexie, don't you? Now, you stay here and I'll come later and pick you up and – Oh, it's so kind of you to offer, Samantha!'

'Oh, no. I'm delighted,' I say. 'It's about time I had a girl for an afternoon rather than just those boys.'

'Right, well, it's sorted,' says Naomi, rushing for the door. When she gets there she turns. 'Hang on a minute,' she says. 'I'll just write down my mobile number. Do you have a bit of paper?'

I tell her I'll fetch one from the kitchen. When I get back to the hall, she's giving Lexie a hug.

'It's so kind of you, Samantha,' she says, scribbling. 'Be a good girl, Lexie. I'll be back early evening. Have a good time!' And she's gone.

Lexie and I look at each other.

'I hope you don't mind that I'm here,' she says, rather nervously.

There's something about her desperate, sad, embarrassed look that suddenly reminds me of her mother when we got caught out after stealing the Monster Munch and Turkish Delight.

'No, Lexie,' I say. 'I'm more than happy to have you. That's why I asked you to stay. Now, would you like something to eat?'

Lexie shakes her head.

'Some more water?'

Lexie shakes her head again.

'What would you like to do?' I ask her.

'Could we . . . could we . . .'

'Yes?' I say.

'. . . could we read *Black Beauty* together?'

'Of course,' I say.

'The end bit of the chapter where Ginger . . . ?'

'Are you sure?' I ask her, and she nods, so we sit down,

the two of us, on the sofa, and I open the pages to find where Lexie has carefully placed her bookmark. '"A short time after this a cart with a dead horse in it passed our cab stand. The head hung out of the cart-tail, the lifeless tongue was slowly dropping with blood; and the sunken eyes! but I can't speak of them, the sight was too dreadful . . ."'

As I read, Lexie's head sinks on to my shoulder. Her hair smells of Green Grass, like her mother's.

The Golden Rule

I'm in the kitchen preparing the picnic when Dougie arrives. Wendy has already come home, bringing Edward, Stanley, Bennie and Jamie, and I have introduced them to Lexie, apart from Stanley who came in in such a rush that he ran up the stairs without saying hello.

'What's up with Stanley?' I asked Edward.

'Desperate to go to the loo,' said Edward. 'Can I go upstairs now?'

'In a minute,' I said. Then I told Edward that the girl standing in front of him was Lexie and that she was the daughter of an old schoolfriend of mine and that I had invited her to spend the afternoon with us.

'Hello, Lexie,' said Edward, without much enthusiasm. 'How old are you?'

'Ten,' said Lexie.

'So am I,' said Edward. He looked at his feet a bit. 'Can I go upstairs now, Mum?' he asked.

'No,' I said. 'Why don't you show Lexie round?'

'Oh, all right,' he said, because he quite likes doing things like that. Once, when I asked him to show Belinda to the kitchen – the phone was ringing so I couldn't – I found him saying things like, 'Now, this is where we keep the spoons,' and opening the cutlery drawer very carefully, before moving on to the sharp knives. Belinda would've been there for hours if I hadn't rescued her.

'Actually,' said Lexie, 'I'd quite like to read.'

'What are you reading?' said Edward.

'*Black Beauty*,' said Lexie.

'Ooh, that sounds scary,' said Edward. 'What's it about?'

'A horse.'

'Oh,' he said, disappointed. 'Mum'll love it. She likes books about horses.'

'Edward,' I said, 'what are you talking about? I've told you about *Black Beauty* a million times. Your granny's even let you look at the old copy she has from a long time ago, yet now you're telling me you don't know anything about it.'

'Yup,' he said happily. 'I've never heard of it.' Then he told Lexie he was reading a book called *The Dark*.

'What's that about?' she asked.

'Funnily enough,' said Edward, very seriously, 'I thought it might have been a love story but, actually, it's a very scary book about some children that get locked in a house at night.'

'I–I'm scared of the dark,' said Bennie, coming forward and taking Lexie's hand.

'Yeah, well, I'm not,' said Edward, and disappeared upstairs in a flash.

'He gets better when you know him,' I said to Lexie.

'It's OK,' said Lexie.

'Do you want to go upstairs and play with him?'

'Would you mind if I didn't?' said Lexie. 'I'd just like to finish this chapter of my book.'

I suggested to Lexie that she went to my room. 'Otherwise you'll have Bennie on your case,' I said, as Bennie smiled at her.

'I'll play with you later,' she said to him, ruffling his hair.

'O-OK,' said Bennie, happily.

So Bennie and I are making sandwiches when Dougie appears.

'Hello, my precious darling,' he says, when he walks through the back door.

I'm about to say, 'Ooh, that's a sweet thing to say to me,' when I realize he's talking to Bennie.

''E-'e-'ello, Dougie,' says Bennie. 'I've finished school now.'

'So Mummy tells me,' says Dougie. 'I bet that was a relief!'

'Wh-why are you here? Where have you been?'

'Oh, you're full of questions today, Bennie. I've been busy getting things for our afternoon trip.'

'Wh-where are we going?'

'Well, that depends on whether or not your mother's bought a cake.'

'No, I haven't,' I say.

'Or made one,' says Dougie.

'I haven't done that either,' I say.

'Well, in that case, I guess we're going on a picnic, which is lucky as I have my picnic kit right here with me.'

'P-picnic kit!' says Bennie, delighted.

'Yes, we're all going for a picnic to the river and we can go swimming!' says Dougie, triumphantly, as if he's the only person in the world ever to have had this idea.

'T-to swim?' says Bennie, alarmed. 'I don't like swimming.' He gets down off the kitchen stool and runs out of the door. 'Ed-Edward!' I hear him call. 'Stanley! Where are you? I want to play with you.'

'We-we-we're up here!' I hear Edward shout, and then a lot of giggling as Bennie scampers up the stairs.

'Oh dear,' says Dougie, raising an eyebrow. 'Why is Bennie's stuttering not getting any better? He never used to stutter.'

'Oh, don't you start,' I say crossly.

'But is there anything you can do about it?'

'What do you expect me to do? Take him back to the beach in Crete and rewind time so that none of it ever happened?'

'He'll grow out of it, won't he?'

'Yes, I'm sure he will. Just be aware that Bennie can be a bit sensitive. And anyway, Dougie, why did you mention the swimming thing? It was tactless.'

'But I am tactless!' Dougie protests, waving a tin of sardines that he has unpacked from a battered rucksack. 'I know you're worried about him but children have an amazing ability to bounce back. Now, have you ever had fresh sardines? They're quite wonderful! You make a fire and you grill them – or do you bake them? Hmm. I'm not sure, but you –'

'Those aren't fresh, Dougie, and we're going for a picnic by the river, not a barbecue.'

'But we could camp! I love camping. I used to go as a child and cook sardines and –'

'It's the middle of the afternoon so we're not camping. And you're avoiding what I want to talk about.'

'Which is what?' Dougie says, innocently.

'For God's sake, Dougie, Bennie's terrified of water now. Can't you understand that? He nearly drowned!'

'Well, I thought if he knew he could swim and therefore not drown, it might give him confidence.'

'But we don't talk about it, Dougie.'

'Why not? That's not like you, Samantha.' Dougie is fingering a fold-in-two can-opener. 'You usually talk about everything, let it all out – that type of thing. Have you talked to John about it?'

I feel a bit miserable now. Why haven't I discussed what happened to Bennie with John? A bad feeling, deep inside, is gnawing at me. 'I'm worried that if I start to talk about it with John, I won't know where the conversation will go,' I say.

'What do you mean?'

'Well, I know John didn't set out to nearly drown Bennie. It could have been me in the sea and, if it had been, I wouldn't want John to go on about it and I know that he probably beats himself up about it but, so far, I haven't said anything apart from the fact that it wasn't his fault.'

'And you believe that, don't you?'

'Yes, of course! But I think we're maybe avoiding having a conversation. I mean, did you ever have a conversation with Maxine that started out in one place and ended up in a totally different direction?'

'I'm not sure,' he says. 'We did once discuss going down the Amazon and ended up having a row over planting the begonias.'

'You see? I'm worried that if I talk to John about how I feel he may take it the wrong way. I worry –'

'About what?'

'About the fragility of everything. I mean, I can see how unhappy Bennie is and I'm trying really hard to help him get over it but . . .'

'Do you think you're trying a bit too hard?' asks Dougie. 'Talk to John! Your relationship's as sturdy as a rock and, actually, Bennie seems perfectly happy.'

'Oh, forget it,' I say, suddenly hurt.

'Why?'

'I don't want to talk about it.'

'Why not?' says Dougie, concerned and irritated at the same time.

I want to tell him about the dream I used to have as a child. One of my favourite things to do when I was about eight was to go swimming in the river. On long hot days, my mother would take Julia and me, in our matching swimming costumes, to what was almost a little lido. It was where the river Thames split. The majority of it swirled off, fast-flowing and dangerous, towards the weir, the lock and then past the gardens of the riverside mansions that were set so far back you had to squint to see them. But off to the right there was a tributary. It wandered, increasingly lazily, past large willow trees and under a small rickety bridge, then sort of stopped and formed a lake, which was surrounded by fields. The landowner had kindly made a picnic area there and put down shingle, which looked rather like a beach. Lots of parents went there with their children in the summer. You had to cross the little rickety bridge to get there – no cars allowed apart from the Mr Softee ice-cream van – and all these ducks and swans used to hang out round the bottom waiting for children to throw bread for them. It was forbidden to jump from the bridge into the river: there was a sign that said, 'No Jumping, Shallow Water,' but no one took much notice of it.

My mother never let Julia and me jump in so, instead, I used to watch the boys leaping off that bridge. They looked so free and comical, like flying monkeys, with their arms spread wide, their legs running in mid-air. They would laugh and scream as they leapt, then crash – *ker-boom!* – into the water. A few heart-stopping seconds later, their heads would emerge from the green, murky depths and they'd be laughing.

I used to dream of jumping from that bridge. At night, when I went to bed still smelling of that slightly dank fresh water, the way a river trout does when you cut it open, I would dream I, too, was flying through the air, lifted by the heat of the day, and then – *ker-boom!* – I would hit that cold, unforgiving water and all the breath would be forced out of me and I would sink like a stone to the bottom. My feet would touch the silty riverbed and my hands would stroke the silky fronds of weed and I would see my hair floating above me and, above my hair, a shadowy but strangely illuminated impression of what life was like on the earth I had left behind. I loved that dream. I found it terribly enticing but the closest I ever got was to stand on the bridge and feed the ducks while boys jumped in, like shot bullets, all around me.

'Do you believe in wish-fulfilment?' I ask Dougie.

'You mean the theory that if you really want something to happen it will?'

'Yes.'

'I don't know,' he says. 'What do you wish for?'

'I used to wish I could dive into a cold river and watch the world from below the water,' I say dreamily.

Dougie looks at me tenderly. 'Bennie's not your fault,' he says. 'You didn't wish for him to drown.'

'No,' I say. 'I didn't wish it. I just . . .'

'Just what?'

'Well, in *Black Beauty* . . .'

'Not this again.'

'. . . in *Black Beauty*, Beauty gets born to a lovely mother and a caring master, has a great time and grows up to be this patient, happy, blessed horse but Ginger, Beauty's friend, is born into a cruel household, no one cares for her and she spends her youth feeling frightened. It turns her into an insecure horse that bites and kicks and –'

'What are you getting at?' he says.

'I don't want Bennie to grow into Ginger because he's frightened. Do you see?'

'No,' he says, utterly baffled. 'I do not.'

'I want him to be Beauty or Merrylegs.'

'Who is Merrylegs?'

'Oh, Merrylegs is a jolly little pony who –'

'Is this relevant to anything?' Dougie says. 'What on earth's going on with you today?'

I'm just about to tell him about Naomi and our childhood game when Edward careers in. 'Dougie!' he says.

'Hi, Edward!' says Dougie, leaping up to hug him.

Edward pulls away. 'Are you coming on this picnic?'

'Absolutely! I've brought all sorts of things. I used to go for picnics when I was a child and –'

'Ah've got things for lunch, Mrs S!' Wendy comes in

through the back door with bags from the car. 'Oh, hello, Dougie,' she says, when she sees him. 'Whatcha been doin'?'

'Hi, Wendy,' he says. 'How are you? Have you lost weight?'

Wendy blushes. 'Dunno. Ah'm great, mate. Now whatcha got for the picnic?'

Dougie brightens.

Then a little voice, from just outside the kitchen door, says, 'Are we going on the picnic yet?'

'Oh, Lexie,' I say, going to the door.

'Who's Lexie?' says Dougie.

'Lexie's a *girl*,' says Edward.

'A girl!' says Dougie, in pretend-shock.

I lead her into the kitchen. She looks a bit vulnerable surrounded by all these boys so I put my arm round her shoulders. 'This is Lexie,' I say to Dougie. 'She's the daughter of my old schoolfriend, Naomi, and she's coming on the picnic with us, aren't you, Lexie?'

Lexie nods.

'Well, hello, Lexie,' says Dougie. 'I hope you like sardines.'

'I don't think I've ever had them,' says Lexie, a trifle warily.

'Well, you must try them. Anyone who is anyone likes sardines, you know.'

'I've got an Arctic Roll,' says Wendy. 'Have you tried one of them?'

'I don't think so,' says Lexie, beginning to smile.

'Well, it's full of jam and ice-cream and it's yum!'

'Goody,' says Lexie.

'Goody?' says Edward. 'What kind of a word is that?'

'Edward!' I say sharply.

'Hello, Lexie,' says Stanley, peering at her from behind his glasses. 'Goodness, you're a girl. Do you want to come and play with us? I think we're going to whistle for wasps in the garden.'

'No, we're not,' says Edward. 'We're going to play Conquerors. I'm going to be the lead conqueror, like Montezuma, and you lot are my subjects.'

'Are you going to get some revenge?' asks Dougie, mock-innocently.

'Of course I am,' says Edward. 'Nothing can beat Montezuma!'

'Would you like to play Conquerors, Lexie?' asks Stanley.

'I don't know,' says Lexie. 'It sounds violent.'

'It *is* violent,' says Edward. 'We all have to pick a name of a conqueror and then we have a battle. I'm usually Montezuma and Stanley is El Cid, but sometimes I'm Nero, although Mum told me Nero was no good because he . . . What did he do, Mum?'

'He fiddled while Rome burnt,' I say.

'What did he fiddle with?' asks Stanley.

'Do you think he fiddled with his wiggle-wiggle?' says Edward, giggling. 'That's what Jamie calls it. When Mum pulls down his nappy to try to get him to use the potty he fiddles with his willy and says, "Wiggle-wiggle." '

'Actually, I could be Cleopatra,' says Lexie. 'She was Egyptian.'

'Did she die in the end?' asks Edward. 'Because in this game you have to die, don't you, Stanley?'

'Yes,' says Stanley, 'but it doesn't hurt all that much.'

'Did Cleo-whatsit die?' says Edward.

'Yes,' says Lexie. 'She was bitten by an asp.'

'What's an asp?' asks Stanley.

'A snake,' says Lexie.

'Yuk,' says Stanley. 'Well, maybe you should be Joan of Arc.'

'But she was burnt at the stake!' exclaims Lexie.

'Oh, you mustn't mind that. It doesn't hurt to die in this game. Bennie dies all the time when we play Conquerors, don't you, Bennie?'

''Es!' says Bennie, falls on to the floor and sticks his tongue out. 'I–I'm dead,' he says, before he closes his eyes.

'And me!' says Lexie, joining in.

With a yelp and a cry, Edward pulls her up and chases her out of the door, followed swiftly by Stanley and Jamie.

'One more word out of you, missy,' yells Edward, 'and you die!'

'I don't know how you cope with any of this,' says Dougie, sighing.

'Neither do I. I certainly wasn't like this before I had the children.'

What Women Are Like Before They Have Children

Here is what women are before they have children: desirable, carefree and fun. Women who have had children can barely remember any of these things. In the backs of their minds they can vaguely recognize that once upon a time their children did not exist. They have a sense that they used to do exactly as they liked. They stayed in bed at the weekend. They read papers and books, listened to the radio, did crosswords and had time to go shopping for dresses, makeup and perfume. They were out late with their friends and went to jazz clubs, kissed unsuitable men and maybe drank too much, then ate an all-day breakfast the next day. When they met a man at a party – and, boy, did they meet a lot of men at a lot of parties – they assumed he would find them attractive.

Then they have children and what happens? Their confidence is stolen, their energy sapped. They go from being someone who likes a few glasses of wine in the evening, maybe friends round for dinner, or sex with their partner to someone who can barely stay awake past ten p.m. They no longer watch the news, Newsnight or Question Time because they're fast asleep. They no longer have sex because they're too exhausted. In fact, women with small children should hang up a sign, saying, 'Hello, I'm a formerly interesting, lively person who has been subsumed by my children. See you in ten years!'

Women who have had perfectly successful careers, perfectly successful lives, are turned into gibbering wrecks by their children. 'When I was working,' they say, 'I ran a department of twenty-five people. I was efficient! But now . . .' You look at their truculent toddler swinging the cat round by its tail and feel sad. For children know our Achilles' heel. They don't do as they're told when they're told to do it. They don't hug and kiss us when we want them to. They don't eat up their vegetables, learn to play the piano, excel at sports and remember not to answer back. Most often, they do the opposite of everything I've ever learnt. So, as a mother, you have a choice: swing along with the good times or fight every battle and end up so miserable that you might as well not have had children anyway.

I have seen women sitting ramrod straight, staring doggedly in front of themselves and nowhere else as their children draw on the *walls around them, swing off the banisters or ride their bikes through the house, and the mother will smile, in a desperate way, and say, 'Oh, yes, Jackson's so lively at the moment!' Then Jackson will smile because he knows how beat his mother is and she will sit and in her eyes there is maybe, just maybe, the last flicker of hope that was Her Former Self.*

Everything changes when you have your first baby. I did not know this because until I had Edward I lived in maternal oblivion. I floated round supermarkets unaware of the chaos around me. I filtered out screaming, wailing and whining. 'Wait till you have children! Then it'll change!' women used to say to me, but I didn't listen to them.

Why not? I ask myself now. Why did I not listen to Julia when she used to plonk a child on my lap and go, wild-eyed, to use my loo, only to be followed by another? 'Can I not even go to the loo on my own?' I'd hear her say. Why did I not think this would happen to me? I'd watch, bemused, as Robert, at two and a half, would throw himself to the floor when I told him I didn't have a blue plastic cup for his juice. 'I wanna boo cup!' he would shout at me.

'But I don't have one, Robert,' I said. 'I have wine glasses, shot glasses, pint glasses, but I don't have a blue plastic cup.'

'Oh, Bobby,' my sister would say, picking him up. 'Auntie Samantha doesn't have children so she doesn't have plastic cups.'

But this would not placate him. 'I wanna boo one!' he'd shout again.

But why on earth would he think I might have one? I was an adult. Adults don't drink out of plastic cups.

Now, of course, I have plastic cups of all hues. And I have plastic plates, plastic cereal bowls, plastic knives and forks with smiley faces on them. All my glasses have been broken. All my sheets have been weed on or thrown-up over, and my rugs, cushions and throws have been used to wrap Beady in when the children are playing 'Poor Beady', which goes something like this. After we have been for our traditional Sunday walk, Edward says, 'Look at poor Beady. She's cold and wet and needs warming up.' It is Bennie's job to find one of my lambswool throws and wrap it round the dog. Jamie rubs it up and down her until Edward proclaims her dry. Wendy shoves it in the washing-machine at 95 degrees, then shrinks it in the tumble-drier until it is only just big enough to wrap a toy poodle. Next time Beady gets wet, Bennie must find another throw and the process starts again.

The wood stove in the inglenook fireplace has gone into storage and, instead, there are boxes and boxes of toys. They must have sex with each other because every day the pile of tractors, diggers, tanks and soldiers grows and grows until I have to buy another toy box. Now there are five where there used to be one.

I used to think that as the children got older, I could get rid of those toys, but no. Edward still has his entire collection of Thomas the Tank Engine and Friends and he will not let Bennie play with them even though Bennie is desperate to play with them, (a) because he loves trains, and Thomas in particular and (b) because they are Edward's. I have had to buy Bennie his own growing set of Thomas and Friends and Jamie his own shape-sorter, which is identical to the one Bennie has because Bennie won't let Jamie play with his, and on it goes.

Other things have changed too. The only books I read are Miffy books, Thomas books and One Gorgeous Baby *books, books about farms, sleepy dogs, lost teddy bears, orphaned lambs, big bears and a really boring one that Bennie loves about a tractor and a digger that seem to be engaged in endless warfare.*

Where I used to be funny, carefree and scatty, I am now terribly together. Somehow I can hold millions of things in my brain simultaneously. I can think about doing the washing-up, unloading the washing-machine, what shopping we need, what Edward and Bennie require for school, Jamie's appointment at the doctor's, John's working schedule, calling the garage to get the car MOT'd, getting money from the bank to pay for Edward's swimming lesson, and how long it will take to get the children to bed all at the same time. When I think of who I was before I had children, I want to kick myself. Instead I carry on – but sometimes I remember the former me, bow down and pray: Dear Lord, make her return one day. Amen.

An hour later the children are still in the garden playing Conquerors. 'You run and deliver the message to the enemy,' Edward is saying to Bennie, 'and then you die!'

'I don't wanna die,' says Bennie, plaintively.

'Didn't you hear me?' replies Edward. 'You deliver the message to El Cid, who is Stanley, and then you die.'

'B-b-but I'm already dead!'

'Oh,' says Edward, sounding disappointed. 'Who killed you?'

'Stanley.'

'Oh, right. Where's Joan of Arc?'

'Here,' Lexie says.

'Right, you run and deliver the message to Stanley, I mean El Cid, and then you can die instead.'

'Can I ride to deliver the message? I'm on a horse, remember?'

'Course. Off you go.'

I move to look out of the window. Lexie is pretending to canter across the garden. She hands a letter to Stanley, who stares at it. He says, 'On guard!' to Lexie, and they have a mock-battle.

Edward canters on the spot in excitement. 'Steady,' he says, to his non-existent mount.

Suddenly Bennie, who has been lying on the grass with his tongue out, gets up and charges at Stanley. 'Y-y-you meanie!' he shouts and, without warning, whacks Stanley's legs hard with the stick he's pretending is a sword.

'Ouch!' yells Stanley.

'Take that!' shrieks Bennie.

'Ouch, Bennie. Stop! It's supposed to be a game!'

Edward canters over. 'I think I've won, haven't I?'

'Yes, you've bloody won,' says Stanley, sulkily. 'But only because Bennie's hurt my legs, which isn't part of the game because I've already killed him.'

'Right, kneel down and I can chop off your head.'

'No,' says Stanley. 'Not until you admit you've won unfairly.'

'I haven't,' says Edward. 'I gave my page a potion that brought him back to life.'

'I never saw you give him anything,' says Stanley.

'Well, I did, so kneel down and I'll chop off your head.'

'No, I will not kneel down,' says Stanley, truculently.

'But Montezuma always chops off heads. He keeps them as prizes.'

'You can chop off mine,' says Lexie, helpfully.

'Oh, all right,' says Edward, impatiently. 'Now kneel down before me and . . .'

Lexie kneels down.

'I take your head as my prize in defeat! Page? Page?' He turns to Bennie. 'That's you,' he hisses. 'You must collect the head of the fallen Joan of Arc and put it on a stake.'

Bennie puts his thumb in his mouth and everyone watches solemnly as Edward raises his sword, then brings it down rather dramatically, but carefully, on Lexie's neck.

'Erggh,' says Lexie, as she falls forward.

Stanley claps, suddenly cheered up. 'That was very good, Lexie,' he says, 'very convincing, wasn't it, Edward?'

'Yeah,' says Edward.

'Thanks,' says Lexie, getting up and smoothing her skirt.

'Do you think it's time for the picnic?' says Stanley. 'I'm starving.'

'Let's go and ask Mum,' says Edward. 'She's been making sandwiches for hours.'

They troop into the kitchen and line up along the wall. I'm just about to tell them it's time to go when I hear Wendy: 'You're a naughty, naughty boy!' she's saying. 'Why have you put my flannel down the dunny?'

Suddenly Jamie scoots round the corner as if on wheels and dashes behind Stanley.

'Are you hiding, Jamie?' asks Stanley.

'Wiggle-wiggle,' says Jamie.

'Jamie's always putting things down the loo,' says Edward to Lexie. 'He put all the kitchen roll down there last week and blocked up the sewage system and Mum had to get these ruddy pipes and poke them down the hole to get it out.'

'They're not called ruddy pipes, Edward,' I say gently. 'They are rodding irons.'

'Then he put Dad's underpants down and Dad had to reach into the loo and –'

'Where's that naughty boy?' says Wendy, thundering

into the kitchen. 'Jamie! Come here,' she yells, 'or you won't get any Arctic Roll and it's yum.'

'Ooh!' says Jamie, giggling.

Now all the children are giggling. I can see that Wendy's finding it hard to keep a straight face. 'Can we go, Mrs S?' she says. 'I'll have to get me flannel out with a stick when we get back.'

Liberty

Twenty minutes later we're there. I spent most of the time in the car telling Dougie about how beautiful the place is that I was taking him to. 'It's sort of remote,' I told him. 'I came across it once when I was taking Beady for a walk. I saw this little lane running down from the main road and worked out it must go to the river. I stopped the car, walked down, and at the end there's a little jetty where you can feed the ducks, then all these fields and the river and a pretty little bridge you cross over. It's lovely and quiet and reminds me of a place I used to go as a child.'

'Sounds great,' said Dougie.

So, now I park the car and we divide the picnic bags into three: one for me, full of salad and wholegrain sandwiches, one for Wendy, with what she bought for the picnic – with my money, I might add – a packet of large Scotch eggs, some mini meat pies, some 're-formed chicken' satay sticks, some precooked cocktail sausages, packets of Monster Munch, marshmallows, two packets of Tunnock's teacakes and a now rather-soggy Arctic Roll; Dougie's has all the juice, beer and water in it.

'Did you get any cucumber or tomatoes or carrots or mini-quiches?' I'd asked when she'd got back from the shops.

'Nah,' she said. 'Couldn't find anything like that.'

'But you did go to Waitrose?'

'Nah, Asda.'

Wendy has an obsession with Asda. John thinks it's because she can buy piles of cakes, chocolates, crisps and sweets at knock-down prices there. I tend to agree with him.

The children pour out of the car, like ferrets out of a sack. I walk casually behind them, letting my thoughts drift. Mmm, how relaxed I feel. It's such a lovely day. The sun's shining, dappling through the leaves and making patterns on the ground. I love this footpath. It's brown and earthy before it turns into fields. It smells almost peaty, woody. I want to lie down on it and feel its silky texture. I want to take off all my clothes and feel the sun and the shadows move across my skin. It's pretty hot in the sun, but cool in the shade. The sky is blue. There's a light breeze. I can see Beady streaking across the field using all the power in her strong black back legs. God, she's fast, that dog.

Today her collar is catching the sunlight, glinting as she runs, nose down, searching for rabbits. Way behind her, in the field two in front of me, I can see Edward, Stanley and Lexie. Stanley has a stick that he obviously wants Beady to chase. I can hear Edward calling her. Like an Exocet missile, without raising her nose from the ground, she changes direction and sets off for the children. She stops dead when she gets to Edward. Stanley calls her and waves the stick. Beady jumps up and down, then splash!

Stanley has thrown it far into the river and Beady leaps off from the bank, lands feet first in the water and sets off, tongue hanging out, to retrieve it. Then I see that

Bennie has joined them. He also has a stick but it's quite small. Beady hauls herself out of the water. She sees Bennie and dances around on her back legs, begging for his stick. I see Bennie going nearer to the water. Oh, God – this is too close for comfort. Suddenly I'm back on that beach in Crete. Edward is standing near Bennie. 'Edward!' I yell.

Bennie is inching towards the edge of the bank. He's not looking where he's going.

'Edward!' I yell again. Why can't he hear me?

Dougie and Wendy have crossed the bridge and are a field behind the children. They are turned towards each other, chatting away, unaware of what's going on. Jamie's on Dougie's shoulders, waving his hands like a fan at a rock concert. Damn Dougie, I think. Actually, damn Wendy. She's supposed to be looking after the children. That's what she's paid for. Why is she jawing on at Dougie, not noticing that Bennie is too close to the river's edge?

I hear a loud splash. Oh, God. Bennie's gone in. I know he has. He's going to drown and there's no Greek doctor to save him. He's . . . But when I look up, Bennie is dancing from foot to foot, no stick in his hand and the dog's in the river.

By the time I get to them, Wendy and Dougie have taken out the picnic things, laid out the rug and are pouring drinks. I have run as fast as I can across the fields because I'm still worried about Bennie.

'Why are you out of breath?' asks Edward, gulping lemonade provided by Wendy, ignoring the elderflower cordial mixed with sparkling water I brought.

'I was worried about Bennie,' I gasp.

'What about Bennie?' asks Dougie.

'He was too near the edge and none of you stopped him.'

'No, he wasn't,' says Edward. 'He's been nowhere near it.'

'I saw him,' I say, having got my breath back. 'Edward, I saw him. He went right up to the edge to throw a stick in for Beady and none of you noticed.'

'Well, I didn't see him,' says Wendy.

'We were a field behind,' says Dougie, helpfully.

'I know that,' I say crossly. 'I saw you two, chatting away and utterly unaware of the danger Bennie was in.'

'He wasn't in any danger, were you, Bennie?' says Edward.

Bennie stares straight in front of him.

'I mean, look, Mum,' says Edward, taking off his shoes and socks. 'Look how shallow the water is.' He gets up and walks down the slope into the river. The water reaches his ankles. 'See?' he says.

'OK,' I say. 'I'm sorry, Edward. I panicked.'

'That's all right, Mum,' says Edward. 'I understand.'

Suddenly I feel lost and lonely. 'I don't know if anyone understands.'

Dougie hears the catch in my voice and takes my hand. 'Samantha,' he says, 'don't blame yourself. You're a mother. You nearly lost Bennie and your need to hold him close, keep him safe, is so strong.'

'You're right,' I say.

'That was pretty profound, wasn't it?' says Dougie cheerfully.

The feeling – oh, God, the feeling. What mother has not virtually ripped out her heart in terror at the thought of her children disappearing? I remember watching Edward once, when he was about four, run down the ramp at the Natural History Museum in London that led on to a very busy road. I was chasing him faster and faster and he was turning and laughing at me as if it was a great game. Then I saw the bus. Edward was heading right for it. 'Edwaaard!' I screamed. He turned and waved at me. Just as his foot was about to leave the kerb, just as the driver's mouth opened in a shout of sheer panic, just as the brakes squealed, just as I was about to sink to my knees and sob, a man appeared from nowhere, grabbed him by his jumper and pulled him back. He reeled him in and held him fast. The next thing I knew I was beating at Edward, at the man, with my fists. 'You stupid boy!' I was shouting. 'Do you know what you've just done?' I was shouting so much and crying so much I could hardly breathe. The man just held Edward and me, then walked away. I never saw him again.

I know I probably worry too much about Bennie but he had the nearest of misses. He sank to the bottom of the sea and maybe there, when he was under the water, he could see everyone above him thrashing around, but perhaps only their legs so that they looked as if they had been cut in two, like a magician's assistant. Maybe he couldn't see his father's face, contorted in pain as he searched frantically through the crashing waves. Maybe, for Bennie, it was terribly calm and peaceful down there. Maybe he didn't feel as I felt – that sense of crushing loss when I thought that John's search for Bennie was fruitless, that Bennie really had been taken away by the waves until the breath had gone from his puppy-fat body and he was floating somewhere, face down, returned to the water, to the endless in and out of the sea.

Then and there I could trace his body in my mind for I know him so well; his feet with their round, curled toes, his legs, quite short and sturdy with blond hairs growing on them, the colour of his skin, marmoreal, almost translucent on his bottom. 'Bottomly Potts, covered in spots,' I used to say to him.

As a younger child, he always had his hand down his knickers. Bennie was always in the habit of taking his trousers and knickers off. He was so unselfconscious about it. I remember how his skin darkened on the small of his back where his birthmark is, the curve of his long back, the slope of his shoulders and the nape of his neck with fine baby hair, and his head, with its blond curls. In my mind I turn him over. I see his knees, squidgy and fat like a carthorse, and his chunky thighs, the pinkness of his infant willy and then his round, full stomach, his chest, his neck and then his face, his dear face, with some freckles, a button nose and clear sky blue eyes and then . . . And then a horrific picture of Bennie comes into my head. I see him lying under water, under the cold grey water, with those once mischievous eyes now dulled and forced open by the demands of the sea, and that perfect skin with its tinge of pink now alabaster and transparent. I see Bennie's naked body entangled in swaying seaweed, his mouth slack, his limbs leaden, dead and destroyed by the weight of the water and I scream. So my advice to all parents is to embrace their sneaky little toes and stinky hot breath and arms whirring round in the night, like little demons manning out-of-control chainsaws. Roll over and grasp your naughty children, hold them in your arms, kiss their tired eyelids, rub their milky tummies and whisper sweet things in their ears for this is what children want. We are the ballast that supports them.

A month after we got home, Jamie had his own mishap. Bennie,

Jamie and I went to the local petting zoo. It's a beautiful place on top of a hill where the children can go into the pens with the rabbits, feed pellets to the goats, touch the cows and stroke the horses. We had gone to bottle-feed the lambs and maybe fit in a tractor ride, but the farm was packed. There were children everywhere, on mechanical diggers, hiding in hay bales in the activity room, stuffing feed into the goats, trying to get on to the Shetland pony and poking the rabbits with bits of straw. Jamie fell in love with the pigs.

When Bennie said he was hungry I took them to the café near the pig pens. I put the two of them at a free table and checked for any possible escape routes. None, except some double doors leading to the loos.

'Bennie,' I said. 'I'm going to get you some sandwiches.'

'J-jam ones?' said Bennie.

'I think they have jam ones.'

'And for Jamie? Can he have jam ones?'

'Yes,' I said.

'And crisps?'

'Yes, and crisps.'

'And cake?'

'Yes,' I said, a bit cross now. 'You can have crisps, cake, juice and anything else you want.'

I dashed to the counter leaving Jamie ripping up napkins and Bennie trying to work the pepper grinder. But the queue was so slow. The man in front of me couldn't decide what to have. He kept picking up sandwiches and putting them back. Ten minutes later, he was still wavering over which juice to get and whether he should go for a KitKat or a Mars Bar. He got his wallet out of his jacket pocket and then his face fell.

'I haven't got any money,' he said. 'I'll have to ask my wife.' He wandered off.

By then I wanted to scream, 'I have two small children who are waiting for their lunch and God knows what they're up to because they're too young to be left by themselves, and as I'm here on my own, I have no choice so hurry up!*'*

He came back with some cash. 'Sorry,' he said to me. I was about to bite a retort when I felt someone tugging at my leg.

It was Bennie. 'I'm starving,' he said.

'I'm just getting your lunch,' I said. I turned to look at their table. There was a mound of pepper and ripped-up napkins but no Jamie. 'Where's Jamie?'

'G-gone,' said Bennie, eyeing the KitKats, placed handily in front of him.

'Gone where?'

Bennie pointed towards the loo. I asked him to go and check on Jamie while I put the lunch, including a KitKat, on the table.

A minute later he was back. 'He's not in there,' he said.

'Of course he's there,' I said. 'There's no other way out.'

But he wasn't. He wasn't in the men's loos or the ladies'. He wasn't in the nappy-changing area or the loos for the disabled. He wasn't in the cleaning cupboard full of Jeyes fluid and mops.

I deposited Bennie back at the table and told him to eat his sandwiches while I looked for Jamie. I scanned the room. Lots of children but no blond ones with mad hair and an orange sweatshirt. I looked at the exit. The doors were swinging. Aha! He's wandered back to the pigs. I strode outside and turned right for the pig pens. No Jamie.

I went to the rabbit hutches. He wasn't there. I went back into the café. I checked on Bennie, now eating jam sandwiches with pepper. I went back to the loos.

The lady at the next table said she hadn't seen Jamie but would I like her to keep an eye on Bennie while I searched?

I went back to the pig pens, the rabbit hutches, the tractors, the goats and the sheep, and then I spotted a member of staff.

'I've lost my little boy!' I said. 'He's two. He's called Jamie and he has mad blond hair and is wearing an orange sweatshirt.'

The man asked where I'd last seen him. 'The loos,' I said.

We went back to the loos. No Jamie.

The man radioed the main office. 'Tell everyone to look for a little boy called Jamie,' he said.

Half an hour later I was slumped on a bale. No one had found Jamie. The park had been temporarily closed as everyone hunted for him. The people manning the office were studying CCTV footage.

'He's gone, hasn't he?' I said to the attendant.

'No,' said the man. 'He's here somewhere. We just haven't found him yet.'

'He isn't,' I said. 'Someone's taken him.'

'No one has taken him.' The man clasped my hand. 'It's not possible.'

'It is!' I said, now close to tears.

Suddenly Bennie appeared with the lady from the next table. He started to cry. 'I–I lost Jamie, Mummy,' he said.

I pulled myself together and put on a smile. 'No, darling,' I said. 'Jamie isn't lost. This nice man is going to find him for us.'

The nice man smiled at me. 'Yes, I am,' he said. He went in the direction of the loos, while I thought about calling the police, calling John. 'John, I've lost Jamie. He may be dead. It's all my fault.' Then the nice man came back. He was still smiling. Wordlessly he took my hand and, with Bennie following, walked me through the double doors to where the loos were.

'He's not here. I've looked,' I said. The man put a finger to his lips.

Then, very quietly, he opened the door to the cleaning cupboard and pulled a mop to one side. There, curled up among the dusters, fast asleep like a dormouse, was Jamie.

'Is this him?' said the nice man.

I nodded, but when we were back in the car, driving past the silent people who watched us sympathetically, I broke down and sobbed. The children watched me, puzzled, as Bennie put what was left of the KitKat into Jamie's dusty mouth.

'Right, let's get on with the picnic,' says Dougie brightly. 'Who wants salad or sandwiches or Scotch eggs or all three?'

'Scotch eggs!' chorus the children.

Jamie crawls over and deposits himself on my lap. Wendy gives him a Scotch egg and he munches it happily. I help myself to salad.

'Actually, I'll have salad, please,' says Lexie.

'Oh, good, someone who likes my salad,' I say, spooning some on to a plate for her.

'I'll have salad too,' says Wendy, unexpectedly.

'Muesli? Salad? What's going on?' I ask.

Wendy doesn't answer.

'I hate salad,' says Edward.

'So do I,' says Stanley.

'I-i-is eating salad dangerous?' asks Bennie.

'No.' We laugh.

'My stomach's so full of blaady green leaves, it feels like it's gonna burst,' says Wendy, lying back on the grass.

Dougie is sitting up, sipping cold beer and looking out across the river. 'Is it moorhens that have white beaks or coots?' he asks no one in particular.

'Coots,' I tell him.

I, too, am lying back with my face upturned to the sun. It's getting hotter and I wonder if my skin is burning. Jamie has his legs in the air and is playing with his toes. 'You're bendy, Jamie,' I say, as I watch him bring one chubby foot to his mouth and suck at his toes. Jamie giggles happily. His mouth is sticky. 'You've been eating marshmallows, haven't you?' I say.

I close my eyes. Mmm. I could just nod off. I'm full of salad, sandwiches and elderflower cordial, and I had a couple of sips of beer. I can feel myself drifting down and inwards. My mind is relaxing, my mouth is relaxing, I've stopped frowning, I'm sinking deeper into the warm earth, I'm –

'Mum,' says a voice, from somewhere above my head.

I open my eyes reluctantly. A huge shadow is looming over me. It's Edward. 'Oh, Edward,' I say. 'I was having a little sleep.'

'It's so hot, Mum,' says Edward. 'Me and Stanley were wondering if we could swim in the river.'

'Of course you can,' I say. 'What about Lexie? Does she want to swim?'

I pull myself up on to my elbows and shade my eyes. Wendy has moved into the shade under the tree and is asleep – I can hear her snoring. Jamie is still up-ended next to me, but I can't see anyone else. 'Where is everyone?' I ask Edward.

'Well, Jamie's next to you . . .'

'Yes, I know that,' I say.

'. . . and Wendy's asleep under that tree over there . . .'

'Yep, I know that too,' I say.

'. . . and the rest of us are paddling with Dougie back at the jetty.'

'Oh, you went all the way there, did you?'

'Well, Dougie thought it was the best place for Bennie to paddle.'

'Did he? That's thoughtful of him. Is Bennie paddling?'

'Yes, he's splashing me and Stanley.'

'He's in the water?' I sit up in panic.

'He's fine,' says Edward. 'Dougie's with him, Mum, and Bennie's laughing a lot.'

'That's good.' Suddenly I feel irrationally happy. It's a beautiful day. It's peaceful. For once, Dougie is doing something active, and Bennie's back in the water for the first time since we came home from Crete.

'Oh, nothing will go wrong today, Edward,' I say.

'But the thing is it's very shallow by the jetty so it's not deep enough to swim. Me and Stanley want to go and swim somewhere else.'

'Like where?' I say, not concentrating on what Edward is saying.

'Well, Dougie says – you know when you cross the bridge?'

'Yes,' I say.

'On the other side of the bridge there's this thing that begins with a T and he says he thinks he saw a tree down there with a tyre on it and we want to go and swing on the tyre and fall into the thing that begins with a T and then we can play Pooh sticks from the bridge.'

'What is this thing that begins with a T?'

'Stand up, Mummy, and I'll show you,' he says.

I stand up, and Edward points to the bridge a bit

further back in the field. There's an obvious fork in the river. The main river continues on to where I'm sitting now but the smaller one snakes off to the right. 'Oh, I see,' I say. 'You mean you want to follow that tributary?'

'Yes, that's the word,' says Edward. 'Can we?'

I strain my eyes. It looks very pretty. I can see a narrow strip of water shaded by willows. Thick plants grow up the banks. 'Is it down there that Dougie thinks the swing is?'

'Yes – me and Stanley have our swimming trunks on under our shorts and Lexie says she can swim in her knickers. Is that all right?'

I tell him it is, but that no one must jump from the bridge and that Dougie must either stay with Bennie or they must all go together, and on no account is Bennie allowed to swing on the tyre and jump into the water or go near any deep water. 'I'll come too,' I say. 'I'll put Jamie on my shoulders and meet you there.'

'Oh, thanks, Mum,' says Edward, and dashes back towards the jetty.

'Take Beady too!' I yell after him. 'She might save you if you're drowning.'

'OK!'

I bend down to lift Jamie. 'Beady might save them,' I tell him. 'She's a very brave and intelligent dog.'

I remember when John and I tested Beady's intelligence. The weekly magazine I work for – or should that be 'worked for'? – ran a competition to find Britain's Most Intelligent Dog. Readers wrote in describing their dogs' supposed braininess and we had to decide which dog was the brightest. There was a terrier who could say 'sausages'.

There was an adorable mongrel called Tilly, who could dance and sing – well, howl – at the same time. There was a collie who could count: he would put his paw on corresponding amounts of chocolate drops. His owner would say, 'Where's the number one?' and this dog would cock his head, look at the chocolate drops laid out in front of him, then put his paw on the single drop. It was amazing. We had a panel of people who judged the evidence and one was a dog behavioural expert who told me how to work out if my dog was intelligent.

'Does it know you're coming home even if you change the pattern of time you arrive?'

'Yes!' I squeaked. I told her it always amazed me that Beady knew what time John was coming home, whether it was three o'clock in the afternoon or midnight. 'About five minutes before he walks in she starts whining and pawing at the door,' I said.

'Does she know who is a member of your family and who isn't?' asked the expert.

'Yes! She counts us in and out. One evening I thought everyone was in the house and Beady kept barking and I kept telling her to shut up, but it turned out that Jamie was still in the garden and I'd forgotten him!'

The dog expert gave me a sheet of tests by which to gauge how intelligent or stupid she was.

That night when John got home I told him about the tests and we got very excited. He said that if Beady was super-intelligent we should enter her for the competition. The prize was free dog food for a year.

'Think about it, Samantha,' he said. 'We probably spend a tenner a week on meat and biscuits for her.'

I didn't think I was allowed to enter the competition because it wasn't open to people who worked for the magazine. 'But I could enter her!' said John, and I didn't have the heart to point out that maybe he might be rumbled: he shares the same surname as me and he's called John, which everyone knew was my husband's name.

Anyway, we did the tests and she turned out to be very intelligent. She could find dog biscuits hidden all round the house. She seemed to be able to memorize which hand we'd put the chocolate drops in, rather than randomly sniffing any hand offered to her, which is what stupid dogs do. We tried the same test on Honey, but he just sat there looking bored.

'You're a very intelligent dog,' John said to Beady. He ended up videoing her sniffing correct hands and finding hidden biscuits, then sent it to the magazine with his entry form. Surprisingly, no one at the magazine tumbled to the fact that he was my husband, but the counting collie still won.

I broke the news that evening.

'I bet you voted for the collie,' said John, accusingly, and I had to lie and say I didn't when, out of guilt, I had.

Only Ignorance

Wendy is still snoring gently under the tree as I lift Jamie on to my shoulders. I can see that Edward, Stanley and Lexie have set off over the fields towards the bridge. They are walking together, arms swinging, swishing through the long grass, which is up to their hips. Edward sees me walking towards them, even though I'm still a field or so away. He waves.

They get to the bridge, turn right and disappear.

Dougie is a bit behind them, near the bridge, walking very carefully with Bennie, who is holding his hand. Jamie is a dead weight on my shoulders. When Dougie sees me coming he slows down and we get to the bridge at the same time. I'm breathless.

'Could you take Jamie?' I ask him. 'My shoulders are hurting.'

Dougie lifts Jamie from me and puts him down on the bridge.

I bend to kiss Bennie.

'I–I–I've been in the water!' he says.

'I know,' I say. 'That's marvellous.'

'Aren't you a brave boy, Bennie?' says Dougie.

Bennie swells with pride.

Then we wander slowly and aimlessly along the river-bank.

I remember how my mother would show us the mallard

ducks and their ducklings, then give us deep, dark warnings of pike, fox and all the other predators who stole little ducklings to feast on their downy feathers and unformed bodies. I always used to ask my mother why she kept telling me and Julia how things died and she said, 'It's not how you were born that matters. It's how you face your death that's important.'

Today, though, I concentrate on the wondrous properties of nature. I point out the willow trees, with their hanging branches and elegant greeny-yellow leaves, to Bennie. I bend towards the slow-flowing narrow water and turn over a leaf to show Jamie the snail hiding beneath it. I point to some water boatmen skidding back and forth across the surface.

'Ooh!' says Jamie, seeing his reflection in the water.

Suddenly we hear a piercing scream.

'Wha-wha-wha –' says Bennie, as Dougie, in one movement, yanks him up off the ground. 'Wha-wha-wha –'

I grab Jamie and we run towards where the scream seemed to come from.

'Which way?' says Dougie, desperately.

'Whee!' says Jamie.

'I think in front,' I say.

'It's not Edward or Stanley, is it?' says Dougie, crashing through a small bush.

'I don't know who it is,' I pant.

The screaming has stopped as suddenly as it started.

Then Edward comes haring round the corner. The dog is right behind him. Something has obviously gone terribly wrong.

'Edward!' I rush towards him.

'Mum!' He skids to a halt.

'Edward, what on earth's the matter? Who's screaming?'

'Lexie,' he says breathlessly. 'She's had a shock. You'd better come.'

'Oh, God,' I say, as we walk on quickly. 'Is she all right? Did she fall in? Have you and Stanley been horrible to her? What on earth –'

'You'd just better come,' says Edward.

'Are you grinning, Edward?' What I'd thought was a grimace of panic is actually a smirk.

'I don't mean to,' he says, smiling openly now. 'Just come and you'll see.'

'But where's Stanley? Where's Lexie? This isn't funny, Edward. If I find that you and Stanley have pushed that poor little girl – who is in my care for just one afternoon – into the water, I'll be –'

'A boat!' says Dougie, as we round the corner.

I stop. There, a few hundred yards or so from us, is a small one-berth boat, bobbing gently on its moorings in a patch of sunshine. Lexie and Stanley are standing on the path next to it. She has her back to it but Stanley is chatting to the person on it.

'Whose boat is it?' I ask Edward.

'You'll see,' says Edward. 'Hey, Lexie! Stanley!' he shouts. 'I'm back. I've got my mum and Dougie.'

Lexie runs towards me. I put Jamie down and hug her because she looks very needy. She's fully clothed and not wet, but she's very cold.

'What's going on, Lexie?' I say, holding her tightly. 'Was it you screaming? You're freezing.'

Lexie buries her head in my chest. 'There's a man,' she says faintly, 'and he was –'

But before she can finish we have got to the boat. Now I can see who Stanley's talking to.

'Gary!' I say, totally taken aback. 'What are you doing here?' For there, in front of me, is Gary White. I'm so surprised I barely register that he's wearing nothing but a towel round his waist.

'Erm, yes, right, er, hello, Samantha,' he says, pulling his towel tighter round his waist.

'Hello,' I say, astounded.

'Gary White,' says Dougie. 'I can't believe it. You're a hero of mine!'

'Oh, thanks.'

'I used to watch all your matches. Do you remember the one against West Ham when you did that fantastic header into the goal? It was magic.'

'Oh, thanks,' Gary says again.

'You had the lightest touch. I used to tell my wife – I mean my ex-wife. The day you retired, well, I cried.'

'It was a bad time,' says Gary.

Lexie is tugging at my T-shirt. 'I am sorry to break up the love-in,' I say, to Gary and Dougie, 'but no one has explained to me why Lexie was screaming.'

Gary blushes and Stanley and Edward are giggling.

'What's so funny, Edward?' I bark.

'I can't say,' he says, giggling even more.

'Stanley?' I ask.

'So sorry, Edward's mum,' he gasps, incoherent with laughter.

Gently I peel Lexie off me. I hold her at arm's length.

'Lexie,' I say, looking into her eyes, 'what made you scream?'

Lexie points behind her at Gary. 'He – he – he showed me his –' She turns away from me to hide her face.

'Wiggle-wiggle!' yells Edward, unable to contain himself any longer. He and Stanley fall to the ground, convulsed with laughter.

'Gary,' I say patiently, 'I'm sure there's a rational explanation for this, but can you tell me right now why you showed a ten-year-old girl your bits? Do you make a habit of exposing yourself to innocent young girls or did your towel just happen to fall off as Lexie came round the corner?'

'I'm so sorry, Samantha. You see, it's a lovely day and I haven't had the boat very long so I thought I'd take it out for a spin because Rowan's with her mother. Then I saw this little offshoot of the river and that bridge and I never expected anyone else to be here so . . .'

'So?'

'So I moored up, got my book out and took my clothes off to sunbathe.'

'You took your clothes off to sunbathe?' I say incredulously. 'Are you mad or ignorant or something? Do you honestly think it's a good idea to be a fully grown man sunbathing naked on a public footpath?'

'Oh, come on, Samantha,' says Dougie. 'The poor man was having a break! It's not the worst thing in the world to sunbathe in the nude.'

'Sorry,' I say, 'but am I the only one who was scared witless by Lexie's screams? I mean, did no one else hear her?'

Gary shifts a bit on his seat. 'I'm really sorry, Samantha,' he says. 'Like I said, it was an accident. If there's anything I can do to –'

'Have you still got your match reports?' says Dougie. 'I'd love to look through them with you.'

Lexie is clinging tighter to me.

'Look,' I say, 'it's been a long day and it's time to go home. Lexie's mother will be at our house soon and I want to make sure she's fine by then.'

'I didn't hear them until the scream,' Gary says. 'If there's anything I can do . . .'

'Can I come and see your Ferrari?' says Edward.

'Yes!' says Gary, looking relieved. 'Samantha, I'm so sorry . . .' His mobile phone rings and he turns to answer it.

'I can't talk now, Mother,' I hear him say as I walk off with Lexie clinging to me. 'Yes, I'm in the boat by the river and . . . No, I'm not on my own. Well, I sort of am but then these people came along . . . Nice people, but I . . .'

'That was a bit off of you,' says Dougie, on the drive home.

'I'm tired,' I say. 'I'm not talking about this now. I'm just going to get Lexie some tea, give her a bath and hope to God Naomi understands.'

'It was an accident,' says Dougie.

'Yeah, it was an accident, Mrs S,' says Wendy, from the back. 'I mean, that's pretty bonkers, isn't it? Seeing the willy of a football star?'

'Former football star,' I say.

'He's a looker, though, ain't he?' Wendy continues. 'I wouldn't mind having a crack at that!'

'Wendy,' I say, 'I've had enough of today. Please just be quiet.'

We drive home in total silence. In the mirror I see the two little ones falling asleep. Lexie is staring straight ahead. What on earth is Naomi going to say?

Poor Ginger

It is nine p.m. and Naomi hasn't appeared. I'm a bit worried about her. I'm also exhausted and so are the children. I've spent the evening cooking. Jamie was tired and hungry so I did him baked beans on toast, but all he wanted was Rice Krispies. 'Bispies!' he kept saying. 'Bispies!' He has them for breakfast, lunch, and at dinner time he treats them like an hors d'oeuvre. Bispies, then cod and chips, lasagne or pizza.

'Why does Jamie like Rice Krispies so much?' Edward asked, eyes out on stalks. Then he remembered that for almost his entire first year, Jamie ate only butternut squash. 'Do you think Jamie has OCD?' he asked.

I was rather taken aback. 'How do you know about obsessive-compulsive disorder?' I asked.

'Stanley told me about it,' Edward said airily. 'Apparently his mum washes her hands at least twenty times a day and Stanley says it's because she has OCD and Stanley's father told him that anyone can get it, which worried me and Stanley a bit because we thought it might be like germs and we might catch it off his parents.'

'Well, does Stanley's father have OCD?'

'I think so. He's always making model aeroplanes so Stanley and I decided that he did have it.'

I spent about half an hour discussing what behaviour

is obsessive-compulsive and what behaviour is probably born of weird habits. 'Stanley's father probably just likes making model aeroplanes,' I said. 'So does Stanley, doesn't he?'

'Yes,' said Edward, solemnly, 'but he might have caught it from his dad.'

'Yes, but it's a hobby, not an obsession.'

'Oh, like me playing Conquerors?'

'Yes, but, actually, that's quite obsessive.'

'Oh. OK, well, is it like me eating ice chocs?'*

I thought for a bit. 'No, that's quite obsessive too.'

'See! I've caught it!' Edward looked aghast.

'I'm only joking,' I said.

When Jamie had had his Bispies and beans and I'd put him in the bath, I produced a feast of burgers, oven chips and vegetables for the other children. Then I had to retidy everything I had already tidied as Bennie and Jamie had tipped an entire box of toys over in the sitting room while I was in the study making up a bed for Stanley. When I came back, I found Dougie reading the newspaper in the Chair, seemingly ignorant to the fact that he had been surrounded by Lego men with no hair, and tractors with only three wheels.

'Ah!' said Dougie, when he saw me. 'Is feeding time at the zoo over?'

'I think so.'

'Was it burgers?'

'Yes.'

'I love burgers. We could cook them on the fire. I'll go and make one in the garden and –'

'They've all been eaten.'

'Oh,' said Dougie, returning to his crossword. 'Well, what are we going to have for dinner?'

I was about to tell him I hadn't thought of that yet when Bennie crawled towards me wielding a truck that had no back wheels. 'H-hello, Mum,' he said happily, suddenly diverting his tipsy truck and parking it between Dougie's legs.

'Brrrr,' said Jamie, copying Bennie with a plastic motorcycle.

'D-D-Dougie's our garage!' said Bennie.

'Am I?' said Dougie, looking up in some surprise from his newspaper again. 'Oh, you two have made a mess, haven't you?' Then he turned to me. 'I'm getting cross with this crossword. Have you looked at it yet?'

'Oh, yes,' I said sarcastically. 'Between saving a child from being scared to her wit's end by a naked man, then trying to tidy the house and feed five children I've completed both the crosswords, cryptic and quick.'

'Have you?' said Dougie, plainly impressed. 'What do you think ten across is then? Essential person or thing, seven letters. Starts with a K and ends with an N.'

I thought about it for a bit. 'Kingpin.'

'God, you're a genius!' said Dougie, as Jamie tried to push a Thunderbird One up Dougie's nose having clambered on to his lap.

'Jamie!' I said.

'Don't do that, Jamie,' said Dougie, sounding a bit stuffed up. 'That Thunderbird One could hurt a man.'

I went into the kitchen to find a note from Wendy stuck on to the board. We used to have a whiteboard where everyone was supposed to write down what we needed for the house for the week – like bin bags, celery, and Edward would write 'ice-chocs'* – and who was doing what and when. We'd write down 'Bennie, swim Mondays' and 'Edward, football Tuesdays', but we had to junk it after Edward and I got embroiled in a running battle over who wrote what. I used to write, 'Edward's feet smell' on it and he'd write, 'No yours do Mummy,' and then, in the end, we got so fevered about it that one evening when I wrote 'Edward has a smelly bottom,' he got so incensed that he grabbed the nearest pen and wrote 'Your a smelly fart' to me. But he'd used one of Bennie's felt tips, not a whiteboard pen, so it wouldn't rub off and I decided that having 'Your a smelly fart' staring everyone in the face all day every day, even though it faded, was not good for morale.

A few months ago, I decided to make a star chart to put on the wall to help Bennie sleep. I phoned John, who was mumbling because he had tacks in his mouth – or, at least, that's what he told me later. 'John!' I said. 'I've cracked it.'

'Er?' mumbled John, above a bit of banging.

'Oh, sorry – are you working?'

'Ner. Er, yer.'

'It's just that I was thinking about Bennie's sleep problems and I remember that when Edward was little and he wouldn't sleep and kept coming to my bed, I made a star chart.'

'Orh.'

'I divvied it up into weeks and days and every night he didn't come into bed he got a star, and if he got seven stars in the week he got a treat like a bag of sweets.'

'Arh.'

'You have to be quite insistent about it, though. For example, if the prize at the end of the week is a bag of sweets then Bennie would not be allowed sweets during the rest of the week. Now, that might be a problem, mightn't it, because would it be fair to let Edward and Jamie have sweets when Bennie can't? But, then again, Edward and Jamie sleep and Bennie doesn't.'

'Mmr.'

'Maybe the prize should be something else. My friend promised her daughter a trip to Disneyland Paris but I think that's a bit excessive and, anyway, I don't want to go to Disneyland Paris do you?'

'Urgh.'

'Hmm, I'll have to think about it but I'll get it all organized. You can see it when you get home and we'll think of a prize.'

'Brr.'

''Bye, then!'

I went to the shops and bought coloured paper, felt tips and a variety of stickers, including stars, footballs and smiley faces. When I got home I told the children what I was doing. 'I'm making a star chart,' I said.

'For me?' said Edward, eyeing the football stickers.

'No, not for you because you're ten and when you're ten you no longer need star charts.'

'But why does Bennie need a star chart?' asked Edward.

'Because he doesn't sleep properly. He keeps coming into our bed and the star chart is to encourage him to sleep.'

'What does he get if he sleeps properly?'

'A bag of sweets.'

'A–a–a bag of sweets?' said Bennie, rather cautiously.

'Yes, a bag of yummy sweets.'

'But that's not fair!' said Edward. 'Jamie and I sleep really well and we don't get any sweets, do we, Jamie?'

'Bispies!' said Jamie, seeing that the cereals cupboard door was open.

'Yes, Jamie, you can have Bispies,' I said. 'Edward, you just have to help me on this one. I need Bennie to sleep properly so it's Bennie who gets the star chart.'

'Yes, but I don't sleep properly either!' said Edward, triumphantly. 'I'm always waking up and stuff so I should get sweeties for not disturbing anyone.'

'I–I–I don't really like sweeties,' said Bennie.

'See?' said Edward. 'Bennie doesn't like sweeties so me and Jamie should get them, but Jamie only likes Bispies so I should get them!'

'C-c-could I have a bike?' asked Bennie.

'A bike!' said Edward, now properly incensed. 'Just for sleeping properly? I mean to say . . .'

'Edward!' I said. 'Would you please shut up and listen to me. I'm making a star chart for Bennie and that's final. If Bennie sleeps properly for a week, we'll put some money – note what I just said, *some* money – aside to get him a bike. OK?'

'I still don't think it's fair,' said Edward, moodily.

But here I am tonight, and now it is nine o'clock and Wendy has gone out, while Dougie has gone back to London, having complained about the lack of bed space in my house.

'Mmm,' he said, at around seven, when I was trying to persuade Jamie and Bennie to go to bed. 'I can't wait to sink into my bed and go to sleep. Should I open a bottle of wine?'

I was trying to squash Jamie into a too-small nappy I'd found in the cupboard as the ones I'd bought earlier were newborn size.

'Yes, don't you think a nice glass of white would be good? I could take the bottle into the garden and –'

'Dougie,' I said, now trying to find Bennie some pyjamas, 'does it look like the right moment to ask me to sit in the garden with you?'

'Oh,' said Dougie. 'I thought the sun was past the yardarm and all that . . .'

'Yes, but unless I'm very much mistaken, there are two children who need to be put to bed, three older children who need to have a bath and be put to bed even if, for Lexie, it's only temporary, and that won't be done until at least seven thirty. As for going to bed, exactly where do you think you'll be sleeping?'

'In my bedroom,' said Dougie.

'That's the thing,' I said. 'Edward's moved into your bedroom because Wendy's got his.'

'Oh,' said Dougie, a bit put out. 'What about the study, then?'

'I was going to put Stanley there because there isn't enough room in Edward's for the spare camp bed. If Naomi doesn't come soon, I might have to put Lexie in the study, and Stanley will have to sleep on the inflatable bed on Edward's floor.'

'Oh, so I don't have a bed?'

'Not unless you bunk up with Wendy.'

'Does she have a double?'

'Yes, but I was only joking.'

'Where's Wendy gone?'

'I don't know,' I said. 'She didn't say. She never does.'

'Do you think she's got a boyfriend?'

I shot him a look.

'Or a girlfriend?'

I shot him another.

An hour later, Jamie and Bennie were in bed and the three older children washed, two in their pyjamas, and Lexie, who had none with her, back in her day clothes.

'I'll go home,' Dougie said. 'I'll have wine by myself.'

'All right,' I said, because I wanted an evening to myself. 'See you soon!'

'Yes,' he said, as he went out of the front door.

When I went back in, I found the three older children watching a film featuring man-eating dinosaurs.

'Ergh! Look at all that blood!' said Stanley, glasses misting.

Lexie was on the sofa, hugging a cushion. I sat next to her and put my arm round her. Her hair still smelt of her mother's perfume.

'Didn't you wash your hair?' I asked.

'No,' she said, in a small voice. 'I don't like washing my hair.'

'Neither do I,' said Stanley.

'Why not?' I asked them.

'I don't like getting soap in my eyes,' said Lexie. 'When Mummy washes my hair she always gets soap in my eyes.'

'So does mine,' said Stanley.

'I wear goggles in the bath, don't I, Mum?' said Edward. 'That way when Mum washes my hair no soap can get in my eyes.'

'Is that true?' asked Lexie.

'Yes,' I said. 'Edward's always worn swimming goggles in the bath and now Bennie does too.'

'That's a good idea,' she said.

Edward looked rather pleased with himself.

'I don't think my mother would let me,' said Stanley. 'She doesn't like things like that.'

'Like what?' said Edward.

'Weird things.'

'Is it weird, Mum?' said Edward.

'A bit,' I said, 'but very practical.'

There was another roar from the television and Lexie pressed into me. 'Is this frightening?' I asked.

'Yes,' she said, clutching the cushion.

'Do you want me to ask Edward to change it?'

'No!' said Edward, as Lexie said, 'Yes.'

'You're going soon, aren't you,' said Edward to Lexie, 'so there's no point in changing it, is there?'

'Actually, your mother should have been here by now, shouldn't she?' I said to Lexie. 'What time did she say she was picking you up?'

'She didn't.'

Stanley said very kindly that he would sit next to Lexie if she was frightened, and Lexie said she'd like that. Edward gave him a withering look.

I went to ring Naomi.

*

Now it's yet another hour later and still no Naomi. In the end I decided to squash Edward and Stanley into Edward's room and told Lexie she should sleep in the study until her mother arrived. I offered her a pair of Edward's pyjamas but she declined and went to bed in her clothes. When I went to say goodnight to her, I found her reading.

'I'm up to the bit where Seedy Sam dies,' she said, yawning. 'Does everyone die in this book?'

'No,' I say, stroking her hair. 'But times were different then. It was a much tougher life for everyone. Now, you should go to sleep and when Mummy comes she can just pick you up, put you in the car and you'll wake up in your bed. Today will be like a dream.'

'I had a nice day, apart from –'

'I know. Just forget about it. It was an unfortunate accident, that's all.'

Lexie's eyes are closing. 'I won't tell my mum about it if you don't want me to.'

'Oh, you must tell her,' I say, stroking her hair.

'Why?'

'Because it's good to tell your parents, or your mother, what's been going on in your life.'

'Why?'

'Because mothers need to know all about their children . . . and, to be honest, Lexie, I feel I must tell your mother what happened in case . . .'

'In case what?'

'I don't know. In case you feel nervous and she doesn't know why.'

'But you said there was no need to feel nervous.'

'Well, there isn't.'

'So why would I tell my mum about what happened, then?'

'Because if it had happened to a daughter of mine when she was with your mum, and that daughter had got upset, I'd want your mum to tell me about it.'

'But I'm not upset now and, anyway, you don't have a daughter,' says Lexie, waking up a bit.

'I know that. I am just saying that *if* I had a daughter, which I don't –'

'I could be like your daughter, couldn't I?' says Lexie intently.

'Yes, Lexie,' I say, stroking her hair again. 'I am sure you'd make anyone a lovely daughter.' Soon after that, she's asleep.

Now it's ten thirty and I'm getting cross. Why is Naomi not here? I hope she didn't expect me to keep Lexie up this late. I telephone her again. 'Hi, this is Naomi. I can't take your call right now . . .' The messaging service again. I suppose I'll just sit and wait.

I'm settling down with a glass of wine and the crossword when I see Beady's ears prick up.

A minute later I hear a knock at the door.

It's Naomi. She's standing on my doorstep, looking frazzled but as beautiful as she was this morning. 'I'm so sorry I'm late,' she says, pushing past me to get inside. 'Is Lexie here? Oh, God, please tell me she is. Is she awake? I didn't mean to be so late but I had so much work to do and the telephone kept ringing and . . .' She looks around the sitting room. 'Where's Lexie? She's here somewhere, isn't she?'

'Of course,' I say. 'Why wouldn't she be?'

'I–I don't know. I've gone mad . . . I'm so sorry. I'm so late and . . . I'm a bit all over the place.'

'She's asleep,' I say. 'We've had a long day and –'

'Asleep? Really? That's marvellous. I felt so awful being so late. Well,' she spies the open wine bottle on the side in the kitchen, 'oh, gosh, what a relief. Can I have a glass of wine? I'd love a drink.'

I pour her one.

'How was the school?' I ask, once she's sat down.

'The school?' she says.

'Yes, the one you had to go and see.'

'Oh, marvellous.'

'You've been there a long time, though, haven't you?'

'Of course I haven't been there all this time,' she says, throwing her head back and laughing. 'You didn't think that, did you? I've been busy, doing things like catching up on my emails and getting some work done. My phone hasn't stopped ringing!'

'I tried to telephone you but I couldn't get through.'

'That's probably because if I'm using it it goes to my messaging service. The office rang and my husband rang and it's been busy, busy, busy. Now, let's talk about you!'

'But we talked about me this morning,' I say, 'and I barely know anything about your life. What have you been doing all these years?'

'Nothing, really. My life's boring. I'm just forty and ancient, but you have all these lovely children! Don't you think children keep you younger?'

'Not in my case.'

'Yes, they do, Samantha. You look great! It's because

you've got young children, isn't it? They keep you youthful. That's my theory anyway.'

'Lexie reminds me so much of you. You're very alike, you know. She has your long limbs, and the same eyes.'

'Does she? Did you have a good time? Picnics always sound fun and Lexie gets bored if she's on her own with me all the time. I bet she loved the attention from the boys, didn't she?'

'Actually, there's something I need to tell you about that happened today that sort of involves the boys, really.' I proceed to tell her about Gary White.

Naomi giggles when I get to the bit where Lexie found him with no clothes on. 'That's brave of him,' she says.

'I thought it was irresponsible,' I say. 'Anyway, it gave Lexie the most dreadful shock and Gary was embarrassed. I'm very sorry but I think she's OK.'

'Don't worry. Worse things happen.'

'I just wanted you to know because . . . I thought it might be important.'

'Did she seem upset when she went to bed?'

'No.'

'Nothing to worry about, then,' says Naomi, stretching back on her chair.

She pours herself another glass of wine. 'Now, tell me about you,' she says. 'I can see many things in your life have changed – loads of kids, lovely man . . . or do you have a secret heartbreak you're nursing somewhere along the line?'

So I tell her about how I was married before to John the First, how we had Edward together and broke up once we'd moved to the countryside. He'd decided he didn't want to be a married man with a child. I tell her how lonely I was until I went to a party in London and met lovely John the Second. The next thing we knew, he'd moved down to join me and Edward in the middle of nowhere and we'd had two more children.

'I thought everything was going to be so tricky but actually we've all muddled along together very well.'

'And does Edward still see his father?' she asks.

'Not really,' I say. 'He came over a couple of summers ago from the States but, well, it didn't work out and he went off travelling. We haven't heard from him since.'

'That's not good, is it?' she says. 'Does it bother Edward?'

'I don't think so. I mean, he barely saw him before that. He calls John, my current John, Dad, and has done for years. He used to see his grandmother but she died that summer. She left Edward a house in Devon so –'

'How lovely! Do you use it?'

'Not really. It's rented out at the moment. I'm sure Edward will go there when he's older. Does it all sound a bit complicated?'

'I think everyone's lives are complicated, aren't they?'

'Well, mine may get more complicated if I get pregnant with a girl.'

'You want more children?' She's clearly amazed.

'I, erm, yes, a girl, really.'

'Fascinating,' says Naomi. 'And do you work?'

I tell her about *Our Fridges, Our Selves.*

'Ooh, I'm very into studies of the self. Did I tell you that when Dad took me to the States we lived in a commune?'

No, I say, she hadn't. 'You haven't really told me anything,' I add.

'Oh. Right,' she says, helping herself to more wine. 'Well, here goes. When we left here, we moved to an island off the east coast. They'd advertised for a carpenter and a friend of Dad's in the States let him know about it so that's where we ended up.'

'It sounds pretty alternative.'

'Well, it was, really,' she says. 'In the commune everyone took care of everyone else, and my father and I were happy there. I had friends of all ages and they taught me loads of things, like how to meditate, how to smoke dope and –'

'How old were you?'

'Only fourteen but everyone was smoking dope then.'

'Even your father?'

'Oh, yes – particularly him!'

'But didn't he mind you doing it?'

Naomi sighs. 'It's hard to explain,' she says. 'We were like hippies. It was free love and free speech, and I lost my virginity on my fifteenth birthday to this sweet Canadian boy called Ryan, and the commune had a party to celebrate.'

'Everybody knew?'

'Of course. It was my birthday present! Anyway, we only did it once because my father met a woman and she decided that communal living didn't suit her so they moved to California. I didn't want to stay in the commune on my own so I went too.'

'Why did they choose California?'

'Clancy – that's the woman's name – had come from

there and she told my father he could get lots of work making bespoke furniture. I think, by that stage, he'd got a bit worried about me living in the commune because he'd stopped smoking dope and I hadn't.'

'So, he took you to California and –'

'I loved it,' she says. 'We lived near San Diego but Clancy had to live in the city for her job so it was just me and Dad for a bit. I went to school there and it was like being in that film *Grease*, all proms and party dresses. The rest of the time I swam in the sea and surfed, and Dad took me riding, and he got loads of work and . . . Do you have any more wine?'

I get another bottle from the fridge.

'What time does your husband work till?' says Naomi, noticing it's past eleven.

'He's designing a set in London,' I say. 'I don't know when he'll get back. He's working all the hours God gave him at the moment.'

'He's a set designer?' says Naomi, opening the bottle. 'That sounds interesting.'

'It is, but it's pretty involving. It's his first really big job so . . .'

'So you're here on your own with the kids?'

'Pretty much.' I ask Naomi to continue her story.

'Everything was fine until my father decided Clancy, who had now lost her job, should move in.'

'Oh dear.'

'Yes. It was a disaster. I'd been very happy on my own with Dad, and then I lost him.'

'You *lost* him?'

'Figuratively speaking . . . I mean, I lost my mother

because she ran off with Fergus, and then I lost Dad to Clancy.'

'Have you seen your mother since that trip we went on to Ireland?'

'No. She writes to me sometimes and I write back but . . . we've really not connected since I last saw her with you.'

'Have you not wanted to see her?'

'Not really. I always preferred my dad and, anyway, my mother chose to abandon me. Before Dad and I left for the States, Mum said she was going to come over and say goodbye, and Dad thought it would be good if we went to some sort of counselling – try to heal the rifts in the family. I guess he knew I wouldn't be seeing her for a while. Anyway, he and I went but my mother never showed up.'

'She never showed up?'

'No. She didn't ring or let anyone know and, to be honest, Samantha, there's nothing much more to say about her.'

'Oh, that's terrible. Thank God for your father, though.'

'Yeah. Well, after Clancy moved in, I moved out.'

'How old were you?'

'Oh, nearly seventeen. I was so unhappy I left home. I met some bloke in a mall where I had a Saturday job in a record shop. He was called Chad – can you believe it? He had a place out in the San Fernando valley near Los Angeles and he seemed to like me, so I moved in with him.'

'How old was he?'

'About thirty, but after a couple of years I left him for Dean. He was thirty-five and he wasn't nice at all but I stayed with him for ages because I was frightened to leave him – I was twenty-five before I plucked up the courage. Then there were a few off-on boyfriends, but when I turned twenty-nine, I met Buck and he was very sweet, but my father hated him because he'd done time in a state penitentiary for drug-dealing and –'

'Buck was a *drug-dealer*?'

'He was a *reformed* drug-dealer. I kept telling Dad that, but he was so angry with me. He told me if I didn't leave Buck he'd never speak to me again, but I wasn't going to be pushed around by him so I stayed with Buck and Dad . . . Well, he stopped returning my calls.'

Naomi pours herself more wine.

'Naomi, that's terrible!'

'It was just over ten years ago and I haven't heard from him since.'

'So he doesn't know about Lexie?'

'Sure he does. I rang and left messages that I was pregnant. I wrote him letters. I even left a message for Clancy. Zip. He sent the letters back unopened but he must've had the phone calls.'

'But what if he didn't? What if he never knew he had a granddaughter?'

'He knows. I saw him in Los Angeles when Lexie was a baby. I was pushing her along in her pram, looking at the shops in Beverly Hills, and I noticed some of my father's furniture in this rather grand interiors shop so we went in. It was lovely, Samantha. He really was talented. He'd made this wonderful armoire and I was telling Lexie about her grandfather when suddenly there he was, staring in at me from outside the shop. He looked at the pram, then took Clancy's arm and walked off down the street.'

'But why didn't you stop him?'

'I ran out and shouted, "Dad," but he and Clancy disappeared round the corner without a backward glance.'

'That's dreadful.'

'Yes,' she says, blinking back tears. 'It was.'

'So he's never officially met Lexie?'

'No.'

'But that's so unlike your father! He used to be lovely. What happened to him to make him so mean? Was it Clancy?'

'No,' says Naomi, in a small voice.

'Well, what was it, then? Buck?'

'Maybe.'

'But surely he can't be that bad? I mean, you told me Lexie's father was a film producer so who cares if he went off the rails as a young man? He's obviously doing well now, isn't he?'

Naomi looks away.

'Well, isn't he?'

Naomi takes a glug of wine. 'Actually,' she says, 'there's something I have to tell you, Samantha, and I need you to promise you won't be angry.' She looks at me from under her fringe, like she used to as a little girl when she'd done something naughty. 'I mean, I really need to trust you.'

'Of course you can,' I say earnestly.

'I need to know that, regardless of what I tell you, you'll still be my friend.'

'Of course! Why wouldn't I? We're Ginger and Black Beauty.'

Naomi is now holding back tears. 'But I'm no real friend to you,' she says, 'because I've lied to you.'

I move to sit with her on the sofa. I take her hand. 'That's all right,' I tell her. 'We all lie sometimes. It can't be that bad. Now, why don't you tell me what's been going on?'

'Oh, you're such a good friend, Samantha!' she says. 'And I'm horrible.'

'No, you're not.'

'I am,' she says. 'I'm damaged. I'm horrible to everyone. In fact, I'm like Ginger. I kick and bite and do awful things to people.'

'Like what?'

'Like lying. I've lied to you about Buck. He's not a film producer. He works on a construction site.'

'Well, what's wrong with that? He brings in money, doesn't he? He makes you happy, doesn't he?'

Naomi nods, gulping a bit.

'And he's a good father, isn't he?'

Naomi is crying again. 'Well, I've rather lied about that too, you see.'

'What?'

She drinks some more wine. 'I'm not sure that Lexie is Buck's daughter.'

'*Not sure?*' I ask. 'Well, whose daughter is she?'

Naomi squirms. 'I'm not sure about that either,' she

says. 'I was seeing a couple of other guys on the side. I didn't tell Buck because he would have gone mad.'

'So any of those men, including Buck, could be Lexie's dad?'

'Well, yes.'

I sit in silence, trying to take it in. Eventually I say, 'So does Buck think he's her father?'

'He did for a while and it was fine, but then some rattlesnake next-door neighbour told him about my carrying-on and he chucked me and Lexie out and told us he never wanted to see us again.'

'But Lexie could be his child, couldn't she? Why don't you get her DNA-tested?'

'Because I know in my heart of hearts that she probably isn't his.'

'You know, Naomi, maybe it doesn't matter if Buck is her father or not. Think of Edward and John. It hasn't mattered to them. Anyway, how do you know he's not the father?'

'She doesn't look like him.'

'In what way doesn't she look like him?'

'Buck's black.'

'Oh,' I say. 'I see. But how did you persuade him she was his child in the first place?'

'I found some research that showed a black-white mix can produce a very white child or a very black child in some circumstances. Anyway, he wanted to believe it. He loved me and Lexie that much.'

'But who does Lexie think is her father?'

'Buck!' says Naomi. 'She doesn't seem bothered by the skin-colour thing and, anyway, I told her the same thing

I told Buck. It's all such a mess. That's why I'm here, Samantha. I've messed everything up and I don't have anywhere else to go and Lexie seems so distant sometimes. My father won't see me, Buck won't see me, so I just gathered up my savings and came home.'

'But what about your job? What about your boss? Have you told your boss you're here?'

Naomi is toying with her wine glass. 'Well, I don't actually have a job, Samantha. I made it up – in the same way I made my husband up.'

'But why?'

'I wanted you to think I was successful.'

'But I'm your friend, Naomi! It doesn't matter to me what you do.'

'Well, you say that but you barely kept in touch with me! You were supposed to be my friend. I sent you letters and I'd sign myself Ginger to make you remember how much you used to care for me.'

'But you said you'd forgotten about that until the other day.'

'Of course I hadn't! How could I possibly forget your happy childhood when I was so abandoned? When I wrote to you, you wrote back when you felt like it and your letters were full of your husband and kids and I thought if I told you the truth you'd look down on me like your mother did –'

'Now hang on a minute . . .'

'And I felt such a failure that I couldn't tell you the truth so I made it up. Then I felt better married to a film producer and I *was* in film PR and I *did* have a father and a husband who cared about me, instead of – of – being

Ginger. Always Ginger. Unloved and abandoned to my terrible fate.'

Naomi collapses, sobbing, on the sofa, her head in my lap, her wine glass tipped up on the floor.

'Oh, Naomi,' I say, stroking her hair. 'Oh, poor Naomi. But you're not Ginger. It's just a story.'

'That's not how I feel,' she says, between sobs. 'I don't know what to do. I'm an emotional wreck. I try to pretend I'm all sorted out but really I'm a walking disaster area. I'm so worried about Lexie and the way our lives are going I can barely think or sleep and we don't have a house and I don't have a job and . . . I've messed everything up.'

'But where are you staying? How are you surviving?'

'I've rented a room in a house in Reading. It's cheap but I didn't know where else to go and then – and then I thought of you. I thought, Samantha will help me, because you're my oldest, bestest friend, and I emailed you from an Internet café, and when you emailed me back I knew you'd help me. I knew if I could just get to your house you'd know what to do. As soon as I saw you on that doorstep, in your jeans and T-shirt, I knew my luck had changed.'

'I don't see how I can help. I mean, do you need some money? We don't have a lot spare but – Hang on, how are you going to pay the school fees?'

'I haven't been to see schools,' she says. 'How on earth could I? There's no way I can afford to send Lexie to boarding-school. I just wrote that email to see if you were around. How could I tell you the truth?'

'But you don't have to lie to me,' I say. 'Why didn't you just ring me and tell me what was going on?'

'I hadn't spoken to you in years! I just thought if I saw you you'd know what to do.'

'Well, I don't. What do you want me to say?'

'I don't know. I just think that you being my friend after all these years, my own Beauty, is an omen.'

Naomi has stopped crying now.

'An omen?' I ask.

'Yes.' She has now rescued her glass from the floor and poured herself yet more wine. 'You were thinking about me, how we were as children. I came home because I had nowhere else to go and I was happiest here. I thought if I found you, found my Beauty, life would . . .'

'Get better?'

Naomi nods. She looks very tired, which makes me feel sorry for her. 'Poor you,' I say. 'What can I do to help? I do really want to help, Naomi. I mean, Beauty did always try to help Ginger.'

Naomi sits quietly for a bit, then says, 'Have you ever felt lost and alone?' I tell her I have. 'Did you have Edward then?'

'Yes.' And then it comes to me. I can offer to have Lexie! Wasn't that what I wanted when I was alone with Edward? A few days' break? A chance to sort myself out? A chance to think straight without having to attend to a young child?

'I've got an idea,' I say. 'Why don't you let me have Lexie for a couple of nights? It's been lovely having her this afternoon and one more child makes no difference to me. Maybe it would give you a break. You could do with one, couldn't you?'

Naomi shakes her head. 'Thanks so much,' she says, 'but I couldn't. You're so kind and I'm sure Lexie's had a wonderful time, but you've got a husband and children who need you and – ' Naomi starts to cry again.

'No,' I say forcefully. 'I can manage all that. Having Lexie's no problem. Listen to me. I've been a single mother. I know how tough life can be. Let me help. It's the least I can do. After all, you've been a good friend to me and stayed in touch and – '

'You don't owe me, Samantha,' she says, tears falling down her face.

'I know that,' I say quietly, 'but sometimes, Naomi, you need to accept help where it's offered. It really is that simple. I don't care about your personal circumstances, I just want to help.'

Naomi's sobs lessen a bit. 'Well,' she says, 'it's true that I've been lonely and tired, and I don't like the house where I've rented the room. It's damp and the man downstairs smokes. Your house is lovely and warm. I wish I could give Lexie what you have – '

'Then let her stay for a couple of nights!' I say. 'She's more than welcome.'

'Is she? Really?' says Naomi. 'Are you sure? Because it would be wonderful to have a couple of days to look for a job and a better house. That's what I've been doing today, I'm afraid. I know I said I was looking at schools and working, but I was going round temping agencies.'

'Any luck?'

'Not yet. They've got my details. Maybe tomorrow I'll look for work as a cleaner.'

'Lexie can stay here, and in a couple of days you can pick her up.'

Naomi looks at me so gratefully it's embarrassing. 'Thank you so much, Samantha,' she says. 'You've always been so good at thinking of the right thing at the right time.'

Then I remember Lexie doesn't have any clothes with her. 'Hang on,' I say. 'Maybe you should take Lexie home now, and in the morning you can explain to her what's happening, pack her a bag and bring her back. She doesn't need much, just some clothes, a swimsuit, a toothbrush and –'

'No need,' says Naomi, jumping up. 'I've got some of her things in the back of the car. We've been travelling so much looking for somewhere to live that I've barely unpacked. I'm sorry, I'm so shambolic, and if you saw my car – I'm not sure what I've got.' She's bit wild-eyed now. 'Possibly some pyjamas and knickers and –'

'That's fine. We'll make do. I can always nip out and buy something for her if she's desperate.'

'No, no, don't do that,' says Naomi. 'I'll see what I can find.' She runs out of the house and comes back a minute later with a battered pink suitcase. 'Look!' she says. 'I wondered where this had gone. I thought we'd lost it and Lexie was so sad, but I found it under the seat. Do you think that's an omen too? Anyway, there's knickers, a dress and some T-shirts. Will that do?'

'Yes.'

'Oh, and there's a toothbrush, a pad of paper and some

other things. I just picked them up and – I'm not sure what else I've put in.'

'It'll be fine,' I say reassuringly.

'Now, I've written her a note explaining what's going on. It's on the pad in her suitcase so if you could show it to her in the morning . . .'

'Absolutely,' I say.

Naomi glances at the clock and gasps. 'Is it really half past midnight? God, I've got to go. Do you really think Lexie will be fine?'

'Don't worry,' I say. 'I'll ring you tomorrow and we'll see you soon.'

She's backing out through the door.

'I'm not sure if you should be driving. Haven't you had too much to drink? Why don't you stay too? You could tuck in with Lexie and explain it all to her in the morning,' I say.

'I can't do that. It's not my car. The man downstairs who smokes lent it to me and I promised to get it back for the morning. He uses it to go to work.'

'Oh.'

'So I must go now.' She blows me a kiss. 'We'll talk tomorrow, my Black Beauty,' she shouts, as she gets into her car. Then, with a jaunty wave, she drives off.

It's gone one before John gets into bed. At first I think he's Bennie but when I roll over I find a man next to me, not a small boy. 'John,' I murmur, half asleep. 'I've had the weirdest day.'

'So have I,' he says, tucking his hands into my knickers. 'Why are you wearing these in bed?'

'I was too tired to take them off. So many things have happened and I want to tell you but – God, your hands are cold! I thought it was warm outside.'

'Not at this time of night.'

'Well, take them away.'

'Sorry, darling. I just wanted to see you, to feel you. Now, what's been happening?'

'Too many things. It can wait until tomorrow.' I close my eyes.

John is nuzzling my ear. 'Are you really that tired?' he whispers, putting his hands in my knickers again. 'I don't think I can wait till tomorrow.'

'Mmm.'

'Really tired?' he says, kissing my neck.

'Mmm, sort of.'

'OK. I'll just go down and check my emails.'

That does it. I open my eyes and pull him back towards me. 'You can't,' I say. 'There's a girl asleep in the study.'

'A girl?'

'Yes, she's called Lexie and . . . Oh, God, it's so complicated but she's my childhood friend Naomi's daughter and I've offered to have her here for a couple of nights.'

'Why?' he says.

I sigh. 'I was Black Beauty and she was Ginger.'

He kisses my neck again. 'I have no idea what you are talking about but, hey, does that mean you've got your wish?'

'What wish?'

'For a girl?'

I reach for John's hands and put them back in my knickers. 'She's not mine,' I say.

'Shall we make one, then?' he says.

'Yes,' I say, 'but you need protection. The timing's not right.'

John groans. 'God, you're serious, aren't you?' He leans over to the drawer in his bedside table.

'Protection?' I say.

'Protection,' he says.

It's two thirty when Bennie comes in. I only know this because I wake up briefly, then fall asleep again, Bennie tucked between the two of us.

'Night-night, Mummy,' he says.

'Night-night, Bennie,' I say. For once, John stays exactly where he is.

A Thief

I wake up way before seven and immediately remember Lexie. Yesterday feels so long ago. I'm about to wake John to tell him about her but he looks too peaceful, with Bennie tucked up against him. Then I hear giggling and two sets of footsteps descending the stairs.

A minute later, the television goes on and I can hear bread being put into the toaster. Oh, bless Edward. He and Stanley have got up to be ready when Stanley's mother arrives. That means it must be about six thirty. I suppose I ought to get up with them, really. Stanley's mother is the type of woman who'd expect that. She's terribly neat and organized, always running focus groups and motivational courses for people working in large companies. Maybe I should get her to motivate me. I've hardly written a word on *Our Fridges, Our Selves*. I wonder if she'd make me play that trust game with John – you have to stand on a table, then fall backwards with your eyes shut. 'But why would anyone do that?' I asked her.

'Because their work colleagues are supposed to catch them,' she said. 'It's called a trust game.'

'Has it ever gone wrong?'

'No,' she said. 'I mean, what kind of people wouldn't catch someone they work with?'

I start giggling. John would be horrified if I suggested we play a trust game. He'd never hold my weight! Maybe

I should suggest it to Adele, Belinda, Liza and all the other mothers. We could go to Starbucks and practise falling on to each other. Not that any of them would feel they had to catch me, I'm pretty sure.

I get up, put on my dressing-gown and go downstairs. Edward is sitting on the Chair, watching a cartoon and munching an alien bagel. 'Morning, Edward,' I say. He doesn't acknowledge me.

Stanley's in the kitchen, poking a knife into the toaster. 'Hi, Edward's mum,' he says. I'm about to tell him it's probably not the best idea to stick a metal object into a live electrical one when he says, 'Now, I know I'm not supposed to stick a knife into the toaster, Edward's mum, but I've turned it off at the plug. Edward told me how he toasts a whole bagel so I was copying him but –' There's a knock at the door.

'My mum!' says Stanley, abandoning the burnt bagel. He tears off to open the door.

' 'Bye, Edward!' he shouts. Still fixated on the television, Edward raises a hand.

I go to the door where Laura, Stanley's mother, is standing in the sunshine. 'What a lovely day,' she says to me.

I hear the alarm clock go off in our bedroom. Damn. I forgot about taking my temperature and now the graph will be wrong because I've done something before I put the blasted misreading thermometer into my mouth.

'Your family's getting up early, these days,' says Laura, who has, in the past, made a point of telling us that she gets up at six thirty as 'The early bird catches the worm.'

This always discombobulates Edward. 'I don't want a worm,' he said to me once. 'Should I?'

'I got up because I heard Edward and Stanley about,' I say.

'Have you had breakfast?' she asks Stanley.

'Yes,' says Stanley.

'What did you have?'

'Well, I tried to have an alien bagel but it got stuck.'

'An alien bagel?'

'It's one of Edward's inventions,' I say.

Just then the study door opens and a sleepy, blinking Lexie emerges. 'Where am I?' she says.

'Hi, Lexie,' says Stanley.

I go to give her a hug. 'It's Samantha,' I say.

'Oh, hi,' she says. 'Where's my mum? Why am I still here?'

I hear another door open. Oh, no. It'll be John, and he won't have any clothes on because he never has when he gets up and he tends to wander round the house in the nude, regardless of who's here.

''Bye then, Stanley,' I say, as I try to close the door. ''Bye, Laura.'

'Samantha!' says Laura. 'I was wondering if I could take an apple for –' She gives a little shriek.

John is standing at the top of the stairs, stretching and yawning. As I predicted, he isn't wearing a stitch.

'Edward! I can see your dad's wiggle-wiggle!' says Stanley.

'John!' I say, pushing Lexie behind me. 'We have company.'

John opens his eyes. 'Oh, hello, Laura,' he says, and disappears into the bedroom.

'I'm sorry,' I say to Laura. 'He didn't know you were here. Now, I'll get you that apple.'

'Don't worry,' she says, and marches Stanley across the road. I can hear Stanley saying, 'The weirdest thing happened to us yesterday when we went for a walk by the river . . .'

I groan as I shut the door.

'Come on, Lexie,' I say, 'let's get you some breakfast and I'll tell you why you're still here.'

An hour later, I have explained to Lexie that her mother came to pick her up last night but that I'd asked if she could stay a bit longer.

'How much longer?'

'A couple of nights, like a mini-holiday,' I said.

'I like the sound of that,' Lexie said. 'I've never been on holiday before.' I told her she didn't have to worry about clothes because her mother had found an old suitcase in the car and put some in it for her.

'The suitcase with the horse picture on?' said Lexie, excitedly. 'I thought she'd lost it. She loses everything.'

'Well, she found it under the front seat and you had some clothes in the boot too.'

'Yes, I do always have clothes with me and I don't think we've unpacked properly yet anyway. Mum told me not to clear my clothes out of the car yesterday because she said I might need them.'

'Why?' I said. 'Is it because you've moved around a lot?'

'No,' said Lexie, screwing up her face thoughtfully. 'I think it's because she thought they might, erm, come in useful.'

'Your mother said she'd written a note for you on the pad in your case so if you want to look at it . . .'

Lexie went and got the pad, then came back into the kitchen. 'Do you know where it is?' she asked.

I flicked through the pad. 'Here.'

'I'll read it out,' said Lexie. She coughed and patted her chest as if she was in a public-speaking competition. '"Dear Lexie, When you wake up this morning you will find that you are still at Samantha's." Well, that's true isn't it?' she said. 'I know I'm still here, don't I?'

'Yes,' I said.

'"Samantha is my oldest friend and I am sure you will have a lovely time with her and her family. She will make you feel safe for she always made me feel safe as a little girl. I'm sorry I've had to leave you but this is a better place for you. I hope you'll come to understand that and, remember, I love you so much and will miss you. Your loving mother, Naomi.

'"PS Keep reading *Black Beauty*. Samantha will explain."'

Lexie paused. 'How long am I staying with you again?' she asked.

'A day or two,' I said, confused. It was a strange note to write when you were going to be away for such a short time.

'OK,' said Lexie. 'Sometimes Mum left me notes back home saying she was going out and she'd be back later but I'd stay awake till dawn and she never was.'

'Oh,' I said. 'Did you have a babysitter?'

'No,' said Lexie, dreamily. 'Usually my dad was home but . . .' her face clouded '. . . we had to leave him, I don't know why, and then I was on my own sometimes and it made me nervous. I'd try to make myself go back to sleep but I never felt safe on my own.'

'Well,' I said, 'you won't be on your own here. There's far too many of us. You'll have a good time, I hope.'

'Oh, I'm sure I will! I'd much rather be here. Our flat's horrible and Mum told me you were nice and I might like being with you.'

John appeared, now dressed, carrying Jamie on one arm and Bennie on his back. 'You're the girl who's living in the study,' he said, and smiled. Then he said he had to go. 'The runners are playing up again,' he added ruefully. Lexie asked him what he did for a living and John told her about his open-air set and how he had to get unicorns to fly through the air, and Lexie told him that unicorns were her favourite animal, and he said she should come and see the play and she said she'd love to. Bennie said he, too, would like to see the play and that he'd quite like to go now, if John would take him, and John just laughed and kissed us goodbye, even Lexie, and told us he'd see us later.

'We've got a trial run tonight,' he said, grabbing a slice of toast and walking out of the door. I followed him. 'It's a dress rehearsal in front of an audience, the first time anyone's seen the whole thing. And when I've finished this play, Samantha, I'm going to take you and the children out for a real family day or on holiday. And I'll treat *you* to a slap-up meal, then maybe a night of hanky-panky because I love you, Mrs Smythe.' With that he swung off down the drive to his car.

I turned back to the house and, through the kitchen windows, saw that Lexie had hoisted Jamie on to a breakfast stool and was pouring milk on his Rice Krispies. He was gazing at her adoringly. I noticed she had put on an apron. The sight of her being a pretend-mother made my heart lurch. Poor Lexie. All she wants is to be part of a family. I resolved then and there that she should become part of ours. That's how you save people, isn't it? I thought. That was how Ginger was saved before life took a turn for the worse. She was shown love and respect, and she became part of a wider stableyard rather than a lonely individual. I shall give Lexie that wider stableyard, that comfy warm stable and warm bran mash to eat at night, I thought. I shall love her back to happiness. I have love to spare, after all.

At nine Wendy comes downstairs. Remarkably, she's dressed.

'Hiya, mate,' she says to Edward, who is still watching the television, then comes into the kitchen and makes for the cupboard.

'Cereal again?' I ask.

'Yeah, that bleedin' horrible muesli,' she says, then sees Lexie. 'Hello, darlin',' she says. 'Did ya mam not come and pick ya up?'

'Naomi did come,' I say, 'but we decided between us that it would be fun for Lexie to stay here a couple of nights.'

'It's like being on holiday,' says Lexie.

'Great,' says Wendy. 'Hey, Mrs S, you gotta girl! Now, what shall we all do?'

I tell Wendy I hadn't thought of doing anything in particular.

'Nah!' says Wendy. 'We gotta girl here who's on her hols and we've gotta have fun.'

I ask Wendy what she thinks we should do.

'Go shopping!' she says. 'That's what girls like to do. I bet you like shopping, don'tcha, little miss?'

Lexie blushes.

'See?' says Wendy. 'And hey, Mrs S, you ain't been shopping for an age!'

'Is that true?' says Lexie.

'Yes.'

'My mum loves shopping,' Lexie continues. 'She's always taking me to Beverly Hills and showing me the dresses she's going to buy me but we never actually buy them.'

'Well, it ain't Beverly Hills here,' says Wendy, 'but we'll pretend it is.' I notice that she's wearing a skirt in a dusky pink colour. It's silky and comes to just below her knees. My God! Wendy actually has a waist and quite shapely legs.

'You're wearing a skirt,' I say. 'You never wear a skirt. You always wear jeans.'

Wendy blushes. 'It's gonna be hot today,' she says.

'It suits you,' I say, and she blushes even more. I'm about to ask if she's lost weight when Edward appears. His eyes are red and his hair is standing on end.

'I'm not going shopping,' he says.

'Yes, you are,' I say to him.

'I–I wanna go shopping,' says Bennie.

'Well, I'm not coming,' says Edward.

'What are you going to do instead?' I ask him.

'I'll go to Josh's house.'

'Who says?'

'Josh's mum. She's on the telephone right now.'

'Christ, Edward! Why didn't you tell me?'

'I just did,' he says.

I rush into the study and pick up the phone.

'Liza,' I pant, 'I'm very sorry. Edward's only just told me you were hanging on.'

'Have you been working out?'

'No.'

'It's just that you're panting.'

'I ran for the phone.'

'That shouldn't make you pant.'

'Well, it does.'

'Maybe you're unfit. I have this trainer –'

'I know,' I say.

'He's called Adam and he's very good. He's looking for more clients.'

'I don't have any spare time or cash, Liza,' I say, 'and, anyway, I walk the dog most days.'

'Where?'

'By the river. I was there yesterday, actually.' I find myself telling her about Gary White sunbathing naked.

'No!' Then she says she has to go as she's due at a lunch meeting in London. 'I'm late,' she says. 'I've done a session with Adam this morning and now I must fly.'

If she's not there, who will be looking after Josh and Edward? I ask.

'Do ten-year-olds need looking after?'

'Who's checking on them?' I say.

'My au pair Basia,' she says. 'Look, please let Edward come over. Josh really needs cheering up. He's been so difficult recently. His school report was dreadful and when I tried to talk to him about it, he wouldn't say anything. He seems so sad and I don't know why.'

'I'll drop Edward round in a bit,' I say, but after she's hung up, I think about what she said. She's right. Josh *is* sad. But why?

Why Children Get Sad

This is a difficult one because children don't come towards you waving a box of Ritalin, saying, 'I'm sad and I know why.' Neither do they come armed with the number of ChildLine telling you they want to talk to Esther Rantzen about their feelings. Sometimes children tell you they're depressed or sad or both at the same time. In fact, there's a huge debate that goes on ad infinitum *among experts about whether or not young children, even toddlers, can experience depression. But how do you know if your child is depressed?*

Being sad is different from being depressed. Depression is inexplicable, long term and difficult to deal with. It is not necessarily logical. Depression is when you can't see why you should bother to get up in the morning. Depression is when you want to spend all your money, then kill yourself. Depression doesn't make sense and no one can snap you out of it. A cup of tea and a hug don't help.

So, I don't think young children get depressed. I think they get down – because adults, parents, sometimes treat them like morons. I have seen Liza with Josh. I have seen her absentmindedly pat his head as she takes a business call on her mobile. I can see him willing her to get off the phone, bend down and kiss him goodbye – or maybe not as that's probably embarrassing, but to do something that reaffirms in Josh's mind that, for this minute, he matters to her above all else. He's about to go into school, and the au pair picks him up, so he won't see his mother again until tomorrow morning, but there she is, buying this and selling that on the phone, utterly unaware of her son's needs. Doesn't she see his face fall as she marches back to the car, forgetting to wave? Now Josh has found a way of getting his mother's attention. He has turned into the Troublesome Boy in the Class.

This is how conversations go between the Teacher of the Troublesome Boy in the Class Who Was Once Not Troublesome At All and the Mother or Father of the Troublesome Boy in the Class.

The Teacher has rung Liza, for it is she, on her mobile.

Liza (snappily): 'Yes? What? Who is this?'

Teacher: 'It's Miss Bland, Josh's teacher.'

Liza: 'Miss Who?'

Teacher: 'Bland. I teach Josh's year at school.'

Liza: 'Oh. Right. Well, is there a problem? I have to be in a meeting in ten minutes.'

Teacher: 'Yes, actually, there is a problem. Maybe I should call you back when you have more time.'

Liza: 'There's a problem? With Josh? What kind of a problem? Has he been fighting in the playground again?'

Teacher: 'No, it's not that.'

Liza (breathing a huge sigh of relief): 'We did talk to him about it, you see. We told him if he kept on doing it we'd take away his PlayStation.'

Teacher: 'Well, what I really want to discuss is his behaviour.'

Liza: 'What's wrong with it?'

Teacher: 'I think it's best if you and your husband come into the school and I can explain it more fully to you.'

Liza: 'Can't you do that now? I'm so fearfully busy and my husband is away.'

Teacher (firmly): 'No, I think you ought to come in.'

The upshot, of course, is that Liza goes into school one evening and Miss Bland tells her what everyone else has long since known: that Josh has turned from being Such a Good Boy into a disruptive troublemaker. She shows Liza his books. They have swear words scrawled all over them. Liza is shocked, especially at the one that says 'Mum is a f-ing cow.'

'Do other children write this?' Liza asks. The teacher tells her no. She tells her that it is only Josh who swears in class and it is only Josh who refuses to do any work during school hours, then hands in shoddy homework the next day.

'But the au pair does it with him!' says Liza, forgetting that the au pair is Polish and has come to learn English. The teacher tells Liza that Josh's marks are plummeting, that he has detention every other day and that, to be frank, no one knows what's wrong with him.

Liza leaves the meeting in tears. She is puzzled, confused, humiliated. When she gets home, she opens a bottle of wine, calls Belinda and sobs down the phone. 'Why is J-J-Josh doing this to me?' She's now on her second glass of wine.

'I don't know,' says Belinda, sympathetically.

'I-i-is Jeremy like this?'

Belinda doesn't know what to say for, of course, Jeremy is not like this at all. Jeremy is the school star. He is always happy, always perfect – maybe too perfect I think sometimes. I don't understand how children can be that perfect, but there you go. Maybe that's just me.

'No, Jeremy isn't disruptive,' says Belinda, 'but then again I am at home with him a lot.'

Liza's warning bells are ringing. 'Oh, so you think it's because I'm not at home very much, do you?'

'No, I didn't say that,' says Belinda, backtracking like crazy.

'You think he feels neglected?'

'I didn't say that either. I meant that I know Jeremy very well, that's all. I don't have to keep playing catch-up with him.'

'Oh, God,' says Liza, wailing again. 'I'm just so busy. You don't understand, Belinda. I have to work this hard. I'm the only person in the office who has a child. If you don't seem willing or you go home early, you never get promoted.'

'But, Liza, you don't get home until eight!'

'That's the same as everybody else. That's even early sometimes! Oh, Belinda, what am I going to do?'

'I don't know. Try to talk to Josh about it? Maybe spend more time with him at weekends? Come home earlier? Get to know his friends? I can't think of anything else.'

Edward groaned when I told him a few weeks ago that he was going to spend a Saturday at Josh's house. 'Oh, no,' he said. 'I don't want to go to his house.'

'Why not?' I asked.

*'He's so snap-mouthed.'**

'What do you mean?'

'If you ask to borrow his rubber, he says, "Why should I let you, Brainache?" then throws it at you.'

'He calls you Brainache?'

'Not just me. He calls Stanley, F-word Brainache.'

'He uses the F-word?'

'All the time.'

'Has anyone told the teachers?'

'I have but I don't want to keep telling them because then Josh will find out and beat me up. He threw a stone at Jeremy. So I don't want to go to his house.'

'I can understand that,' I said, 'but he used to be a nice boy, didn't he?'

'Oh, yes,' said Edward.

'So there must be reasons why he's not nice now, don't you think?'

'Maybe he doesn't wear lucky trousers like I do.'*

'I don't think it's to do with that. Imagine if you didn't see me for more than an hour in the morning.'

'Why would that happen?'

'Maybe I had to work or something. Would you like that?'

'No, I wouldn't like it one bit and neither would Bennie and Jamie. We'd miss you and no one would pack our lunch, would they?'

'But I'm not going to do that,' I say, as his eyes fill with tears. 'I'm just saying imagine if he was you. How would you feel?'

'Miserable.'

'Yes, miserable and sad, and what might you do then?'

'Kill myself.'

'Apart from that.'

'Look after Bennie and Jamie.'

'Well, that's sweet of you to say so but might you feel angry?'

'With you?' Edward thought. 'Yes, I might.'

'Do you think you might be badly behaved and naughty?'

'I suppose so.'

'So that's how Josh is. And he needs friends because he's sad and cross. He never sees his mummy and he's lonely. It might help him feel better if you went to play at his house.'

Edward was quiet for a long time. 'I still don't want to go there,' he said eventually.

'He has a PlayStation.'

'When I am going?'

'I don't mind Josh, really,' Edward says, when I'm off the phone. 'I like his PlayStation and I don't want to go shopping.'

I tell Edward we'll drop him off on the way to the shops and pick him up on the way back.

'OK,' he says happily, and that's that.

We're in the middle of the largest department store in our local shopping centre when my mobile rings. I'm trying on a dress that I could tell was too small before I put it over my head, and Lexie is in another cubicle trying on some pedal-pushers, when Adele's number flashes up. Wendy seems to have grabbed half the shop to try on and has locked herself into another cubicle with Bennie and Jamie.

'Adele?' I say, wriggling the skirt part over my hips. 'I'm trying on clothes. Can you call me back?'

'No,' she says. 'I need to talk to you now.'

'Why?' I say. 'I can't get this bloody dress on. If I pull any more, it's going to split.'

'Why don't you try a bigger size?'

'It's the biggest they've got. I don't think they do dresses to fit a she-elephant like me.'

'You're not a she-elephant – and I know why you're buying new clothes. It's because you're going out with Gary White.'

'I'm not! Who told you that?'

'Liza. She said you'd seen him naked. Did you?'

'Well, not me,' I say. 'I –'

'Are you having an affair with him?'

'*No! Absolutely not!*'

'So how did you see him naked?'

'I just told you. I didn't. I saw him semi-naked. Didn't Liza tell you what happened by the river?'

'Yes, but it sounded so improbable.'

'It's true,' I say. 'God, news travels fast, doesn't it?'

Just then, Lexie comes in, very pretty and summery in the trousers and a pink top. 'You look lovely,' I say.

'I haven't had any new clothes for ages.' Then she says she's going to try on a dress Wendy picked out for her.

'Who are you talking to?' says Adele.

'Oh, my friend's daughter, Lexie. She's staying with us for a couple of nights.'

'Oh, typical you, Samantha.'

'What do you mean?'

'Picking up life's waifs and strays.'

'Lexie is not a waif or stray. She is my friend's daughter and she is having a mini-holiday with us while her mother relocates from LA to here.'

'Why on earth does she want to do that? You can get great non-surgical facelifts in LA.'

'Because she's from here and she wants her daughter to go to school here.'

'Anyway, I rang to ask on behalf of Belinda if you want to come to her first Colour Me Wonderful party in two days' time. It's at her house, it starts at eleven a.m. and you can bring the kids but none of the rest of us are, so –'

'I'd love to come,' I say quickly. 'The children can stay with Wendy. It won't go on that long, will it?'

'A couple of hours, maybe. Oh, and will she actually look after them? Where is she now?'

'Here, trying on clothes.'

'Ha! They must do clothes in she-elephant sizes then.'

'Actually,' I say, 'she's lost weight.'

'Impossible!'

'No. She has a waistline.' I tell Adele I have to go. 'This dress is stuck,' I tell her. 'I'm going to need both hands to get out of it.'

I hang up and tug at it. It really is stuck. I wiggle some more. It's straining at the seams. If I pull at it any harder it will start to rip. I gaze at myself in the mirror. It's not a flattering look, really – off-white bra, huge boobs, bulging shoulders, saggy underarms and a dress stuck round my hips with a hint of some flesh-coloured knickers peeking out. Christ! I can't even get my underwear to match.

The door to the cubicle opens and Jamie toddles in, wearing a pair of high-heeled shoes and a pink feather boa round his neck. He is giggling. Bennie follows him, in a tank top, a skirt and his clumpy trainers. He has fastened a comb with a flower on it in his hair. 'I'm a girl,' he says. 'I've got lipstick.'

It's true. He has. 'Who put it on you?' I ask.

'W-Wendy,' he says.

'Where is she?' I say.

'Here!' says Wendy's voice. 'Ah'm using the full-length mirror. Come and see what you think.'

I pull my T-shirt over the top of the dress, which is now round my middle, and go out into the communal changing area. Wendy is standing with her back towards me. She's wearing a midnight blue dress that has slightly puffed sleeves and a low neck. It is nipped in at the waist, and drops to her knees in a tulip shape. She has let her blonde hair fall to her shoulders, put on some makeup and some strappy summer wedges. 'You look amazing!' I say.

'Do I?' she says.

'Yes! You've lost so much weight.'

'Yeah, but you can still pinch an inch, Mrs S,' she says.

'Maybe, but before you had, well . . .'

'A tyre round me middle?'

'Erm, yes. And now you have an inner tube.'

'Yeah, well, Ah've been dieting, Mrs S, y'know.'

'It's working. Really.'

Lexie appears in a rather sophisticated red spaghetti-strap ruffled summer dress, with sprigs of white flowers on the fabric.

'Oh, Wendy!' says Lexie. 'That dress really suits you!'

'And that one suits you, princess.'

Lexie stands in front of the mirror. 'I like it a lot,' she says. 'What do you think, Samantha?'

I tell her I like it but there's something I'm not sure about. 'The red looks good with your colouring but . . .'

'But what?' says Wendy. 'It's perfect.'

'I preferred you in the pedal-pushers and the pink top. It's a more age-appropriate look.'

'Balls to that!' says Wendy. 'You're a man-magnet in that red dress, Lexie!'

'Yes, and she's also a ten-year-old who has better things to do than be a "man-magnet".'

'But I was wearing stuff like that at Lexie's age,' says Wendy.

Lexie notices what I'm wearing. 'What about your dress?'

'Oh, I don't like it.' I'm retreating into my cubicle. 'It's not my style.'

'Oh, c'mon, Mrs S!' says Wendy. 'Why've you dragged that dirty T-shirt over the top? That dress's got a pretty neckline, hasn't it?'

'I can't do the buttons up at the top and now it's got stuck over my hips and I can't get out of it.'

Lexie's eyes widen. 'Can't get out of it?' she says. 'What are you going to do?'

'I'll have to get it cut off and pay for it, I suppose.'

'No!' says Wendy. 'Ah'll help ya.'

We go into the cubicle, where Bennie and Jamie are solemnly taking everything out of my handbag, rubbing hand cream on their faces and drawing on the mirror with my lip-gloss.

'What are you doin', naughties?' says Wendy.

'We–we're decorating,' says Bennie.

'Don't ruin my lip-gloss,' I say, as Jamie starts jabbing the end into the carpet.

''Ip doss,' he says.

'He's really talking now, Mrs S, isn't he?' says Wendy. Then she bends down, giving me a good view of her tanned cleavage, and tugs at the dress. There's a tearing noise and then, thank God, it's off.

'It ripped,' I say.

'Don't worry about it,' says Wendy. 'No one will know it's you.'

'But I should pay for it, shouldn't I?'

'Don't be a wally. Ah'm gonna get this dress and you can buy Lexie that stuff you want to get for her and no one'll notice that dress was too small for ya.'

'But that's immoral,' I say.

'Bullshit! These stores rip you off anyway. That's what

me mam always used to say. Jeez, we're spending a fortune in here and you're worried about one dress. Forget it.'

On the way home in the car, Bennie and Jamie squabble over the feather boa I bought Lexie. It was like a booby prize, really. Lexie was upset when I told her I was only getting the pedal-pushers and the T-shirt. 'But the dress was pretty too, wasn't it?' she said.

'Yes, but I prefer you in the other outfit.'

'But the other outfit's plain, isn't it?'

'I don't think so.'

'That's what Wendy said.'

Wendy was waving at me from the checkout. She was buying the midnight blue dress, a low-cut top and some hipster jeans. 'Well, maybe Wendy doesn't really understand that you're ten, not sixteen.'

'I don't want to be ten any more. I want to be sixteen.'

'Well, you can't,' I said. I told her I'd buy her the boa. 'I had one just like this when I was your age and I loved it.'

'Oh,' said Lexie, sulkily.

She hasn't said a word since we left the shop. I watch her in the rear-view mirror. She's staring out of the window and refusing to appear interested in anything, which is odd as Bennie and Jamie are about to rip up the boa.

'Th-this is mine,' says Bennie, trying to take it out of the bag.

''Smine,' says Jamie, finding the other end.

'M-my feathers,' says Bennie, ripping a handful off.

''Smine.'

Jamie is biting the feathers. He has a few stuck round his mouth. He looks like a chick.

'Jamie!' I say. 'Stop that!'

Wendy, who is sitting in the passenger seat, leans back to Jamie and grabs the boa.

''Smine!' yells Jamie, bursting into tears.

'M-my feathers!' yells Bennie.

They cry all the way to Josh's house.

When we arrive Edward is at the door. When he sees the car he flies out.

'Mum!' he says, as he throws himself into my arms.

'Edward!' I'm surprised. He hasn't flung himself into my arms for ages.

'Can we go now?' he says.

'Is Liza there?'

'Who's Liza?'

'Josh's mum.'

'No. It's that woman who speaks funny and whose name begins with a B.'

'Basia.'

'Yes. She's there.'

'Well, I'd better go and say thank you to her.'

'What for?' says Edward. 'She hasn't given me anything to eat and I'm starving.'

'Well, did you ask for some food?'

'Yes! She just gave me sweets!'

'I thought you liked sweets,' says Wendy, who has got out of the car and is standing behind me.

'I do,' says Edward, 'but not when there's nothing else to eat. Josh doesn't have a single apple in his house.'

Just then Josh appears. 'Going, are you?' he says.

'Yeah,' says Edward.

'Say thank you to Josh,' I say to Edward.

'No,' says Edward.

'Didn't you have a good time?' says Josh, too casually.

'Not really,' says Edward. 'You didn't let me play on the PlayStation and that's all you've done.'

'Oh, poor little Edward,' says Josh. 'You're too stupid to play my games.'

'Josh!' I say.

'I'm not stupid,' says Edward. 'I was bored!'

'Only cos you didn't understand it, mummy's boy.'

I'm so shocked, I don't know what to say.

'I'm not a mummy's boy!' says Edward, stepping closer to me.

'Yes, you are. Look at you trying to hide behind her now.'

'Josh!' I say again.

'What?' he says, in a challenging fashion.

'That's enough,' says Wendy, now moving towards Josh. 'Edward isn't stupid or a mummy's boy. It's you who's stupid for playing the daggy games all day.'

Josh stares at her.

'We're going now, Josh,' she says, 'and we ain't coming back.'

'Good,' he says, as we get into the car.

'H-hello, Edward,' says Bennie, once his brother has squashed into the back.

Edward doesn't say anything. He just looks out of the window in the opposite direction from Josh.

'Are you having an argument with that big boy?'

'No,' says Edward, sullenly.

'Is he not a nice boy?'

'No.'

'D-did you eat some sweets at his house?'

'Yes.'

'H-have you got any left?'

'No.'

'Mummy,' says Bennie, as I reverse out of the drive, 'E-edward isn't talking to me. Words won't come out of his mouth.'

'Just leave him alone,' I say. 'He's had a tiring day.'

Suddenly Lexie turns to Edward.

'I put two fingers up at that boy like this,' she says, flicking a V at everyone in the car.

'Did you?' says Edward, rather gleefully.

'Yes,' says Lexie, defiantly.

'Like this?' says Edward, copying her.

'Yes,' says Lexie.

'L-like this?' says Bennie, waving two fingers the wrong way round.

'No, that's V for Victory,' says Lexie. 'You have to do it the other way.'

'I am not sure anyone should be making V-signs,' I say.

'But that boy was rude to you,' Lexie says. 'I heard him through the window. My mum says that if someone's rude to you, you can make that sign at them.'

'What does it mean?' says Edward.

'It means "f–"'

'It means "Stuff you",' I say, butting in.

'Yeah,' says Wendy. 'It means, "Sod off, you daggy person," and that boy really is a dag. What's wrong with him?'

'I don't know,' says Edward. 'He wasn't very nice to me.'

'He wasn't nice to you the last time you went round either,' I say.

'Why did you go, then?' asks Lexie.

'I didn't want to come shopping.'

A Humbug

Tonight I'm exhausted. I've spent hours clearing up the clothes and makeup the children got out. I've cooked, washed-up and ferried glasses of water from one child to another. I've found Edward a book to read – 'Not *Black Beauty*,' he said. 'Something more violent' – I've read to Jamie and Bennie, and helped Lexie finish her next chapter of *Black Beauty*. I've also telephoned Liza. I don't usually make a fuss but tonight I couldn't help it.

I kept thinking of Josh and how malicious he was to Edward. I spent an age wondering if I should interfere. All the late afternoon and early evening, as I watched Bennie running around in his blue Power Rangers outfit that used to belong to Edward, I thought about what I should say to Liza. Josh should be doing this. He should be having fun. He should be here, using Beady as a teleporter to a different world with Bennie. I don't suppose Josh has much fun.

Then I saw Edward dressed up as a yellow-dog-meets-a-vampire. He had on his ancient Hallowe'en outfit that no longer fits him on his top half and Bennie's yellow fluffy dog outfit on his bottom half with the yellow dog's head lolling round his nether regions. Lexie had abandoned her new clothes pretty quickly and ended up borrowing an oversize dress from Wendy, which she cinched in at the waist with a belt. She also borrowed an old hat of my mother's from the seventies – a sort of silk turban – and wandered around looking like a film star. Jamie wore nothing but a pair of my high-heeled shoes and the feather boa. I watched them play in the garden for ages and, as I watched them, I thought about Josh. Then I went inside and telephoned Liza. She wasn't there so I left a message.

'Liza,' I said, 'it's Samantha and I need to talk to you. It was very kind of you to invite Edward over but, actually, I don't think he had a particularly good time, and when I went to pick him up, Josh was very rude to me and him. I don't want to make a big deal of it but I do think you should know. Maybe we can have a chat when you get in. Thanks so much.'

By eleven Liza hasn't rung. I've spent two hours staring at my computer, willing myself to work on *Our Fridges, Our Selves*. I've written all the rock-star copy, which is good, but am now struggling with the fridge belonging to a television presenter. I start writing about it as if it's a contender in *Through The Keyhole*: 'Now, this skinny little minx has nothing in her fridge apart from champagne and caviar. See? Who could possibly exist on that?' Then I stop and think. Have I done the wrong thing in telephoning Liza? Maybe I should ring Adele and ask her. But it's too late now so I sit and think about the children. Why are Josh and Lexie so sad? Are my own children sad but I can't see it?

I'm just pondering this when Bennie comes downstairs to the sitting room, crying. He stands before me, arms out, and I pull him on to my lap. 'Why are you crying, Bennie?' I ask him, kissing the top of his head.

'Wh-where's Daddy?' he says.

I've hardly thought about John all day. In fact, wasn't today his run-through? I feel guilty. I should have called and wished him luck. 'Oh, Bennie,' I say sighing. 'Daddy isn't here yet, darling. He's at work.'

'I want him here, Mummy,' says Bennie, sniffling and cuddling into me.

'I want him here too,' I say, 'but Daddy's only going to be working hard for a bit longer.'

Bennie snuggles into me some more. I can smell his breath – milky and sweet. He rubs his hands up and down my arms, a sure sign that he's about to nod off. Then he says, rather sleepily, 'Is – is work like school, Mummy?'

'Yes, quite like school.'

'B-but I hate school.'

'I know, darling, but it will get better, I promise. You've got all the summer holiday to look forward to and . . . Do you know? Edward used to hate school and now he loves it.'

'That's cos he's got Stanley. But that big boy isn't his friend, is he?'

'No – and you've got friends, Bennie,' I say encouragingly. 'You'll see them in September when you go back.'

'No,' he says sadly, 'I haven't got friends.'

'Yes, you have.'

'N-no, I haven't. I miss you and Jamie.'

'We miss you too, darling,' I say. 'But, Bennie, you're a little boy and everyone likes you.'

'Edward told me I haven't got any friends.' Bennie looks so sad it breaks my heart. He starts crying again. Edward? Blast him!

'Bennie,' I say, 'Edward isn't telling you the truth. Don't listen when he says silly things like that.' I kiss the top of his head.

'I'm so tired and sad, Mummy,' he says. 'Can I sleep with you?'

Bennie puts his curly blond head on my arm and starts stroking his own arm as he always does when he really, really wants to go to sleep. I know I should say no. I promised myself Bennie wouldn't sleep with me any more, but now the combination of Bennie, his soft, downy skin and his rhythmic stroking makes me feel very tired.

'Of course you can,' I say. 'I'll carry you to my bed, then come downstairs, lock up and I'll be in bed with you, OK?'

'Cuddle,' he murmurs, when I take him upstairs, so I lie with him for a bit as he fusses and twitches, moving this way and that. He opens his eyes occasionally to check I'm still with him and, finally, he falls asleep. He rolls on to his back and I see his body relax.

On the way downstairs, I pass his room only it doesn't look like Bennie's room any more because, although it's full of stuffed animals and crumpled bedlinen with Thomas the Tank Engine on it, John's alarm clock sits on the bedside table and his robe is tucked in the corner of the room behind the big Eeyore Dougie once bought Bennie as a birthday present. Oh, poor John, exiled to the Land of Luminous Stars and Pokémon Figures. I stand and look at Bennie's room: dinosaurs grimace from the shelf, the rabbit in Bennie's alarm clock is waving its paws about, the arms showing the time. Books like *Thomas Saves the Day* and *The Tale of Peter Rabbit* litter the floor and there, alongside them, is a pair of John's abandoned boxer shorts. I go into the room and pick them up, then lie on the bed with them. It's rather comfortable. Maybe John should sleep with Bennie and I'll sleep in here. No, that wouldn't work. He gets in so late.

I look up at the stars, winking at me. There are planets too. There's Saturn and Jupiter. Now where did I get this kit? Then I remember it wasn't me who bought it for Bennie but Wendy.

Where *is* Wendy? I look at Bennie's clock. One rabbit paw is above the eleven and the longer one is on the nine. Eleven forty-five? Where does she go every evening? I thought we'd bonded a bit today, yet she's gone off in her new midnight blue dress without a word. And where's John? Why does he have to work so late every night? I suddenly feel rather peeved.

Wendy used to like to stay in with me. She used to eat nachos and drink beer and now she's off looking like a sex-kitten and I don't see her for love or money. A ghastly thought occurs to me. I'm suddenly convinced that John and Wendy are somewhere together. That would explain why Wendy has lost weight and why neither of them gets home before midnight. Jesus! Maybe they're having an affair. Maybe they're having sex right now in John's car, pulled off the M40 into a lay-by. Maybe Julia's right. John's fed up and bored, so much so that he's screwing our au pair, who was formerly the size of the Incredible Hulk. No, surely not. I must call Julia. She'll know. Oh, God, she's in Los Angeles.

I get up and go to Wendy's room. What am I looking for? I don't know. I feel so confused. Why did I ever let her into our lives? I look around. Hmm, what can I see? Endless pairs of G-strings. John always said he didn't like G-strings. He said they were naff. And now he's probably pulling Wendy's off with his teeth. The thought makes me feel faint so I sit down. Then I notice something on the floor. It's a letter. Should I open it? It's immoral to read people's letters but then I think about John and Wendy in the lay-by and pick it up.

Dear Wendy,
Thank you so much for enquiring about vacancies at Midway WeightWatchers. We are happy to tell you that we do have some vacancies on our Tuesday night sessions and all other sessions. We here at WeightWatchers appreciate the effort it takes to lose weight. By enquiring about our sessions, Wendy, you have already taken a significant step towards making a commitment to losing weight. We hope you decide to join us, Wendy, as it is only with the help of a plan such as one supervised by WeightWatchers, that your weight will come off and stay off! Discover how to make small, positive changes for your weight loss success. People who attend WeightWatchers meetings lose three times more weight than those who go it alone. Start your story today.

So Wendy's going to WeightWatchers! She never said anything. I feel really bad. Oh dear, poor Wendy. She's obviously been embarrassed about her weight for a while. And tonight's a Tuesday night! So that's where she's been. She's not with my John, she's on some scales in Midway church hall. Hang on a minute. It's nearly midnight. Surely she's not still discussing the pros and cons of eating a hamburger. No. She's definitely with John, then.

In my head, I construct a scenario in which Wendy has gone to WeightWatchers and John has picked her up from Midway and *then* they've gone to a lay-by off the M40. No, maybe not a lay-by. Maybe they've gone to the woodland off Midway Hill. Maybe they've been discussing her weight loss. 'Don't I look so much better in me keks, Johnno,' she'll be saying. Oh the thought of it!

Just as I'm about to get really upset, I see a note stuck behind Wendy's pillow. A *billet doux*! I reach down for it and am about to open it when I hear the phone ring.

I jump and run to the stairs, only to hear an Australian voice say, 'Yeah. Hi . . . Everything's good . . . Yeah, sure, tomorrow's bonza . . . Yeah, she's here, I think. Maybe she's upstairs with Bennie.

'Mrs S!'

'Ssh, Wendy,' I say, in a stage-whisper, as I come down the stairs towards her.

'Ah've been out!' she stage-whispers back.

'I know,' I say.

'Ah've been going to WeightWatchers. I didn't tell you before cos I thought you'd laugh at me but I got weighed tonight and Ah've lost ten pounds. That's over half a stone, Mrs S! Great, isn't it?'

'Well done you,' I whisper.

'I was so happy that me and me mates from Weight-Watchers all went to a bar and drank vodka cos that's what WeightWatchers say we can drink! There's two units in one shot of vodka compared to one point in a glass of wine and two points in a pint of lager, but you get drunk quicker on vodka, don'tcha?'

'Right,' I say.

'Oh, your hubby's on the phone. Naughty boy,' she says.

Naughty boy? I pick up the phone.

'Samantha, my darling.' John sounds slightly the worse for wear. 'I've been waiting on this telephone for fucking ages.'

'Sorry,' I say, surprised – he never swears. 'I was upstairs with Bennie.'

'Ah, my boy!' he says. 'My cutest, most beautiful boy. How I love my baby, how I –'

I cut him off mid-flow. 'I can hear music behind you. Where are you?'

'In heaven,' he says.

'Where?'

'I'm just inside Heaven, that nightclub off Sloane Street.'

'You're in a nightclub? In London? Why?'

'It's a long story, darling, but, look, I can't come home tonight.'

It takes a moment to sink in.

'Samantha?' he says, slurring a bit. 'Don't be cross. I'm just saying I can't come home tonight because –'

'Why not?' I interrupt. 'You always come home, however late it is. You always say you can't stand not being with us, and the children will want to see you in the morning.' Maybe he's ill. 'Are you ill?' I say. 'Do you need help? What's going on?'

'No, darling,' says John. 'I'm fine. I just can't come home because it was the dress rehearsal for the play and it went so well, my darling, and everyone clapped and I got a standing ovation and it looks like we're going to go to Edinburgh and – please don't be angry with me. Be happy for me. Please.'

'I *am* happy for you,' I say, sounding anything but, 'I'm ecstatic, but why can't you come home? We have champagne here. We could celebrate!'

I can see Wendy in the kitchen, trying to make herself a cup of tea. She keeps dunking the teabag in the cup but failing to find the bin when she takes it out. She tries five times before she succeeds.

'Oh, God, Wendy's drunk,' I say. 'She's making a terrible mess in the kitchen.'

'Wendy's *drunk*?' He sounds delighted.

'Yes, she's been to WeightWatchers and they told her she could drink vodka and now it looks like she's had a whole bottle with her new WeightWatchers friends.'

'*Really?* That's brilliant. Hey, Samantha, maybe you should get drunk. It's great. I'm drunk now. That's why I can't get home.'

'Well, it may be great that everyone's drunk, but I've got four children here and tomorrow I've got to do something with them because it's the summer holidays.'

'I'm sorry. I've put you right in it.'

'It's OK,' I say. 'I just wanted to celebrate your play and get drunk with you at home.'

'But it was an amazing evening!' says John. 'Really it was. The stars shone. The unicorns flew. I've never felt so happy.'

'Oh,' I say.

'But I missed you so. I wish you could have been there. I'm so sorry, darling.'

He sounds truly remorseful. 'It's OK,' I say again. 'I'm

really happy everyone liked your set. Truly I am. Well done.'

'Oh, thank you, my darling Samantha.'

'But where will you sleep?'

'I'll stay at Charlie's. She says she has a spare room.'

'I don't want you to do that, John,' I say.

'It's fine. Stop panicking.'

'I'm not. I just don't want you to stay the night in a strange woman's house.'

'She's not strange. She's perfectly normal.' Then I hear him turn away from his phone. 'My wife thinks you're strange!' I hear John and a female voice giggling. 'Look, Samantha, Charlie's here. Talk to her and you'll see how normal she is.'

'No, John, I –'

'Hello? Is that Mrs Smythe? It's Charlotte.' She sounds young, giggly, drunk. I can hear John talking excitedly in the background.

'Oh, sorry,' continues this fresh, youthful voice, 'John says I should call you Samantha. Can I call you that? Or Sammie?'

'No, don't call me Sammie. My ex-husband called me that. Samantha's fine.'

I hear more giggling.

'Well, Samantha, your husband can stay with me. I have a spare room and I promise to feed him breakfast and look after him.'

'Oh, don't bother,' I say breezily. 'Just send him home to his wife and *children* as soon as you can.'

'Oh, yes, Mrs Smythe – I mean, Samantha. I know John misses them a lot.'

Misses *them*?

I hear rustling and John is back on the line. 'See?' he says. 'Nothing to worry about. I'll be home as soon as I can because there's a party tomorrow night to celebrate so we'll have to come up to town.'

'A party?'

'Yes, you must come and see the play and meet Charlie. You'll love her. Everyone does. I've already asked Wendy to babysit. Hey, we'll have fun! I love you, Samantha. I love you.' And then he's gone.

Wendy appears, clutching her tea. 'Hubbie out on the tiles?' she says.

I nod morosely.

'Cheer up, Mrs S. He'll get bored of her in the end. Mind you, that's what me mam said about me dad when he met a floozy half his age. Now they're married with two kids so, hey, what do I know?' She staggers up the stairs to bed.

I go up after her. I feel dazed. I take my clothes off, put my nightie on, cream my face. I look in the mirror. I see a woman who is ageing. I have bags under my eyes and lines round my mouth. My skin is slack and slightly discoloured. God, is that a double chin? My neck used to be smooth and pale. Now it's lined. I inspect the pot of the cream I've just put on. I put it on every night without fail and have done for years. The cream says it's 'anti-ageing' so why do I look old? In theory, I should look terribly young – so how come when I went to have a facial with Adele the lady in the white coat said, in her estuary accent, 'Your skin is very dehydrated.' I said, 'Well, it bloody well shouldn't be,' and she reeled back with shock. I told her I spent half my life putting on lotions and potions and, as they didn't work, there was no point in buying the ones she was peddling because they are nothing but placebos. 'I might as well go out and rub sheep fat on my face,' I said to her. She ran out of the room then, and all the other therapists gave me odd looks as I left the salon. I look harder at myself. It's not often I do that. I like being blissfully oblivious of what I look like. In my mind's eye I have a picture of myself as tall and slim (ha! how wrong can you be?), with an aquiline if somewhat large nose, nice mouth, high cheekbones, brown hair that is going grey, which I cleverly disguise by paying the hairdresser enormous amounts of money to colour it. I see myself as about twenty-eight, which is how old I was when I got pregnant with Edward. Since then I don't think I've looked at myself at all. I always feel quite shocked when other people, such as the children, seem to know what I look like better than I do.

Once, Edward said, 'You've got spots, Mummy.'

And the other day apropos of nothing, Bennie said, 'P-podgy legs, podgy legs, you've got podgy legs!'

'No, I haven't!' I said hotly.

'And a wobbly tummy!' he said, pushing it with his little hands.

'That's because there've been babies in it,' I said.

Bennie kissed it. 'H-hello, baby!' he said gently.

Then Jamie tottered in. 'H-hello, Jamie,' said Bennie. 'Do you know that Mummy's got a baby in her tummy?'

'Well, I haven't just now,' I said to Bennie, 'but I've had you three in me and that's why – Ow!' I felt a shooting pain in my stomach. I looked down to find that Jamie had given me a nip. 'Jamie!' I said, as he toddled off to the bathroom.

'I don't think he likes babies, Mummy,' said Bennie, a bit sadly.

I pick up the phone and call Julia. On the seventh ring, she picks up. 'Hiya,' she says jauntily in a fake-American accent. 'This is Julia Smythe. Can I help you?'

'Julia,' I say, 'what's the matter with you? Why are you answering the phone like that?'

'Hello,' says the voice. 'Who is this, please? How can I help you?'

'It's me, Julia. Your sister.'

'Oh, Samantha,' she says, suddenly all English and Julia-like again. 'Sorry. All Americans talk like that and I'm practising so that when people ring me on this number they don't get put off by my English accent.'

'Julia, I need to talk to you,' I say. 'John hasn't come home and I've been crying for the last half-hour. He's drunk and he's in a nightclub called Heaven and then he's staying up in town with a girl called Charlie who he works with.'

Julia is silent for a bit. Then she says, 'Hmm. So John's working hard and not coming home. Is that the problem?'

'Yes!' I say. 'I think he might be having an affair with this Charlie.'

'No,' she says immediately. 'Not John. Your life together may be chaotic but, Samantha, it's not in John's makeup. He loves you. He saved you, remember? When you were on your own with Edward? He's not having an affair. You know that, don't you? So what are you really worried about?'

'Maybe I'm overreacting. I'm just so worried about Bennie, I'm probably putting it all on John.'

'So you don't think John's avoiding issues?'

'No. It's not John who has night terrors and stutters.'

'Yes, but, Samantha, Bennie's fine. I'm sure of it. Children are much more resilient than we give them credit for.'

'Funny, that's what Dougie said.'

'Oh,' says Julia, momentarily silenced. 'Well, he's right. Actually, if Dougie taught me anything, it's that we're all past masters of avoiding issues. We all do it. Look at me. I only told Dougie I was going to LA as I left. I was burying my head about ending it because I didn't want to hurt him and he wasn't talking about the fact that we weren't suited, really, and maybe you and John are doing the same.'

'Burying our heads in the sand?'

'Yes.'

'But I'm so busy. The children are on holiday and I've got Naomi's daughter Lexie here –'

'What?' says Julia. 'You mean that girl you knew as a child who thought she was Ginger?'

'The very same.'

'Christ, she was the Queen of Avoidance.'

'What do you mean?'

'Oh, you could never see it but she was so manipulative. She never faced up to the fact that she kept leading you astray, and when anyone confronted her with it she blamed her sad home life.'

'No, she didn't!'

'Oh, yes, she did. Ask Mum. She never liked her. In fact, she was relieved when Naomi moved away.'

'That's not true.'

'It is and you know it. Naomi was bad news then and I bet she's bad news now. If you want to sort things out with John, you need to talk to him and spend some time with him, which means you'd better jettison her daughter and concentrate on your marriage and your own children. John needs you now. Take it from someone who knows. Apart from that, have a nice day!' She rings off.

Hard Times

It's seven fifteen and the loathsome thermometer is in my mouth. Bennie's still asleep. He looks so peaceful. He's lying on his back, legs splayed out, arms open, palms up. He shouldn't be here, I think. He may be peaceful now but for the majority of the night he wriggled this way and that like a child possessed. Consequently I have barely slept. When I did drop off, I dreamt that John had left me and gone off with an inflatable pink doll, which was very disturbing.

I get up and look at myself in the mirror. My eyes are swollen. I feel terrible. I'm about to go back to bed when I hear the television. Ah, so Edward's up. Of course he is. He's always up. I have only ever known Edward to wake up after me twice in his entire life and both times it was because we were travelling and he had finally succumbed to jet-lag.

I put on my pink dressing-gown and go downstairs. Edward gives me a wave and a smile. I go to sit down next to him and rub the top of his head. 'Do you remember the time you woke up after me when we went to the Maldives?' I say.

'Mmm,' he says. I gaze at him, taking in his mop of now-ruffled hair, the freckles on his face, the scar on his nose from when he broke it on holiday last year doing a 'Super-Scooby back slip' as he called it, which means he tried to do a back flip, miscalculated and ended up smashing his nose on the side of the swimming-pool. Very painful. Lots of blood.

'That was just after I met Dad.'

'Mmm.'

'Before we even knew there was going to be a Bennie or a Jamie.'

'Mmm.'

'When it was just you and me, and Dad lived in London . . .'

Just then, we hear a muffled bang. 'What's that?'

'Jamie falling out of his cot?' Edward suggests.

'No, that's more of a thud. He wails when he falls out.'

'Wendy turning over in bed?' says Edward, giggling.

'No. Listen. There's something else.'

We sit still. What's that noise? It sounds like water rushing from one side of the house to the other. 'It's water,' I say. 'Somewhere near the washroom.'

Edward and I creep through the hall to the washroom. Hmm, nothing there.

'I can hear something dripping,' he says.

We go to look in the kitchen. Beady wakes, startled, then leaps up wagging her tail.

'Hello, Beady,' says Edward, giving her a hug. 'Is there leaky water in here?'

Beady wags some more and licks Edward's face.

We look in the sitting room. Nothing. The study. Nothing. The games room. Nothing. The bathroom. Nothing. Then we look in the laundry room. 'Oh dear,' says Edward.

'Oh, God.' There, pumping out of the back of the washing-machine, is a ton of hot, soapy water.

'It's like a geyser,' says Edward.

'What's the matter, Samantha?' a voice says.

I turn. Lexie is standing there in a too-small nightdress with a Care Bear on the front. Her legs are long and thin. She's like a beanpole. I hadn't realized how skinny she is. She looks like a little fawn, all big-eyed and leggy. I feel instantly protective. I go over to give her a hug. She stands woodenly for a minute, then hugs me back. It feels nice.

'We seem to have a leak, Lexie,' I say. 'We'll get a plumber in to fix it.'

Lexie looks beyond me into the laundry room. 'It looks like a geyser,' she says.

'That's what I said,' says Edward, proudly.

I tell them to gather up some towels and put them on the laundry-room floor to soak up the water and that I'll ring the plumber.

'Shall I make myself some breakfast?' asks Lexie, sweetly, after she's put a couple of towels down. 'I could make you some too, if you like.'

'Yes,' I say. 'That would be lovely.'

'No,' pipes up Edward from where he is spreading towels. 'Look at the good job I'm doing. I'll make Mum breakfast because I know what she likes.'

'Well,' I say, 'it's very kind of you both to offer and, yes, I'd love something to eat so maybe you could make it together.'

'What would you like?' says Lexie, as the water soaks rapidly through the towels.

'Hang on,' says Edward and rushes off. The next thing

I know, he's back with a pad and pen. 'Would Madame like some toast?'

'Mmm,' I say.

'And what would Madame like on her toast?' says Lexie, getting into the swing of things and talking with a fake French accent.

'Oh, Marmite, I think.'

'Marmite?' she says. 'That's disgusting.' Then she sighs. 'But if Madame wants Marmite then that is what she will have. I shall make you Marmite on toast.'

'There's a girl at school who eats Marmite three times a day,' says Edward.

'Toast?' I say brightly. 'Is anyone getting it?'

'I'll make the toast because I know how the toaster works,' says Edward to Lexie. Then he turns to me. 'And would Madame like a coffee?'

'Oh yes,' I say.

'With milk?' says Lexie. 'I shall make it right now.'

'No,' says Edward, crossly. 'You know Madame hates milk. I'll get her coffee.'

'Would Madame like some fruit, then?' says Lexie. 'I can cut Madame up some apples and bananas.'

'Well . . .' I say.

'I'll cut Madame up some apples and bananas,' butts in Edward.

'What am I supposed to do, then?' says Lexie, a bit annoyed.

'You can set the breakfast table,' says Edward. 'That's what girls do.'

'Edward,' I say warningly.

'What?' he says, looking a bit hurt.

'Lexie,' I say, 'could you please get me some orange juice?'

'Yes!' she says happily.

'I'll get it,' says Edward. 'I know where it is in the fridge.'

'No, Edward. I asked Lexie to get it, thank you.'

'All right,' says Edward reluctantly, and off they go to the kitchen.

The water is still gushing into the laundry room. I'm going to have to phone the plumber. It's nine o'clock now. I wonder if he'll be up. Now, where is his number? Hmm. I open my address book and look under P for Plumber. Plumridge. Parsons. Potts Garage. Post Office. No plumber. What was his name again? Was it Mr Micklethwaite? I look under M. Merrybridge. Mappins. Mitchell. Murphy. Midwife. None of them is a plumber. Maybe I put him under H for handyperson. Horseman. Hopple. Heppiatt. Helpline for smoking but no handyperson. God, how irritating. Now, who would have his telephone number? John! I'd better ring him. For a moment I wonder if it's too early. He was up late, he was drunk – Sod it. It's a good excuse to call him and I like the idea of waking him up. After all, I've been up for hours.

John picks up on the third ring. 'Hi, my darling,' he says. 'How are you? I've been thinking about you ever since I woke up. How are the boys? Oh, and Lexie. I'm missing you so much. I'm – Hang on a minute, darling.' He turns away from the telephone. I can hear him saying something muffled to someone, and something else, a rumbling sound. It might be traffic. Where is he?

Maybe he's on his way home! Maybe he missed us so

much he couldn't sleep and now he's at the nearest station on his way here.

'Samantha? Are you still there?' he asks.

'Yes,' I say excitedly, 'but where are you? Are you on your way home?'

'No, sorry, I'm at a café,' he says. 'It was such a lovely morning, I couldn't sleep and I was rather hungover and wanted something to eat – I'm so excited about the play. I can't tell you how good it looked. I'm longing for you to see it.'

'When are you coming home?'

'I'm not sure. I've got another run-through this morning and then they're making a decision about whether or not to take it to Edinburgh.'

'Is it good if it goes to Edinburgh?'

'Yeah, it's great. But it means me and Charlie'll have to go up there almost immediately.'

'But why? Don't you just transfer what you've done in London?'

John laughs. 'No, it doesn't work like that. We'd have to go up, rebuild a whole new set and adapt it to the space. I can't tell you how difficult it was to get this one right.'

'Oh,' I say, trying not to sound disappointed.

'You're cross, aren't you?' says John.

'I'm not sure.'

'Please don't be. It would just be for a couple of weeks and maybe you could come up. I've really missed you all. I can't wait to see you and kiss you and do lots of other things to you.'

'OK, I'm not cross, just missing you, and I was a bit unhappy when you told me you were staying at that girl's house, but now I know you only went there for a few hours and –'

'Hang on a minute, darling,' says John. 'I've just got to –'

I hear more muttering. This time there's a girl's voice and a chink of glasses.

'Where actually are you, John?'

'At a café,' he says. 'I told you.'

'But are you on your own?'

'Oh. No,' he says shiftily.

'I can hear a woman's voice and the glasses clinking,' I say. 'What's going on?'

'Charlie's here. We're having champagne.'

'At nine in the morning?'

'It sounds bad, doesn't it?'

'Bad? It sounds really, really self-indulgent. I mean, I'm sure it's lovely to sit in the sunshine on a summer's morning after the night before and drink champagne with an attractive female but it's hardly fair, is it?'

'Where does fairness come into it?' he says evenly.

'Because I'm at home!'

'I know you are.'

'Yes, well, I'm at home and one of your children has spent the night with me, wriggling like a worm on acid, and the other is refusing to do anything but watch television, and now the laundry room has sprung a *tsunami* of a leak and I can't find the plumber's number and you're at a café drinking champagne.'

'Oh, poor you,' he says. 'I'm so sorry. I've got the plumber's number in my phone so I'll hang up and find it, then call you back.'

'Yeah, great. Chin-chin and all that,' I say.

Damn John. Damn him, damn him, damn him. I'm about to shout this at the telephone when Lexie comes in. ''Ere is your juice, Madame,' she says. She puts it on the step to the laundry room.

'Thanks, Lexie,' I say.

'We 'ave ze table set in ze kitchen for Madame if you care to join us for a spot of *petit déjeuner*.'

'Marvellous.'

'We 'ave ze toast, ze fruit salad, ze café . . .'

Just then the telephone rings but before I can pick it up Lexie grabs it. 'Ze French 'Ouse,' she says, as smooth as butter. 'Can I 'elp you?'

I hear the person at the other end put down the phone.

'I wonder who that was,' I say.

'Oh, sorry,' she says, blushing and looking younger than her ten years. 'I didn't mean to scare whoever it was away. I was just playing a joke.'

'I know,' I say. 'It doesn't matter. It was probably no one of any importance.'

Two hours later there is a very loud knock. Lexie and Edward run to open the door.

'I shall open eet for you, Madame!' yells Lexie.

'No, I will!' shrieks Edward, trying to elbow her, and me, out of the way.

'Calm down!' I roar, as they pound up the hall, Beady barking at their ankles.

'Ooh, runnin', runnin'!' says Jamie, who is still in his pyjamas, perched on the arm of the sofa. He is somehow managing to balance a bowl of Rice Krispies, which

Wendy has given him, on his lap and wave his spoon above his head.

'Watch that cereal!' I say to him.

'Bispies!' He giggles, jiggling his bottom this way and that.

'Those Rice Krispies will fall on the floor,' I say.

'On da foor,' he says, as the bowl smashes.

'Wendy!' I yell as Honey slinks across the floor for the milk. 'I'm not sure why you gave Jamie a china bowl with his breakfast in it but it's broken and the plumber's here and I need to get the door.'

'All right, Mrs S!' yells Wendy, from somewhere. 'Ah'll be right with ya.'

'Has anyone opened the door yet?' I shout.

'I've got it,' yells Edward.

'No, I have!' retorts Lexie.

'Wh-what about me?' says Bennie, emerging from my bedroom where he has been lying in bed and watching television. 'I'm cold.'

'That's because you've got no clothes on,' says Lexie. Bennie is standing stark naked at the top of the stairs.

'Wendy!' I call again. 'Bennie has no clothes on!'

'All right, Mrs S!' she shouts back.

''Oney, off milka!' yells Jamie, from the sitting room.

I go back into the room to find the cat licking the milk off the floor from around the shards.

'Wendy!' I yell again. 'Where are you? Now the cat's licking up the milk and –' Jamie gets down and starts to lick up the milk with the cat. 'Christ! Jamie's licking up the milk too and there's china on the floor.' I swoop down and grab him.

'Noo, Daddy,' he says.

'I'm Mummy,' I say. 'Daddy's not here.'

'Ooh, Mummy.'

'I'm c-c-cold,' says Bennie again, from the stairs.

There's another, even louder knock.

'Christ, Edward,' I yell, 'haven't you opened that bloody door yet?'

I hear a bolt draw back, then Edward yelling, 'Ow! Get off me, Lexie!' and Lexie saying, very sweetly, 'How can I help you?' to whoever is at the door.

'I've come to do your plumbing,' says a gruff male voice.

'Ah, come in,' she says. 'I shall get the lady of the house for you.'

The plumber comes in as I emerge holding Jamie, whose pyjamas are covered with milk.

Just then Wendy appears in a boob tube and her new jeans. She is also carrying some clothes.

'Hiya, mate,' she says, grabs Bennie and disappears into my bedroom.

'God, it's like a football team in here,' the plumber says.

'Yes,' I say.

'Now, what seems to be the problem?'

I show him into the laundry room. The water isn't so much pouring out now as trickling, but the floor is wet.

'Oh, right,' he says. 'Let me think. You don't happen to have a cup of tea, do you?'

Lexie says she'll go and make him one.

I take the plumber his tea and find him crouching

behind the washing-machine with a torch. 'I don't think you have a leak,' he says.

'Oh,' I say. 'That's odd, because about two hours ago I saw water pouring out from behind this machine.'

'Well, I can't find a leak.'

'So you say,' I say patiently, 'but there was lots of water and the floor's wet.'

'Yeah, but this room is dug below floor level, isn't it?'

'Yes.'

'Rooms like this always have damp floors.'

'Not this one. I've lived here for six years and it's always been as dry as a bone.'

The plumber stands up. 'I don't know what else to do,' he says.

I tell him to stay there a minute while I grab Lexie. 'Come with me,' I say to her.

When we're in the laundry room, I ask her to tell the plumber what she saw earlier on. 'There was water pouring from behind that machine,' she says, pointing. 'I saw it and so did Edward.'

'Ah, so you and your mummy are saying there's a leak, are you?' asks the plumber.

'She's not my mummy,' says Lexie.

'But there is a leak,' I say.

The plumber, now looking confused, asks us to leave him alone for a bit. Lexie and I go back into the sitting room, where Bennie and Jamie are playing with their cars. Edward is in the kitchen, helping Wendy make chips.

'Do you know when my mum's coming back to get me?' asks Lexie, suddenly.

'No,' I say, taken aback. 'I mean, sorry, yes, of course I do. She's coming today, I think. Why? Are you missing her? Aren't you happy here? I can ring her and ask her to come now if you like.'

'No, I didn't mean that,' says Lexie, quickly. 'I like it here. I'd like to stay longer.'

'Well, it's nice having you, Lexie,' I say, 'but I'm sure your mum must miss you. You can come and stay any time, though.'

Just then, as the plumber appears from the laundry room, we hear the most terrible noise. It's the sound of screeching brakes outside the window, a terrible thud and then a most awful wail – a high-pitched scream. The sound of an animal in pain.

'Oh, my God!' I run to the door.

'What is it?' says Lexie, right behind me.

We open the door to find Gary White outside. He looks as if he's seen a ghost.

'Gary!' I say. 'What are you doing here?'

'I–I . . .' His mouth opens and shuts like a goldfish's but no more words come out.

'Gary, what is it? We heard this terrible noise like a hurt animal. What's happened?'

Gary points desperately to the road.

I follow his finger and see his Ferrari, with something black and lumpen near the back tyre.

By now Wendy and Edward are at the door.

'Oh, hello,' says Edward to Gary. 'What's happened to your car? Have you hit a badger? Mummy hit one once. She made us bury it and cried for days. We could bury your badger next to it, if you like.'

Gary shakes his head wordlessly. 'Oh, Samantha,' he says. 'I'm so sorry.'

'Sorry for what?' I ask, and then, all of a sudden, I know. 'Oh, my God. Beady.'

Gary nods.

Edward reacts immediately. 'Beady!' he yells, and runs straight to Gary's car. 'Beady! Beady! Beady!' he says.

'She just ran out,' says Gary. 'I'm so sorry. I wasn't going fast. My mother rang and I went to answer the phone. I swerved but she . . .'

'How bad is it?' I say, fighting tears.

'I don't know,' says Gary. 'I think I got her with my rear tyres. I don't know what to say. Oh, God, I'm so sorry.'

Edward is crying and cradling Beady's head. She's lying limply on the ground. 'She's alive,' he says, 'but I think she's very hurt.'

Beady looks at me with her big brown eyes and tries to wag her tail.

'Oh, Beady, my love.' I bend down to stroke her. 'Let me look at you.'

She flinches as I try to move her back legs. The front ones seem fine but she can't stand.

'Oh, Beady,' I say again, as she licks my hand.

'Oh, Beady,' repeats Edward, sobbing now. 'I love you, Beady. Please don't die. You're the best dog in the world.'

'O-o-oh, Beady!' Bennie's behind me now. 'P-p-poor Beady!' He's very distressed.

'Wendy,' I say, 'you'd better take the children back indoors.'

'No, she's my dog!' yells Edward. His head sinks into

her fur. 'If she's going to die I'm staying right here with her.'

'B-B-Beady going to die?' says Bennie, starting to cry.

'My woof-woof ow,' says Jamie, tears rolling down his cheeks.

'Oh, no – poor Beady,' says Lexie.

'Nah, she's not gonna die.'

'I beg your pardon?' I say, looking up at Wendy.

'Nah, she's all right. She's probably cracked her pelvis. I saw that on me dad's cattle ranches all the time. Stupid buggers, they'd get stuck in the fences, go this way and that until their pelvis snapped in two, like a dingo breaking a baby's bones.'

'Wendy!' I say. 'For goodness' sake!'

'All you gotta do is go to the vet. He'll set it and she'll be right as rain in a couple of weeks.'

'Really?' says Edward, looking at Wendy doubtfully.

'Sure as eggs is eggs. We just need to get her in the car and off you go.'

'I'll drive you,' says Gary, still upset but relieved too. 'It's the least I can do.'

'No,' I say. 'We could be there all day. I'll take her.'

'I want to help, Samantha.'

I close my eyes and take a deep breath. 'Gary,' I say, 'I don't want to be rude but you've just run over my dog and you're the last person I want with me at the vet's.'

'I'll come with you,' says Edward.

'Me too,' says Lexie.

'M-me too,' says Bennie.

'No,' I say. 'I'll take her with Edward. She's Edward's dog. I need the rest of you to stay here.'

'But I want to come,' says Lexie, looking hurt.

I take her in my arms. 'Lexie darling,' I say quietly, 'I really need you to do me a favour.'

Lexie nods.

'I need you to stay with the little ones and look after them because they're cold and hungry and I don't want them to come to the vet because Wendy's cooking chicken nuggets and chips. I need you to help them have a happy day. Can you do that for me?'

Lexie looks doubtful. 'What if something happens to Beady?' she asks.

'I won't let anything happen to Beady. But if anything *is* going to happen to Beady, I'll call Wendy and she'll bring you all over so you can say goodbye to her.'

Lexie is crying too now.

'But she's going to be fine,' I say quickly. 'Can you be a big girl for me?'

Lexie kisses my cheek. 'Poor Beady,' she says, then takes Jamie's hand. She, Wendy, Jamie and Bennie go inside.

Bennie gives me a sad little wave on the doorstep. 'I love you, Bennie,' I say.

'I–I want to come.'

'We won't be long, and Lexie's going to play with you.'

Bennie's face brightens and he disappears.

By now the plumber has appeared. 'Oh, poor dog,' he says. 'Whose is it?'

'Mine,' I say.

'You taking her to the vet?'

'Yes.'

'Do you want some help putting her in your car?'

Gary moves the Ferrari to the side of the road, leaving Beady exposed in the middle. She looks very sorry for herself.

'Broken her pelvis?' says the plumber.

'Think so,' I say.

'That's not good.'

Gary gets out of his car. 'Samantha, I really want to go with you to the vet,' he says. 'I want to be there to help. I wasn't going anywhere special, only to the shop, and I feel so bad about it. If only I hadn't answered the mobile.'

'Gary,' I say, 'I've already told you. I don't want you to come.'

'Yeah,' says the plumber, squaring up to him a bit. 'She doesn't want you.'

'But I want to help!' says Gary.

'You know what would've been a help, Gary?' I say, trying not to get angry or cry. 'It would have been a major help if you didn't drive that bloody Ferrari round these little lanes too fast while talking on your phone. It's illegal, you know.'

'I don't!' says Gary, hotly. 'Your dog ran out and –'

'Blimey, are you Gary White?' asks the plumber, his mouth wide open.

'Yes, I am,' says Gary, not really looking at him.

'Gary White who used to play in the Premier League?'

'The very same,' says Gary, now smiling at him.

'I'm your biggest fan, mate. You were magic. I used to tell my wife you had wings on your boots.'

'Oh, you're too kind,' says Gary.

'No,' says the plumber. 'You were my hero. I remember when –'

Just then Beady whimpers.

'Oh, no,' says Gary. 'Samantha, please will you let me help you to get the dog into your car at least?'

I nod wearily.

I reverse my car out of the drive and position the boot as close to Beady as possible. Edward finds a rug on the back seat and lays it out.

'Now, we've got to move her gently,' says the plumber to Gary. 'She could have internal bleeding and we don't want to make it worse.'

They slide their hands under Beady and start to lift her. Beady yelps and bares her teeth. The plumber looks nervous.

'She won't bite you,' Edward tells him. 'Beady has never bitten anyone.'

'Stroke her, Edward,' I say, as the plumber and Gary lift her higher.

Poor Beady closes her eyes and yelps again.

'She's one hurt dog,' says the plumber.

Eventually they slide her into the boot. Edward clambers in with her and she puts her muzzle into his lap. 'I'm going to stay here with her,' he says, kissing her forehead. 'I can calm her down.'

I start to move off. As I leave, I wind down the window to thank the plumber.

'No problem,' he says. 'I'll send the bill to your house. Oh, and there *was* a leak, a dodgy connection with that washing-machine, but I fixed it.'

'Thanks again,' I say.

'Samantha . . .' Gary begins, but I drive off before he can say anything else.

Just as we're about to turn right at the junction, Edward's head bobs up in my rear-view mirror. 'Mum, I want to say something.'

'What is it?' I ask him.

He pauses, then says, 'It's Lexie's fault, you know.'

'How can it possibly have been Lexie's fault?'

'She let Beady out.'

'No, she didn't.'

'Yes, she did. When the plumber came. She opened the door and that must have been when Beady got out.'

'We all opened the door, Edward, don't you remember?'

'No, we didn't. Lexie opened it because she's a fathead* and I don't like fatheads!'

The Parting

Edward and I spend what seems to be the entire day at the vet's. When we get there, his eyes all red from crying, the officious woman at the desk is so unhelpful I feel like shouting at her.

'Name?' she says to us, as we walk through the door.

'Smythe,' I say quickly. 'Our dog's in the back of the car and –'

'Name of pet?' she says, not looking up from her computer.

'Beady.'

'Beady Smythe,' she says, tap-tap-tapping very slowly.

'Our dog's very hurt,' says Edward. 'She –'

'What seems to be the problem with her?' says the receptionist, still not looking up.

'I don't know,' I say. 'That's why I am here.'

'Doesn't know,' she types in.

'No, I do know,' I say. 'She's been run over and –'

'Been run over.'

'And –'

'She's bleeding to death!' yells Edward.

'Possibly bleeding to death.'

'It's an emergency,' I say desperately. 'She really needs to see a vet right now.'

At last the receptionist looks at us. 'I'll see if a vet is available, Mrs Smythe.'

'A vet *has* to be available. It's an emergency! Our dog's dying.'

'Well, it's a very busy morning.'

No one is there but us. 'But no one else is here.'

'That's true, Mrs Smythe, but one vet has had to go out and see a horse suffering from an attack of colic and the other is performing a complicated operation on a budgerigar.'

'A *budgerigar*? How can you operate on a budgerigar?'

'That's the point, Mrs Smythe,' says the receptionist. 'It's a very labour-intensive procedure and all the nurses are helping.'

'So you're telling me no one can see our dog?'

Edward starts to cry again.

'I'm not saying that, Mrs Smythe,' says the receptionist. 'I'm going to speak with the vet now, if you would take a seat.'

Edward and I sit down.

'Beady's going to die,' says Edward. 'I'm going back to the car to be with her.' I tell Edward that's a good idea. I sit and stare at the walls. They are covered with posters advertising Happy Chappy dog biscuits and dry catfood. Poor Beady.

I'm just wondering whether or not I should call John to let him know when an attractive young man in a white coat appears in front of me. 'Mrs Smythe,' he says, 'I understand you have a sick dog with you.'

I stand up. 'Yes,' I say. 'She's in the car with my son and she's been run over. I daren't move her and –'

'Right,' he says reassuringly. 'Well, I'm the vet and I'll

come out now with my nurse to help move her and we'll take a look at her.'

I follow him out to the car. Edward sees us and waves. He opens the boot. 'She's still alive,' he says to the vet, as Beady tries to wag her tail at me, 'but she's very sad. She keeps whimpering.'

The vet is joined by a nurse.

'Now, what's your name?' he says to Edward.

'Edward.'

'You get out and stand with your mum and the nurse.' Edward nods. 'We'll carry Beady into the clinic after I've had a quick look at her.'

Edward and I watch as the vet tries gently to move Beady's back legs. She yelps. He turns and asks the nurse to stroke her head while he looks further. He moves Beady's back legs again. She yelps a bit louder. The nurse, who can't be out of her early twenties, strokes Beady and talks to her. The vet moves Beady's front legs, then tries to rotate her pelvis. She lets out such a yelp of anguish that Edward shouts, 'Stop, you're hurting her!'

The vet turns to explain that he has to do these things to help our dog. 'I think her pelvis is probably broken,' he says.

'Is that bad?' says Edward.

'It's not good,' says the vet, 'but she'll live.'

He tells Edward that he and the nurse will now take Beady into the surgery. 'We'll give her a general anaesthetic, then operate to set the bone,' he says. 'I'll also check the rest of her to make sure there's no internal bleeding as that's actually more serious.'

'Do you think there is any?' says Edward, anxiously.

'I'm not sure,' says the vet. Then he sees how upset Edward is. 'I don't think so. I think she'll be fine.'

He and the nurse pick Beady up gently and carry her into the building and then to the consulting room, where they lay her on a high table. She looks very nervous, so Edward strokes her.

'Is she your dog?' the vet asks Edward.

'Yes,' says Edward. 'I love her so much. She can swim and chase sticks and she's always happy.'

'Well, she'll be as good as new in a few weeks' time,' says the vet. 'Now, the best thing you and your mother can do is to get some lunch while we operate. It'll take a couple of hours and then you can come back, see your dog and I'll tell you how it's gone. OK?'

Edward nods. 'Will we be able to take her home then?' he says.

'She'll have to stay here for a while so we can keep an eye on her.'

At three o'clock we go back to the surgery. No one is there so Edward and I sit and wait. Edward looks at a *Beano* he finds under a pile of magazines and I pick up a copy of *Fruit Garden*. After about twenty minutes the young nurse appears.

Edward leaps out of his seat. 'How's Beady?' he says. 'Is she still alive?'

The nurse smiles, and says that the vet will come and see us soon. Twenty minutes later, he appears. Edward leaps up again. 'Where's Beady?' he says. 'Is she –'

The vet nods and smiles. 'Do you want to come and see her now?' he says.

We troop after him to where Beady is laid out on the operating table. She is covered with a plastic sheet, her head lolling on the table, eyes closed. She has a plastic tube coming out of her mouth.

'She's dead!' says Edward.

'No, no,' the vet says hurriedly. 'She's not, just sedated. You have to sedate animals when you operate on them so they don't feel anything. It's the same as what happens to humans.'

'Is it, Mum?' Edward asks.

'Yes,' I say.

'Have I ever had that done to me?'

'No, it's only if you've had major surgery,' I tell him.

'Like if you lost a leg?' he says.

'Yes,' I say.

'But Beady hasn't lost a leg?' he asks the vet.

The vet laughs. 'No,' he says. 'She'll be fine. There was no major internal bleeding, which is good,' he says, 'and actually, apart from the pelvis, she's in pretty good nick.' He asks if we throw a lot of sticks for her and Edward nods. 'Well,' he says, 'you'll have to be gentle with her for about six months. She's had a tough time and it'll take a while for her bones to knit together.'

'What does that mean?' says Edward.

'It means only walks on the lead, no jumping up, no running around and lots of rest. Do you think you can help Beady get better?' he asks Edward, very seriously.

Edward nods enthusiastically. 'When she comes home, she can live in my room,' he says. 'That way I can keep an eye on her.'

The vet tells me they'll need to keep Beady in for at

least a couple of nights and that I should call in the morning to find out how she is.

As we leave his surgery the vet says to Edward, 'I think you must be the best dog owner I've met all year.'

Edward blushes with pride.

We're walking through the waiting room when the receptionist grabs us. 'You need to pay your bill, Mrs Smythe,' she says.

'My bill?' I say, confused.

'Yes. You have to pay to see the vet.'

'I know that,' I say, 'but I don't have any money or cards with me right now. Can you send me the bill?'

The receptionist purses her lips and stares disbelievingly at me as I try to explain that our dog was run over unexpectedly, I left the house in a rush and consequently didn't bring my handbag. Edward and I only managed to have lunch because I found a ten-pound note in my back pocket.

'So you can't pay?' she says.

'I can,' I say, 'just not now.'

The receptionist tells me to wait. 'I'll have to talk to the vet,' she says.

Edward and I sit down again. Another twenty minutes go by and no one appears. I decide that Edward and I should leave.

'Come on, Edward,' I say. 'Let's go.'

'We can't!' says Edward, horrified.

'Yes, we can,' I say. 'That stupid battleaxe of a receptionist can send us the bill at home. Look, it's four o'clock. We need to get back to the others. They'll be worrying.'

Edward looks at me dubiously as I head for the door. I hold it open as he gets up reluctantly to follow.

'*Mrs Smythe!*' says a voice. The receptionist has returned.

'Yes?' I say.

'I have the vet here now,' she says.

'Great,' I say. 'Finally. We've been here for hours, you know.'

'Yes, well, he's been busy restitching your dog as she developed a complication he needs to tell you about so I'm sure we're sorry for wasting your time but –'

The vet comes in.

'Is she all right?' Edward asks him.

'Yes,' says the vet. 'But this is why we need to keep an eye on her. She had some internal bleeding that we'd missed but we've sorted it out and stabilized her and . . . It's been a long day for everyone, Edward.'

'Right, Mrs Smythe,' says the vet, wearily. 'Our receptionist tells me you can't pay your bill.'

'I can pay my bill. It's just that –'

'Do you know who ran over your dog?'

'Yes,' I say.

'Will you be claiming damages from this person?'

'I hadn't thought about it,' I say. 'Gary White ran over my dog. His daughter goes to Edward's school and he's sort of a friend. I'm sure he'd offer to pay but I hadn't thought of asking him because it all happened so quickly that I didn't pick up my bag and –'

'Gary White the footballer?' says the vet, perking up.

'The very same.'

'Will you be contacting him about it?' the vet asks.

'Maybe you could ask him to drop by and pick up your bill. I'm such a fan.'

'Yes, I'll ask him,' I say, sounding weary myself now.

'If not, we'll just send it to your address, if that's OK with you.'

'That's fine.'

We're reversing out of the drive when the vet appears again. I stop and wind down the window. 'If Mr White does come in,' says the vet, looking embarrassed, 'do you think you could ask him to give me his autograph?'

'Yes,' I say, and drive off.

'Does everyone know Gary White?' asks Edward.

'It looks that way.'

'Cool.' Edward rests his head on the seat back and promptly falls asleep.

John's Manly Talk

On the way home I remember I'm supposed to be going to London for John's first-night party. Damn. What time is it? Four fifteen. What time was the party supposed to start?

I find my mobile, which I'd hidden in the side pocket of my car. Nine messages are registered on it. Nine? Who on earth are they all from? No one ever messages me.

I dial 123.

The first five are from John, all saying a variation of 'Why aren't you talking to me?' and 'Call me asap,' and 'What time are you getting to London?'

I delete them all as I'm still angry with him.

The next is from Dougie, announcing he's very depressed and is on his way to see me.

Then Wendy's saying that all is fine at home but could I call John as he's driving her 'mad as a snake' by calling home continually.

Dougie again, wondering how many sleeping-bags I have in the house. 'Never mind,' he ends cheerfully. 'I've just talked to Wendy and she's found two so we'll be fine. Oh, and I hope Beady isn't dead. Mind you, you could get another dog, couldn't you? I've always thought beagles were fun. Love you, Samantha. 'Byeee!'

I pull into the driveway. Edward is still asleep. I love him so much, everything about him, from his over-large feet to his squiggly eyebrows. For a moment I think about him and his life, which makes me sigh. We've been through so much together. I know he finds it hard with Lexie here. I think of how cross he was this morning when they were vying to make my breakfast. Edward can't stand his access to me being blocked by anyone else. Yet he's kind to his brothers, especially Jamie. He loves John, even though he's not his father. But in his heart of hearts he yearns to be with me. Maybe all my children do. Maybe all children do.

I see Lexie come to the back gate. Her face lights up, and my heart jolts. Poor Lexie. She's sad. She feels alone and unloved, and I've offered her a little branch to cling to, but, I realize, as I look at her face, I cannot help her. Only Naomi can. The thought makes me want to cry. I want to help her but my children need me, John needs me – or I need him. I have nothing left for someone else's child.

I'm almost in tears when Lexie gets to the car. She is opening my car door, her arms widening for a hug.

'Samantha!' she says, getting on to my lap rather awkwardly and folding herself into me as much as she can. I try not to cry. 'What's the matter?'

'Nothing,' I say.

'Are you crying? Oh, please, don't cry.'

'I'm not crying, Lexie. I'm fine. It's just that I –'

'Is it Beady?' she interrupts. 'Oh, please don't say Beady's dead. Is she? Is she dead?'

'No,' I say. 'She's had an operation and she's resting at the vet's for a while.'

'Oh, good – because I think it was my fault.'

'No, Lexie,' I say. 'It wasn't.'

'But you don't understand,' she says. 'I opened the door for the plumber. It was me who let Beady out. I'm always getting everything wrong.'

I sit back from Lexie, as far as I can in our cramped space. 'No, you're not. You mustn't think that. It was an accident. Any one of us could have left that door open.'

'But it was me,' she says, 'and you know it, and now you're going to ask me to leave and then you'll never see me again.'

'No,' I say, feeling terrible now. 'I'm not going to ask you to leave. I mean, you're going to have to go with your mother when she comes to get you but then I hope you'll come back as often as you like.'

'You won't want me,' she says. 'No one ever wants me.'

'That's not true!'

'Isn't it?' she says. 'My mum told me my granddad doesn't want me and my dad doesn't want me and I don't think she wants me either.'

'She does want you, Lexie! She loves you!'

'Does she?' says Lexie, looking away. 'Where is she, then?'

'She's looking for a job. She'll be here tonight or tomorrow.'

'Oh.'

Just then Bennie's little blond head pops round the back gate.

'I like it here with Edward and Bennie and Jamie,' says Lexie, 'and I don't want to go home with Mum because I don't have a home. I just want to stay here with you – and you want a girl and . . . Please, Samantha.'

'Lexie . . .' I say, but it's too late because Bennie is bombarding the side of the car with a shower of gravel.

'L-l-let me in!' he yells. 'Where's Beady? Where's Edward? Open the door now, Mummy.'

I open the door and Lexie shifts on to the passenger seat. 'Edward's asleep in the back,' I tell Bennie, 'and Beady had an operation but the vet says she'll be fine.'

Sh-sh-she'll be fine?' repeats Bennie, looking worried.

'Oh, yes.'

He gives me a hug. 'I love her,' he says sadly. 'I love Beady so much.'

I close my eyes and kiss the top of his head. 'I know,' I murmur. 'We all love her.'

'Who do we all love?' says a jocular voice.

I open my eyes to see Dougie standing next to my door. 'Oh, Dougie,' I say.

'Are you having a party in there?' he says. 'Can I join in?'

Bennie laughs. 'W-we are having a party, Dougie,' he says. 'I like parties.'

'I'm coming out,' I say to Dougie, and extricate myself from Bennie, who bashes his head on the car ceiling.

'Ow, Mummy,' he says. He sidles over and gets on to Lexie's lap. She kisses him and Bennie snuggles into her, closing his eyes.

When I'm out of the car Dougie gives me a hug. 'Oh dear,' he says. 'Wendy told me what happened. Are you OK?'

'Not really,' I say. 'It's been a horrible day.'

Dougie holds me tighter. 'Do you want to have a cry?' he says.

'Not in front of the children,' I say. 'I've got to keep it together.'

I tell him about everything – John staying in London, the water disaster, Beady, but can't tell him about Lexie asking to stay because she's listening.

Dougie sighs. 'What a day,' he says.

'And I've got to go to London for John's first night and a party. I should have left by now and –'

Bennie's cornflower eyes snap open. 'Wh-where are you going, Mummy?' he moves off Lexie's lap into the driver's seat.

'Nowhere right now,' I say.

'Are you going to L-l-london?' he says, his eyes filling with tears.

'Bennie,' I say, a bit frustrated, 'I have to go and see Daddy.'

'I want to go and see Daddy,' he says. 'I haven't seen Daddy for ages.'

'Well, you can see Daddy in the morning and –'

'I–I feel sick,' says Bennie, bending over out of the car door.

'Oh, don't be sick on me, Bennie,' says Lexie.

'Thick!' says Jamie, appearing with Wendy in tow.

'Who's sick?' says Wendy. She sees Edward, who is now stirring, in the back of the car. 'Is Edward sick?'

'No, it's Bennie,' I say. 'I don't think he wants me to go to London.'

'Don't be a wally!' Wendy says to Bennie. 'Your mam's gotta go to London, else your dad might run off and leave her.'

'Wendy!' I say.

'L-l-leave her?' says Bennie, clearly terrified.

'Yeah,' says Wendy, ignoring me. 'Your dad'll leave her and all you lot cos your mam hasn't spent any time with him in days, so stop being so silly, Bennie.'

'B-but I'm sick,' says Bennie, pretending to retch out of the car again.

'No, you're not,' says Wendy. 'You're being a wally.'

'Bennie!' says Edward, now fully awake. 'Why are you being sick?'

'D-Daddy's leaving us,' says Bennie.

'Is he?' Edward asks me, mildly interested.

'No,' I say, 'he is not leaving us. It's just that I need to go to London tonight –'

'London!' wails Bennie, bending over again.

'– to see Daddy's new play and celebrate with him.'

'Oh. Right,' says Edward. 'And who will look after us?'

'Wendy,' I say.

'Oh,' says Dougie, a bit put out. 'I was hoping Wendy and I could take Lexie and Edward camping. Didn't you get my message?'

'What message?' I ask. 'You mean the one about sleeping-bags?'

'Yes.'

'Of course I have some,' I say, 'but how on earth was I supposed to know that that was your code for "Can we go camping"?'

'Well, can we?' says Edward, getting out of the car, falling to his knees on the gravel and pretending to beg. 'Can we?'

'Yes, can we?' says Lexie, getting out of the car and kneeling next to Edward.

'Oh, look how much they want to go!' says Dougie.

'Now, listen here, kiddios,' says Wendy, putting Jamie on the gravel and ignoring him as he puts small stones thoughtfully into his mouth, 'your mam needs a break. She promised your dad.' She turns to me.

'You go and put on your makeup and find a nice dress. Me and Dougie will deal with this lot.'

'What about the camping?' says Dougie.

'We'll put a tent in the back garden and make a fire,' says Wendy. 'I used to do that on me dad's farm. It's bonza fun.'

'I want to camp in the woods,' says Edward.

'Well, you can't,' says Wendy, scooping Jamie up. 'Now, Bennie, you get out of the car and we can get the tent ready.'

He looks quite excited for once.

'Thanks, Wendy,' I say gratefully, as I bolt for the back door. 'I'll be upstairs,' I say to Dougie.

'I'll make you a tea.'

I'm in shock as I go upstairs. What's happened to Wendy? My God, I'm so grateful. Maybe I've misjudged her. WeightWatchers is doing her the world of good. But I'm so tired. It is now five and I'm never going to get to John's play. It starts at seven thirty and it'll take me at least two hours to drive to London and I'm not bathed or changed.

I look in the mirror. I'm a wreck. My hair's all over the place and I have dark bags under my eyes. All I want to do is sink on to my bed, which is calling to me. 'Samantha,' it is saying, 'come and lie down on me. I'm clean and I smell nice and I'm comfortable and comforting and I can soothe your frayed nerves.'

'Oh, bed,' I say. 'How much I want to lie on you! I want to sink down into your feathered softness and sleep for ever.' Maybe I could give myself half an hour. I'll miss the beginning anyway – I'm sure he won't mind if I sneak in during the interval. He probably won't even know. So I sink down on to the bed. The window is open and the curtains are flapping in the breeze. I can smell the evening air, like a faintly rose-scented perfume. I can feel the warmth of the day, still present, wafting over me. I close my eyes. Oh, this really is very nice.

I let my thoughts drift. Where shall I let them go? I'm not sure. They drift towards Lexie. Poor Lexie, my thoughts say, poor, poor Lexie. There's nothing you can do about her, though. You cannot keep her but you can call Naomi. You can talk to Naomi about her. That is what you must do. You must tell Naomi when she comes to pick Lexie up that she must find a more settled life for her. We're not children any more, we have responsibilities, and Naomi must embrace hers. She must stop hanging out with the cigarette-smoking man from the flat below. She must write to her father and make amends. She must find out who Lexie's real father is. You will tell Naomi to stop playing the victim. Oh, yes, say my thoughts, this is how you will help Lexie. This is how you will be her salvation. You can save her, say my thoughts, you can save her, you can save her, you can . . . I am just drifting into a lovely doze when the phone rings.

'Hello,' I say sleepily.

'Oh, my God, Samantha! Why haven't you rung me? I've been calling all day. I was so worried about you. Are you still cross? Please don't be cross with me. I love you, Samantha, and I miss you and – why haven't you left yet?'

'Hello, John,' I say pleasantly. I'd forgotten I was cross with him – that all seems such a long time ago. 'I was just having a lovely doze when you rang.'

'A lovely doze? You're supposed to be here by half past seven! That's when the play starts.'

'I know,' I say dreamily, looking out of the window. 'There's a tractor cutting the grass on the hill already. Is it time to make hay?'

'Time to make hay? What are you talking about? How on earth am I supposed to know?'

'You used to.'

'Are you on drugs, Samantha? I've been ringing you all day. Where on earth have you been?'

'The vet.'

'The vet?'

'When the plumber came Beady ran out of the door and got run over by Gary White.'

'The dog's been run over by Gary White? Gary White as in famous-footballer-Gary-White?'

'Yes.'

'Oh, my God! Is she all right?'

'No, she's not. She's been run over.'

'Is she dead?'

'She's had her pelvis pinned and she has to stay at the vet's for a couple of nights.'

'Oh, poor you. The children must have been distraught.'

'They've all cried all day.'

Suddenly I feel a bit tearful.

'Oh, darling,' says John, 'I'm so sorry I wasn't there.'

'Me too,' I say.

'Are you still cross with me?'

'I'm too tired to be cross and I just want to see you.'

'Well, get up now and find a pretty dress, come up to me and I'll look after you.'

'I don't have a pretty dress.'

'Yes, you do. That white summer one. The plain one. It looks so fresh on you. Why don't you wear that?'

I know which dress he's talking about. 'OK,' I say.

'I've put a ticket out for you at the box office and I'll ask them to sneak you in when you get here, and then we'll go to the party. I'll drive us home and make love to you and everything will be OK. How does that sound?'

'Lovely,' I say. 'John, I need someone to look after me right now.'

'I know,' he says. 'I am that man.'

'You're being surprisingly manly too,' I say.

'Now, my love, I have to adjust the lights but I'll see you soon.'

He blows me a kiss down the telephone.

I blow one back.

A Strike for Liberty

It's now six. I'm ready. I've ironed my dress and put it on, tied up my hair and let little tendrils float down by my face. I have put on some makeup – a bit of powder, blusher, bronzer and something called 'Sparkling Nude' on my eyes. I have looked at myself long and hard in the mirror. I might look quite good. Maybe I won't compare too badly to Charlotte. She may be young, pretty, glamorous or, God forbid, sexy, but I'm a woman of experience, a woman of the world, a mother of three. I have seen inside celebrities' fridges, for God's sake! I shan't let Charlotte get to me. I shall stay feeling nice and relaxed. It's a summer's evening and I like nothing better than a long, dusky evening spent with the man I love. If I didn't have to get to London, everything would be perfect.

I waft into the garden. I can smell sausages cooking on the fire. I can hear murmuring and giggling from the tent. Jamie is in what was supposed to be the vegetable patch. Edward and Lexie poke their heads out of the tent.

'Hi,' says Edward, smiling.

'Hi,' says Lexie, also smiling.

'Are you going to London, then?' says Edward. 'You look mighty pretty.'

'Yes, mighty pretty,' says Lexie.

'Thanks,' I say.

'We're being like Red Indians in our tepee,' says Edward.

'Right,' I say.

'And that's how Red Indians speak. I heard it on a western,' he says.

'I think you'll find it's the cowboys who say things like that,' I say.

'No, it isn't,' says Edward, affronted. 'It's the Indians, isn't it, Lexie?'

'Yes,' says Lexie, equally affronted. They both pull their heads back into the tent.

Someone is tugging at my leg. Jamie. 'Mama?' he says, waving his hands above his head, clenching and unclenching his little fists. 'Carreee me . . .'

'You're speaking so well, Jamie,' I say, 'but I can't carry you because you're covered in mud and I've just put a nice clean white dress on.'

'Carreee me,' says Jamie, waving his hands more determinedly.

'Wendy!' I yell. 'No, Jamie. I'm sorry. I can't think of anything I'd rather do than carry you but not right now.'

'Carreee me!' roars Jamie, now crying.

'Wendy!' I shout more loudly. 'Where are you?'

'She's gone out,' says Lexie, her head popping out of the tent.

'What?' I say.

'She and Dougie went to get some vodka whatsits.'

'But the shop's half an hour away! I've got to go. They both know that. Why are they doing this to me? I've got to get to London.'

'It's all right,' says Lexie. 'Edward and I said we'd hold the fort, didn't we, Edward?'

'Yes,' says Edward, from inside the tent.

'But you can't do that,' I say. 'It's illegal. They may not be back for an hour.'

'Oh, we'll be fine,' says Edward, sticking his head out too.

'But you're not fine, are you?' I say. 'Here's Jamie wanting a carry and you're both fiddling around in a tent!'

'Well, I'll carry him, then,' says Edward, extricating himself. 'Now, Jamie, where do you want to be carried to?'

Jamie giggles.

'Where?' says Edward.

'Dada,' says Jamie.

'You want to be carried to Dada?'

'He's not here, though, your dad, is he?' says Lexie.

'Nooo,' says Jamie, making his funny face where he sticks his lips out in a pretend pout.

'Nooo,' says Lexie, laughing. 'Neither's my dada nor my mama for that matter.'

'Me your mama?' says Jamie.

'Ooh, yes,' says Lexie, laughing even more.

Now I'm laughing too.

'Oh, you are funny, Jamie,' I say. 'Now, listen. I have to go and you two are in charge until Dougie and Wendy get back, which shouldn't be too long. I'll leave my mobile number on the pad next to the phone and if anything goes wrong you must – Where's Bennie?'

Just then we hear a piercing wail.

'Oh, my God,' I say. 'Not Bennie again! What on earth's happening? Why is today a disaster?'

Bennie appears from the kitchen door. 'I–I've hurt my hand,' he says piteously.

'Oh, God, Bennie.'

'What have you done to it?' says Edward, putting Jamie down and going to Bennie.

Bennie waves it in front of Edward's face.

'Did you shut it in the door?' says Lexie.

The tops of Bennie's fingers are bright red. 'Bennie,' I say, sinking down to inspect them, 'what have you done? Have you burnt them?'

'Yes,' says Bennie, tears falling down his face. 'I–I've hurt my hand.'

'How did you do it?' I ask, taking him into the kitchen and turning the cold tap on.

'On the iron in the laundry room,' says Bennie. 'I went to see if the water was still there and I touched the iron.'

Oh, my God! I left it on – I never leave it on! John does, and gets an earful from me about it, but now . . . It's because I was in such a rush.

'I'm so sorry, Bennie. I left the iron on and you touched it. Haven't I told you a million times not to touch the iron?' I'm suddenly irrationally cross with him. 'Bennie, why did you touch it?' I say. 'I've got to go out and now your fingers are all hurt and – Christ! Why can't it be easy for me to get out of this house? All I want to do is see your father.'

'It's hardly his fault,' says Edward, who is now standing behind me. 'I mean, who left the iron on?'

'I did,' I say crossly, 'but you shouldn't have been left in charge. Look what's happened! You and Lexie were so busy being Red Indians no one bothered to look after poor Bennie!'

'How on earth were we supposed to know Bennie was going to burn himself?' says Edward, aggrieved. 'It's hardly our fault. When Wendy went out, she didn't say, "Oh, and look after Bennie because he's in the laundry room playing with an iron your mum left on."'

'We didn't know,' says Lexie, backing him up. 'We would have stopped him if we did, wouldn't we, Edward?'

'Yes!' says Edward.

'Ow. My hand!' wails Bennie.

Ten minutes later I have switched off the iron and Bennie still has his hand under the tap. I can see the clock creeping towards seven and I want to cry but poor Bennie's fingers are so red and painful, it would be unfair.

'Poor Bennie. Will you be OK if I leave you with Wendy and go to London?'

'N-no.' He sniffs. 'I – I want you to stay with me. I'm hurting, Mama.' He buries his little head in my chest. 'S-stay with me, Mama, please?' he says.

He starts to cry again. I kiss the tears from his eyes. 'I suppose I'll have to,' I say resignedly. 'I'll just call Daddy.'

I go to the phone and ring John's mobile. It goes straight to his answerphone.

'Hi,' I say. 'I love you, and I'm sorry, but I can't come tonight. It's nearly seven and Wendy's disappeared with Dougie to buy vodka and I'm absolutely furious but there's nothing much I can do because Bennie's burnt his hand on the iron and . . . I don't know what's happening, John. I feel like I'm disappearing – we both are. I'm vanishing into my children and you into your play. I'm sorry. I wanted to see it. I wanted to see you. I –' *Bleep.* The telephone cuts out. 'I just wanted us to have some fun together, that's all,' I say, and put down the receiver.

When I get back into the kitchen, Bennie isn't there.

I wander out into the garden. I can hear voices. One belongs to an adult male.

'Dougie!' I say, as I'm about to round the corner. 'Where the hell have you – Oh!'

It's not Dougie in the garden. It's Gary White. He's standing by the fire, clutching a bottle of wine.

'Gary!' I say, shocked. 'What are you doing here?'

'I, erm, I, well, I rang,' he says awkwardly.

'When?'

'Earlier. Dougie was here. I wanted to say sorry, Samantha, and I didn't know what to do and Dougie suggested I come round and . . . I brought you this.' He hands me the bottle. 'How's your dog? Is she OK? Is there anything I can do?'

'She'll be fine,' I say. 'Her pelvis was broken but she'll survive.'

'I'll pay,' says Gary. 'I'll go in and pay – or have you already?'

I shake my head.

'Right, give me the address and I'll go tomorrow.'

I'm just about to tell him about the vet wanting an autograph when Bennie appears with his hand held out in front of him.

'What's wrong?' Gary asks, bending down to look.

'I – I hurt my fingers,' says Bennie.

'Poor Nennie,' says Jamie, emerging from the tent with a singed sausage.

'Poor Bennie indeed,' says Gary. 'Now, you don't want to eat that do you, Jamie? It's burnt.'

'Can I go for a ride in your car?' asks Edward.

'Not now, Edward,' I say.

'Can I, then?' says Lexie.

I shoot her a look. A couple of days ago she was screaming about Gary because he had no clothes on and now she wants to go for a ride in his car.

'No, you can't either, Lexie,' I say. 'It's late.'

'Maybe you both can another day,' says Gary, looking in a rather concerned way at me. 'Shall I open the wine?'

'No. I will. You'll never be able to find the corkscrew. The last time I needed it, it was in the fish tank. Would you like some?'

'I'm on the wagon.'

'Did you have a problem?'

Gary grimaces. 'All footballers have problems. I wasn't the worst.'

'So this is all for me?'

'Yes, but isn't Dougie here?'

Now it clicks. 'Oh, so you've come to see Dougie, not me.'

'Well, he said you wouldn't be here and I was on my own and he asked me over.'

'So you didn't come to apologize?'

'Yes,' he says, 'I did. I hoped I'd catch you but if you'd left I'd've left you a note.'

'After drinking the wine that's supposed to be my present?'

'I told you, Samantha, I don't drink. Look, open the wine. Have a glass and I'll . . .' he looks round the garden '. . . I'll get your fire going again. It's gone out.'

'All right,' I say, and go to look for the corkscrew, just missing Wendy and Dougie coming back through the gate.

I glower at Dougie through the kitchen window. He's hugging Gary as if he's known him all his life.

'Gary!' he's saying. 'So glad you could come! How wonderful to see you. We've been out getting alcohol. Oh, the fire's gone out. We put some sausages on and then –' He spies Jamie toddling towards him eating something that looks like charcoal. 'Ah, I see the sausages are done. Now, Samantha's gone to London and –'

'Nah, she hasn't,' butts in Wendy.

'What do you mean, she hasn't?' says Dougie, looking as if someone's shot him.

'Her car's here.' She motions towards the drive.

I smile secretly in the kitchen. Ha! That'll wrongfoot Dougie.

'Her car's here?' says Dougie. 'How can it be?'

'She hasn't gone,' says Gary. 'Bennie burnt his hand and he wanted her to stay so she did.'

'You mean you've *seen* her?' says Dougie. 'She really is here?'

'Yes. She's gone inside to open the wine I brought.'

'Christ!' says Dougie, and walks towards the kitchen.

He finds me casually chopping some mint that's been languishing in the fridge for a week.

'Samantha!' he says, in his panicked voice. 'What are you doing? Why haven't you gone to London?'

'I'm making a dip,' I say. 'I'm going to do a cucumber and mint dip for some crudités because that's what people eat at parties, isn't it? As you invited Gary to your private party in my back garden I thought the least I could do was make you some food.' I give him my biggest and most gracious smile.

'Oh, God, it's not like that,' he says. 'Gary rang earlier to speak to you and you weren't here so I told him that and he said he wanted to bring you a present to apologize and I said he should bring it round even if you weren't here and then I thought he might like to chat to me because he said he was on his own. I love football. I'm impressed by ex-footballers. I'm pathetic.' He hangs his head. 'And, anyway,' he continues, 'why aren't you in London? Gary said Bennie burnt his hand. What on earth happened?'

'Oh,' I say. 'What happened? You and Wendy went out for almost an hour to look for booze without telling me, which meant I didn't know the children were unsupervised and Bennie burnt himself.'

'On what?'

'On . . . something,' I say.

'But on what?' says Dougie, anguished. 'I couldn't bear to think it's my fault.'

'Actually,' I say, relenting, 'it was my fault. He did it on the iron I'd left on. But you and Wendy had no right to go out and leave the children on their own.'

'But you were here.'

'Yes, but that's not the point, is it, Dougie? Wendy's job is to look after the children on the odd occasion I actually might need to go out. I mean, how hard is that? You knew how important it was for me to get to London. John didn't come home last night. Did either of you think about my marriage? No. You were too busy thinking of yourselves.'

'Oh dear,' says Dougie. 'You're really cross, aren't you?'

'I'm more than cross. In fact, I'm really upset. I cannot believe you'd be so irresponsible, although God knows why I expect you to behave any better. You've always been irresponsible . . .'

'That's unfair,' says Dougie, bridling. 'Anyway, why don't you go to London now? Go, Samantha! Go and see John.'

That does it!

'For God's sake, Dougie!' I yell. 'I'm a mother. I cannot just leave my children. I cannot walk out on Bennie when he needs me. Don't you get that? The moment when it was remotely possible for me to leave has gone and that's your fault.'

'I'm sorry,' he says.

'And to invite someone to my house without telling me! That really takes the biscuit.'

'I thought you wouldn't mind!' Dougie protests.

'But you didn't think, did you?'

I take a sip of the wine. It's really very good.

'Is it OK?' asks Dougie, trying to look winningly at me.

'Yup,' I say, a bit grumpily. '"Here I am, ruined in the prime of my youth and strength, by a drunkard and a fool."'

'What?' says Dougie.

'It's from *Black Beauty*,' I say tearfully. 'Here I am, all dressed up, and now everything's ruined because you and that idiotic Wendy went to get some booze.'

Dougie puts his arms round me. 'My poor Samantha,' he says. 'You didn't get to go to the ball, did you?'

'No,' I say, even more tearfully.

'I'm so sorry – and you're right. I *am* useless. I've always been useless but I'm devoted to you.'

'Well, you've got a funny way of showing it.' I sniffle. 'I haven't been out for weeks and I'm really worried about John and –'

'You need a night's fun, that's what,' says Dougie.

'No,' I say. 'I need a magic carpet to whisk me up to London so that I *can* go to the ball.'

'Oh dear,' he says mournfully. 'Well, that won't happen, but, hey, why don't we have a ball here? We could find that electric extension lead and move the CD-player into the garden. It's a warm, light evening. We have a fire, wine and food. We have guests –'

'One guest.'

'We can have fun!' he says. 'Stuff London. I'm so sorry you've missed John's play but why don't we make the best of it? And Gary's a nice bloke, isn't he?'

'I don't know,' I say sulkily. 'He drives too fast, he turns up uninvited in people's gardens and he ran over my dog.'

'But he didn't mean to run over Beady. He can stay for a bit, can't he?'

'Only if you don't talk about football.'

'I promise,' says Dougie, crossing his chest. 'Now, what do you say?'

'I've got nothing else to do.'

'And you're all dressed up,' says Dougie.

So he goes out into the garden to get Wendy to help him move the stereo and I ask Gary to help me with the drinks.

He almost trips over himself with excitement. 'Yes, of

course, whatever you say,' he says, all in one breath, and pretty soon we're dancing and eating crudités, and Bennie's taking off his clothes, for some reason, giggling, thoughts of his hurt hand now banished.

About an hour later we're breathless and sitting by the fire. Wendy has shown Dougie how to do a Haka, which was odd as I thought the Haka was something Maoris did, but when I said so to Wendy she looked at me as if I was an idiot. 'Anyone from the Antipodes can do it,' she said. She spread her legs, crouched and said, 'Ha!' threateningly.

Gary has done his impression of how footballers' dance, which involved him pogoing up and down and punching the air. I attempted a salsa with Dougie, and when Lexie saw us whirling around, as Dougie is rather good at the salsa because he and Maxine used to go to communal lessons in the village hall, she made Edward try to dance with her.

'Oh, come on, Edward!' she said, trying to prise him off Bennie.

Edward was pretending to hunt Bennie down with a pointed stick. 'I'm coming at you with my pointed stick!' he was saying.

'Why?' asked Bennie, still stark naked and running round the fire with his fingers raised above his head as if he were a demented bull.

'You're a bull and I'm a huntsman!' said Edward, chasing him.

'Oh, don't be a huntsman, Edward, come and dance with me instead,' pleaded Lexie.

Edward stopped dead in his tracks.

'Dance? With you?' he said, then spotted me and Dougie on the other side of the fire. 'You're dancing, Mum,' he said and grabbed Lexie's hand. They executed such a funny dance – hopping here and colliding there – that Dougie and I had to stop and watch.

'Oh, God,' said Dougie, stifling his laughter as Edward trod on Lexie's toes.

'Ouch!' said Lexie.

'You're not twirling the right way,' said Edward, trying to force her round to the right.

'I can't do that! My arms are jumbled up!' said Lexie.

Then naked Bennie appeared at Lexie's side, apparently recovered from the anguish of his burnt fingers. 'I–I'll dance with you, Lexie,' he said.

'You can't,' said Edward, pushing him out of the way. 'I'm trying to teach Lexie to dance.'

'Edward!' I said, as Bennie tried to prise Lexie's hands from Edward's.

Edward gave up and stalked off to sit by the fire as Lexie and Bennie jiggled around.

'I–I'm going to do my bottom dance,' Bennie told Lexie.

'Not your world-famous bottom dance?' I said to him, knowing what was about to happen.

'Bennie's going to bend over and waggle his bum in your face!' said Edward.

'How horrible!' yelled Lexie, and ran off round the garden, pursued by Bennie and Edward. Then, right at the back, little Jamie, now also naked, appeared unexpectedly from the flowerbed.

'Jamie's got no clothes on!' yelled Lexie.

'M-maybe he's going to do a bottom dance too!' yelled Bennie.

'Let's all do bottom dances!' shouted Edward, and started to take off his trousers.

I intervened. 'Not now,' I said, motioning to Lexie. 'We have a young lady present.'

'Who?' said Edward.

'Lexie,' I said.

'Oh, she won't mind.'

But I had remembered what happened by the river the other day. 'I don't think it's appropriate, Edward,' I said. 'Why don't you put another log on the fire and come and sit down?'

So, now we're sitting down. Jamie is lying on his back, waving his legs in the air and Bennie is counting his toes for him.

'L-look, Jamie,' he says. 'You have ten toes, see? One . . .'

'Un . . .' says Jamie.

'Two . . .'

'Doo . . .'

'Three . . .'

'Tee . . .'

'Not tee, Jamie,' says Bennie. 'Three!'

'Tee!' says Jamie, giggling, and Bennie leans forward to hug him.

'God, your children are sweet,' says Gary. 'That Jamie looks like a little angel.'

'He's not really,' I say, 'but thanks.'

Dougie yawns. 'I don't know why but I'm tired,' he says.

Edward comes over and sits on his lap.

'You're squashing me,' says Dougie.

'Don't be tired, Dougie,' he says. 'It's only ten.'

'Ten!' I exclaim. We sit and look into the fire for a while longer. About twenty minutes later, I remember that I must put the little ones to bed. I look around and can't see them. Then again, I can't see anything much because the light has faded, except for the fire.

'Jamie?' I say. 'Bennie?'

'They went into the house with Wendy,' says Lexie.

I go in and find Wendy opening another bottle of wine in the kitchen. 'I thought you were having those vodka shots you went out for,' I say accusingly.

'I am,' she says defensively. 'I just thought I'd bring you out some wine.'

'Why?'

'Oh, y'know. I want you to have a nice night. I feel bad about letting ya down. Me and Dougie shouldn'ta gone out. If we hadn't, you woulda got to London and seen John, and Bennie wouldn'ta burnt his hand and . . . I'm sorry.'

I feel touched. 'I'm a bit sad I didn't get to London but –'

'We're having a good time here, eh?' she says enthusiastically. 'Aren't we, Mrs S?'

'Yes, but I need to put Bennie and Jamie to bed now.'

'Done it!' says Wendy, beaming proudly.

'Where's Bennie? Is he in my bed?'

'Nope. I told him he's gotta sleep in his own. I was pretty tough with him, Mrs S.'

'Oh, my God, what did you do? Lock him in his room?'

'Nah, I just told him if he didn't sleep in his own bed he'd be in Big Trouble and he'd not go and see Gary's sports car. That did the trick.'

'Oh, right,' I say. Thanks.'

'So, let's take this wine and some candles outside and have a girly natter, eh?'

'All right,' I say faintly. 'Let's.'

When we get back to the fire, I find that Dougie is talking football with Gary while balancing a ball on his finger. 'Why didn't you go abroad?' he says, concentrating on the ball. It falls off repeatedly and he has to catch it.

Gary is hunched forward, staring into the fire. 'I don't know,' he says. 'I was so young when I made it big I didn't really know what I wanted. I just married my childhood sweetheart and we got a house in London, then a bigger one and we had a daughter, then got an even bigger house and my wife, my former wife, got an architect in and she didn't want to move . . . I was earning a fortune. I was having a good time and I don't suppose I thought it would stop.'

Just then his phone rings. 'It's my mother,' he says to me. I raise my eyebrows.

'Hi, Mum,' says Gary. He makes a gesture of helplessness with his hands. 'Yes, I'm fine . . . No, Rowan isn't here . . . Yes, I'm with friends . . . Yes, the lady with the girl who . . . Yes, I did apologize . . . No, I don't think anyone took a picture . . . No, I'm sure it won't be in the tabloids . . . Yes, we're having dinner now so I have to go.' He puts down the phone and sighs.

'Does your mother call you every day?' I ask.

'Yes,' he says.

'My mother never calls me,' says Dougie, 'and Samantha's mum is always on a cruise.'

'Lucky you,' says Gary.

'Why do you answer?' I ask him.

'Because I'm all she has,' he says. 'She's always been pretty hands-on . . .'

'That means interfering,' says Dougie.

'Even when I was little it was her, not my dad, who encouraged me to play football. My dad was always happier in the potting-shed. He wanted a family life but she wanted fame and fortune.'

'And which did you want?' I ask.

'I always wanted this,' he says.

'This?' I say. 'You mean all these children and chaos?'

'Yes,' he says. 'I'd love a rural life. I've spent so much of my time in cities. I grew up in London but I always wanted a big house and garden in the countryside. That's why I bought the Dower House. It was a dream, really. I imagined me and my second wife sitting by the fire with friends and spending summer nights walking through the woods trying to find badgers and –'

'Find badgers?' says Edward, appearing on the other side of the fire.

'I've never seen a badger,' says Lexie.

'Can we go and find some?' says Edward. 'Can we?'

'I don't know,' I say. 'It's very late.'

'Oh, it'd be easy to see one at this time of night,' says Dougie, airily. 'You have to take a torch, then hide in the wood and wait.'

'Can we go and see them?' asks Lexie. 'Oh, please,

Samantha. It would make me so happy to see badgers at night.'

'All right, you can go,' I say, 'but don't be ages because I want you both in bed before midnight.'

'Midnight!' says Edward. 'That's the latest I've ever been up.'

As they leave, Dougie gives me a cheery wave.

''Bye, Mum!' says Edward.

''Bye, Samantha!' says Lexie.

Gary has chosen not to go with them. 'I'll stay here and keep Samantha company,' he said, but Wendy opted to see the badgers. 'I've never seen those critters before,' she said. But as they are leaving she turns. 'Oh,' she says, 'I forgot to tell you John rang. He sounded cross. 'Byee!'

I go back into the garden, deflated. John rang and I didn't know about it. What on earth is wrong with Wendy? Why doesn't she tell me these things? I go back in, find the telephone and call John. He doesn't answer. I leave another message. 'Sorry,' I say. Sorry, sorry, sorry. In the kitchen Gary is drinking a glass of water and looking very thoughtful. He goes to the fridge and sees the wall charts.

'No snogging dog,' he says, looking at Jamie's chart. 'Does Jamie often snog the dog?'

'Yes,' I say, smiling, but then I remember that Beady is at the vet's with a broken pelvis. 'Oh, God, it's been such a day.'

'I know,' says Gary. 'Look, come and sit by the fire. I've stoked it up and poured you some more wine. Come and relax.'

We go back out to the fire. For a while we say nothing. I sip my wine. He sips his water. Then I remember what Gary had said earlier. 'Did you really have a drink problem?' I ask.

'Yes,' he says simply. 'I had a lot of money. I was very young. I started playing football when I was five. At sixteen I was playing in England's youth team. At eighteen I went professional. It's amazing and horrible at the same time.'

'What's the amazing bit?'

'The money. The adulation. I wasn't academic but I could play football, and that meant the other kids in my class looked up to me. And I loved to play. That feeling when you score a goal . . . indescribable.'

'What was the horrible bit?'

'My marriage broke up. I married Sian when I was nineteen. She was the trendiest girl in our class. My mum liked her. I think she thought she'd steady me but we were so young. We had a life, though – parties and clubs – and then she got pregnant with Chantal. I loved that girl, but I wasn't around much. I was off playing football and . . .'

'Having affairs?'

'Loads,' he says. 'Everyone was. But it was embarrassing because one girl went to the press and –'

'Sian left you.'

'Yeah, and she took Chantal. I've barely heard from her since. I wrote letters but they kept coming back so I've just assumed Chantal doesn't want to know me. I've always sent money for her to her mum but . . . I hurt her. I hurt them both. I hurt everyone.' He stares into the fire. 'I just wanted us to be a family,' he says, 'but I was so busy all the time. I mean, how do you manage it?'

'I suppose I made the decision to be around my children, really,' I say. 'It's not easy, especially if you've been successful, but for me families are about shared experiences, about day-to-day intimacy. You can't buy that. You can't dip in and out of it. You're either there or you're not.'

'Oh, God, now I feel really bad,' says Gary.

'But everyone loves you,' I say. 'Even the vet wants your autograph!'

'Does he?' says Gary, brightening.

'Yes, and all the mothers at the school gates . . .'

Gary laughs. 'I did notice,' he says.

'Well, don't you like all that? Isn't it part of your life? Everyone telling you how marvellous you are and how much they admire you?'

Gary thinks for a bit. Eventually he says, 'But I want to be anonymous. Everyone thinks they know me but no one really does and, hey, I'm a bit old to be relying on my mother, aren't I?'

'Yes.'

'I just want a life where no one recognizes me or expects anything from me. I want something normal. I haven't had normal for a long time.'

'Is that why you moved here? To get away from everything?'

'Yes!' he says passionately. 'I thought I'd find a new life where I wasn't just this famous footballer but a proper person like you – kids, marriage, a dog – and I moved down here because I thought it'd give me and Blondie a chance . . . but it didn't, did it? As soon as I told her we were leaving London, she'd gone off with my accountant.'

'Maybe she fell in love,' I say. 'Maybe it wasn't really your fault.'

'She married me for the money,' he says bitterly. 'That's what my mum always said about her. She never liked Blondie. She called her "that bloody gold-digger". I met her a few years after me and Sian had split and she seemed fun, different. She's Australian and I liked her brand of directness.'

'Like Wendy,' I say.

'Yes, she is a bit like Wendy!' He laughs. Then he stops. 'We were happy for a while, I mean really happy, but eventually she became disillusioned with me.'

'Why?'

Gary looks straight at me. 'Maybe there's a lot to be disillusioned about.'

'Have you read *Black Beauty*?' I ask.

'No.'

'You should,' I say. 'It's all about families even though it seems to be about horses.'

'I'm not following you.'

'Well, it has noble Beauty and sad Ginger in it and . . . actually, talking of Ginger, I haven't heard from Naomi. She's Lexie's mum and she should have rung but she hasn't. That's odd, isn't it?'

'Still not following,' says Gary.

'Oh, Naomi's my friend and –'

'Hang on a minute. Somebody did ring.'

'Yes, my husband,' I say.

'No, a woman.'

'How do you know?'

'I answered the phone. I hope I didn't do wrong but

you were outside saying goodbye to Dougie and I thought it might be important.'

'Well, who was it, then? Was it Naomi?'

'No, it was . . .' Gary screws up his face '. . . Belinda! She says she'd rung to remind you about a party you're supposed to be going to tomorrow.'

'A makeup party.'

'A *makeup* party?' Gary is trying not to laugh.

'Don't ask,' I say.

'Well, she said that the party isn't being held at her house but at someone else's so your friend can get away from her kids.'

'Whose house, then?'

Gary screws up his face again. 'Can't remember.'

'Was it Gail? Liza? Nicki?'

'Nicki! The message was that you're all going to be made up at Nicki's house.'

We're quiet for a bit. Then Gary says, 'Do you think Lexie's mum will come back?'

I stare at him. 'What are you talking about?'

'Well, you know, animals abandon their young. They give them up to other animals or leave them under bushes, and I was wondering if your friend is going to come back.'

'Why wouldn't she?'

'Maybe she feels she can't cope.'

'Possibly,' I say, 'but there's no way she'd do that. Anyway, what makes you think she might?'

'Because I've seen it before. A friend of mine's mother went off for a weekend and was tracked down in South Africa three months later. She'd had a nervous breakdown and just cut loose. He ended up living with the neighbours for years.'

I feel a bit confused now. 'Are you telling me that in your humble opinion a woman you've never met isn't going to pick up her daughter?'

'It happens.'

'Not often,' I say, 'and there's no evidence in this case that it will.'

'Apart from the fact that Lexie is obviously disturbed,' says Gary, 'and her mother hasn't rung. My mother would never do that.'

'Yes, but Naomi's probably busy and your mother rings a bit too frequently, doesn't she?'

'Better than not at all. If I were you, I'd call her mother and tell her to come and get her or you'll be in touch with Social Services.'

'What are you talking about? You couldn't possibly think that's a good idea.'

'Why not?'

'Because Naomi's her mother. They'd take Lexie away and who on earth would benefit?'

'Maybe Lexie. Maybe Naomi. Maybe both.'

'How? Why? They'd be separated. Their bond would be broken. It would be a dreadful thing to do.'

'What bond? Have you seen any evidence of it?'

'Have you?'

'Of course I haven't,' he says. 'I haven't met Naomi or seen them together. All I know is that people with secure family lives do not go bonkers when they glimpse a man wearing no clothes.'

'Wait a minute . . .' I say.

'Listen to me,' he says. 'There's something wrong with that girl. You didn't see her by the river. I know I had no clothes on but you'd think I'd deliberately exposed myself to her she went so insane. That's not the action of a settled child.'

'Gary,' I say, 'where's all this coming from?'

'I've been reading some books on child psychology,' he says. 'I've been trying to work out why Chantal doesn't like me and Rowan doesn't seem that keen either.'

'That's all well and good,' I say, 'but you know nothing about Naomi. She's merely having a break. It's hardly a criminal offence – and who are you to judge? As you say, you have one daughter you don't see, two ex-wives and a daughter you have on the odd occasion. What would you know about bonding with a child?'

As soon as I've said it, I regret it. Gary goes very quiet.

'I'm sorry, Gary,' I said, 'I really am. I don't know why I said that.'

'No, you're right,' he says quietly. 'I'm no father and I don't know what I'm doing with my life. I married Blondie because I thought she loved me for me. I gave up football because I thought I'd find something else I was good at where I could be as successful but in a quieter way.'

'It's not very quiet to drive a bright red Ferrari, is it?'

'No – you see? Another of my theories smashed. I want to stay here, and for Rowan to go to the local school, but will that happen? Of course it won't. I thought if I spent some time with Rowan, she'd grow to love me but she barely knows me. She has all the toys in the world and her own pony, but she's still as quiet as a church mouse with me. Blondie's looking for a new house with lover-boy and I don't even know where they're thinking of moving. Knowing my luck, it'll be as far away from me as possible.'

'Oh,' I say. 'Sorry.'

'It's not your fault. I'd love to be you. I was watching you tonight dancing barefoot in your pretty dress with a man who cares for you, and then I saw the love on the faces of your children and – do you know something, Samantha Smythe, mother of three? You're a well-loved woman. I think you're the most-loved woman I've ever come across and I haven't even met your husband yet.'

Right on cue, I hear the phone ring.

Hours later, when Gary has gone home in his red Ferrari, when I have left a message for Naomi that she must pick up Lexie tomorrow, when Dougie, Wendy, Edward and Lexie have come back with happy faces, tinged with sadness because the badgers weren't playing ball, when Dougie and Edward have sunk into sleep in the tent and Wendy and Lexie are in their beds, John comes home. He slips into bed, cold, smelling of alcohol, cigarettes and sweat, and I breathe him in. He reminds me of a different life, one I used to inhabit with him, and he kisses me. His chin is scratchy and stubbly and he says he's sorry for staying out the night before. I tell him I was angry with him but now I'm not, and then I tell him how tired I am and how so much has gone on and how worried I am that we're not communicating any more. He kisses me again and says he's sorry again and he says trust me, trust me, trust me, and I tell him I do trust him, and then I kiss his words away and we make love as if we'd never touched each other before. And when we've finished and we're lying there in the moonlight, he asks me if I still love him and I tuck my head into its usual place on his shoulder, stroke his chest and tell him I love him more than the moon, the stars, the sun and all the planets put together. He's smiling, but just as he's about to speak, the door opens and Bennie comes in.

'D-d-daddy!' he says delightedly, and nestles down between us. At some point in the night John must have slipped out for when I woke in the morning he was gone, and I wondered if he'd been there at all.

The Devil's Trademark

John has left me a note. I find it under my thermometer, which I suppose, when I think about it, is the best place to leave it.

Dearest Samantha,
I have left for Edinburgh. The play was such a success last night that the promoters have decided to take up the offer of running a second version of the show in Princes Street Gardens. Can you imagine? I feel like I'm producing the equivalent of Cirque du Soleil. The play will be up there for the whole of August to coincide with the Festival, but Charlie and I are just going to set it up in advance. Once it's running smoothly I'm all yours. I know I haven't been around much lately and I'm really sorry. I miss the children so much that I didn't even mind Bennie coming into bed last night. It was so wonderful just to feel his skin against mine and smell his stinky breath. Bear with me, darling. I'll be back in a couple of days for a quick visit. Don't give up on me, Samantha. I'd never give up on you.

What does he mean 'don't give up on me'? Why would I? Is there something he hasn't told me? But how could he possibly tell me anything? We've barely seen each other lately. I'm beginning to get angry. Why does he think it's OK to waltz off to Edinburgh without even saying goodbye? If I ever go anywhere, which I rarely do, it takes me weeks to organize it. I have to write a dissertation on who does what, who needs what, what they all do and don't eat, after-school clubs when and where, and I even write down really stupid, easy-to-remember things that John always forgets like 'Children Must Brush Their Teeth Every Night' and 'Wash Their Hair' and 'Cut Fingernails' and 'Edward Must Use Soap When He Washes', and then I wonder if, in fact, John is brain dead. I went away for three nights once to see an actor's fridge in Scotland, and when I came back, the children were smelly and unwashed.

'Why do you smell?' I asked Bennie.

'I don't,' he said.

'But you do,' I replied, wrinkling my nose.

'Oh, we haven't had a bath since you left,' Edward said airily.

'Why not?'

'Daddy didn't give us one.'

Jamie had something that looked suspiciously like a toffee stuck in his hair, which Edward said must have been there for at least a couple of days as that's when they last had toffees, and Bennie's scalp was dandruffy.

'Why have these children not been bathed?' I asked John.

'What?' said John, looking (a) tired and (b) very confused.

'Why do they smell so bad? Why does Jamie have a toffee in his hair?'

'I've been looking after them single-handed,' he said.

'I know,' I said. 'I do it all the time and they don't stink when they're with me.'

'Do you know how hard it is to get them into the bath?'
'Yes.'
'Do you know how much they squabble and bicker?'
'Yes.'
'Well, how on earth was I supposed to get them into the bath, then?' he said angrily.
'You put them in together.'
'But they hate each other,' he said. 'They're awful. How on earth is anyone supposed to deal with that?'
'It's sibling rivalry,' I said. 'Every family has to deal with it.'
'You're mad,' he said.

How to Deal with Sibling Rivalry

In our house, Edward hates Bennie but loves Jamie, and Bennie hates Edward and Jamie but sort of loves them too but Edward sort of more because he's bigger and cool, and Jamie loves everyone. This means that most scenarios involve a tortuous system of cajoling and setting one off against another. John has not grasped this. I have explained it to him a thousand times but he still refuses to believe that looking after children can be so complicated and, potentially, devious. So I have written a plan for him to explain it all.

The Rule of Toys

All children will, de facto, *want the toy another child is playing with. Even though they have a million toys that are all the same and all broken, when faced with a decision about which toy to play with, they will only want to play with the toy that a brother is currently playing with. This goes for all children and all toys. If, for example, Bennie is playing with a truck and Jamie sees, he will waddle over and try to take it. He will say, 'Me want truck,' and Bennie will say, 'No, this is my truck, Jamie,' and carry on playing. Jamie will sink to the floor wailing. If no truck is forthcoming from Bennie, Jamie will reach out and pull his brother's hair. Bennie will drop the truck and yell, 'Ow! Jamie pulled my hair,' and run into the room where a parent (usually me) is cooking. He will howl until this parent goes into the sitting room and sorts out the battle. By this time, of course, Jamie is happily playing with the truck.*

What is the solution?

Suggestion (a): *Find Bennie an identical truck to play with; this does not work as Bennie only wants his original truck and will not be fobbed off with a doppelgänger.*

Suggestion (b): *Find Jamie an identical truck; this is hopeless for same reason as before.*

Suggestion (c): *Ignore them and let them battle it out; this is possibly the worst solution and I should know because I have tried it. The battle will soon rage out of control.*

Suggestion (d): *Get Edward involved. This is not a bad idea as Edward has the weight and age-related gravitas to stop a battle. Interestingly, Jamie and Bennie will often take a telling-off from him as they will not from their parents (i.e. me).*

Sometimes it is worth persuading Edward to wade in – he doesn't need much persuasion as he is constantly trying to police the family. Off he'll go: 'Bennie, you have this truck and, Jamie, you have this one!' he'll say. Nine times out of ten, the younger two accept his authority.

Suggestion (e): *If the Edward-is-boss technique doesn't work, the best solution is to cut and run. Tell the children that as they cannot play nicely no one can have the truck, then put it on the mantelpiece. This solution brings short-term problems (crying, wailing, gnashing of teeth, accusations of unfairness) but the long-term result is pretty good: the children tend to wander out into the garden and start digging up the shrubs . . . quietly.*

The Rule of Going to Bed

In our house no child wants to go to bed before the others. Neither will they get undressed/get into the bath/allow themselves to be washed/clean their teeth/get dry/put on their pyjamas/go upstairs unless the others do too. This would be fine if they were triplets, but as they are different ages they have fixed ideas about the bedtime hierarchy. Edward, for example, cannot see why he should have a bath and go to bed at the same time as his brothers. 'But Jamie has a bath at six and is in bed by seven!' he'll say, when I plead with him to get into the hot soapy water. 'I am ten,' he'll say. 'I want a hot bath to myself.' I will then say that of course he can have one to himself but only if Jamie is allowed in it. Bennie only wants to bath with Jamie, but Jamie hates bathing with Bennie because Bennie tends to splash water in his eyes. He only wants to get in with Edward, whose bath is too hot for him.

Once I have managed to get two out of the three bathed (generally Bennie sits it out), I have to get them to brush their teeth. Bennie wants to use Edward's blue toothbrush with a Power Ranger on it, but if he does, Edward will say, 'Arrgh, Bennie's put germs on my toothbrush!' Then Bennie will spy that Jamie has grasped his toothbrush – although how he knows I have no idea: I deliberately bought Bennie and Jamie identical toothbrushes to prevent this kind of argument – and start wailing and yelling. Then Jamie will run off with Bennie's supposed-toothbrush and hide it somewhere and . . . it's all hopeless and no one's teeth get done at all.

Then I have to put them to bed. Bennie wants Edward to read him a story, as does Jamie, but Edward never wants to read to them. We will all go upstairs and Jamie will find about six books and pile them on his bed, then take Edward's hand and lead him to the pile. He'll get under his duvet, pop his thumb into his mouth and stare at Edward until Edward starts Jamie's Postman Pat *annual. 'One day, there was snow in Greendale . . .' Edward will say, and Jamie will snuggle into him. Edward will give me a desperate look and say, 'Do I have to read all of it?' Jamie will get bored with* Postman Pat *after page three and push* Miffy *in front of Edward's nose. Eventually, Edward will put a tape on for Jamie and creep out of the room.*

He then has to run the gamut of Bennie, who has been waiting patiently in his room with his two carefully chosen books. Edward knows how to play the game when it comes to Bennie. He'll read Bennie's books in such a monotone – 'Thomas-the-Tank-Engine-was-in-his-engine-shed' – that by page five Bennie has either fallen asleep or insisted I take over.

If Edward is in a non-helpful mood he will not venture up the stairs at all. Instead, come seven o'clock, when I'm trying to get Jamie and Bennie to bed, he'll say, 'It's not my bedtime yet,' and Bennie will hear and say, 'I'm not going to bed until Edward does,' and Jamie will catch on and park his bottom solidly on the floor.

What is the solution to this?

Suggestion (a): *Persuade them to go to bed at the same time – useless. Edward is quite correct in pointing out that, at ten, he should not be expected to go to bed at the same time as a two-year-old.*

Suggestion (b): *Make it a competition. This is a good idea that often works. If I have managed to get them into the bath and cleaned their teeth, I can usually get them up the stairs by pretending to be a monster that bites the bottom of the slowest child. The children love this game – even Edward who reverts to being four.*

They tear up the stairs and I crawl after them making loud growling noises. Once they're in Jamie's room, at the top of the house, I close the door and tickle them, and if I'm very, very lucky, they will all stay with me and listen to stories. Then I have to make another game to get them to put on their pyjamas ('I'm the pyjama-ripping monster') and then another to get them into bed ('I'll suck your noses off') and then, eventually, the two little ones will fall asleep. Edward and I will go back downstairs and collapse for half an hour.

Suggestion (c): *Give up. This is often the most alluring solution, especially on a Saturday night when there's no school the next day and I'm tired. I turn the television on, sit in front of it and hope that the children will follow suit. Then, at ten, I can wake up, find them asleep and bundle them off to bed.*

There is a problem with this solution. I have woken up to find them all wide awake. Once Bennie had made a trap that involved sticking a plate with Sellotape on to a box next to the kitchen door and it was all very complicated and dangerous. On another occasion Jamie had scribbled on the walls with Edward's felt tips while his brothers had had a fruit fight.

'What's the matter with you all?' I shouted at them.

They gave me a look of triumphant defiance.
It was terrifying.

But just as I'm musing about how the children love and hate each other at the same time, the thermometer bleeps. Oh, good. Time to take it out of my mouth, get up and have a coffee. I reach for my booklet to record my temperature. I look at the thermometer.

Crikey – my temperature's shot up and the thermometer is now deigning to read it in centigrade again! Yesterday it was 36.8 C and now it's 37.6. I put a dot on the graph and join it up. Yes, my temperature has risen so I'm about to ovulate. I read my booklet to find out what to do next. 'You must now test for ovulation,' it says. I grab a test stick, go into the bathroom and wee on it, come back and place it in the specially designed monitor. 'It will take up to three minutes for the monitor to read your result,' says the booklet.

Two minutes later, it shows a green light. 'If the monitor shows a green light,' says the booklet, 'you must have sexual intercourse within the next 24-hour period. The green light indicates that your womb is ready to be impregnated with a girl.'

Oh, my God, the time is now! Finally my *How To Get A Girl* kit is telling me I can conceive one. I'm so overwhelmed that I sit and stare at the monitor.

Then I panic. Do I really want another child? I'm not sure John and I are coping with the ones we already have – or that I'm coping that well with Lexie either.

Then the thought hits me. How on earth am I going

to get a girl? *John is not here.* Not only that but he's miles away, probably somewhere up the M1 with bloody Charlotte, talking about revolving unicorns. And the thought of not getting a girl because John has spent much of the summer away from the family and is now thoughtlessly on his way to Edinburgh incenses me so much that I decide my kit is now trying to tell me something. It is saying this: if John does not come back and have sex with you he doesn't love you and you are destined never to have a girl.

'It's now or never,' I say to myself, as I pick up the phone. 'John,' I say into his answer-machine, 'you have to do something momentous for me right now. My girl kit has gone green. Sparkle Smelly-bum Smythe is hours away from being conceived but to get her you have to come home and make love to me within twenty-four hours. I know you're on your way to Edinburgh. I know this is a lot to ask but, John, you'll only be a day late and that one day away from your job could save our marriage.'

After I've put the phone down I wonder if I've been a bit over-dramatic. Will our marriage fail if John doesn't come back? I don't know. I only know that it's of the utmost importance that he comes back to me.

The phone rings.

'Hi, Adele,' I say, disappointed.

'What's the matter?' she says.

'Nothing, really. I was waiting for John to ring.'

'John?'

'He's gone to Edinburgh and I've barely seen him and . . . I'm feeling a bit sorry for myself.'

'Well, you shouldn't be. You're the talk of the town!'

'I beg your pardon?'

'Everyone's talking about you.'

'At this time in the morning?' I say.

'Yes. I've already had Liza on the phone.'

'Oh.'

'And then Belinda rang.'

'Double oh.'

'Then Nicki and Gail rang and . . . well, let's say it should make for an interesting morning.'

'An interesting morning?'

'The makeup party. Belinda says she phoned last night to remind you but –'

'Yes, she did. I totally forgot.'

'– Gary White answered your telephone.'

'Yes, he did.'

'But what was he doing at your house?'

'He ran over Beady and he came to say sorry.'

'He what?'

'He ran over Beady and the plumber had to rescue her and I had to take her to the vet's and it was awful.'

'I'm not following, Samantha. Nothing in your life makes sense.'

'That's true.'

'Why was the plumber in your house?'

'Because John was out for the night and there was a leak, which didn't have anything to do with John being away although, right now, I'm wondering if it was an omen.'

'What type of omen?'

'A bad one. John's job is a bad omen. My ovulation kit is flashing a green light at me and he isn't here!'

'What ovulation kit?'

'The one that's going to help me get a girl.'

'Jesus Christ, Samantha,' says Adele. 'You're not trying to have another child, are you?'

'Absolutely,' I say.

'Well, you'd better go to Belinda's party and explain all this because I've got no idea what you're talking about.'

'Why?' I ask, confused.

'Because Belinda thinks you're having an affair with Gary White.'

'What?'

'That's what she told Gail and Nicki – oh, by the way, did Belinda tell Gary the party's at Nicki's house so she can get away from the kids?'

'Yes.'

'And Liza's going to have your guts for garters because apparently you left a rude message about Josh on her answering-machine and, anyway, she thinks she's the only one in the valley allowed to have an affair.'

'But I'm not having an affair and I didn't leave a rude message. I just wanted to let her know how rude Josh was to me, not the other way round.'

'Well, she's furious and I suggest you come right now to the party because, unless I'm very much mistaken, you're going to get a lot more done to you than just a makeover!'

Two hours later I'm at Nicki's house. It's a large mock-Tudor mansion on the outskirts of our nearest town. I've never particularly liked it – it has an indoor swimming-pool and a gym and is a bit too nouveau-riche for me – but inside it's welcoming enough, for Nicki has staff. She has a gardener and a Thai lady who cooks, cleans and babysits all at the same time. Her name is Ping – actually, I don't think that's her name at all but it's what Nicki calls her. Ping seems devoted to Nicki. I see them together often – out in the garden looking at herbs, trying on dresses in shops in town. Well, Nicki tries on the dresses and Ping does up the zips. In her own way, Nicki is maybe devoted to Ping. I think she stops Nicki being lonely. And Ping is the most fabulous cook, which is, unfortunately, wasted on Nicki, with all her mad diets, but to give her her due she doesn't let her own food-mania stop Ping cooking delicious food for the rest of us. So, I love going to Nicki's for lunch, even though I've only been invited twice, because Ping makes such mouthwatering things: prawn balls and *tom yam* soup and fantastic salads laced with coriander and lemon grass. She also makes these lovely savoury biscuits. In fact, today in Nicki's house sitting at her retro Ron Arad table, I'm waiting for some. Nicki won't touch them because they have wheat, dairy and sugar in them, all three of which are a current no-no.

'Have you made any lovely biscuits, Ping?' I said, and she went bright red, then asked after the children. I told her I'd left them at home with Wendy and my friend Dougie. I remember how cross they all were, even Lexie, who obviously thought it was her divine right as a fellow member of the female sex, to come and try on makeup with me. 'Oh, please, Samantha,' she said. 'I want to know what season I am.'

'No, Lexie,' I said. 'Not even Adele's daughter, Nancy, is going. It's for grown-ups.'

'But I'll behave, I promise! You'll hardly notice I'm there!'

'That's not the point. No one else is bringing their children so I'm not going to either.'

'But I'm not your child,' she said pleadingly. 'I'm your friend's daughter so surely it doesn't count. You could say there was no one else to look after me.'

'But there is and, anyway, why on earth do you want to come to a boring makeup party?'

'I've never been to one before!'

'Well, neither have I. Anyway, you're too young to wear makeup and –'

'Have you heard from my mum?' Lexie said sulkily.

'No,' I said, 'but I'm going to ring her right now.' I picked up the phone, dialled Naomi again and left another message. 'Hi, Naomi,' I said chirpily. 'Lexie was wondering where you are,' I noticed Lexie shaking her head as I said this, 'and I was wondering when you're coming to pick her up because you were due here yesterday. Give me a call and let me know. Bye.'

'Are you going today?' said Edward, in a rather startled way.

'Looks like it,' said Lexie.

'Oh dear,' said Edward.

'Why?' said Lexie.

'Nothing,' said Edward, then gave her a wink. 'When exactly today might you be going?'

'Don't know,' said Lexie.

'Might you be able to Play That Game with me?' said Edward.

'What game?' said Lexie.

'You know.' He winked at her again.

'Oh, right. *That* Game,' said Lexie, winking back.

'Why are you two winking?' I asked.

'No reason,' said Lexie, breezily.

'Edward,' I asked, 'are you and Lexie planning something I don't know about?'

'No,' said Edward. 'It's just that there are lots of things we haven't done yet that we thought we might do.'

'Like what?'

'Erm, a new game of Conquerors,' said Edward.

'We've got a role for Jamie,' said Lexie, now giggling, 'and we want to try him out.'

'Yes, we want Jamie to play the page's assistant,' said Edward, the picture of innocence. 'We thought it was unfair if he didn't get a go too. Come on, Lexie, let's go and find him.'

Later, before I left, I asked Wendy to keep an eye on Edward and Lexie. 'They're up to something,' I said, as Wendy rolled her hair into curlers in front of her bedroom mirror.

'Do you think my hair'd look nice curly?' she asked.

'Yes,' I said, 'but please watch those older children. Something's going on.'

'How can ya tell, Mrs S?'

'Because Edward's being nice to Lexie and he keeps winking at her.'

'Maybe he fancies her.'

'Don't be ridiculous, he's only ten, and yesterday he was calling her a fathead for letting the dog out.'

'What's a fathead, Mrs S?'

'Oh, someone who's a bit dense. Anyway, keep an eye

on them all. Dougie's here somewhere, probably still in the tent or trying to fry his sardines on a dead fire, so he can help.'

'Rightio.'

Then, as I left, I realized that Wendy was wearing yet another blue dress – turquoise with a low back and ruched front.

'Gosh, that dress is a bit risqué for this time in the morning, isn't it?'

'What does risqué mean?'

So now I'm in Nicki's house, listening to Adele telling us about the things she likes. We're seated round the large coffee-table, which is festooned with a variety of make-up palettes. I'm opposite Liza, who, so far, has ignored me. Nicki is next to me, and Gail hasn't arrived yet. A couple of other women are listening to Adele, but I don't recognize them. Belinda is sorting out some colour charts, which resemble the ones you get from paint companies.

'Hmm,' says Belinda, holding one up to Liza's face. 'Now, is that you?'

'Is what me?' snaps Liza.

'This bronze foundation. I think it's you . . . I've just got to go and check my notes. Hang on a minute.'

Liza rolls her eyes at Adele, who ignores her as she's sipping green tea and talking non-stop to anyone who will listen about makeup, alternative remedies, face and body products, shopping, drinking two and a half litres of water a day, walking, exercising in general, scented candles, charity lunches, her daughter Nancy, travelling first class, getting her hair done, facials, collagen injections in her lips and, her latest fad, micro-dermabrasion.

'Can't you talk about anything else?' says Liza, after about fifteen minutes.

'It's a makeup party,' says Adele, smoothly. 'What else would you like me to talk about?'

'I don't know. What about food?' says Liza.

'Hate food,' says Adele. 'Makes you fat.'

'I agree,' says Nicki, nodding fervently as Ping appears with the delicious biscuits.

I take two. No one else takes any.

'OK, let's talk about sex, then,' says Liza.

Adele looks at her meaningfully. 'That's not my bag, really. Too personal for this time of the morning.'

'Oh,' says Liza. 'What *is* your bag, then?'

'I've told you,' says Adele, evenly. 'I like beauty treatments, rejuvenating body balms and spending days at the spa.'

Adele is always off to spas for therapies, or driving up to London to pick up the latest skin creams, have a Brazilian at Heidi Klum or getting Nico at Daniel Galvin to retouch her highlights. 'What highlights?' I said to her once. Adele has ash-blonde, dead-straight hair. I once made the mistake of joining her on a spa morning. Her husband, Charles, the merchant banker who never has anything to say to me, had given her two day passes for the latest Tibetan place near Gerrards Cross.

'It'll be full of middle-class, middle-aged women,' I said.

Adele raised an eyebrow. 'What are we, darling?' she said.

'I mean, boring ones who actually care what colour their walls are and peer over the fence into their neighbour's garden.'

But, still, we went and spent the day thumbing magazines, drinking peppermint tea and eating salad, and I noticed that, while my hair goes into fuzzy curls the moment it gets a whiff of moisture, Adele can dive into the pool and come out the other side with her hair as sleek and straight as ever. 'I should seriously dislike you,' I said to her, and she flicked a piece of rocket at me.

'You should join a gym with a spa, or a spa with a gym,' she said, looking at me.

'Oh,' I moaned, looking down at my less-than-taut physique. 'I know, but I can't afford it.'

'Why? What do you spend your money on?'

Everything We Spend Our Money On

I had a memory the other day, when the newspapers thudded on to our doorstep, as they do every day, that once upon a time I actually read them. Now I spend all day looking at them and wondering, 'When will I have time to read you?' But whenever I sit down to do the crossword someone always decides they want something. My mother does the Guardian *Quick Crossword every day.*

As soon as her newspaper's through the door she's on it like a terrier. At eight fifty-five, she'll ring and say, 'I've done all of it bar three down, darling. Have you done yours yet?' and I'll reply, 'No, I haven't because I had to get up, get the children breakfast, find their school clothes, make Edward his packed lunch, persuade Bennie to get into the car, pick up the teabags that Jamie had started to bury in the garden, take the children to school, prise Bennie off me and persuade him to walk through the gates, put Jamie back in the car and retrieve the car keys he'd stuffed down the side of the driver's seat, which took the skin off my hand, and then come home.'

'So you haven't thought what a landlocked southern African country, six letters, is?' she'll say.

'No,' I'll reply. 'I haven't even looked at it.'

'Pity.' She'll ring off.

Anyway, John and I have a contorted relationship with newspapers. Sometimes, when I realize we have no money in the bank, I say things like 'We've got to cut down!' then panic and make lists of incomings and outgoings. The incoming list is short: John's salary (quite a high figure) and my salary (minuscule). Then I list the monthly outgoings:

food £800
alcohol £200
electricity £100
babysitting £100
running two cars £200
oil for the central heating £150
man who comes and does the garden occasionally £50
children's activities £100
children's clothes and shoes £100
newspapers £90

I often look at it and will it to get shorter, but it never does. John looks at it and says, 'Nearly a thousand pounds a month on food! Ridiculous!'

'We're a family of five,' I say. 'The boys eat a lot.'

'Well, they're eating too much then,' John will say.

If I buy a packet of six chocolate croissants, Edward will come home from school, find them in the drawer, eat four and give the remaining two to Bennie and Jamie. He will then turn to me and say, 'We've run out of chocolate croissants. Can you get some more tomorrow?'

'How do we cut down?' I ask John. I remind him that Bennie spends most of his life ferreting for food in the fridge. He wanders in, grabs a carton of apple juice, takes the top off, drinks the lot and then puts the empty carton back. Then he might decide he's still thirsty and drink half a pint of milk. Then he'll scramble up the fridge shelves and eat whatever he finds on the way: a tube of Frube, a slice of pork pie, a bite of cheese, cucumber, a cherry tomato and half a cookie he left there yesterday. Then he will abseil back down, rub his tummy, take off his trousers and leave the kitchen without closing the fridge door. This means that everything goes off rather quickly. Luckily Jamie eats only Rice Krispies but as he has about ten bowls a day, we get through a heck of a lot of them.

Yet John persists in endeavouring to minimize the grocery bill. He'll look at my list and substitute £800 for £1000 on food. 'Surely we can manage on that!' But it's not John who 'edits' the fridge. It's me. I watch the food disappear. The more we buy, the more they eat.

I bought a packet of real fruit lollies the other day and put them into the freezer. 'Ooh,' said Edward, when, on his eternal search for 'ice-chocs', he found the lollies instead. 'Can I have one?' he said. He had one, Bennie had one and so did Jamie. Then Stanley came over and he had one and somehow, in the space of forty-eight hours, the whole lot had gone.

The next week I decided to buy two packs. Edward found them again and the same pattern was repeated, except that Adele and Nancy were over. Adele didn't have one, of course – 'Sticky, calorie-packed things,' she said – and then Stanley came over again, and forty-eight hours later two packs had gone.

That's how it works in this house. Chocolate croissants, packets of crisps, baguettes, yoghurts, ice-cream, punnets of strawberries, steamed asparagus, cucumber after cucumber, carrot after carrot, they all go into the endless bottomless black holes that are the children's stomachs.

In the end, I agree that yes it is ridiculous to spend so much on food and John will look triumphant, but in my heart I know that we'll never stick to £800.

Sometimes I suggest 'We could cut down on the newspapers,' and John will look horrified. For ages I wondered why, but now I know. The newspapers prove we exist. We may not have the time or energy to read them, but they are there, symbolizing the people we used to be, people with time and brains and a genuine interest in the workings of the world. And if we cancelled the newspapers, it would mean that the children with their myriad demands, needs and empty stomachs had won.

But, in fact, we have already lost. As soon as I had pushed Edward out of my body I lost everything I had been before.

Adele has her expensive foibles and knows it. Her current insecurity is that she has turned forty. She spends much of her life staring into the mirror, pouting – 'to see if the collagen injections are working' – and pulling up the skin from her cheekbones to decide if she should have a facelift.

'A facelift at forty?' I say. 'But you're too young, aren't you?'

'No,' she says. 'Everyone's having it done. They all have Botox and facial scrubs and non-surgical facelifts and that's what I want.'

'Why?'

'I want to look young again.'

'But you do look young and, anyway, we're getting older. That's how life is.'

'I want to look like a Hollywood actress.'

'But we're not Hollywood actresses. We're mothers and housewives.'

'Hollywood actresses have facelifts all the time. All those celebrities, when they have babies they book in for a C-section and have a tummy tuck at the same time!'

'No!' I said.

'That's how they stay so slim. I should have had one when I had Nancy.'

But Adele is so slim, I don't know why she worries so – but worry she does. She worries about the fact that she's just spent a grand on micro-dermabrasion. 'Can you tell?' she says, pointing to her face.

'Tell what?' asks Liza.

'My skin!' she says. 'It's great, isn't it?'

'What have you done to it?'

'Micro-dermabrasion.'

'I'm not sure it's made much difference,' says Liza.

Adele looks very put out.

Luckily, Belinda comes back from the kitchen, followed by Gail. 'Makeup can make a real difference,' she says, picking up on the tail end of the conversation. 'Honestly, my Colour Me Wonderful kit can make you look ten years younger.'

'Can it?' says Gail, taking off her coat and sitting down. 'Hi, Samantha,' she says, spotting me. 'Haven't you been a busy girl?'

'Who's going to be first?' says Belinda. 'We can talk about everything later.'

'Can I?' says Nicki. 'It'll stop me wanting to eat those biscuits.'

I take another. 'Aren't you going to have one?' I say to Adele. 'They're delicious.'

Adele pats her tummy. 'A second on the lips is an inch on the hips.'

'Oh, for God's sake, I'll have one!' says Liza. 'It's only a bloody biscuit.'

I shoot her a grateful look, which she ignores.

'Ladies!' says Belinda, warningly. 'I'm about to do a colour consultation and I want you all to pay attention.'

'Yes, miss,' says Gail.

'Now, Nicki must move into the light,' says Belinda, carefully manoeuvring Nicki's chair towards the window, 'and I have to consult the colour charts to see what palette would suit her.' She looks down at them. 'Hmm,' she says. 'You're blonde and pale and . . .'

'Surely she's summer?' says Gail. 'I mean, Nicki actually looks like a summer's day.'

'Actually, it's my favourite season,' says Nicki.

Ping comes in. 'Prawn balls, Miss Nicki,' she says.

I pop one into my mouth. Delicious. 'You're an amazing cook,' I say to Ping, who smiles and blushes again. I hand them round. Again, only Liza and I take one. 'Liza,' I say, 'I really think we should talk.'

'About what?' she says, refusing to look at me.

'About what happened when I left you that message because –'

'I don't think Nicki is summer at all! I think she's spring!' Belinda exclaims.

'Oh,' says Nicki, disappointed. 'I so wanted to be summer.'

'No, no, no! Spring is lovely,' says Belinda. 'It's all light pastels and pinks.'

'I like pink,' says Nicki, 'especially when it comes to lipstick.'

'Hallelujah!' says Gail.

'Why don't you all go back to chatting while I do Nicki's makeup?' says Belinda. 'Then you can see the difference my Colour Me Wonderful system makes to Nicki's appearance.'

'What's wrong with my appearance?' says Nicki.

'Just go with it,' says Gail, then turns to Adele. 'Gosh, your skin's amazing! What have you done to it?'

As Adele starts off on her micro-dermabrasion story again, I sidle towards Liza with the plate of prawn balls. 'More?' I say, smiling in what I hope is a conciliatory fashion.

'No, thanks,' she says coldly.

'Look, Liza,' I say, 'please stop being so cross.'

'Why?'

'Because I can't see what I've done to upset you.'

'Can't you?' she says. 'Do you know what I do, Samantha?'

'You're a banker.'

'Do you know what that involves?'

'Yes,' I say patiently.

'Do you know how a job like that affects my life?'

I tell her that, no, I don't suppose I do but maybe, if she told me, then I would understand better than she thinks I do.

'I get up at six every day. Before I leave for work I have to shower, wash my hair, get dressed, then blow-dry my hair. I have to do this every morning because I have to look professional – and do you know why I have to look professional every day?'

I shake my head.

'Because that's how everyone else looks. Every day I have to wear a different outfit from the day before. The men don't, as they assume no one notices what they are wearing, but the women – we all know if a blouse or a brooch has been duplicated. Every night, I put out a different set of clothes, change my bag and jewellery, make sure my nail varnish isn't chipped and that it matches my lipstick. I do this every single day of my life, except at weekends and on the occasional day off and the whole process of getting ready can take up to two hours. Do you understand what I'm saying?'

'Yes,' I say meekly.

'Then I have to make sure Basia has got Josh up and fed him some breakfast, drive him to school and get to the station to catch the nine five. If I miss it there isn't another till nine thirty, which doesn't get me to London until ten thirty, which is too late for someone who runs a team in a bank.'

'But surely people will understand you being late occasionally. I mean, you have a child –'

'That makes no difference,' says Liza. 'I'm the only

person in my office with one. Well, the men do but they also have wives.'

'And you have a husband.'

'Have you met my husband?' she says.

'No.'

'That's because he spends the week in London,' she says. 'He stays up there in our flat because he's too tired to commute.'

'When do you see him?'

'Weekends,' she says, 'and the occasional night out in town.'

'When does Josh see him?'

'He doesn't, really.'

'Oh. Aren't you tired as well?'

'Yes, but I'm a woman and a mother and my feelings, apparently, don't count.'

'But you get time to work out, don't you?'

'I do that as many mornings as I can – do you know why?'

I shake my head. I want to say, 'For sexual reasons,' but manage to stop myself.

'Because every woman in my office goes to the gym every day. They all look great.'

'But so do you.'

'Only because I work out, and on those days I get up at about five.'

'God, it sounds dreadful!'

'It *is* dreadful. So, you see, Samantha, not everyone is like you. Not everyone can fiddle around in jeans and a T-shirt every day writing books about fridges and having a nice time with the children. Some of us have demanding jobs so we don't have time to reassure our children that we love them, and when a child behaves badly because he wants more attention – which his mother is perfectly aware of but can do nothing about – that mother does not appreciate being told her son is dysfunctional by a stay-at-home mother because there is no solution. If there was, I'd have found it by now. OK?'

'I'm sorry,' I say, feeling rather awkward. 'I was sort of trying to help. I didn't mean to upset you.'

Liza puts her head into her hands. 'It wasn't helpful,' she says. 'I cannot be like you. I don't want to be like you. I like my job and I like the money, and as for Josh, I don't know what to do.' She sighs. 'I'm sorry he was rude to you, Samantha, really I am. I did talk to him about it but I lost the battle with him a long time ago. Maybe boarding-school will sort him out. I can't.'

'Is it that bad?'

'Yes,' she says.

'You know,' I say, 'there has to be a solution. Maybe you need to draw a line in the sand and stick to it. Maybe if you said to Josh that every Saturday, say, was your day with him and he would have your undivided attention it would help. He'd know that he was going to have a whole day with you, rather than snatched hours here and there.'

'But I often have to work at weekends,' says Liza. 'If I take a morning off, like this, I have to catch up on Saturday. Then there's the shopping. I have to buy clothes and get food in and Adam's around to do fitness training . . .'

'That's what I am saying. Rearrange your life. Ask Basia to do the food shopping. Buy clothes in town in your lunch break. Tell Adam you don't work out at weekends, and ask your husband to make the same commitment to Josh on Sundays.'

'I can't see Luke agreeing but –'

Before we can go any further, Belinda announces she's finished. Liza and I were so busy talking we failed to notice that Belinda and Nicki had left the room, but now Belinda has walked in followed by Nicki. She stands aside and there is Nicki for all of us to see. She is now wearing a long, pastel-pink floaty dress, with bright blue eye-shadow and baby pink lipstick.

'I present spring!' says Belinda, with a flourish.

Nicki looks dreadful but she can't have seen herself as she's smiling away, oblivious to her appalling makeup.

'Nicki is promoting spring,' says Belinda, as if she's the host of a game show. 'She's wearing – hang on.' She stops to consult her charts. 'Erm, she has "naturally nude" on her face and, um . . .' She juggles the charts. '". . . blue yonder" on her eyes with azure mascara and "ooh baby" on her lips. All these colours are part of the spring palette of the Colour Me Wonderful range and are available to buy as a set. If I could possibly have another volunteer – let's say you, Samantha – I can show off a different palette.'

'Why me?' I say, horrified.

'Because you're dark,' says Belinda, 'so you'll either be winter or autumn.'

'I don't like wearing makeup,' I gabble, 'and I'm talking to Liza about something important.'

'Samantha, this is a makeup party and you must take part,' says Belinda, sternly.

'I don't have much choice, do I?' I say.

'No,' says Belinda. She picks up her palette. 'Do you ever wear mauve eye-shadow?'

'No.'

'Maybe you should. My reading of you is that you're autumn.'

'What does that mean?'

'Oh, it's all mauves and greens and ruby blush and smoky amber lipstick.'

'I'll look like a traffic-light.'

'No,' says Belinda, 'you'll look ten years younger. Gary White will think you're magnificent when I've done your makeup.'

I'm about to tell her she's barking up the wrong tree when she announces, 'Samantha is autumn!'

'Of course she's autumn,' says Adele. 'She has dark hair and pale skin.'

'Well, she could have been winter,' says Belinda, defensively. She gets up and leads me into Nicki's bedroom.

'Sit down here in the light,' she says, 'and let's have a real chat while I do your face. Now, turn this way . . .' I turn my head to the right '. . . and I'll sponge some autumn mist foundation on you.'

While she does that, I tell her everything about Gary White. 'I'm not having an affair with him,' I say. 'I can't believe you think that.'

'I don't,' she says. 'It's everyone else. Mind you, he did answer your telephone last night.'

'He ran over my dog! He came to apologize.'

'Well, you know how everyone gossips.'

'Haven't they got anything better to do?'

'No,' says Belinda. 'I mean, I do. I've got the kids and this new business but most people have nothing. Their children are at school. They don't work. We live in a little valley and Gary White is the most sensational thing that's moved here in ages and, it seems, he has the hots for you. He could have gone for anyone – Adele, Liza – but he went for you. Now, that's gossip worthy!'

'But why?'

'Because it's *you*!'

'What's wrong with me?'

'Oh, nothing,' she says, now stroking ruby blush on to my cheekbones. 'But you're pretty casual and you have lots of children. I watched Adele at the school gates that day. She was desperate for him to talk to her and he barely looked at her. You've captivated him.'

'Not true,' I say. 'He isn't interested in me. If Adele turned up at his house he'd ravish her.'

'Would he?' she says. 'Is he a good ravisher?'

'I wouldn't know,' I say. 'You have to believe me, Belinda. I have so much on my plate at the moment that an affair with anyone is out of the question – and, anyway, I wouldn't do it to John. I cannot see why you've all decided I'm having an affair. I would have thought Adele knows me better than that.'

'Maybe she's jealous,' says Belinda.

'Of what? She's always saying she doesn't want my life with all the children and the mess and, anyway, between you and me, we're trying for a fourth child, a girl, really. I bought a kit on the Internet.'

'Did you?' she says. 'Oh, how exciting! Please get pregnant quickly and we can have our babies together. I do so like being pregnant with someone else. Have you told anyone?'

'Well, I'm not pregnant yet, so no.'

'But you must! It might even persuade Adele to have another. Maybe that's the problem – maybe she should have another child.'

'I don't think she wants to,' I say – but Belinda's off.

'I'm finished,' she says, and catapults me back into the sitting room. 'I present autumn!' she says.

Adele stifles a giggle and Liza is grinning.

'Oh,' says Gail. 'Well, hello, autumn. Would you like to look in a mirror?'

Adele is rolling her eyes in mock-horror.

'Yes,' I say. Gail passes me one from her bag.

Christ! What's happened to me? I barely recognize myself. I look like a heroin-addicted marionette that's been in a car crash.

'What do you think?' says Belinda, enthusiastically.

'Erm,' I say.

'Will Gary like it?' says Nicki, innocently.

'Oh, Samantha has something to tell you about that,' says Belinda.

'Do I?'

'Yes!' says Belinda. 'She's not having an affair with Gary White. In fact, she doesn't think he even fancies her.'

'Well, that's what we all thought until it became obvious that he does,' says Adele.

'No, he doesn't.'

'OK! Let's make a list,' she says. 'Number one, he stopped to talk to you, and only you, outside the school gates. He didn't even look at the rest of us. Number two, he's invited you for dinner. Number three, he's invited your children to come and see his Ferrari. Number four, you've seen him naked. Number five, he comes round to your house in the evening and answers your telephone. Shall I go on?'

An hour later we have all been made up, except Adele who says she has a skin allergy, and we're going home. Adele gets into her car and speeds off. I stare after her with Liza. 'What's wrong with her?' I ask.

'Don't know,' says Liza. 'Maybe you hit a raw nerve.'

'What?'

'Oh, all that not-having-an-affair thing. Maybe she really does like Gary White.'

'But she barely knows him.'

'Yes, but she's as insecure as the rest of us. And she's probably bored. Why do you think she's always messing about with how she looks? She's so beautiful – I'd be dancing on the rooftops if I looked like her.'

'But you're beautiful too,' I tell Liza, 'if not when you're done up as winter, I have to say.'

'I'm not sure either that kohl round my eyes and brown eye-shadow is quite my thing . . .'

'But why would that make Adele cross with me?'

'Because you don't make any effort but you've bagged the most eligible man around.'

'But I haven't!'

'Well, it doesn't look that way to the rest of us.'

'What can I do about it?'

'Nothing,' says Liza. 'Everyone thinks I'm having an affair with Adam.'

'Are you?'

'Of course not. I haven't got time and, despite my husband's failings, I love him.'

'Why do people think you're seeing Adam, then?'

'Because they've got nothing better to do. And I spend time with Adam – he's good-looking and flirtatious, but I'm too exhausted to have sex with him, or anyone else.'

And, with that, she drives off.

Ruined and Going Downhill

By the time evening comes, much of my makeup has worn off. When I'd got home Wendy and Dougie laughed so much that Dougie had tears rolling down his cheeks.

'You look dreadful!' he said. 'Like the bride of Frankenstein or something!'

'Thanks,' I said.

'I could do ya better makeup than that!' said Wendy.

Even Edward and Lexie thought it was funny. 'Why do women wear makeup?' said Edward, when he saw my purple eyes.

'That isn't flattering,' said Lexie.

The children spent the rest of the afternoon playing outside. Often I'd see Edward and Lexie huddled in the corner of the garden. When I asked Wendy about it, she just said, 'Oh, they're being kids together, Mrs S,' but then Dougie said he thought they might be discussing their camping night.

'What camping night?' I asked.

'Oh, hasn't Wendy told you? We thought it might be fun to go camping tonight. We've borrowed another tent from a friend of Wendy's.'

'She goes to WeightWatchers with me,' said Wendy.

'And we've got a stove and some paraffin lamps I found in your garage. If we take some sleeping-bags and duvets . . . Well, it *is* the holidays. I thought it would be fun.'

'Do Edward and Lexie *want* to go?' I asked.

'Oh, yes,' said Dougie. 'Edward's already put in a request for two plates of baked beans and Lexie says her mother has never taken her camping.'

'Has Naomi rung?' I asked. 'She's supposed to be picking Lexie up today.'

Dougie and Wendy shook their heads.

I called Naomi again. 'Hi, this is Naomi. I can't take your call right now . . .'

'Naomi,' I said, 'ring me about picking Lexie up. I really need to know what your plans are. It's Samantha, by the way.'

I told Dougie and Wendy I couldn't get hold of Naomi, and the next thing I knew, it was seven o'clock and they were all getting ready. Dougie told me he'd take his mobile. 'Look,' he said, 'if Naomi shows up ring me and we'll come back.'

'*I*'m not coming back,' said Edward.

'We're *all* coming back,' said Wendy, and off they went.

It takes me an age to put Bennie and Jamie to bed. Bennie does his I-just-want-to-be-with-you routine and, once he's out of the bath, scoots up the stairs to my bed. I leave Jamie on the sofa wrapped in a towel and looking at a book, then follow Bennie. He's lying on John's side, blond hair spilling over the pillows. He looks at me with his cornflower eyes and smiles. For a minuscule moment he's just like his father, same shape face, same blue eyes, same mop of hair. Suddenly I miss John, and sit down on the bed with a sigh.

'What's wrong, Mummy?' asks Bennie. 'You look funny.'

'It's because I've got that makeup on.'

'Will Daddy like it?' he says.

'I don't know.'

'I'm missing him,' he says, rather sorrowfully. 'Is he coming back?'

'I think he'll be here tonight,' I say. 'Or I hope he will.'

'Will he?' Bennie says, eyes widening with excitement.

'I don't know. I just hope so.'

Is he coming back tonight? I need him to come home. I want to tell him how tired I am, how worried. God, what a week it's been. There's been Lexie and Gary and the dog, and everyone seems to need me so much that I've barely had time to think. And now everyone thinks I'm having an affair with Gary and I need to tell John before someone else does. I don't suppose he's registered the fact that Gary White has moved into the area. For what does John know of anything that's happened this week? Nothing. And what do I know of his life? Nothing.

This play has been one of the biggest events of my husband's life and I've been looking after children, mine and other people's. Christ, Naomi hasn't seen me for years – I could be a child-batterer, an alcoholic or a drug addict. I could be locking her daughter in the coal hole and feeding her bread and dripping, like her mother did to her. She hasn't even rung. Poor Lexie. Of course she's disturbed.

I'm so incensed that I decide to call Naomi again. She has to come and get Lexie. The phone rings.

'Naomi!' I say into the receiver.

'No, sorry,' says a female voice with an American twang. 'It's only me.'

'Julia.'

'Don't sound so pleased to hear from me.' She sounds hurt. 'I've got some exciting news.'

'Great.'

'Did I tell you I'm studying with Zachary Hofman Junior?'

'Erm, I can't remember.'

'Well, he's amazing. Really amazing. He's an expert on childcare and he's very intelligent and he's done all these studies and written all these books. He goes on tour lecturing to everybody in the States and he goes on television and he rebirths people.'

'Oh.'

'And I think he can help you – I mean help Bennie. I told him about the stuttering and he said he'd cure Bennie when we come over.'

'When "we" come over?'

'Zac and I are flying home in a week or two.'

'You and Zac?'

She giggles. 'We're an item and I want the children to meet him as soon as possible because I need to tell them I'm staying in LA for a year to finish my studies.'

'Won't they be upset?'

'Samantha, they're virtually grown up. The eldest two are at university and Robert's about to finish sixth form so he can decide whether he wants to stay in the UK or move to LA with the younger three. Anyway, I'm not going for ever. You've got to grab the bull by the horns sometimes. You can't live your life pleasing other people all the time.'

'*I* do.'

'Well, maybe you should think about changing,' says Julia. 'Have you had that talk with John yet?'

I tell her I haven't.

'Why not?'

'I'm waiting for the right moment. I haven't seen him much lately, and when I do I'm tired, and so much has gone on he doesn't know about that I don't know where to start.'

'That's key avoidance behaviour,' says Julia. 'You've got to pin him down.'

'Yes,' I say, 'but now I'm worried I'll say the wrong things.'

'Why?' says Julia.

'Because I'm angry with him. He hasn't been here all week. He's gone off and had a good time while I've stayed here with the children, and now I've got Lexie and I can't find Naomi, and Gary White has run over Beady and . . . Actually, I'm seething but I feel guilty about it.'

'Oh,' says Julia. 'Well, maybe John needs support rather than anger.'

'That's why I'm avoiding talking to him,' I say, and hang up.

Thank God for the children. I turn to give Bennie a cuddle but he has fallen asleep. A line of saliva is dribbling out of the corner of his mouth. 'Oh, Bennie,' I say. 'You're so lovely when you're fast asleep.'

Then I hear gurgling from downstairs.

Oh, my God! Jamie's still in the sitting room! I find him surrounded by books. 'Buddles all gone,' he says dolefully. He has the cafetière, which someone had left next to the sofa, and has obviously been pouring cold coffee all over the floor. At least it didn't have too much in it. I pick him up and carry him upstairs.

'Nice,' he says, laying his head on my shoulder and kicking a bit. 'Nice cuggle,' he says.

I close my eyes and breathe him in. 'I love you, Jamie.' I can see in the mirror on the wall that his eyes are closing so I take him to bed. I slip a pull-up nappy over his bottom, and pop him into his teddy-bear pyjamas, the ones that he loves so much, and then gaze into his bluey-green eyes. 'Night night,' I say, kissing the top of his head.

'Nice,' he says, and dozes off.

Then I go back to Bennie. I peel off the duvet to find him stark naked. 'Bennie,' I say, to his slumbering form, 'I have to move you. Your daddy is coming home. We have to make a sister for you, so you have to sleep in your own bed.' And then I sit next to him, stroke his back, as he likes me to do, and whisper in his ear, 'I know we nearly lost you, Bennie, and I know you were very frightened and that that's why you want to sleep near me every night. I'm sorry, so sorry, and I understand how terrible it must have been for you, but now is the time to leave that beach, the sea and that wave behind, and go forwards. I promise I will never let anything like that happen to you ever again.'

Bennie opens his blue eyes and smiles. I lead him to his room, help him put his pyjamas on, then tuck him in tight and hold him for a minute. He goes to sleep just like that.

*

Two hours and two glasses of wine later, I'm feeling pleasantly jolly. I've decided that I must convince myself John is coming home and prepare everything, leaving nothing to chance. So I have lit candles around the house, prepared a rocket salad and laid out a plate of Italian cheeses, Parma ham and salami that Dougie brought from the deli in the nearby town. 'What lovely food!' I said, when he pulled the carefully wrapped parcels out of his bag. I opened up the first to find a creamy block of Taleggio. The second was pungent, crumbling, aged Parmesan, and the third was stuffed with pink, pungent meat sprinkled with oil and pepper. The fourth contained rosemary focaccia.

'Yummy,' I said. 'How kind of you.'

'It's for our camping trip,' said Dougie, looking a bit uncomfortable.

'Oh,' I said, crestfallen. 'I thought it was for me and John.' I told him I didn't have anything much in the larder, what with the washing-machine leaking, the dog getting run over and the makeup party . . . Dougie said I could have everything as long as he could take some bread and Parmesan for himself.

'Thank you,' I said, as I popped it all into the fridge. 'You've saved our relationship!'

I decide to make a fire outside. How did Gary do it? He got paper, sticks, firelighters and logs from the garage. Right. I fetch today's paper, scrunch it up into little balls and put them into the bottom of the brazier. I break off some sticks from the old cherry tree and lay them on top. Then I find the firelighters and add them. I go indoors to get the matches and help myself to another glass of wine, feel a bit peckish and slice myself some Taleggio. I wash it down with more wine, then I have a slice of peppered salami, then another and another. I find the matches, pick up the wine bottle and go out to light the fire.

The firelighters catch immediately, throwing huge flames into the air, which soon settle to caress the sticks. I sit down to watch them. I lean in to put a log on, then close my eyes.

CRASH!

'Shit!' a voice says.

I leap up and run to the driveway. Gary White's Ferrari is crumpled into my gatepost.

'Shit!' says the voice again. Then, 'Hello, Samantha, my petal!'

'Gary?' I can hardly see anything in the dark. 'Is that you?'

'No, it's another man who drives a red Ferrari and often comes to see you.'

'Are you OK?' I walk towards the car. I can hear him but not see him. Why is Gary White such a disaster area? 'Where are you?'

'In the driver's seat and I can't open my door. I'll get out of the passenger side.'

A minute later Gary appears. There's a torch in the garage so I fetch it, turn it on and shine it at him. It makes him look like a ghost.

'Turn it off, will you?' he says. 'I can't see anything.' He lurches forwards and falls into me. We stumble and, as I try to balance, he pulls me close to him, steadying himself.

I can smell alcohol. 'Gary, have you been drinking?'

'Gary White, had a fright, in the middle of the night,' he sings.

'Gary, you *have* been drinking, haven't you? Why? *And* you're driving!'

'No. I mean, yes,' he says. 'Can I come in? I need to talk to someone and I thought of you!'

'Gary, you don't drink.'

'I do tonight, darling,' he says, lurching towards the gate.

'Gary, that's the wrong way!' I tell him to go into the back garden. 'There's a fire. I'll bring more wood.'

'And wine!' he says.

He's probably had enough but I tell him I'll bring some.

When I get back he's sitting with his head in his hands.

'What's the matter?'

'It's not good, Samantha, not good at all.' He slurps some wine.

'No, it isn't,' I say. 'You've fallen off the wagon.'

Gary starts singing 'So Long, Farewell' from *The Sound of Music* very loudly.

'I must go to bed,' he rants. 'Only, I'm not going to bed. I won't! Every Good Boy Deserves Fruit . . . I learnt that in a music lesson. See? I'm not just a stupid footballer, am I?'

'Gary, what on earth's going on?'

'What's going on? You mean what's not going on, don't you?'

'OK, what isn't going on, then?'

'Nothing's going on. Nothing's good. I mean, you're good but nothing else is. Not even my car. It's a pile of shit, destroyed by your bloody gatepost.'

'Actually, Gary, your car destroyed my gatepost.'

'Who cares? Who cares about my car? Who cares about anything?'

'Well, I care about –'

'She's leaving.'

'Who is?'

'Rowan. Blondie's taking her away to live in Australia.'

'Blondie's what?'

'Aren't you listening, Samantha?' Gary says, pouring more wine. 'Ro-wan-is-leeea-ving.'

'I can hear what you're saying, Gary, but I don't understand why Rowan's leaving. You've only just moved here. I thought she was going to go to Edward's school and you'd have her at weekends and –'

Gary drinks some more wine. 'I know that,' he says, 'but it was a false dream.' Then he starts singing again, and I wait patiently for him to finish.

'It turns out that Blondie only let me have Rowan for weekends so she could spend time on the Internet looking for a house in Australia and now she's taking me for a ride. At that he bursts into a terrible rendition of 'Ticket to Ride'.

'Poor Gary,' I say quietly.

He takes my hand and kisses it. 'Samantha,' he says, letting go and looking into my eyes. 'What would I do without my Samantha, eh?'

I tell him I'll go and get him some food.

'And more wine,' he says, as his mobile phone rings. 'Argh! Go away, Mum!' He throws it into the fire.

In the kitchen I find I'm a bit disconcerted. Did Gary White just throw his mobile phone into the fire? He did. And did he just call me his Samantha? Yes. I pour myself some wine. I'm not his Samantha. I'm somebody else's Samantha so I cannot be Gary White's. What do I know of him? That he drives too fast, that he ran over my dog, that he sunbathes naked, that he has an overprotective mother and that he's sad, but he's hardly my responsibility. In fact, I'm tired of being responsible for everyone, of being everyone's Samantha and, as I think about this, I feel tears in my eyes. What have I done since we left Crete? I have tried to put this family back together. I have rallied round Bennie, kept him safe from harm and let him do what I've felt he should do, which is, namely, to be with me most of the time and get in and out of my bed, and although it's my job as his mother to love and protect him as the horses do for their foals in *Black Beauty*, I now realize that Dougie's right about Bennie. I need to stop mothering him so much. I need to get him to stand on his own two feet again and I cannot do that if I'm sorting out Gary White's life, looking after Lexie and trying to bring up everyone else as well. I now know I cannot do it any more. I cannot make Lexie better or give her a proper life or offer her a permanent home. I cannot save Gary's disastrous marriage and his relationships with his two daughters. It's time I looked after myself, my husband and my own children. I must go back outside and tell

Gary I can't help him, but I can try to make him see what families need.

To do this, I decide to stop drinking. I must stay calm. I pick up a tray, put the salad, breadsticks, meats, another bottle of wine and a corkscrew on it, with a large glass of water. Maybe I should make a pot of coffee. I go into the sitting room for the cafetière and I notice the red light of the answerphone flashing. My heart sinks. John's phoned to say he hasn't left Edinburgh, that he's not coming home. I don't listen to the message.

When I get back outside, Gary is lying on his back, staring up at the sky. 'I've just thrown my mother in the fire,' he says.

'I know.'

'Is that a terrible thing to do?'

'The phone's insured, isn't it?'

'I don't care about the bloody phone. I just can't talk to my mum right now.'

'Probably because you're drunk and you don't want her to know.' Gary is still gazing at the stars. 'I bought my elder daughter a telescope once so she could see the star formations and the planets but she didn't want it.' He turns to lie on his side, elbow on the ground, propping his head. 'Actually, I bought her loads of stuff she didn't want. In the end she wrote and asked me to stop. Well, her mother did, which is much the same thing.'

Now he looks as if he's about to cry. 'I'm frightened, Samantha,' he says. 'I've lost one daughter and I really don't want to lose the other.'

'Gary,' I say, as he gets up to help himself to more

wine, and then forks some cheese and Parma ham on to a plate. 'I don't think you understand what makes a family.'

'What?'

'I don't think you understand what makes a family. You have an inkling of the mother–son relationship – although I have to say your mother calling every day is over the top.'

'Well, she can't now, can she?' he says. 'I've just cremated her.'

'I don't think you really know what love is.'

'What are you talking about?'

'You just called me "my Samantha".'

'What's wrong with that?'

'I'm not your Samantha.'

'I didn't mean it in a bad way.'

'I know that, but I'm John's Samantha and my children's Samantha, and sometimes I'm not sure if you really grasp these concepts.'

'What concepts?'

'The reason I'm my family's Samantha is because I'm there for them all the time. You can't just be there once in a while. You can't throw money at people and think it will make everything OK.'

'I don't!' he says. 'I only bought Rowan a few things –'

'You bought her a pony and she's allergic to horses.'

'I didn't know that!'

'But you should have done, shouldn't you? You thought that buying her a pony would somehow bridge the space between the two of you. You think you can solve everything by paying for it.'

'Like what?'

'My dog, my gatepost. You even use your car as a bargaining tool.'

'I do not!'

'Yes, you do. Every time you think you've done something wrong when it comes to me and my children you offer them a ride in your Ferrari. Family relationships are based on more than that. What happens between mothers and children and fathers and children is more complicated than you understand.'

'What do you mean?'

'More than just a football match where you're either winning or losing. I'm not sure that you've grasped the dynamic of a family.'

'Oh, God,' he says. 'You're about to go on about *Black Beauty* again, aren't you?'

'You could do worse than read it,' I say. 'It's about the alphabet of family relationships.'

'It's about horses,' he says.

'No, it's a book about growing up and how to treat other people. It might help you understand things about family rules and structures, and belonging to someone who really cares about you.'

'But what's the point?' he says. 'Rowan's leaving.'

'The point is that if you really want to be in Rowan's life, if you want to right the wrongs between you, you have to be there for her. You have that chance.'

'What chance?'

'To show her how important she is to you. That's what children need to know – that they're more important than the fame you once had or the things you can buy them. They need to know they're important to you above and beyond everything else. You have to prove to Rowan that you can be kind, compassionate and understanding.'

'And how am I going to do that if she's moving to Australia?'

'I don't know,' I say sadly.

We sit in silence for a while, listening to the night.

'Gary!' I say. 'You could move to Australia! There's nothing keeping you here. You don't have a job and you don't need one. Just think about it – you could open a bar or do anything. You're always saying you want a new life, you want to be anonymous, you want a chance to be you. Well, this is that chance!'

Gary smiles.

'You see?' I say, pleased to have cheered him up. 'It's not such a bad idea, is it? You could be near Rowan and surely Blondie would let you have her at weekends, if you've gone all that way to be near her. You could sunbathe and surf and – hey, if you didn't buy a Ferrari you might manage to be low key.'

'But I've just bought a house,' says Gary.

'So what? It's just bricks and mortar. Sell it.'

'But I like it.'

'Well, you'll like another.'

'What about my mother?'

'You said it yourself. You've cremated her. Anyway, she has your father, doesn't she? Maybe it would be good for them to get their own relationship back. You're too old to be tied to her apron strings.'

I'm really getting into it now. 'You say you want to

understand what it is to be a family but you're putting your house and your mother above your happiness with Rowan. Stop being so short-sighted. You have money and freedom, everyone likes you and loads of women fancy you. You'll have no problem.'

Gary shifts his chair right up next to mine. 'Do loads of women fancy me?' he says.

'You know they do.' I slap his hand playfully. 'Within a few years you'll have made loads of little Garys.'

'You're crazy,' he says. 'It's such a big step to take and, well, I'd miss you.'

'No, you wouldn't,' I say. 'You barely know me.'

'But I *feel* I know you,' he says earnestly. 'This summer's taught me so many things, Samantha, and I really love you. You're so unlike my mum. She was always bossing me around and telling me what to do, but you give your children freedom and it's magical. That's why I love being here with you and your family. You've been such a good friend to me and I couldn't bear to leave you.'

'Gary,' I say, taking his hand, 'it's not me you love. I'm unavailable because I love my husband so there's no point in you thinking you love me.'

'But I do – as a friend!' he says. 'You're my best friend.'

'Gary, we've only known each other a few days. Friendship takes years.'

'But what about Dougie? You're friends with him.'

'I've known him for a very long time.'

'And Naomi? The friend who's abandoned her child with you? Why are you friends with her?'

'I told you. She's my Ginger.'

'But why aren't I your Ginger?' he says. 'I'm desperate and drunk and sad and –'

'You can't be Ginger,' I say to him carefully, 'because I already have my Ginger and, in my own way, I'm trying to save her. I can't save all of you.'

'Who am I in the book?' says Gary, a bit desperately. 'Surely there's someone who doesn't need saving?'

'You aren't even in the book.'

'But I've started reading it like you said. Doesn't that mean something to you?'

'Yes, it means good things,' I say, 'but to be part of that book, you have to have been in my life for a long time. Love and life are precious, and friendships are very important to me, and although it's been an experience knowing you, the most dangerous thing people can do is to enter the lives of others and dabble with them, then not be there in the end.'

'Do I do this with you?' Gary asks.

'I don't know, Gary,' I say simply. 'All I know is that it's not here in this back garden with me that your future lies. You do see this, don't you? You are simply not in that book.'

Plain Speaking

I don't know why we didn't hear the latch of the gate click, the squeak of the hinges as it opened, feet crunching over the gravel on the garden path, but the next thing we know, Dougie has appeared, closely followed by Wendy, Lexie and Edward. Lexie's eyes are hollow, tired and red.

'Jesus Christ!' says Dougie. 'Is that Gary's Ferrari?'

'Ask Gary,' I say, 'and why are you back? Is everything OK?'

Lexie comes to me and puts her head on my lap. 'Are you all right, darling?' I ask.

'Not really,' she says. 'I got afraid.'

'Well, course ya did, little nipper,' says Wendy. 'It was so dark I couldn't even see to get me keks off so we came home.'

'Oh dear.'

'Yes,' says Dougie, airily, 'in my long history of camping disasters, this one would be in my top five. We got to the woods and Wendy and Edward made a fire while Lexie and I put up the tents, and everything was fine. We cooked baked beans. We toasted the marshmallows. We told stories.'

'Spooky ones?'

'Not especially. Ask Edward. They weren't spooky, were they, Edward?'

'Not specially,' says a voice behind me. I turn to see Edward whirling a large stick round his head. 'They weren't spooky at all, really,' he says, coming to brandish his stick next to me. 'We just made them up, and I made up one about warlocks' – he stabs the stick into the air – 'and witches' – jab – 'and mummies!' Jab, jab, jab. 'But Lexie got a bit scared. Especially when I told her we had to turn off the paraffin lamp cos it smelt. She was worried about wild animals coming to eat her but I told her that was impossible because I was going to hit them with my stick!' Jab! Jab! Jab!

'Edward!' I say. 'For God's sake, stop messing about with that bloody stick.'

'Why?' says Edward.

'Everything's fine, Samantha,' says Dougie. 'Lexie asked to come home so here we are.' Then he turns to Gary. 'What happened to the car?' he asks.

'Is that *your* Ferrari?' asks Edward.

Gary nods.

'Phew,' says Edward. 'I'm glad Lexie and I had a go in it before you crashed it.'

There is a silence before the significance of what Edward has said dawns on me. 'What?' I say.

'Oh, nothing,' says Edward, suddenly winking at Lexie like a demented owl.

'God, I'm such an idiot. That's what you were up to this morning, winking at each other. You were arranging to go to Gary's and ask him to take you for a ride in the Ferrari, weren't you?'

'No,' says Edward.

'Lexie?' I say.

She won't look at me.

'Gary, did Edward and Lexie have a ride in your Ferrari?'

'Don't ask,' he says, sighing wearily.

'I have to,' I say.

'OK, then, yes.'

'Today?'

'Yes.'

'Where was I?'

'I think Edward said you were at the makeup party. He showed up with Lexie and I took them for a spin. What's the problem?'

'What's the *problem*?' I am incensed. 'They were supposed to be at home with Wendy and Dougie.'

Wendy and Dougie are looking at their feet. Lexie is sitting up now and watching everyone very carefully.

'Wendy,' I say slowly, 'were the children with you or not?'

'Well, I thought they were,' she says shiftily.

'But they weren't, were they?' I say.

'The little two were, weren't they, Dougie?'

'I don't know,' says Dougie. 'I'm not the one who's paid to look after them.'

'Dougie!' says Wendy.

'Sorry.' He shrugs.

'So, where were the elder two?' I ask.

'I thought they were upstairs playing on the computer, but when I went to call them for lunch they'd gone and I didn't know where they were.'

'You didn't know where two children who were supposed to be in your care actually were?'

Wendy blushes bright red.

'And what were you going to do about it? Call me? Call the police? Where did you think they were?'

Wendy hangs her head.

'I don't see why everyone's making such a fuss,' says Edward. 'Wendy was on the phone and Dougie was doing the crossword so me and Lexie went to Gary's cos we were bored.'

'You and Lexie just walked out of the house, went down the busy road and up the hill all by yourselves without telling anyone where you were going?'

'Yes,' says Edward, 'and it's not a busy road and we had to go today because you said Lexie's mum was coming to get her and she hadn't seen the Ferrari.'

'And what if something had happened, Edward? What if you'd got run over? What if –'

'But nothing happened, Mum.'

'Can't you see how irresponsible you've been? I've spent the last ten years bringing you up to be a responsible, honest boy, and this is how you repay me? Sneaking around, lying, winking and not telling an adult where you're going. I don't know what's wrong with you, Edward. I've been all by myself, your father's been away, I've spent a fortune trying to save your dog and all you're interested in is a bloody Ferrari! I'm ashamed of you, Edward, and I never thought I'd hear myself say that.'

'Right!' says Edward, close to tears now. He storms off to the house.

'Edward!' I say.

'Mrs S . . .' says Wendy, tentatively.

'And as for you and Dougie . . . !' Words fail me.

'Ah'm so sorry,' says Wendy. 'I was organizing this weekend do for WeightWatchers and –'

'Wendy,' I say, 'I'm sick of WeightWatchers. If you're so keen on it, why don't you go and work for them?'

'Well, now you come to mention it,' says Wendy, affronted, 'they wrote me a letter a few days ago asking me if I'd be their area representative and I might say yes!'

'Great,' I say, as she stalks off to the house.

'Samantha,' says Dougie, 'I think you're being a bit harsh –'

'And I've had it with you too,' I say. 'God, you're such a romantic. You invest so much emotional energy in things that are past – your failed marriage, your days as a Boy Scout. You didn't even tell me that Julia had finished with you. I'm your friend and you won't talk to me. Why don't you concentrate on things in the present or things that may happen in the future? Why don't you start to live your life?'

'Right, I will,' says Dougie, 'but without you because you're being unbearable.'

'I haven't finished with you!' I shout, as he walks away.

'Well, we've finished with you!' he yells back. 'I'm going to say goodbye to Wendy and go back to London!'

I sit down by the fire, deflated. Lexie shuffles over to me. Absentmindedly I stroke her hair and she closes her eyes.

Gary moves into view. 'I'll go, shall I?'

I nod.

'I'll get someone to come and move the car in the morning.'

I nod again.

'I'll walk back, shall I?'

I make no reply.

'Well, 'bye, then, Samantha,' he says. 'Er, 'bye, Lexie.'

Neither of us responds.

After we hear the gate shut, Lexie says, in a small voice, 'I didn't mean to cause trouble.'

'I know,' I say wearily.

'Am I in trouble?'

'No,' I say.

'Is my mum coming?'

'I don't know.'

'I don't want to go home, Samantha.'

'Oh, Lexie . . .' I hold her in my arms for quite a long time.

Two hours later John comes through the gate. The fire is down to the embers. The wine bottles are empty. The food is eaten. It's chilly. My limbs feel leaden and numb. I want to reach out and hold him, but I'm half asleep. I want to kiss him and tell him everything that's happened, and I want him to reach out for me. I want to feel him envelop me in the strong arms I know so well. I want to inhale him and run my hands over his body and through his hair, and I want him to comfort me, but the words won't come. Instead, the sight of his face makes me want to cry. He stoops and kisses my forehead, soothing, warming, relaxing.

'I'm back, Samantha,' he says.

'Yes, you are,' I say. 'It's a miracle.'

Then he bends down and sees that Lexie is sleeping at my feet, curled into a ball. He looks at her quizzically, then his face softens. He picks her up and carries her into the house. I rise and follow him. The next thing I know I'm in our bedroom and John's there too. Bennie is lying on the bed.

'Oh, God,' says John. 'Why's Bennie in our bed?'

'I don't know.' I'm confused. Wasn't he in his own bed earlier tonight? Or was that a completely different day? I groan. 'He must've crept downstairs when I was outside.' I smile at John. 'I can't believe you're here. You've come all the way back from Edinburgh just for me.'

'Yes, I have,' he says shortly, 'and now Bennie's in our bed, out for the count. I've spent hours in the car and –'

'Actually,' I say, remembering what's gone on this evening, 'that's the least of our worries. I've had the most awful night –'

'So have I, Samantha,' he says. 'As I said, I've just driven back from Edinburgh to make this girl you're so keen on, and I've left Charlie all by herself. I've come back here to find no food, no wine and you with someone else's child asleep in the garden. Do you know what I think?'

'I'm sorry?' I say. John sounds angry and I don't understand why. 'Look, John, I've had an awful night. I've had a row with Wendy and Dougie and Edward's in a mood and Dougie's gone back to London and why are you so angry?'

'Because it's like a bloody circus here! I've come back

to see you, to be with you and have sex with you, and now I don't know why I bothered. This whole thing's a mess.'

'What's a mess?'

'Well, I come through the gate expecting a hero's welcome and what do I get? Bennie's in our bed. I thought we were supposed to be dealing with that.'

'Yes,' I say, '*we* were. I can't do it by myself, you know.'

He continues as if he hasn't heard me. 'I ask myself again, why did I bother?'

'Well, why did you?' I ask, a bit cross myself now. 'I mean, you've been away having a marvellous time so why did you come back? It's hardly my fault I fell asleep. I've been having a very difficult time and – '

'I came back because you were so desperate.'

'I beg your pardon?'

'You've spent months sticking thermometers in your mouth and peeing on sticks and – it's hardly been very romantic.'

'Oh,' I say, furious now. 'Well, I'm sorry I haven't been very romantic but, unlike your good friend Charlie who has been handily available to drink champagne with you at nine in the morning, I've spent the last few days looking after our children as usual, in case you hadn't noticed!'

'Oh, it's always the children, isn't it?'

'What does *that* mean?' I'm shocked.

'It's always the children with you. Bennie's hurt his hand so you can't come to the party. Bennie's upset so he has to sleep with us. I'm always last on your list, Samantha.'

'That's not true,' I say. 'It's just been difficult recently. This summer's been more stressful than I can say and I haven't been able to tell you about it because either you come home too late or you're just not here.'

'I've been working to earn money for us,' he says, 'and, anyway, it's always a difficult time in this family.'

'I'm sorry I'm not looking after you properly,' I say, 'but I was labouring under the impression that you were an adult and therefore able to look after yourself. Now I know that's not the case, I'll make sure I give you what's left of my highly sought-after attention.'

'I didn't mean that,' he says. 'I just meant that Bennie's been taking up so much of your time –'

'Because Bennie's upset. You know he is.'

'Do I, Samantha? Do I really?'

'Yes,' I say to him, suddenly crying and shouting at the same time. 'Bennie's upset because he nearly drowned!'

'That was months ago!'

'*He nearly drowned!* Don't you get it?'

'I know he nearly drowned. Do you think I don't? You probably even think it was my fault.'

'Yes,' I say quietly. 'I do.'

Now it's John's turn to be shocked. 'I'm sorry,' he says, staring at me. 'You think it was my fault?'

'Yes.' God, what am I saying? Why am I saying all these things? 'You let go of him.'

'What?'

'*You let go of him!*'

'I didn't mean to! It was an accident. It could have happened to anyone.'

'No, it couldn't!' I say – and suddenly I can't stop

myself. Everything that's been left unsaid over the last few months comes pouring out. 'I would never have let go of him! Nothing would ever make me let go of my children! You threw him too high in the air and you risked the life of my treasured Bennie and now you dare to come back into this house and tell me that the little boy you dropped to the bottom of the sea because you couldn't be bothered to hold on to him has no right to be in this bed. You terrified him! He hasn't been the same since and I've spent all my time trying to help him because that's what I'm supposed to do as his mother. You, his father, think you can shrug off responsibility for him, go back to work, stay out all hours and have boozy breakfasts, then assume that driving back from Edinburgh to have sex with me absolves you from all this. Well, it doesn't, John Smythe. It really doesn't.'

John sits absolutely still. 'Is that how you feel?' he says.

'Yes.'

'Well, I might as well go, then,' he says, walks out of the bedroom and slams the door.

I collapse on the bed, racked with sobs. Why did I say those things? Now I've driven my husband away. I realize suddenly that I must stop John leaving so I get off the bed and – *Brriinngg.*

Damn the bloody phone! What time is it? Two a.m. Who rings at this time of night? I'm tempted to leave it but it might be an emergency so I pick it up.

'Samantha,' says a far-away voice. 'It's Naomi.'

'Naomi!' I spit. 'Where the bloody hell are you? What time do you call this?'

'I got your messages.'

'About bloody time too,' I say angrily.

'I meant to call. It's just that –'

'Now, you listen to me,' I interrupt. 'If you don't get your lazy, selfish bottom back to my house by tomorrow lunch time, I'm calling Social Services.'

'*What?*'

'You heard. Get here or Lexie will go into foster care. Do you understand what I'm saying?'

'Yes.'

'It's time you stopped messing about and got out of the stables. You're not tragic Ginger any more and I'm not Black Beauty. You're Lexie's mother, so grow up and take some responsibility for once.'

I slam the phone down to find that Bennie is stirring. Thank God he's slept through John and me rowing. Christ, what if he'd woken up and heard us?

'Mama?' he says, still half-asleep.

'Oh, my Bennie,' I say, curling around him protectively. Somehow, some time, I fall asleep crying.

A Talk in the Orchard

When I wake up in the morning John is downstairs making the children breakfast. I lie in bed listening to the clatter of pots and pans. I have a sinking sense of dread and misery. I know I must go downstairs and talk to him but I'm scared of what I might find. If I remain here I can pretend that nothing has happened, that I didn't say those terrible things to John, that maybe even we did make love and create a girl but . . . I look at my *How To Get A Girl* kit. The green light is no longer shining. I've blown it. All this waiting and hoping and trying and making John drive back from Edinburgh, yet now everything's a mess and it's all my fault.

Suddenly, Edward bursts in. 'Are you still cross with me?' he asks.

'What?' I say. God, I can barely remember that I *was* cross with him.

'Oh, good, you're not – because Daddy is. He's downstairs tossing pancakes on to the ceiling and one's got stuck but another one caught fire and he said the sh-word.'

'Oh,' I say.

'He's not supposed to say it, is he?' says Edward.

'No, he's not.'

'So can you come down and tell him that cos when I told him he was swearing he looked really fed up with me.'

I get up and put on my dressing-gown. The sinking feeling is worse. I have to make things better because if I don't . . . Well, John will go back to Edinburgh, Charlie and champagne breakfasts, and I shall be left here, alone and desperate. So, as I walk downstairs I rehearse what I'm going to say. 'John, I'm very, very sorry and I was very, very wrong to say what I said and although I am glad we cleared the air [did we?] I should have said things more tactfully and I don't believe you deliberately wanted to drown Bennie but any mother's instinct is to protect her child and, really, I'm a dim-witted numbskull who should be made to say sorry every day for a year to atone.' There. Then I'll tell him about everything that's been going on, how hard it's been and how sad I feel about having to tell Lexie she must go back to her mother. 'Everything's just built up, John,' I shall say, 'and I took it out on you, which wasn't fair but it's because I love you so much.' Will that do it?

But when I get to the kitchen, John refuses to look at me.

'Hi,' I say brightly, feeling wrongfooted.

'Hi,' he says, in a very cool voice, searching in the fridge.

'What are you looking for?' I say. 'Can I help?'

'Oh, no,' he says. 'You see, being in my forties, I'm quite capable of finding some orange juice in this kitchen without your help.'

'There's none in the fridge,' says Edward, cheerfully, heading out of the back door. 'Mum didn't get any.'

'Oh,' says John.

'Have the little two and Lexie had breakfast?' I ask him.

'Yes,' he says.

'Edward says you made pancakes.'

'Yes.'

'Actually, where are Bennie and Jamie and Lexie?'

'In the garden.'

'I didn't hear Bennie get up.'

'No.'

'Oh, John,' I say, 'I'm so sorry, really I am. I said some unforgivable things.'

'Yes, you did,' he says.

'I didn't mean them. Please forgive me. I don't know what to say . . .'

'Obviously not.'

I go to him and take his arm. 'John,' I say, 'please look at me. We need to sort this out. Relationships can be broken by this type of thing.'

'You think ours is that fragile?' he says coldly.

'No,' I say, rather desperately, 'but I said some terrible things.'

'Like the fact that I deliberately nearly killed *your* son?' he says.

'I didn't mean it like that.'

'Well, Samantha,' he says, as he turns away, 'you'd better think pretty carefully about what you did mean or I can't say where we might end up.'

'What do you mean?' I ask, panicked. 'I was just trying to have a conversation. We were avoiding things.'

'Everyone avoids things,' says John, staring out of the window. 'Hadn't you noticed? Wendy spends her life avoiding the fact that she's overweight.'

'Actually,' I say, 'I need to talk to you about Wendy

because she's going to WeightWatchers so much now that –'

'And Dougie spends his life avoiding the fact that he's an adult, and your friend Naomi is avoiding being a mother. Now, I don't think any of this is good but sometimes, Samantha, we have to avoid things because they're just too painful to think about. OK?'

'OK,' I say, in a small voice.

Then John turns to me for the first time. He looks pretty angry. 'And you, Samantha,' he says, 'are avoiding the fact that you are a bloody martyr. And now I'm going outside to play with my children – safely – if that's all right with you.'

But now it's midday and John is pulling up in the lay-by near my childhood home. 'I don't know why you agreed to this,' he says frostily. He's barely spoken to me since he walked out of the kitchen. He spent hours outside with the children showing them where he was going to make the tree-house, then playing leapfrog, hide-and-seek and Conquerors. The children and he ran about screaming and laughing . . .

'I don't know why you arranged to meet Naomi here but it's your decision, as per usual.'

'I couldn't turn her down. When she called this morning she sounded so desperate and –'

'But she's manipulating you,' he says quietly. '"We have to meet by our tree." Honestly, she's being ridiculously melodramatic. You'll do Lexie no favours by letting her mother manipulate you. You can't save everybody.'

'I was just trying to help,' I say. 'Is it really that bad?'

John doesn't answer.

The children are in the back of the car. They're very quiet. Edward is half asleep, Bennie is snoring in his seat, as is Jamie. Only Lexie is awake. She has her battered suitcase on her lap and is staring out of the window, pretending not to listen. I feel like crying as I watch her. I think of her saying goodbye to Wendy. When I told Lexie we were going to meet her mother, she ran to Wendy and flung herself into her arms.

'Don't worry, little mate,' said Wendy. 'Keep in touch, eh?'

'But I'll see you when I come back to visit, won't I?' said Lexie.

'Don't think Ah'm staying here much longer. Ah think Mrs S wants me to leave . . .'

'Wendy,' I said.

'Ah'll go and pack,' she said, and walked upstairs to her bedroom.

'Is Wendy going?' Lexie asked me.

'I think so,' I said.

'And that's my fault, isn't it?' Lexie had wailed. 'I wish I hadn't been afraid of the dark because then we'd never have come back from the woods and you wouldn't have found out that me and Edward had gone to see Gary White and Wendy wouldn't be in trouble.'

'It's not that,' I said. 'Wendy would have left anyway. Everything has its time to end, Lexie.'

'So it's my time to end, is it?' asks Lexie.

'Yes, it is,' I said. 'You need to go back to your mummy.'

'But I want to stay and finish *Black Beauty* with you.

Can I? Please?' I told Lexie we would finish it together. We sat on the sofa and read the last chapter.

'My troubles are all over, and I am at home; and often before I am quite awake, I fancy I am still in the orchard at Birtwick, standing with my old friends under the apple trees.'

When I turned to say, 'The End,' Lexie was crying.

'Why are you crying?' I asked her, but I knew.

'I want this to be my home,' she said. 'I don't want to go back to that flat in Reading. It smells of cigarettes and I don't like the man who lends Mummy his car. I want to stay here and go swimming and camping, and I promise I won't let Beady out again. I really won't.'

'It's nothing to do with Beady, Lexie,' I said. 'This is so hard to explain to you but . . . we all have our lives and there are people we belong to. Much as I'd like you to belong to me, you don't. You belong to your mother and the two of you need to be together.'

'But why can't we be together here?' she asked.

'Because you have to find your own place,' I said. 'She's probably found a nice clean new flat and a job, and you're probably going to be living nearby and we can see you all the time.'

'Then why don't I just stay here and Mummy can visit me?'

'Because I'm not your mother,' I said.

'But I don't want to be with my mummy,' she said. 'I want to be with you and Edward and Bennie and Jamie. Why can't I?'

I held her and my heart hurt as if it was breaking in two. I told her I loved her but she was crying too hard to hear.

So now we're parked near the old orchard with the apple trees that runs along the bottom of the road. A silver hatchback pulls up.

'I think that's Naomi,' I say to John. He doesn't reply.

I turn to Lexie. 'Your mother's here,' I say, touching her hand. Lexie pulls it away and gets out of the car.

'Do you want me to wake the boys up,' I ask her, 'so you can say goodbye?'

She shakes her head.

As we walk towards the silver car, Naomi gets out. She sees us and waves. I wave back.

'There's your mum,' I say encouragingly. Lexie still doesn't say anything.

We get to Naomi, who is flushed. 'Oh, Lexie, oh, Samantha,' she says, 'isn't this a glorious day?'

We stare at her.

'Aren't you going to hug me, Lexie?' she says. Lexie shakes her head. 'Been having too much of a good time, eh?' she says. 'I told you Samantha was a wonderful person. Bet you don't want to come home now.'

Lexie nods. I reach to stroke her hair but she moves sideways and I miss. I let my hand drop to my side. If Naomi notices, she doesn't say so.

'Do you know why we're here, Lexie?' she says. Lexie shakes her head. 'We're here to find Samantha's and my den. We had a camp here in this orchard, didn't we, Samantha? We came here all the time and carved our names in a tree.'

'Actually, we carved "Ginger" and "Beauty",' I say.

Naomi blushes. 'Our alter egos. Yes, we did.'

'Why are we looking for them now?' I ask.

'Don't be angry with me,' she says. 'I've been on a journey and this might be where it ends. I want Lexie to see somewhere that made me happy.'

'I've been on a journey too,' I say, 'and it definitely ends here.'

'What kind of journey have you been on?' asks Naomi eagerly.

'One involving my family.'

'Me too! I went to Ireland to find my mother.'

'I thought you were looking for a job and somewhere to live.'

'Well, I meant to,' she says, 'but then I realized I'd never be able to move on in my life if I didn't have it out with my mother.'

'For God's sake, Naomi,' I start walking into the orchard, 'what on earth did you think that would achieve?'

'I don't know,' she says, 'but it doesn't matter because I didn't find her.'

We wander through the trees for maybe ten minutes, inspecting them. Lexie follows us silently. Naomi keeps glancing at me, as if she wishes to say something, but I refuse to meet her gaze. 'It never used to be so overgrown,' she says. 'I remember when we came down here and ate the blackberries and raspberries. You used to pretend to be Beauty and take the berries off with your mouth. And I remember copying you. You had to be really gentle or else you got prickles in your gums.' Before I can answer, she exclaims, 'There! The camp was there.'

I look to where she's pointing. I see two trees close together. One seems to be a tall apple tree. 'Why do you think it's there?'

'Because I'm sure there are steps on that left-hand tree,' she says. 'Can you see them?' I tell her I can't. 'Yes, you can!' she says, as we get closer. 'Look at the trunk.'

'Oh, yes,' I say. We look up. There is some wooden debris in the tree.

'This is what's left of it,' says Naomi. 'Your grandfather built this, Lexie. See these bits of wood? They were once the floor. Oh, he was so clever. Now, let me see . . .' Naomi starts to climb the tree. 'We sat up there and . . .' She pulls herself further up and rubs at the bark. 'Oh, my God!' she says. 'It's here, Samantha! Our names are still carved into the tree.' She climbs down and we change places. 'It's only a few steps up,' she says. Then she turns to Lexie. 'That's funny, because when we were little it felt miles up but, really, it's only a few feet. We must have been tiny.'

I pull myself up the tree using the toeholds Gordon Cooper made in that bark all those years ago, and as I climb I'm transported back to when Naomi and I were children, life was good and Naomi's parents were still together. A few more steps up, I see where Naomi has rubbed away the lichen. There it is, all these years on, the heart, and in it, in our childish writing, the words 'Beauty' and 'Ginger'.

'Do you see it?' yells Naomi.

'Yes,' I say, blinking away tears. I trace the names with my finger, then climb down. I step aside, and Lexie starts to climb up.

'Isn't that amazing?' Naomi calls up to Lexie. 'It must be nearly thirty years since we did that. Can you imagine? I was up there thirty years ago, scratching my name with

Samantha's in the tree, and now here we are as if nothing's changed! We were the best of friends, the very best, and my parents were together and life was –' Naomi looks at me. 'Were you crying up there, Samantha?'

I move away from the tree and Naomi follows me.

'You have been crying! It's because you care about me, isn't it? We can be friends again. I'm back. I'm still your Ginger! We could even re-carve our names in the tree. Would you like to do that?'

I shake my head.

'Oh, come on, Samantha!' she says. 'Remember, "*Here we are – ruined in the prime of our youth and strength – you by a drunkard and I by a fool.*" Isn't that what the book says before Ginger and Beauty part? But it doesn't have to be that way. We don't have to part! This isn't the end of our story. I won't die this time. We can be reunited, can't we? Like we always wanted to be. We're Beauty and Ginger once more, aren't we?'

'No, Naomi,' I say, now that Lexie's out of earshot. 'We're not. We're adults and I haven't been ruined by a useless man and I'm sorry if you feel you have but I have other people to look after now. I'm sorry, I really am, but you need to move on. You need to let go. I have nothing more to offer you.'

'Let go?' says Naomi. 'How can I? I'm holding on to nothing. I have nothing to hold on to.'

'But you do, Naomi,' I say. 'You have Lexie to look after and you have to stop living in the past. Lexie needs you. Can't you see that?'

'Yes, but I need you!' says Naomi, wildly. 'I came home to find happiness and now you're ruining everything. I've been rejected by everybody. Don't you know how that feels?'

'No, I don't but, Naomi, Lexie hasn't rejected you.'

'But where are we supposed to go? How can you turn us away? Look, you offered me friendship and you're snatching it away.'

'No, I'm not. I'm not responsible for your happiness. We carved those names a long time ago. Now I barely know you.'

'Yes, you do! It's me. I haven't changed and I need you!'

'No, you don't,' I say. 'You only need me to look after Lexie for you. But, really, if you want to sort yourself out, you have to find a new life for yourself. Stop trying to relive the past. I'm sorry your mother left you and I'm sorry you weren't able to find her, but what about your dad, Naomi? Make it up with him. Give Lexie a home near him in the States. I'm sure if you went to see him you'd find –'

'Find what?' yells Naomi. 'I'm abandoned. People always abandon me. You're abandoning me and Lexie, and I don't know how you can bring yourself to do it! You, a mother of three, with all your bloody proselytizing about your happy household and you can't even give my daughter a home!'

'No,' I say, 'because she's your daughter, not mine.'

Lexie is walking towards us.

'Did you see them?' Naomi asks, as she rejoins us. 'The names? Did you see them carved in the tree?'

Lexie nods silently.

'See?' Naomi says to me. 'We were best friends and now you're turning us away!'

'I'm sorry,' I say to Lexie, taking her hand and squeezing it, 'I really am, but I can't help you right now, Lexie, even though I really want to. I just can't.'

I hear the car horn beep.

'I have to go,' I say, dropping her hand. 'I do love you, Lexie, and I hope one day you'll understand that.'

'Samantha!' says Naomi. 'Please don't go! Beauty, don't leave me!' I reach forward to hug Lexie but she shrinks away.

'I'm not Beauty,' I say, to Naomi. 'I'm sorry. I'm merely Samantha Smythe.' I walk back towards the car. As I emerge from the orchard, I see Edward leaning out of the car window, whirling his arms.

'Come on, Mum!' he yells. 'You've been ages. Dad says we can go and get ice-chocs.* Can we?'

I wipe away the tears, and as I walk towards the car, John is watching me.

Epilogue: How It Ended

Later on that day, when the night drew in and the children were in bed, John took my hand and led me upstairs.

'It's time to make up,' he said.

I leant over and kissed his lips. 'John,' I said, 'I still need to say something to you.'

'And I have something to say to you,' he said.

'I was so horrid to you and I'm sorry,' I said. 'I'm so, so sorry. I should never have said what I did. I should never have accused you of deliberately hurting Bennie. I know you'd never hurt your children and I don't know why I said it.'

'Well,' he said, sighing, 'I want to tell you that you have a point. I did nearly drown Bennie. I didn't mean to –'

'I know,' I said fervently.

'– but I did and you're right. It's also true that I've been working so hard I haven't been here for you and the kids –'

'We've missed you so much, but I do know why you've been working so hard.'

'– and, to a certain extent, I was running away from you and the children because I felt so guilty about what happened on holiday, but I don't want to do that any more. I want to clear the air. That's why I stayed here today, to spend some time with you and the kids.'

'But you've barely spoken to me.'

'I was hurt. You can understand that, can't you?'

'Yes,' I said. 'But I was so cross about you partying that night with Charlie.'

'Well, it was fun working with her, but I found out that I don't want to go out every night and party. I'm too old. I just want to be here with you.' He rolled towards me and started kissing my neck and shoulders. 'Mm, I missed everything about you,' he said, putting his hand between my thighs.

'What about my *How To Get A Girl* kit? It's not the right time. We're out by twenty-four hours.'

'Oh, sod it,' said John. 'Let's be reckless for once.'

So we were and afterwards I finally told him everything – about Gary White, how Lexie caught him sunbathing naked, how he ran over our dog and why I didn't come to London to the party, how Gary came round for the evening after the laundry room flooded and then how he came round drunk last night and crashed his car into the gatepost.

John asked about Lexie so I told him how unhappy she was. Then I told him I was letting Wendy go, and why, and he nodded and said I was doing the right thing. Eventually we were yawning. Then John leant over and started kissing me again and, this time, for once, all thoughts of the kit went out of the window.

A month later, and John has just returned from the garden centre with Edward. It's their second trip in two weeks. I can feel the heat of the sun ricocheting off the parched earth. Poor thirsty earth with its yellowing grass and unyielding soil. What a summer. So hot. Everything is wilting, even the strawberries Edward and I planted a few weeks back.

'I knew they'd die,' Edward said to me, fingering their shrivelled leaves.

'How could you know that?' I asked.

'It's because I'm unlucky,' he said.

'What do you mean?'

'Stanley said it's obvious I'm unlucky. It's because I put my underpants on first and that's an unlucky thing to do.'

'Well, what does Stanley put on first?'

'His vest.'

'You don't think it was the heat of the sun that killed them, then?'

'No,' he said. 'It was the underpants.'

But today Edward is in the garden, looking at John's plans and carefully planting out some cut-and-come-again salad leaves.

'These seedlings look great,' he says to me.

'Yes, they're very good in salad,' I say. 'But we must water them.'

'Oh,' says Edward, dismayed. 'Wendy would like them, wouldn't she?'

I say that she would, and we'll take her some in her new flat near the WeightWatchers centre.

'Why did she leave?' asks Edward.

I tell him, as I have many times before, that Wendy decided that, although she loved us, she wanted to try out a new job. 'She'll be earning decent money and she has her own place now, sees her friends and –'

'So it wasn't to do with me and Lexie going to see Gary White, then?'

'Well, it was a bit,' I said, 'but in the end, Wendy wasn't really concentrating on the job here properly. Maybe childcare wasn't for her.'

Edward thinks for a bit. 'But she was fun,' he says. 'Even though she always got up too early* to take us to school.'

'Yes, that's true,' I say. 'She *was* fun and she left you all those fish as a present, but sometimes people have to move on.'

This reminds Edward that Gary has also left the village. 'Why do people leave?' he says.

'Like I said, they move on.'

'Shame about his car, though,' he says. 'I never thought they'd get it off the gatepost.'

It happened the day after we came back from saying goodbye to Lexie. John had gone back to Edinburgh and I was in the garden when a blue hatchback drew up outside and Gary got out.

'I'm so sorry about your gatepost,' he said, a bit embarrassed. 'But thanks for the other night, for the advice and everything. It got me thinking so I called my mother and told her I was moving to Australia to be near Rowan and she told me to go for it. She said she thought it was a very good idea, and it was about time I made my own decisions in life. That's amazing, isn't it?'

Just then, Edward appeared. 'Hello, Gary,' he said.

'I've got something for you,' said Gary. 'Come with me to the car.'

A few seconds later I heard a squeal of delight and a

lot of barking. Then Edward came back with Beady on a lead. 'Gary picked her up for us!' he cried.

Beady looked as if she wanted to jump up and lick us, but her hind leg was obviously still painful.

Edward crouched to hug her and then Beady licked his face. 'I've missed you, Beady,' he said. Then, out of the blue, he leapt up and threw his arms round Gary. 'Thank you,' he said. 'This is the best present a boy could have.'

Gary blushed and said he had to go. 'Take care of your mum, Edward,' he said, and hugged him. Then he hugged me. 'I paid the bill,' he said, 'and I gave the vet my autograph. Oh, and tell Dougie if he sends me those match reports in Australia I'll sign them for him . . . You'll be talking to him soon, will you?' he asked.

'Of course. Why wouldn't I?'

'He stormed off . . .'

'Yes, but that's Dougie for you. We go back a long way. He's in my book, Gary. He always will be.'

Gary sighed, got back into his little hatchback and drove off.

Two weeks after we'd said goodbye to Gary, I was in the garden with Julia. She'd come back from Los Angeles with Zachary Hofman Junior the previous night. 'We were going to drop in on the way back from the airport,' she said, 'but we were so tired.'

'That's a shame,' I said. 'You missed all the fun.'

Today she was going to the airport to pick up her children who were flying down from Scotland. 'I'm so nervous,' she kept saying to me. 'I haven't seen them for ages. I'm worried they won't like Zac.' I was sure they would because I couldn't see why they wouldn't. He's tall with a beard and looks like the depictions of Jesus Christ you see in stained-glass windows. If he'd been living in a different era he'd probably have been wearing sandals.

'You don't mind him spending time with Bennie, do you?' she asked. I didn't: as soon as Zachary Hofman Junior had come through the door, I'd known he might be able to help us. He'd looked up when Bennie said 'H-h-hello, Auntie Julia,' and when he saw Jamie, who was still wearing the feather boa that Lexie had forgotten to take with her, he had given me a broad smile and said, 'Hey, interesting kids, Julia's sister!' Then he asked if I minded him 'hanging out' with them a bit and I said he should be my guest. The last time I saw him, Jamie was wearing full makeup, which I assume he'd stolen from my bathroom cabinet, and Bennie was running around stark naked, yelling, 'And this is my wiggle-wiggle!'

'What do you think he's doing?' I asked Julia.

'Oh,' she said, 'haven't I told you about his methods? Well, with Jamie he's probably probing his tendency towards transgender behaviour, and with Bennie he may be doing some regression therapy. Has he pretended to drown him in the bath yet?'

'Why would he do that? Bennie's terrified of water.'

'It's like being reborn or something,' said Julia. 'I've seen Zac put disturbed children back into fake wombs made of blankets and stuff, then hold them really tight and they have to force their way out as if they're being born again.'

'What's the point of that?'

'He thinks it helps them regress to a time when their

life was happy and uncomplicated and that, if they go through the rebirthing experience, it undoes all the misery that's happened since.'

'Does it?'

'He won't rebirth Bennie. No, with Bennie he might have to take him back to the moment when he was drowning and then replace that memory of being abandoned with a positive one. Bennie will stop stuttering. The man's a genius.'

Just then Adele appeared with Nancy in tow. Jamie ran out of the house waving his arms at her.

'Jamie! What on earth's happened to you?'

'Apparently he's exploring his transgender issues,' I told her, and introduced her to my sister.

'My friend Zachary Hofman Junior is doing some studies on how children relate to objects that are deemed healthy for the other sex but unhealthy for their own,' Julia told Adele.

'Really?' said Adele, clearly fascinated. 'I've heard of him. Isn't he that man from LA who does seminars and stuff?'

'Yes,' said Julia, excitedly. 'He's pushing back the boundaries of children's behaviour as we know it. He's a fascinating man. Honestly, if you give him a minute, Jamie will be twirling around in a nightie!'

'I'm not sure I want Jamie twirling around in a nightie,' I said.

'That's because you're putting your own structures of masculinity on him,' said Julia, earnestly. 'Zac believes that, until children are at least ten, they should be given the freedom of self-expression.'

'We could all do with some of that,' said Adele. 'In fact, that's why I've come round. I've decided to make a major change in my life.'

'Like what?' I asked.

Adele blushed. 'Well, Belinda's five months pregnant and she can see that, with no childcare, it'll be hard for her to keep running that Colour Me Wonderful business so she's asked me to go in with her.'

'No!' I say.

'It makes sense, though, doesn't it?' says Adele. 'I love makeup and I like talking to people and . . . I've been bored, Samantha. I've only got Nancy and I know I don't want any more children. I spend all our money having treatments and going to spas and I thought, well, maybe I should do something with my life. I could expand the business. I could train in micro-dermabrasion, and I know how to do facial scrubs and stuff. Liza's going to help too. She'll bring clients down from London on her days off for skin treatments and makeovers.'

'But I thought she didn't have any days off.'

'She does now. She's told her boss she needs to spend more time with Josh, and she's told her husband to pull his weight. I think she's got rid of Adam and is planning to go running with Gail instead.'

Out of the blue, we hear a scream, then some mad laughing and a soaking-wet Bennie comes out of the house pursued by Edward.

'What's going on?' I ask.

'I've just been inside,' says Edward, 'and I saw that friend of Auntie Julia's make Bennie go underwater in the bath. It was very scary but when Bennie came up from the water the man hugged him really close and wrapped him in a towel and now the man says Bennie's cured.'

'I'm cured. I'm cured,' sings Bennie, and it turns out that he probably is. He hasn't stuttered since.

This evening the sun is still hot as it goes down behind the hill. I sit and watch it disappear. The house is quiet but I can hear the hum of a combine harvester moving this way and that across the field. Is it that time of year already? Time to bring in the crops and then autumn will be upon us. I hate saying goodbye to summer – those long evenings and the children playing outside. But they're in bed now. Only John is in the garden, banging away at bits of wood, soon to become a tree house.

A pair of ginger ears is twitching at the bottom of the field just below my window. This is Honey's favourite time of year. He waits until the combine has passed then off he goes, moving stealthily and silently until he finds what he's looking for. I've watched him do this before. Move. Pounce. Kill. That cat's a machine.

The combine turns at the bottom of the field to come back towards the house. I switch on my computer. Time to write more copy for *Our Fridges, Our Selves* but I can't concentrate. Everything has changed.

Will there be a happy ending for Lexie? I don't know. I don't think so. I've only heard once from Naomi since that day in the orchard. She wrote me a rather stiff email to say that she and Lexie had gone back to the States, and that although she had tried to see her father, he had still refused to meet her. He had, however, sent some money, which Naomi was thinking of using to send Lexie to a boarding-school in Massachusetts. 'It's a good school,' she wrote. 'It will give Lexie what she needs. I can't give her stability. I've decided I need to come over and find my mother and, if I do, I'll drop in . . .' Maybe Lexie will come back to us one day but I hold out no hope. It's dreadful to know that I have failed.

As the sun sinks finally and the air cools, I feel almost unbearably sad. I know, deep down, that I will never see Lexie again.

Five Months Later: My Last Home

It's nearly Christmas, and Bennie, Jamie and I are snuggled up on the bed.

'What shall we do now, Mama?' says Bennie, as he watches the rain fall outside the window.

'What do now?' says Jamie.

'I don't know,' I say, yawning. 'I guess we could play a game or something.'

'What game?' says Bennie.

'I don't know.'

'Shall we play the name-the-baby game?'

'We can't play that until we know if it's a boy or a girl.'

Edward suddenly appears with a letter for me. 'I think it's from the clinic,' he says.

'What clinic?' I say.

'Oh,' he says. 'They rang the other day. They said it was about the baby and I was supposed to tell you that if you didn't ring back they'd send you a letter.' He waves it at me. 'Shall I open it?' he says.

'No, you mustn't yet. You must fetch Daddy.'

Edward nods. 'I'll go and get him.'

I hear him running down the stairs two at a time. There's a pause, then two sets of feet are pounding back.

'Edward says there's a letter from the clinic,' says John. 'Oh, God, I have to sit down.'

We all look at the envelope.

'Shall I open it?' says Edward.

John and I nod. John stares at me. 'Samantha,' he says, 'don't get your hopes up. We didn't use the kit.'

'I know,' I say. 'It's all right. I don't mind.'

'Here goes,' says Edward. 'The result of your amnio . . . amnio . . . amnio . . . What's this word, Mum?'

'Amniocentesis probably.'

'OK. "The result of your amnio-thingy is one in a thousand for Down's syndrome and as to the sex of your child –"' Edward breaks off. 'Ooh,' he says. 'Now's the moment we've all been waiting for . . .'

'Edward!'

'"You will be pleased to know that your baby is a . . ."'

'Edward!' I say again.

'". . . your baby is a . . ."'

'What is it?' says John.

'A girl!' says Edward. 'Your baby is a girl!'

'Oh, my God!' I promptly burst into tears.

'Oh, my God,' says John.

'Yes,' says Edward happily. 'We're going to have a sister! We're going to have a girl in the family.'

'A girl?' says Bennie. 'A girl like Lexie?'

'Well, not quite like Lexie,' I say, trying to gather myself. 'This girl will be a baby, our baby.'

'Ooh,' says Edward. 'Talking of Lexie, I've just remembered something.' He disappears.

'Don't say he's actually got us a present,' says John, now pulling Jamie and Bennie on to his lap and hugging them in a rather emotional way.

Edward reappears clutching something. 'I was supposed to give this to you ages ago,' he says. 'I promised

Lexie I would but I forgot.' Then, from behind his back, Edward produces a book. 'It's Lexie's copy of that book she liked. She asked me to give it to you before she left but I put it down the side of my bed for safe keeping and . . . I'm really sorry, Mum. Have I done wrong?'

'No,' I say. 'How could you do any wrong, my Edward?'

Edward hands it to me and I open it. In her childish writing, Lexie has scribbled, 'To Samantha from Lexie xxx'.

'Well,' I say, 'are we sitting comfortably?' The children nod as Edward flops down on the bed. John kisses me and gets up. 'And you,' I say to him, pulling him down again. 'You need to hear this if we're having a girl.'

John kisses the top of my head and settles himself next to me.

'Right,' I say, 'I shall begin.

'"The first place that I can well remember was a large pleasant meadow with a pond of clear water in it . . ."'

Glossary of Edwardisms

accurate It always sounds as if Edward might be using this in the correct context – as in 'I am being very accurate today' – but actually it means the opposite. If I have made an arrangement with Stanley's mother that the children will get together, then say to Edward, 'Do you want to go to Stanley's house or ask Stanley to come here?' Edward will say, 'I don't mind, it's up to Stanley.' And when I say, 'But why can't you decide?' he says, 'Because I'm being very accurate today,' whereas, in fact, he is being indecisive and not at all accurate.

alien bagel This is what Edward likes for breakfast. It is, essentially, an entire bagel put into the toaster and blasted until it singes. An alien bagel is never cut in half – too tricky, too time-consuming. It never has any butter or jam on it. It is just a plain toasted bagel.

anything that rhymes This is impossible for Edward. We will play a rhyming game, more often than not with Stanley, who is very good at rhyming, and Edward will *not* get it. If I suggest making up limericks, Edward and Stanley become overexcited and squeal, 'Ooh, yes, ooh, yes.' So I will start, 'There was a young chappie called Eddie,' and Stanley will say, 'Who was always and for ever ready.' I will say, 'He got on a horse.' Stanley will say, 'And it shied, of course,' and then Edward will pipe up, 'And he fell off and hurt himself!' When Stanley and

I point out that the last line might be something like, 'So no longer was poor Eddie steady,' Edward says, 'But I would've fallen off and hurt myself, wouldn't I?'
discussing He means arguing. He says things like 'Why are you and Daddy discussing about who looks after the babies more than the other?' and I say, 'Edward, we're not discussing it, we're arguing about it.' Then Edward will say, 'But when I argue with you, Mummy, you tell me to calm down and have a discussion about it.' Then he looks very confused.
early/late Late/early. Edward gets muddled with these. For example, he will say things like, 'As a special treat, can I stay up early, Mummy?' or 'I got up very late this morning,' and I will remember that I heard him looking for the television remote control at about five thirty. Then I will say, 'But didn't you get up at five thirty, Edward?' and he'll say, 'How do you know?' and I'll say, 'Because I heard you,' and he'll say, 'I got up a bit late, didn't I?'

Actually, another moot point I'm always discussing with Edward and Stanley, is why the birdcage is unused. I found them outside with it once, ceremoniously dropping bread on to its floor. 'What are you doing?' I asked.

'We're going to wait for a bird to come and eat the bread, and then we're going to catch it in the cage,' said Edward.

'But that's impossible,' I said. 'It's got huge bars. No bird would stay in there.'

'Why have you bought it, then?' said Edward.

'Seems like a silly birdcage if you can't keep a bird in it,' said Stanley.

'It's ornamental,' I said.

'What does "ormanental" mean?' said Edward.

fathead Fathead. Edward likes to use this word especially when it comes to his brothers but he insists on pronouncing it as it is spelt – fath-ead.

hand-burger This is a hamburger, but not in Edward Land. There is logic to this. As Edward put it to me: 'Mummy, I know why they are called hand-burgers. It's because you hold them in your hand.'

ice-chocs Edward's word for choc ices, which he loves above and beyond all other ice-creams even mint choc chip, his second favourite, and chocolate, his third. He hates strawberry, although he is rather partial to fresh ones.

interactive It's impossible to find a real word to take the place of Edward's term 'interactive'. Instead, I shall give examples of the context in which he uses it and you can fill in with whatever alternative you feel appropriate. Let's say Edward has spent his week being very busy *doing things*. This is rare. Edward likes to do very little in the way of organized activities. This is what he'll say: 'On Monday I did football and on Tuesday I went to Granny's house and on Thursday I did rounders and then tomorrow Stanley's coming round and it's been a very interactive week, hasn't it, Mum?' In this context, interactive would imply that it is referring to *something*, as in the business of the week, and a word you could use to replace it would be 'active'. But sometimes he will use it in an entirely different context. If, for example, he has friends round and they are chatting with John, and I come in and say something like, 'Can you be quiet for a minute, please, and tell me what you want for tea?' Edward will look at his friends and say, 'My dad's more interactive than my mum.' In this context he means that his father has, at this one given moment in time, been more receptive and involved with Edward and his friends than I have. I think the word that should be used in this context is 'involved' but I personally wouldn't use it because it's *bloody well not true*, as everyone knows.

life savers Light sabres, but used only in context with *Star Wars*. For a while, Edward called them 'light savers' but now he has perverted it even further to 'life savers' but, yet again, this seems convincingly logical. They are seemingly made of light and save the lives of the Jedi knights who yield them. Perfect, really.

the lucky trousers Strictly speaking, there is nothing grammatically incorrect with Edward talking about his lucky trousers. I got them through a mail-order catalogue and they started off being way too long for him but now they are miles too short. Not that this bothers Edward because he loves them. They are blue sweatpants, ripped to shreds round the hems. He learnt to ride a bike, scored a hat-trick at a football match, whistled for a wasp and caught one with Stanley when he was wearing them. John has tried very hard to bin them but Edward always retrieves them and takes them back to his bedroom.

the museum The cinema, as in the context of 'Let's go to the museum to see the new Harry Potter film.'

ormanental see *early/late*

people's names Edward steadfastly refuses to call people by their proper names until he has met them, ooh, about a billion times. Therefore, he knows Dougie's name but he still doesn't know the name of Stanley's mother. 'Hello, Sophie,' he'll say to her, when she comes to pick Stanley up. 'Her name is Laura,' I'll mutter to him under my breath. 'But she looks like a Sophie!' Edward will say. Or he insisted on calling the gardener Oscar. His real name was Oliver and he came weekly for about a year until John decided a gardener was too expensive – 'Twelve pounds an hour!' he exclaimed, when he saw the bill for trimming a hedge. Anyway, Edward told me that Oliver liked being called Oscar. 'What do names mean anyway?' he asked happily.

runway Motorway. I don't know why Edward calls it the runway. I think it's something to do with the motorway being long, wide and fast, as if we're going to take off.

snap-mouthed Edward uses this when someone is being rude to someone else – as in to me when I ask him to clean up his room for the fiftieth time: 'There is no need to be snap-mouthed with me.'

Acknowledgements

I would like to thank Polly Roger Brown for all her support and for finding me a quiet place to write. I would also like to thank Jose Antonio and Bienvenido for letting me use that quiet space. Much thanks also to Cherry and Brian for the use of their front room and to Noel Flanagan for his office. Once again, I could not have done this book without the creative input and staunch support of my editor Louise Moore at Penguin. I am indebted to Clare Ledingham for her impressive editing skills, as well as Hazel Orme, and to Bridget Hancock for being my sounding board and unofficial editor.

Thanks to my family and friends but of course my most special thanks must go to my children and to Michael, who I love so very much. My final thanks must go to my agent, Kate Jones; she was my mentor, my friend and an all-round unique and wonderful woman. She will be sorely missed.

Read on for more about the
Smythe family from

Lucy Cavendish's

new novel coming soon from Penguin

Prologue

It happened one Wednesday morning. I was doing the laundry, drinking a coffee, listening to the radio. It doesn't really matter which. Maybe I was sitting down trying to do the crossword, for, on most Wednesday mornings, my two eldest sons Edward and Bennie are at school and their younger brother Jamie is at nursery. But, on that Wednesday morning, as I was maybe sitting down with a cup of something hot, the telephone rang. Perhaps I tried to leave it. I do sometimes when I have a few minutes to myself, for then the telephone seems like a squat toad bleeping and burping at me. But this time I didn't. I picked up the receiver.

'Hello,' said a nervous voice. It was the nice lady from the nursery. I knew she was nice because she sneaks Jamie an extra Rich Tea biscuit at the end, when everyone is leaving.

'Mrs Smythe?' she asked, even more tentatively.

'Yes,' I said.

'I need you to come to the nursery.'

'Come to the nursery?' I repeated, feeling rather confused. 'Why?'

The nice lady from the nursery sighed.

'I don't want to explain on the telephone.'

'What? Is Jamie OK? Has something awful happened to him?' I suddenly had visions of Jamie walking out into the road and being hit by a car, or somehow toppling into a pond they don't actually have. I've read about these things. Children go to nurseries and never come back.

'No, Jamie's fine,' said the nice lady quickly, too quickly. 'I just need you to come right now.'

The nursery is five minutes away. As I drove there my heart was beating so fast I could barely hear myself breathe.

When I got to the gates, a member of nursery staff motioned for me to park my car alongside the playground. Jamie was waiting there. He seemed totally fine, if a little forlorn.

'Jamie,' I said. I bent down to hold him. He would not look at me.

'Jamie?' I said again.

The nice lady came into the yard.

'Come with me into the office,' she said. She gave Jamie a pitying look. 'One of our staff members will take care of everything out here.'

We went into her office and sat down. Her on one side of the desk, me on the other.

'It is very hard for me to tell you this, Mrs Smythe,' she said gravely, 'but I am afraid that you will have to take Jamie home.'

'Take Jamie home?'

'Yes.'

'What, right now?'

'Yes. He is going to have to stay at home for the time being, I'm afraid.'

'Why?'

She sighed again.

'Jamie committed a misdemeanour today that was so awful there may be an investigation into it by the nursery.'

'What on earth did he do?'

'He hurt another child.'

'What do you mean "hurt"? What did he do?'

'He lunged at a child with the sharp end of a paintbrush and tried to stick it in the child's eye. If one of my staff members hadn't been nearby he could have blinded someone.'

'He must have slipped!'

'No,' said the nice lady, kindly but firmly. 'He didn't slip. I was there and I saw it. He meant to hurt that child. It was alarmingly deliberate.'

'No, not Jamie!' I said, defensively, shocked. 'Which child was it?'

'It was Isla. I don't know why he did it. Isla wasn't even that near him. She'd just toddled over there. She's barely more than a baby girl . . .'

The words 'baby girl' hung in the air.

'Mrs Smythe,' she continued, looking embarrassed. 'I am not sure how to help. Jamie's behaviour has been . . . well, it's changed, if I can be frank. He's quite aggressive with the smaller children, and I have found recently that he's become very disruptive . . .'

'I'll take him home,' I said, maybe a bit too abruptly.

'And you also need to know that Isla's parents have the right to make an official complaint.'

'I'm going now. I'll take him home.'

'Isla was very badly bruised and quite hysterical. Jamie didn't try to harm her just once. We pulled him away but he was going for her again. I have had to tell her parents this. They may ask for an investigation. We are a state nursery. There are procedures we have to follow . . .'

I got up.

'I'm going,' I said. 'Don't worry. I won't bring Jamie back.'

The nice lady started wringing her hands in a concerned fashion.

'This gives me no pleasure, Mrs Smythe,' she said. 'I have, in the past, found Jamie to be a most charming child . . .' but it was too late, for now I was out of the door.

I took Jamie by the hand and marched him out of the playground. I gave the young girl who had been overseeing everything a falsely jaunty wave.

'Everything's fine,' she said. 'Not even a murmur.'

'Thanks,' I said.

I didn't speak to Jamie as I put him in the car, but he soon spied what it was he wanted. I watched him carefully through the rear-view mirror. I could see him leaning over towards the baby seat. Then suddenly he reared up, opened his mouth as wide as he could and yelled, 'Wake up, Baby Sparkle!'

My new-born baby daughter's grey-blue eyes snapped open and filled with tears.

'Waaaa!' she cried.

'Jamie!' I said.

Jamie sat back into his car seat, popped his thumb in his mouth and smiled to himself.

This is how it all started.

1. Distinguishing Features

Jamie is sitting in an over-large chair wearing a tight pink gingham dress. I am sitting next to him trying to ignore this fact. I am wearing a skirt – I never wear skirts – and a shirt that I have ironed – I never iron – and I am hoping that, with my ironed shirt and smart skirt, the child psychologist sitting opposite me might take me a bit more seriously than before. I am here not simply because of what happened just under a year ago, but also because, after the paintbrush calamity, Jamie's behaviour has got worse.

This change in Jamie – revealed in his insisting on using baby talk even though he is four years old (such as saying 'my' instead of 'I' and 'sike' for 'like'), trying to drink his milk from a baby beaker, and sometimes becoming aggressive towards his brothers when he gets cross – has caused undeniable ripples in our family. Where once we were all united, now we are pulling in different directions.

We are a large family. There are six of us in the Smythe household, and we all have different needs and desires. My husband John, who is my second one as I was married to a different John before him, wants me. I want him, but I also want my children. Edward, the eldest and son of John the First, wants me, as do Bennie, Jamie and, of course, Baby Sparkle. I have, over the years, cut myself into ever-decreasing portions to satisfy their need for my love and attention. I have, I think, done well. Sometimes I even catch sight of myself in a random mirror and, although I am shocked by what I see – a wild-haired woman shedding children as rabbits do kittens, all reattaching themselves to me as I shoo them away – I realize I look like a mum. I act like a mum. I sound like a mum. I shout like a mum. And I have, after all these years, given myself a teeny bit of space and told myself I am good at this. I eased Edward and me through the parting of his father. I then eased John the Second into our lives with barely a ripple (hmm, I think), and have gone on to pop out three more babies.

Yet here I am with my Jamie, and life is not as it is supposed to be. I was so shocked after he nearly blinded Isla that I telephoned John when we got home, feeling nearly hysterical, imagining that, somehow, he would feel nearly hysterical too.

'Isla's parents will call the social services,' I said to John in a panic down the telephone. 'Then they'll come to our house and take the children away at midnight . . .'

'No they won't,' he said, surprisingly reassured considering I had just told him his youngest son had been excluded from nursery. 'Jamie's just suffering from a bit of sibling rivalry. He didn't actually hurt Isla.'

'The nice lady at the nursery says she's bruised. He lunged at her, twice!'

'Maybe he was just a bit fed up.'

'Fed up?' I said. 'Have you got any idea how bad this is?'

'No,' he said calmly, 'because I am here in London working so I wasn't at the nursery and I didn't see the bruises on Isla. Did you?'

'Well, no, not exactly,' I said, wrong-footed, 'but the nice lady there said there'll have to be an investigation. She said they have to write all these things down in a book and if the child is badly hurt then procedures happen.'

'There won't be any investigation,' said John. 'It's all fine.'

But it wasn't really. Isla's parents were not at all happy about what Jamie had done. They asked the nursery to look into what had happened, and I spent an awkward morning with the nice lady on one side of me and Isla's parents on the other. John couldn't come to the meeting as he was working, so I went on my own and squirmed in embarrassment as I apologized to them profusely, explaining that Jamie had recently had to cope with the birth of a baby sister, but they remained hurt and unmoved.

'Isla's our only child,' they said.

'I'm so sorry,' I said.

The upshot was I decided to keep Jamie out of nursery and to monitor his behaviour. John, it has to be said, did not agree with my decision.

'What's he going to do now?'

'He'll be with me and Baby Sparkle. In that way I can help him to adjust.'

'He doesn't need to adjust,' said John. 'He'll get over it.'

'I can't trust him with other children,' I said. 'You should have seen Isla's parents. They were not at all happy.'

'Jamie's always been the easy one in the household,' said

John. 'Do you not think you are overreacting somewhat?'

It is true that before Baby Sparkle was born Jamie was a happy-go-lucky soul, who could occasionally be quirky. Our eldest son Edward, who is now nearly thirteen, was immensely difficult as a small boy. He was cross and angry and couldn't speak properly. Bennie's also had his problems. Two years ago he nearly drowned in a freak accident on holiday and has since developed a stutter. However, despite the semi-traumatic state the Smythe family seemed to live in, Jamie waddled through life merrily eating butternut squash and, oddly, not liking sandpits.

Since the paintbrush incident, however, he has started shouting and becoming rude. He calls people 'stupid idiots' all the time, he refuses to eat and he swears. When the telephone rings, he picks it up and shouts 'Bugger off!' into the receiver.

At first, everyone thought it was funny – angelic Jamie with his blond hair, green eyes and cute face shouting 'Bugger off!' was amusing, but now we are all sick of it.

'Why does Jamie tell my friends to bugger off when they ring?' said Edward, who was lolling on the sofa watching the television. 'Why doesn't he bugger off?'

My mother told me I should grin and bear it. 'All children feel cross when another baby comes into the family,' she said. 'Your sister refused to stop using a potty for years after you were born.'

But then everything got much worse. For a start Jamie kept stealing all Baby Sparkle's clothes. It started with her knickers, which meant he has spent most of the last year waving baby knickers above his head, once he'd found out they were too small to fit on his bottom. Then, when he realized that if he were smaller he too could wear gathered-up silky little pouffy underpants with roses on, he virtually stopped eating. I'd find all sorts of things to tempt him with – bagels with melted cheese on them, delicious creamy fish pies, meaty shepherd's pie topped with piles of mash. I tried yoghurts and croissants, and chopped-up bits of fruit and fromage frais. I cut up paw-paws, pineapple, melon, bananas. I made puddings and tarts and soufflés and stews. I flash-fried steaks and baked lamb chops and peeled prawns. I then scoured the shelves of the supermarket and even put things such as Cheestrings, Cheezy Dippers and pizzas into my shopping basket. All to no avail. And now the weight has fallen off him and he looks so skinny and tiny I'm amazed I haven't had a visit from the social services on the charge of starving my child.

When we went out for a walk once, Jamie and I met the nice lady from the nursery and I could tell she was shocked by how he looked.

'Jamie!' she said, her hands flying to her mouth.

'I am so thin!' he announced to her. He then ran his hands over his tiny skinny body.

As Baby Sparkle emerged from her Babygros and began to be put in dresses, Jamie started wanting to wear dresses. When I drew the line at this behaviour, he stopped eating again, even pushing bowls of Rice Krispies away, until one day I bought him a dress. We went to the shop and I pretended we were looking for a dress for Baby Sparkle. 'Look at this lovely dress,' I said pulling out a purple one with a discreet bow at the back. 'This would look nice on Baby Sparkle, wouldn't it, Jamie?'

'I think that might be a bit big for your baby,' said the helpful shop assistant hovering behind us and peering into Baby Sparkle's pram.

'She's a big baby,' I said.

'She doesn't look that big,' said the shop assistant.

'It's for me!' yelled Jamie crossly.

After that Jamie and I got into a sort of code. He made up an imaginary friend called Sophie and we'd often go and shop for her. For a while this worked very well. Jamie seemed to be able to express himself in the form of Sophie, and this imaginary Sophie seemed a far more reasonable person than her alter-ego. 'Sophie likes a bit of butter on her bread,' Jamie would say pertly when I'd ask him what he'd like to eat for dinner, and he'd say he would not like anything but he was sure Sophie would love some toast. He'd then eat rounds and rounds of toast to keep up with Sophie.

'God I love Sophie,' I said to my mother one day after Jamie had devoured some baked beans, scrambled eggs and a cup of milk followed by two yoghurts, because Jamie told me that 'Sophie likes yoghurts.'

But soon things started to go awry with Sophie. For a start, she gradually became more and more demanding.

'Sophie would like a Flower Fairy cup,' Jamie would say when we were in the toy shop. 'Sophie would like a tea set. Sophie would like a pink bathrobe.'

In the end I told Jamie that Sophie couldn't have *everything* she wanted, and the next morning Jamie woke up and clamped his mouth shut again.

'I've made toast with butter on for Sophie,' I said in my most persuasive voice one lunchtime. 'Sophie's about to eat it all up.'

'No she isn't,' said Jamie. 'Sophie's got too fat. She's on a diet now.'

And that was that.

The nice lady at the nursery, who I contacted for help as I thought she might know about these matters, suggested I go and see my doctor. After much thought, and some persuasion on my part, Jamie was referred by the doctor to a child psychologist.

I don't hold out much hope though. When I first went to see the child psychologist a month ago – 'Hello Candace,' I said, noticing that her name, Candace Harris, was typed neatly on the questionnaire I was asked to fill in all about Jamie's behaviour – I felt we got off on the wrong foot. She said, 'Please call me Miss Harris in front of your child,' and I felt I had been scolded like a little girl. Later on, Candace, who I from then on called Miss Harris, explained to me that she always felt it worked better for the children if the parents called her by her surname, as it meant she maintained a position of authority.

'Is that important?' I said to her.

'Yes,' she said. 'If I want Jamie, for example, to sit down and try to vocalize what is going on in his life, in his head, then he has to respect me, and in order for him to respect me I have to be perceived as being in a position of authority over him.'

'But he doesn't do anything I say,' I said. 'If I asked

him to call me Mrs Smythe do you think he'd behave himself a bit more?'

Candace–Miss-Harris looked at me as if I were mocking her.

'Of course not,' she said coldly. 'You can hardly expect your own son to call you by your surname.'

'Oh, I just thought it might help,' I said.

Candace–Miss-Harris didn't say anything. She just watched Jamie who, at that first meeting, insisted on having a dummy in his mouth, even though he'd never used one before.

'Is this your baby daughter's dummy?' Candace–Miss-Harris asked me.

'No,' I said, 'she doesn't use a dummy.'

'So where did Jamie get it from?'

'My mother bought it ages ago for the baby but I never used it. Jamie found it in a cupboard. He's just playing with it. He likes to play with it. He keeps it under his pillow. Is that not good?' I asked, seeing how cross Candace–Miss-Harris looked.

'It is an inappropriate object for a boy of four years old to play with,' she said. 'He should be playing with toys that ask questions of him, not baby things.' Then she turned to Jamie. 'Give me the dummy, Jamie.'

Jamie just looked at her. He shook his head.

'Dummy please, Jamie,' she said again, giving him a stern look.

Jamie stared out of the window.

'Give Miss Harris your dummy, Jamie, will you?' I asked him in the most conciliatory tone possible.

'Could you let me do the talking please, Mrs Smythe?'

said Candace–Miss-Harris. 'Jamie, I want that dummy now. I have asked you nicely twice and if you don't give it to me I will come over and take it off you myself.'

Jamie just looked at her and kept on sucking in a determined fashion.

'One, Jamie, two, three . . .'

Suddenly Jamie spat his dummy out and, at the same time, flew like a demon over to Candace–Miss-Harris, and he moved so rapidly that no one could have predicted what he was about to do. He sunk his teeth into Candace–Miss-Harris's outstretched arm.

'Arrgghh!' she screamed, clenching her fist in pain.

'Oh God, I'm really sorry, Candace,' I said.

'Miss Harris,' she said through gritted teeth.

'Jamie,' I said to him, now holding him firmly by his arm. 'That is very naughty of you to bite Miss Harris. What on earth has got into you?'

'Bugger off!' he screamed. Then he ran out of the door.

I turned to Candace–Miss-Harris.

'I am so sorry,' I said. 'He doesn't usually bite. I mean, he did try to stab a girl's eye out with a paintbrush, but the doctor's told you all that, so . . .'

'Clearly, there is a lot of work to do here,' said Candace–Miss-Harris through her grimaces. 'Come back again next week.'

I nodded meekly and then followed Jamie.

So this time, in our second session, I am trying to show Candace–Miss-Harris that I am in control. I am trying to say to her, through my smart new clothes, that instead of being a frazzled mother of four I am, in fact, totally organized and cool and sanguine. I am hoping that my skirt and ironed shirt are showing Candace–Miss-Harris that I am the type of mother who can make a nutritious breakfast which all my children eat at the table with nothing spilled anywhere, certainly not on me, get them all out of the door for school and then put on my superbly neat and ironed clothes for a trip to the psychologist. In fact, I am hoping to give the impression of a mother who is so supremely together that I actually put on my neat, clean, ironed clothes *before* breakfast. That's how bloody controlled and together I am and, as I think this, I smile confidently at Candace–Miss-Harris.

But at this moment Candace–Miss-Harris seems to be staring intently at Jamie, who is smiling back at her in a helpful fashion.

'How are we today, Jamie?' asks Candace–Miss-Harris.

'Happy,' says Jamie fluffing his dress up around his legs.

'Jamie, why are you wearing a dress?'

'I like my dress,' he says. Then he cocks his head to one side and opens his big green eyes. 'Is your name Sophie?' he asks, smiling at the psychologist.

'Sophie?' she asks, looking at him and then looking down to write some notes. 'What does the name Sophie mean to you, Jamie?'

'Sophie's his imaginary friend,' I explain.

'No she's not!' says Jamie angrily, his eyes glinting. 'She's my real friend. She is Sophie and I am Dorothy from Oz and mummy is Truly Scrumptious.'

'Ah,' says the therapist meaningfully and writing yet more notes. 'You like watching these films, do you?'

'Oh yes,' says Jamie.

'He doesn't watch them that much, Candace,' I say. 'I just let him when he's tired because . . .'

'My name is Miss Harris,' says Candace–Miss-Harris.

'Sorry,' I say.

'I want mummy to wear a white dress like Truly Scrumptious.'

'You want mummy to look like the character in *Chitty Chitty Bang Bang*?'

' 'Es,' says Jamie.

'Why is that, Jamie?'

'I want her to look like a dolly. I like dollies.'

'He likes to line them up in his cot,' I say.

As soon as I say the word 'cot', I realize I've said the wrong thing.

'Cot?' asks Candace–Miss-Harris, her eyes flashing. 'At the age of four?'

'Well, he loves his cot,' I say apologetically. 'He just adores it and I didn't think there was a problem with that really because it's such a big one and . . .'

'Will you please let Jamie answer, Mrs Smythe?' she says. 'Jamie, why do you still sleep in a cot?'

'Girls like sleeping in cots.'

'So, do you think you are a girl?'

Jamie shoots me a look and then starts struggling to get off the chair.

'Which little person is really supposed to wear a dress in this family, Jamie?'

Jamie struggles some more.

'Come on, Jamie,' says Candace–Miss-Harris. 'I can help you.'

'No,' he says. 'I wanna go! I wanna go!'

'All right, Jamie,' says Candace–Miss-Harris, suddenly rather weary. 'Why don't you go? There are some toys in the waiting room and Nicole, the lady at the reception desk, will play with you.'

'I want mummy to come,' says Jamie truculently.

'Well, I need to talk to your mother.'

Jamie comes towards me and starts tugging at my hand.

'You come with me mummy,' he says.

'No,' I say. 'I have to stay and talk.'

Jamie starts to cry. He tries to get on my lap. I stroke his hair and pull him towards me.

'I need some help, Jamie,' I say. 'We both do. I just need to do this. OK?'

Jamie looks at me. Then suddenly we hear a gurgling from outside the room. I remember the baby is there. She has been sitting quietly on the floor in the reception area this past half-hour playing with a plastic toy Nicole gave her. Jamie follows my glance until he sees his little sister. His face contorts into an angry, scrunched-up ball.

'Twinkle, twinkle, little willy. Baby Sparkle is so silly. Baby Sparkle's a bum-bum!' yells Jamie. Then he runs out of the door, slamming it behind him.

'I'd better go,' I say to the psychologist.

She nods. She is taking notes. 'I have observed everything that's come up today. I am writing up what I think.'

'Same time next week then?' I ask her desperately.

She nods again.

I go back into the waiting room. The receptionist gives me a sympathetic smile.

'Your baby's been marvellous,' says Nicole, retrieving the plastic ball from Baby Sparkle who raises her arms for me to lift her up. 'Your little boy . . . he's waiting for you in the hall.'

I thank her and go towards the hall to get Jamie.

'Shall I book you in for next week?' she calls after me.

'Yes,' I say, but I am lying. I know we won't be back next week. We won't be back at all.

We are too far gone for all that.

When I get home to our old brick and flint cottage in our quiet valley tucked away between a crease in the Chilterns, John is up in the attic.

'How did it go?' he yells down at me from the very top of the house. 'Did she find out what's wrong with Jamie?'

'No,' I yell back as I watch Jamie put the *Chitty Chitty Bang Bang* DVD on. 'He wants me to dress like Truly Scrumptious and he called Baby Sparkle something rude in front of the psychologist.'

'What?' John shouts. 'I can't hear you.'

'Come downstairs then,' I retort.

There is no answer from John so I go into the kitchen to watch Baby Sparkle from the window. She is asleep in the back of our car that is parked in the driveway. We often leave her to sleep in the driveway where we can see her. It always seems such a shame to move her when she is so happy in her car seat. Her babyish head lolls over to one side, her pert little mouth is open and she is heavily breathing in and out. I love watching her sleep. I love the way she twitches and jerks until she finally goes off into this deep, utterly uninterruptable torpor. I feel John beside me. He has come downstairs. He puts his arm around me.

'You know, I don't think there's anything wrong with Jamie,' he says, quietly kissing the top of my head. 'It's just taking a bit of time for him to get used to the baby being around, that's all.'

'Why do I feel so miserable then?' I ask as I sit down at the table. 'You have no idea how it all sounds, how guilty I feel.'

'Why do you feel guilty?'

'Who lets him wear dresses? Who lets him sleep in a cot? I do. When I told her Jamie still sleeps in a cot she gave me such a look.'

'Maybe she has a point,' says John.

'Well, thanks,' I say, sinking my head down. 'Thanks for the support.'

John sighs. 'Samantha,' he says. He tries to stroke my hair. I push his hand away.

'I'm tired of this, John,' I say. 'You know, Baby Sparkle isn't really a baby any more. She's over a year old, yet Jamie still likes wearing dresses and he has an imaginary friend who is spending all our money and neither of them will eat.'

John laughs. 'What's wrong with that?' he says.

'Oh come on,' I say wearily.

'He'll adjust. I'm sure he will.'

'What if he doesn't? What if he has become seriously psychologically disturbed by Sparkle's arrival. I've heard of siblings who are so scarred by the rivalry in their childhood that they have never spoken to their sibling again. My sister Julia told me that her friend's brother took a knife to her throat when they were little and said he'd kill her unless she sang every verse of *All Things Bright and Beautiful* for him.'

'Oh God,' says John. 'Who on earth knows all the words to *All Things Bright and Beautiful*? It's about a million verses long.'

'Actually, it's only four.'

'Is it?' says John, sounding astounded.

'That's not the point. According to Julia, those siblings never spoke to each other again.'

'Well, at least Jamie's not that bad,' says John.

'I think he is,' I say. 'I think he's really disturbed.'

'Yes,' says John, 'I know that's what you think. In your mind, he's disturbed.'

'What do you mean by that?'

John doesn't answer.

'I don't believe this,' I say, turning towards him. 'My God, you think it's just me. You think I am over-worrying.'

'Yes I do, to a certain extent,' he says simply.

'How can you be so relaxed about this?' I ask, almost shouting. 'I mean, has the thought ever occurred to you that maybe we are seeing a psychologist because he is disturbed. Or do you think we are going there because Jamie and I have nothing better to do?'

'No,' says John slowly. 'It's just that I . . .'

'You haven't even been to one session with us. How come this is all my responsibility? I need some help and if you won't help me, and bloody Candace–Miss-Harris won't either, then I'm going to have to find someone who can.'

'Oh, Samantha,' says John, kissing the top of my head. I let him this time. 'I am trying, you know.'

'We've got one summer,' I say to him. 'He starts school after this summer and he cannot still be swearing and sleeping in a cot by the end of it. Something has to happen, John, and you have to help me. They are *our* children, not just mine.'

John and I then turn to watch Baby Sparkle, who is still asleep.

'Look at that peaceful baby,' says John. 'See? She's fine.'

Suddenly, Jamie appears from the sitting room. He has taken off his dress and is clad in nothing but a pair of light-blue knickers.

'Hello, Jamie,' says John.

Jamie looks at John. He looks adorable, as he can do sometimes. He gives his most winning smile.

'I'm watching *Chiccy Chiccy Bang Bang*,' he says to John, batting his eyelashes at him.

'I can see that,' says John.

'I'm not wearing any clothes.'

'I can see that as well. Aren't you cold?'

'No.' Then he says he wants to whisper something to John. 'I wanna tell you a secret.'

'What?' whispers John loudly, bending down and cupping his ear.

Jamie leans forwards and says, rather loudly, 'I want mummy to wear a Truly Scrumptious dress.' He then sits back looking very pleased with himself.

John looks at me and raises an eyebrow.

'God, John,' I say, 'I just don't know how we got here. I really don't.'

Lucy Cavendish

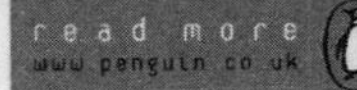

Photograph © Harry Borden

Becoming a novelist

Samantha Smythe, the heroine of my trilogy of novels, took a while to come about. I have spent most of my working life in journalism and, like most journalists, would dream of writing a book while I edited copy. I used to sit wondering what I could write a book about. I longed to turn my usual one-thousand-word articles into something longer and more thoughtful but life kept getting in the way. I got married. I had children. I got tired. I just about managed to hold on to my job, but life was changing. Pretty quickly I realized an office life wasn't going to work for me. I missed my children like an ache. Everything was so manic. With my eldest son, I'd drive to Canary Wharf where I was working, drop him at his nursery, tear into the office (probably with my skirt tucked into my knickers), grab a coffee and then sit down and try to pretend I was a cool, calm and collected editor.

'Life kept getting in the way. I got married. I had children. I got tired.'

At 5.30 p.m., I'd start sneaking frantic peeks at the clock. I had to pick my son up by 6 p.m., or meet with an understandable chorus of disapproval from the nursery staff. At 5.45 p.m., just as I'd be gathering my coat, my boss would come over with some intricate query that needed sorting out that second. I'd sit there gawping like a goldfish with no air and then try to answer the problem in a nanosecond, when it probably needed a good hour's thought, and then I'd run madly back to the nursery to drive a fractious, over-tired baby home.

'My work was suffering, my child was suffering and my marriage.'

In truth, my life wasn't working. Like many women I felt I wasn't doing either job properly. I was just about holding it all together but my work was suffering, my child was suffering and my marriage – well, I barely saw my husband. It was obvious something had to change. This is where Samantha Smythe came in. She started life, not that I knew it then, as a character in a set of columns I did, first for the *Sunday Telegraph* magazine and then for the *Evening Standard*. In these columns I'd write about my own life as a working mother. Somewhere along the line these columns morphed into a semi-fictitious state, so that the 'I' character could comment quite freely on what she saw mothers actually going through. The 'I' person went on play dates, took her children on holiday, went off to see cranial osteopaths, etc. She started having a life above and beyond my own in her search to experience every facet of being a wife, a mother – the ultimate juggling machine. The columns generated a lot of response. I always knew there were tons of women out there juggling their lives. I just didn't know that so many of them felt the same way I did. Something in the columns obviously resonated, so when an agent approached me about writing a book I could see it was a very exciting prospect. At first I thought I'd do a guide – or a sort of polemic really – on how to bring up children. I started off by writing five thousand words on what happens in my family life every day, but as the book went on and I wrote further it became obvious to me that I wasn't writing a guide at all but a novel, with the 'I' character at the centre of it. That novel – my first – became *Samantha Smythe's Modern Family Journal*.

Samantha Smythe and her family

People ask me every day if Samantha is me. She certainly started out as me. I used her as a mouthpiece to explore my life, a life that I felt was pretty representative of many other women's lives. But gradually, as the book changed from fact to fiction, Samantha started having a life of her own. She became a better person than me. She is kind. She is always there to listen. She is very supportive. She tries not to be judgemental. She is a very good person. She is also supposed to symbolize every woman. Like every woman, she tries to do the best by her husband and children. She is the one who makes the packed lunches and reads bedtime stories and knows on which day swimming lessons occur. She feeds the dog and strokes the cat and

'She certainly started out as me. I used her as a mouthpiece to explore my life.'

washes the socks and cleans the kitchen. She helps out her friend Dougie who has got divorced. She tries to balance her abandoned sister. In this, the second book about Samantha, she also tries to help her old friend Naomi who reappears in her life, somewhat out of the blue. How can she deny help to Naomi? After all, they played at being Beauty and Ginger from *Black Beauty* when they were younger. They *loved* each other.

Samantha also loves her husband, John – even if he is sometimes errant. In fact, Samantha really *does* love him and this relationship turns out, eventually, to be of much importance in the books. I always wanted John to be a real character, not a cardboard cut-out. It was absolutely vital that he wasn't the typical two-dimensional, useless man often portrayed in fiction. John loves his children as much as Samantha does.

He tries to help, to be supportive. He too can cook and clean and hold his children when they cry and read them bedtime stories. However, in this second book, John is working away in London. He has, in effect, had to abandon his family, and thus is on the periphery of what is going on at home. I think this is true of many marriages – they have a rock solid base, it's everything else that gets in the way. Like any couple, John and Samantha may argue but they know how strong their relationship is, how much it works. They are each other's greatest supporter and defender, but they are also honest with each other. They can dare, within this strong marriage, to challenge each other, to say things that are hurtful but sometimes necessary. For example, in this book John can see how manipulative Naomi is being. He has the honesty to tell Samantha this, even though she may well not want to hear it.

The other main characters are, of course, the children. When I first started writing these books, I had no idea how strong a character Edward would become. I just love Edward so much. I can see him in my mind's eye and he makes me laugh and cry at the same time. For me, Edward is at the heart of my first book. He is Samantha's son by another man. He is a part of her past that John the Second, Bennie and Jamie can never really know about. Edward is always on a journey. In this book he is reaching an age when he begins to question things and his inquiring mind becomes almost hyperactive when Naomi's daughter Lexie comes to stay. Edward knows how much Samantha wants a girl in the family. He knows that she craves more feminine-based company sometimes. Edward can therefore understand, in his own way, why Lexie has come into his family. Yet Lexie confuses Edward. She is the same age as him but is a thoroughly more complicated character. He wants to like her – and often he genuinely does – but she unnerves him and unsettles his sense of time and place. Edward doesn't really like change and yet that is what Lexie represents to him.

I hope that readers can experience Edward as I do. I wanted the children to be real, fleshed-out characters. I read so many books where the children are almost in the way but this is a book about a family, and that family includes children. As this book is the second part of a trilogy, it also focuses on Bennie. Book three will focus on Jamie as both he and Bennie grow into their characters.

Edward will still be very present though! I think it's impossible for him not to be. Again, I get asked if the children are based on my children and to a certain extent they are but, yet again, their characters have become their own and what happens to them certainly does not happen in my own children's lives. My eldest son, I have to say, loves me reading the books out to him. I think he feels flattered that he is the inspiration for Edward. He is very happy that I write really, as is my middle son, who in some ways is Bennie to me.

'I get asked if the children are based on my children and to a certain extent they are.'

Sometimes people ask me why Samantha doesn't have a job. She does have a job of sorts, but she doesn't have an office life. Once again, I didn't really choose it that way for Samantha. When I first thought about her she had a job, but as I began to write about her the nuances of her life with her children and John the Second became more interesting than any office relationship could be. I began to like the fact that she wasn't interested in designer clothes and the glass ceiling. I love the fact that she embraces her life. She has wobbles – we all have wobbles – but she always tries to help people. She may be frantic and life may overtake her sometimes but she is the kingpin in the home that everyone revolves around. She is the consummate warm-hearted wife and mother. In *Lost and Found* we also see Samantha as the friend. Like many women, she has a friend who she loved as a child but lost touch with. When this friend reappears, Samantha has to help her. She just cannot turn Naomi away, even though it means Samantha will have to learn to say no sometimes in the end.

'Life may overtake her sometimes but she is the kingpin in the home that everyone revolves around.'

Samantha has, in many ways, inadvertently chosen the stay-at-home route, but this has left her free to be a very useful canvas. She can, as a character, express what we are all feeling. In *Samantha Smythe's Modern Family Journal* she is in the same position of many of us – that of not having a traditional nuclear family. She must balance the needs of her eldest son with those of her second husband and her other two children. This book deals with what it means to be a mother to all these children, each with their individual needs. It also looks at the particularly modern phenomenon of the non-nuclear family.

Lost and Found deals with Samantha's family rather differently. At the beginning something truly shocking happens to Bennie. He nearly drowns and, in a way, it is John's fault. But this is not said until the very end. Samantha has to live with her anger towards John, for she knows that if she opens up this particular can of worms many other accusations may emerge. Will John turn on her? Tell her how disappointed he is that she never made it to the opening night of his play in London? So Samantha festers for months. She spends her time trying desperately to conceive a girl while helping Bennie get over his stutter. Then Naomi appears with Lexie ... well, this is something Samantha can really get her teeth into. She is Samantha the martyr, helping not just her own children but someone else's as well. However, this leaves her increasingly emotionally confused.

Life as a writer

Sometimes I have no idea how I manage to write though. My daily routine seems so full of everything else: there's the breakfast to get ready and the children to get to school. They go in three different directions because of their various ages. I also have a baby at home. By the time I get back there's the baby's nappy to change, the house to clean, the washing up to do, and the laundry and the bedrooms to tidy.

And then there are the animals, for I have realized I am an animal freak. In fact, the older I get, the more animals I seem to acquire. We started off with a cat we were given by our next-door neighbour when her relationship broke up. My eldest son had casually said one day, 'Oh, I do like your cat', and the next thing we knew the cat came over the fence, our neighbour drove off in the opposite direction and the cat was ours. He is a big tomcat and rather aggressive, and we are all terrified of him.

Then, one Christmas, I saw some puppies advertised in the local paper. The children had been begging me for a puppy for years so I went to see them, and they were all black and tumbling over each other and they smelled divine and so ... one girl puppy became ours. She is, of course, Beady in the books, and she is as lovely as Beady. My best friend actually said, 'You've put your dog in the book!', and I told her I was happy to as I have now immortalized her for us and I'm very happy about that.

Currently we also have some fish (won at a fair and growing bigger and bigger by the day), some chickens (who strut about our garden and don't lay eggs for some reason), and also a horse. We are in the process of getting two kittens and another puppy, and my husband keeps talking about pigs in a loving fashion and eyeing the field behind our house. So, once I have done the animals, fed them, groomed them and, if I am very lucky, ridden the horse occasionally, I sit down to write.

'I had children crawling underneath me and pulling at me and asking me to get them juice every five minutes.'

When I first started writing books, rather than stringing a set of columns together, I found it incredibly enjoyable but also incredibly difficult. I was pregnant for most of the time I was writing this particular book. I spent a lot of time closing down my computer and lying on my bed pretending to 'think', whereas really I was falling asleep. Then, when I wasn't sleeping, I became convinced I wasn't really sure where I was going with it or what I was trying to say, and so everything got very convoluted. I'd have one character in two places at the same time. Then I got into a rut of making them explain *absolutely everything,* which became rather annoying for me and would also be, I was sure, for any potential readers. I realized quite quickly that my piecemeal way of writing, squeezing in an hour here and an hour there, wasn't really going to work. I was also writing in the house, which meant I had children crawling underneath me and pulling at me and asking me to get them juice every five minutes.

At this point two things happened: my husband downsized his job to spend three days a week at home and I was offered a peaceful Portakabin by the river in which to write. Suddenly I had time and space, so I became very disciplined and abandoned my husband for huge tranches of time while I went, with the baby kicking away inside me, and created Samantha and her world while looking at swans drifting down the Thames. It was an incredibly lovely thing to do. I immersed myself in her. I am still immersed in her. I began to realize what fun you could have with characters, how they each become their own person. This is why I am not Samantha. She is her own person.

What's next …

Well, there is even more of Samantha. I am still not done with her. Book Three progresses Samantha and her family's life even further. It is set in a new place and has a whole new cast of characters, bar Dougie of course.

'She is on her own with three boys and the baby girl and no John.'

In Book Three the Smythe family go to Devon on holiday to stay in Edward's granny's house near the sea. John is supposed to be coming for the entire time but, of course, he ends up with a job designing lighting for a puppet show. This puts immense strain on the Smythe family. Jamie is being very difficult, dressing in girls' clothes and demanding the earth for his imaginary friend Sophie. Samantha is at the end of her tether. She is on her own with three boys and the baby girl and no John. But almost as soon as she gets to Devon she meets Noel Rideout, a neighbour, who turns out to have been an old friend of Janet's. He is not a love interest in the traditional way. He is around seventy years old. Yet Samantha becomes enchanted by him and his knowledge of moths – a knowledge that seems to enchant Jamie as much as it does Samantha. Noel, however, has a secret, one that threatens to destroy

Samantha's belief in everything ...

This third book deals with what it means to belong. Samantha goes on her journey – a literal one to Devon – and becomes captivated by Noel because he shows her the magic of the place where he lives. Samantha hasn't actually done anything pro-active in years, so when Noel suggests she prove her commitment to the village of Lower Strand, where the novel is set, she leaps at the chance. She puts on a fete to help an old lady save her house. It is not this simple though – life never is. Edward is turning into a recalcitrant teenager. He falls in with Noel Rideout's Bacardi Breezer-drinking granddaughter Isobel. Bennie makes a new friend, and the mother of that friend proves to change both Samantha and Dougie's life.

It is the final Samantha Smythe book. Her journey is complete – not the geographical one the reader may expect, but a far more complex one – one that involves discovering long-dormant emotions she forgot she even had ...